To An

Merry Christmas
2021

Early one morning, just as the sun was rising
I heard a maid sing in the valley below
"Remember the vows that you made to me truly
Remember how tenderly you nestled close to me.
Oh don't deceive me: Oh never leave me.
How could you use, a poor maiden so? "

English folk song 1787

Books by Alex Willis

Non-Fiction

Step by Step Guitar Making 1st and 2nd editions

Standalone fiction

The Penitent Heart

The Falcon, The Search for Horus.

Crichtons End

The Road Home

Buchanan Series

Book 1   The Bodies in the Marina

Book 2   The Laminated man

Book 3   The Mystery of Cabin 312

Book 4   The Reluctant Jockey

Book 5   The Missing Heiress

Book 6   The Jockey's Wife

Book 7   Death on the Cart

Book 8   Death Stalks by Night

BUCHANAN

The Mystery of Cabin 312

Alex Willis

First published in Great Britain by Mount Pleasant Press 2018
This edition published by Mount Pleasant Publishing 2020

ISBN-13:978-1-913471-14-9

Text set in Garamond 12 point.

Cover photo © Nancy Willis 2017
Cover Layout © Alex & Nancy Willis 2018/2020

Acknowledgement

I would like to extend my gratitude to, Rosemary and Seymour for their help in turning my high school English into a readable story. And also to Barry, Michael, Simon and Nancy for their help with the cover.

This book is dedicated to.

Y'all right? Your usual, Jack?' said Jade, as Buchanan walked into Starbucks.

1

Buchanan had lost count of the times he'd woken in a sweat during the night. He couldn't shake the dream. Nor the image of the demented look on the face of the driver of the oncoming car. His shoulders twitched as he made an involuntary move to avoid the tree of his nightmare.

He let out his breath, turned on his side and squinted at the bedside clock: Five-fifteen. Gently rolling back the bedclothes, he eased himself into a seated position. He stretched, yawned and winced. The pain in his ribs where the seatbelt had grabbed him and stopped him from going through the windshield still hurt. The doctor had prescribed bed-rest and sleep, had told him it would get better over time, and to take it easy.

'Jack, why are you up? You remember what the doctor advised?' said Karen, his wife of thirty-five years.

'Yes, dear. I remember what the doctor advised.'

'Bed-rest and sleep. Why won't you take his advice?'

'There'll be plenty of time to rest when I'm dead.'

'Oh, Jack, stop being so melodramatic and lie back down.'

Buchanan shook his head and reached for his dressing gown. 'I can't sleep, I'm going downstairs to sit in my recliner and think.'

He glanced at the front door and saw a postcard sticking out from under the hall rug. He bent down to pick it up and realised it must have been there for a couple of days. When he read it, he saw to his delight it was a postcard from Jill and Stephen. It was posted from their hotel in Mauritius. *Having a wonderful time, might just stay here forever, love to you both, Jill and Stephen.*

◆

He relaxed into his recliner with a cup of fresh coffee. For the umpteenth time he tried to remember what had happened during the accident. But, no matter how hard he tried, all he could muster up from memory was the Bach prelude he'd been listening to, the grill of the oncoming Mercedes and the face of the other driver – his eyes like those of a man possessed. Buchanan thought he would like to give him a driving lesson – right at the end of his fist.

Reaching over to the side table he picked up the Viking River Cruise file that Karen had put together. He wondered how he was going to fill the time as they sailed through the canals of the Netherlands and Belgium. At least they'd purchased the Silver Beverage Package, and he was sure he'd have no trouble getting his money's worth at the bar.

He opened the folder to the details of their itinerary. Tuesday morning fly from Gatwick to Amsterdam. The first couple of nights in the Radisson Blue hotel with a self-guided walking tour of the city on Wednesday. Thursday, they were to be bussed to the cruise ship.

They'd booked a river view stateroom with a balcony. The boat wasn't something to go to sea in thought Buchanan, but perfect for the wide European canals and locks. Another walking tour through the city of Amsterdam, then back on board for cheese and wine tasting, followed by cocktail hour. Buchanan was beginning to think the next twelve days were going to be just fine. He was finally going to have a proper holiday without the need to feel any collars. What could go wrong? The miscreants of his previous case had been suitably dealt with, and Jill – she'd called him 'Dad'.

♦

Buchanan's tummy rumbled – time for something to eat. He wandered back into the kitchen, dropped two slices of bread in the toaster while turning on the radio for the morning news. Boris was at it again, muddying the political waters, and here it was, early 2018 with just about a year to go till the UK exited the EU. On one hand he was praising the PM while on the other he was setting an agenda that would suit his own position post-Brexit. The words *Friends,*

Romans, countrymen, I come not to praise Cesar but to bury him came to mind.

Regardless of his upcoming holiday, there was still the pending issue of his retirement. Karen had said she was looking forward to them moving in to their own house and the possibility of him retiring. The Assistant Chief Commissioner was also pushing for the same result, as had the former crime commissioner. Buchanan being signed off sick for the next several weeks by the police doctor had given him a window of time to consider his position, and to plot his campaign of resistance.

'Coffee smells good,' said Karen.

'Thought you were going to sleep in?'

'I was.'

'I thought I'd turned off the alarm?'

'You did, it was someone getting out of bed that woke me, I couldn't get back to sleep afterwards.'

'Sorry – you could always go back for an hour, I'll wake you.'

'Are you kidding? I've got the packing to complete. Thanks,' she said, taking the offered cup of freshly-made coffee.

'Can I help?'

'You can help by staying out from under my feet.'

Buchanan wondered about retirement, both of them in the house at the same time. He was now, more than ever, determined to stay working. But what would he do if there were no cases for someone of his stature to investigate?

'It's not my decision to be off work, you know I'm never sick.'

'Never? What about when you had your appendix out, or how about the time you caught pneumonia?'

'They weren't my fault.'

'All right, what about the fight in Porter's bar?'

'I was just doing my job. They shouldn't have run out into the street and got run over by the police car.'

'And what about the car accident? Are you sure you were paying attention to your driving?'

'All right, three occasions in thirty-four years, and what was my reaction? I went straight back to work, that's what I did.'

'Jack, you hit a tree at sixty miles per hour. You're lucky to be alive.'

'All right, I'll take my medicine like a good boy. I'll only go back to work if the doctor says I can.'

'All I'm trying to say is, you're human, take advantage of the time off you've been given. This holiday you have booked is just what we both need, time for us to rediscover who we are as a couple. Time to relive memories, time to cuddle.'

He took the coffee cup from her hands and pulled her to him. 'I love you, Mrs Buchanan. Yes, we'll relive memories and to hell with the job, it can wait.'

'Good. I think I will take you up on your offer – just an hour mind you. I've only got today to finish packing and I've got a hair appointment as well this afternoon.'

Buchanan returned to his recliner and winced as he relaxed back into it. Not only did his ribs hurt, but his collar bone was badly bruised. He grinned as he saw his resignation letter sitting on the sideboard. Because of the accident he'd never managed to deliver it. As far as his employers were concerned, he was still employed, off sick with an additional two weeks' leave available. That is if he wanted to take it. *Take time off and recuperate* the Assistant Chief Constable had said, *take advantage of your situation, go on holiday, take up painting, write a book.*

Write a book! What nonsense. He had written more words in his reports during his career to date than Shakespeare ever did during his whole life. And besides, where would he even start? What would he say?

Then there was Hanbury's suggestion: *take up golf, get you out in the fresh air, keep you fit, old man.*

4

Keep me fit? What tosh, thought Buchanan, as he took a sip of his coffee. Bet you'd never see the ACC out on the golf course. The best way to keep fit was to be on the job looking for criminals.

♦

'What time did you book the taxi for, Jack?'

'Six-thirty, the flight doesn't leave till ten-fifty.'

At six thirty-five, Buchanan secured the house and they were driven off to the airport. The M23 was blocked due to an oil spill so the driver made a detour through the quiet side roads and still managed to drop them off at eight-thirty. They checked in, dropped off their bags, went through security and commenced their holiday by going for breakfast.

'Right, my dear,' said Buchanan. 'What do you fancy?'

'Coffee and doughnut?'

'You do know me well, but not this morning, my dear. I'm on holiday. It's a full English for me.'

'In that case, I'll join you.'

'Let's sit by the window,' said Buchanan, pulling out a chair for Karen to sit down.

'Aren't they a lovely couple?' said Karen, looking over the top of her menu.'

'Which couple?'

'Over there, the table in the corner.'

Buchanan turned to look, then froze. His face turned white.

'Jack, what's the matter? Can you breathe?'

'That's him – that's the shite that ran me off the road!'

'How can you be sure?' she said, turning to look for her husband's phantom driver.

'I'm sure, I never forget a face, especially the one that nearly killed me.'

'You're still in shock. The doctor said you might have flashbacks and confusion.'

'I'm not confused. That's the bastard who nearly killed me.'

'Look away, take a deep breath and relax. Have you taken your medication this morning?'

Buchanan looked back at Karen, closed his eyes as he took a deep breath. 'No, I forgot.'

'Thought so. Here, I've got your prescription in my handbag.' Karen opened the pill bottle and handed her husband a little blue pill 'Here you are, drink it down with water.'

'Thanks, I guess I needed that.' He turned and looked at the couple again. 'You could be right, I suppose I am a bit stressed. Though –'

'Breathe deeply and relax. They're just a couple off on their holidays.'

'OK. I suppose they would be if they really are a couple.'

'What do you mean, if they really are a couple?'

'For one thing, you'd think they would look a little happier.'

'Oh, Jack. Remember when we used to go on holiday?'

'No, it's been too long.'

'I'd be looking forward to lying about by the pool and you'd –'

'Be thinking about work.'

'Exactly. Is that what you're getting at? And I suppose as soon as they get to their hotel, he'll relax, and all will be well?'

'Uh-huh, bet he's a – tell you what –'

'What, another game of yours?'

'No, not exactly. Remember the game my team sometimes play at Starbucks?'

'You mean guess the occupation?'

'Exactly, I'll start.'

'OK, the floor's all yours.'

'First, the lady. I think she's his – no, though he is married, I don't think she's his wife, more likely a secretary.'

'And they're on a business trip? He's married and they're having an affair?'

'How did you guess that? You must be a detective, my dear.'

Karen smiled. 'Thanks, do I get the job?'

'And who'd make my dinner?'

'You make me sound like a domestic servant.'

'Sorry – my humour engine's a bit off kilter this morning.'

'I'd already noticed. But I'd agree with you he's married although not to the lady. She probably is – no wait a minute, we're assuming too much. I think we should start again.'

'Good, it's always a good idea to look at a problem from a different perspective.'

'Is that what you do?'

Buchanan shrugged. 'For a start he's wearing an expensive suit, not quite what you'd wear to go on holiday, unless you are Prince Charles.'

'Prince Charles? What's he got to do with it?'

'Ever see him in shorts and flip-flops?'

'No, of course not. He's got an image to maintain.'

'That's what I'm getting at. Our friend over there is dressed for a business conference or similar. Look at his shoes, bet they never came off a shelf at Clarks. The tie is pure silk and the suit Savile Row. Look at his hands, especially the right one. That's a fraternity ring.'

'You think he's a mason?'

'Can't tell from here. Could be some sort of university secret society.'

'Now you're stretching credibility. A gold ring it certainly looks like, but a university secret society?'

'His tie – just look at the design.'

'It's just a tie.'

Buchanan shook his head. 'That's a university tie, not sure which one though.'

'Blue with gold stripes? Jack, it's just a tie.'

Buchanan shook his head, 'No, Karen. There's something about it that is niggling the little grey cells.'

'Are you going to start speaking with a French accent?'

'What?'

'You're quoting that great Belgian detective again.'

'*Ah, Monsieur Poirot, n'est-ce pas?*'

'*Mais oui, c'est Monsieur Poirot.*'

'Wish I could speak French as good as you.'

'You can, I'll teach you while we are on holiday.'

Buchanan shook his head. 'Let's wait till we get home, don't fancy trying it out in the Netherlands.'

'We'll be in Belgium in a few days. French is one of the major languages, what could be better?'

'Ach, we're supposed to be on holiday, let's not talk of work.'

'All right, what else do you think of our couple? Are you done working out what he's about?'

'Probably an executive going to a meeting, maybe giving a sales presentation to the European investors.'

'That why he's taking his secretary instead of his wife?' said Karen. 'Maybe they work for the same company and they just happen to be on the same flight.'

'So, you don't think they're a couple after all?'

Karen shrugged. 'Look at their carry-on bags. They're side by side, just like ours.'

Buchanan looked down at his carry-on bag, then over to the couple. 'I'll concede you that. What about her, what stands out to you?'

'The dress, no woman is going to wear that to a business meeting. More likely to be going down to meet friends for coffee or going on holiday.'

'Then why is he wearing such an expensive suit?'

'Disguise. Suppose they are having an affair. His wife drove him to the airport. He told her he was going on a business trip, that's why they don't want to be noticed.'

'Why not sit apart, then no-one would notice?'

'I'd say they do work together and they're going on a business trip together. He's got the important part, she's probably his PA, and – Jack, it's time to board.'

2

The plane climbed out of the cloudy sky and into brilliant sunshine. Buchanan closed his eyes and thought of the days ahead, wondering what he would do to fill the time.

♦

'Jack, time to wake up, we're landing.'

'Already?'

'You've been asleep.'

'I needed that.'

'Feel better?'

'Yep, ready to relax.'

'That's my Jack. *Oops.*'

'What's the matter?'

'Nothing – nothing at all.'

Buchanan looked to see what had caught Karen's attention. Seated five rows forward in the business class were the couple they'd seen in the airport restaurant. 'This is getting interesting,' he said.

'Jack, we're on holiday – remember?'

'Yes, my dear. But something isn't right. My knower knows something.'

They walked through the immigration hall, collected their suitcases and exited through the green lane.

'Here, put this on your lapel,' said Karen, handing Buchanan a cruise ship sticker.

Within minutes they were greeted by the Viking cruise line representative.

'Mr and Mrs Buchanan?'

'Yes,' said Karen.

'Good morning. My name is Felicia. Welcome to Amsterdam and Viking River Cruises. If you'll follow me, I'll show you where to wait for the coach to your hotel.

Buchanan smiled as he saw the mystery couple join the line waiting to board the same coach.

♦

'Jack, I want you to promise me something,' said Karen, as she brushed her hair in front of the hotel-room mirror.

'What's that?'

'I want you to promise me you will remember you are on holiday and will not bother that couple. If they want to have time away together, it's none of our business.'

Buchanan was staring down at the canal and the narrow roads that ran parallel, wondering how often bicyclists ran into unwary pedestrians. At the sound of Karen's voice, he turned away from his daydream. 'Sorry, what was that you said?'

Karen shook her head. 'Are you here, or are you off down some dark alley, chasing an axe murderer or investigating some other sort of gruesome crime?'

'I am here. I'm just marvelling at how many bicycles there are on the streets of Amsterdam and how they manage to avoid each other and the pedestrians.'

'You didn't hear the tour guide's warning?'

'No, what was it?'

'She said to watch for bicycles when out walking, otherwise you can get run over. There are reputed to be over eight hundred thousand of them on the streets.'

'Is that what you were saying?'

'No – I was saying, I want you to promise you'll leave that couple alone and not bother them. They've as much right to their privacy as we do ours.'

'OK. No problem, but –'

11

'No buts, Jack. I want you to be here with me, not off on some wild goose chase.'

'All right. Shall we go for a walk? We've got two hours before dinner time.'

'Dinner time? We're on holiday. Dinner time is when we make it.'

Buchanan smiled. 'Then, in that case, let's go for a drink. It's been a while since I tried Dutch beer.'

The lift doors slid slowly back and Buchanan, in his haste to down a cool beer, almost knocked over the female half of the mystery couple.

'Oops, sorry, are you all right, Mrs –?'

'Yes, thanks, I'm fine.'

'Please excuse my husband, his first holiday in years,' said Karen. 'He's a bit over-enthusiastic to get started.'

'That's all right.'

'Are you on the cruise?'

'Yes, sort of. Karl has business meetings in several cities in Holland and Belgium and, since this cruise visits them all, he booked this holiday as a way of travelling between them yet staying in the same floating hotel.'

'Smart man,' said Karen.

Buchanan smiled.

'In that case we'll probably see you around,' said Karen.

'Yes, I suppose we will.'

'OK, see you later.'

'*See you later?* What was that all about? I thought you said we're on holiday, just the two of us?' said Buchanan, as they made their way over to the hotel entrance doors.

'I've been married to a detective too long, my dear, you've rubbed off on me.'

'Hmm. C'mon, let's go to the bar, I need something cool to drink.'

'Then can we go for a stroll?' asked Karen.

♦

'Where shall we start?' said Buchanan, as they stepped out of the hotel being mindful of the passing bicycles.

'How about we just turn left and see where we end up? Let's see what we find, everything is so different, it won't make any difference which way we go.'

'I'd often wandered, with an empty heart. Till I saw you, now no more to part.'

'Thanks, Jack.'

They turned left and meandered down to the canal. After a few lefts and rights Karen realised where they had ended up.

'Do you realise where we are?'

'No, should I?'

'You must be really relaxing, we're in the red-light district.'

'I had noticed. But since it's only five o'clock the windows are all empty. I've been told it's a completely different show at night.'

'Trust you. Shall we head back? I need to freshen up before we eat.'

♦

'What shall we do about dinner?' asked Karen, as she took one last look in the mirror.

'We passed a nice restaurant this afternoon, the one by the church, remember?'

'Oh yes. We could sit outside and watch the world go by, I'd like that.

They retraced their steps from earlier and were soon seated at a table in the T Loosje restaurant.

'Jack, this is so exciting! Do you realise how long it's been since we ate outside?'

Buchanan looked off into the distance, searching for an elusive memory. But like the proverbial bar of soap in the bathtub, every time he tried to grab it, it was gone again.

'You can't remember, can you?' said Karen, a grin growing on her face.

He shook his head.

'I'll tell you. It was twelve years ago. We were in Edinburgh at one of your police do's. It was August and there was a heatwave. I remember we sat outside because you wanted to smoke.'

'Those were the days.'

'You're not still missing smoking, are you? I thought you were over that?'

'Sometimes, when I get a whiff of someone's smoke, it brings back the old desires, now these,' he said holding up an open tube of fruit gums, 'are my cigarettes.'

'They smoke something else here in Amsterdam,' said Karen.

'So they do, but it's legal here. Not sure if it makes any difference to crime statistics being legal. People still get addicted, and unfortunately some go on to more addictive substances.'

They were interrupted by the waiter wanting to know if they would they like something to drink and were ready to order.

'I'll have a Heineken and a burger,' said Buchanan.

'Could I have a Pinot Grigio, please? And I'll have a burger as well,' said Karen.

They watched a mother with a child on the crossbar cycle past while they waited for their food.

'What shall we do tomorrow?' said Karen, as she took a sip of her wine. 'We have a full day to do whatever we want,'

'Not sure. There seems to be so much to see. Did you have anything in mind?'

'I had a look at the city map while you were resting this afternoon. I'd like to go to the Rijksmuseum. Then in the same area there is the Van Gogh museum with a Dali and Banksy exhibition in the Moco museum. They're all within walking distance from each other. We can get a day ticket for the tram if you think it's too far to walk.'

14

'Sounds fine to me. Bit odd though, coming all this way to see a Banksy.'

'Also, if there is time, I'd like to go to the Eye film museum and up to the top of the A'DAM tower. They have a huge swing up there, it swings right out over the edge of the building.'

'I'll watch you,' said Buchanan, 'but I'll keep my feet firmly on the ground.'

'We'll see. Shall we head back to the hotel?'

♦

'I'll meet you at the front door, I need the toilet before we go wandering,' said Buchanan, as he pushed his chair back from the breakfast table.'

'OK, see you in a few minutes,' said Karen.

Buchanan was back in five minutes. 'Still want to go to the Rijksmuseum?'

'Yes, please. But first I would like to do some window shopping, then we can take a tram to the Rijksmuseum.'

'I'm not really interested in walking round streets,' said Buchanan. 'It's a bit like the day job.'

'There's the architecture of the converted warehouses for a start, then there's the Amsterdam museum. It's a bit too far to walk considering your recent accident.'

'Where do we get the tram tickets?' Buchanan asked Karen

'The hotel reception said to buy them on-board.'

'Where are we going next?'

'The Amsterdam museum, it's not far.'

♦

'Look at that statue,' said Karen, as they walked through the Amsterdam museum.

'Was Goliath really that big?' asked Buchanan. 'Makes David look quite puny.'

'Is that what you saw yourself as?'

'What, as a policeman? I suppose in the early days I might have felt a bit overwhelmed, but not anymore. Anyway, what does any of it matter? I'm just a has-been, an old thespian who doesn't realise the final curtain has descended.'

Karen looked at him. 'You really don't want to retire, do you?'

'I'll have to someday, I suppose.'

'But not just yet, is that what you are saying?'

'I – look, let's get going, we don't have all day.'

They boarded the number 5 tram, found a seat and watched the city pass by.

'Jack – look!'

Buchanan shook himself out of his day-dream. 'Look at what?'

'The flower markets. I'd like to see those and maybe buy some tulip bulbs for the new house.'

'Sounds fine to me. But wouldn't that be better to wait till the end of the holiday? We have a day and a half at the end. That way you won't have to find somewhere to store them in our cabin?'

'Makes sense. You know something?'

Buchanan's attention went into overdrive, Karen was about to make one of her profound statements. 'Yes, I know lots of things, anything in particular you were referring to?'

She ignored his friendly barb. 'I was thinking, when you retire, we could do a lot more of this, the going on holiday business. For instance, Amsterdam is only a couple of hours away from Eastbourne. We could just pop over for a long weekend anytime we fancied it.'

'Yes, we could. But who'd look after the dog?'

'Jack, we don't have a dog.'

'I'm talking about my black dog. The one who comes to visit from time to time when I get to feeling sorry for myself.'

'When you retire, I realise there will be a time of readjustment for you. I'm sure it won't be easy but when you let go of the need to sort out the world's problems you'll find there's another side to life. You deserve it after all these years.'

Buchanan thought for a moment. 'I can accept that. I think this is our stop – that looks like the museum over there,' he said, pointing.

Karen put her arm though his and leaned on his shoulder. 'I love you, Jack, you'll get through it – we'll get through it, together.'

'Thanks.'

They exited the tram, crossed the road and entered the Rijksmuseum.

'Karen – isn't that – who did she say she was?'

'Who are you talking about?'

'The woman in the hotel, the one who was with –'

'Jack,' said Karen, looking in the direction of Buchanan's gaze, 'there's no woman over there. C'mon, follow me, you need something to occupy your mind.'

Karen walked through to the next exhibition room. 'Well, what do you think? Could you see me pouring you a cup of tea from that teapot?' she said, as they stopped in front of a glass case full of teapots from around the world.

'Thanks, I'll just take mine black in the auld mug.'

'You really do need a holiday,' she said, pulling him to her in an embrace. 'Be patient, things will get better. Remember, you're supposed to be recovering from a near death experience.'

They meandered through the apartheid exhibition and out into the sun.

'What's next?' asked Buchanan.

'An exhibition about a one-eared painter.'

'Van Gogh?'

'Yes, and after that, there's the Dali and Banksy exhibition to see.'

Since Buchanan wasn't really paying attention to the Van Gogh paintings, Karen steered them out into the sunshine and over to the Dali exhibition.

'What's got you smiling?' she asked.

That,' said Buchanan pointing to a Dali quote on the exhibition wall.

'*There is only one difference between a madman and me. The madman thinks he's sane. I know I am mad.*' Karen read out. 'Is that what you feel about yourself?'

He shrugged. 'No, it just appeals to me at the moment.'

'Let's go get something to drink, I saw a sign for the café when we were walking over. You get us a seat, and I'll order the tea. Would you like cake to go with your tea?' asked Karen.

'Yes, please. If they have it, I'll have a slice of chocolate.'

Karen was back in a few minutes with two teas and two slices of cake. Dark chocolate for Buchanan and a raspberry sponge for herself.'

'Cake all right?' she asked, as Buchanan played with his.

'She's here.'

'Who's here?'

'Our mystery woman.'

'Where?'

'The table in the corner. Over by the entrance door. She must have been in the Ladies; her drink was already on the table.'

'So, you did see her, earlier.'

'Yup,' said Buchanan, smiling. 'I'm not going mad after all.'

'That's my Jack.'

'Shall we get going? We have a busy day tomorrow. We're going on our cruise.'

'Don't forget we have the canal cruise round the city first and a walking tour after, remember?' said Karen.

They got up and walked over to the exit, finding themselves going down the escalator with the mystery lady.

'Enjoy the museum?' asked Buchanan loudly.

Karen turned to look at Buchanan to ask why he was talking so loudly, then realised he was addressing the mystery woman.

'Oh, it's you again. Yes, thanks, did you?'

'Very much. Did you see the Banksy exhibition?'

'Yes, but it's not quite my thing. I preferred the Van Gogh paintings.'

'So, I wasn't imaging things.'

'Have you been trailing me?'

'Please excuse my husband,' said Karen. 'He's recovering from a car accident and is still getting used to being up and about.'

'Yes, you did mention that earlier. If you'll excuse me, I have to get back to the hotel.'

'She was a bit short with you, Jack. Wonder what you said. It was as almost like you were asking her to bare her soul.'

'She's hiding something,' said Buchanan, rubbing his hands together.

'Jack – remember we are on holiday, and you are fifty percent of that we.'

♦

'How did you sleep?' asked Karen, yawning.

'I slept very well, must be the fresh air,' said Buchanan, already dressed and standing in front of the window.

'You sure it wasn't the double whisky you had before coming to bed?'

'Who knows? All I do know is I feel great. Fancy a coffee?'

'There's a kettle in the room, coffee's in a cup on the dresser.'

'I didn't mean that coffee. I meant real coffee.'

'Where are you going to find a Starbucks round here?'

'I already have. It's only a couple of streets away.'

'You win. I'll have a large latte and whatever sticky bun you think I'll like.'

♦

'That didn't take you very long,' said Karen, sitting up in bed adjusting the pillows.

'I said it was only a couple of streets away. I got you a chocolate chip muffin.'

'And what about you?'

Buchanan grinned and putting his hand in the bag brought out two sugared doughnuts. 'What have I said? Why are you smiling?'

'Something silly just popped into my head.'

'And what would that be?'

'President Kennedy's speech where he called himself a jelly doughnut.'

'That goes back a few years. Just like us. Thirty-five years this year. Oh, shoot, I'm sorry,' said Buchanan, 'with all that's been going on I've completely forgotten it's our anniversary in three days.'

'That's all right, you've been quite stressed with your accident.'

'I'm sorry, Karen. You and the doctor are so right. I do need this time off.'

She smiled at him. 'We'll get through it together.'

'What time do we board?' asked Buchanan.

Karen leaned over to the bedside table and picked up the travel folder. 'Looks like we have time for a look around. The coach will be here at twelve to take us to the ship. What would you like to go see?'

'You said earlier that you wanted to see the A'DAM tower, you know the one, the tower with the film museum underneath.'

'Fine. Let me get dressed and I'll meet you downstairs for breakfast.'

♦

'How do we get across the river, Jack?' asked Karen, as they stood and looked at the tower on the far bank.

'The ferry, I suppose. Let's follow the crowd and see where they get on.'

'Lead on, my fine travel guide.'

'Are you all right?' asked Buchanan.

'Never felt better, it's the fresh air and the water. I'm so looking forward to getting on board and relaxing.'

'Look,' said Buchanan, 'the ferry is free, and we have company again.'

'Are you referring to a certain blonde with the pink ski jacket?'

'Wonder why she's always on her own?'

'It will be as she said, *Karl has business meetings to attend.* I expect we'll see them at dinner this evening.'

'Have you seen anything about seating arrangements for dinner?'

'I did look, but as far as I can determine it's a case of sit where you want. Why?'

'Just wondering. Remember the fuss we had with seating when we did the cruise on the Med?'

'Jack, that was years ago, things have changed. Besides this is an informal cruise, we wear what we want, as long as it's smart casual.'

'Good, I'll wear my pyjamas.'

'You don't wear pyjamas.'

'I know, just being silly. Looks like we're arriving. Watch for the bicycles as we get off.'

They once again followed the crowd and disembarked from the ferry.

'Could we have a look at the old canal barges?' said Karen.

'Fine by me.'

'Then we can finish the day by going to the top of the A'DAM lookout tower.'

Buchanan turned and looked up at the tower. What caught his attention was the huge structure leaning over the edge at the top. 'Is that the swing you were talking about?'

Karen looked at what had caught Buchanan's attention. 'Yes, looks like fun to me.'

'You'll no catch me on that. I read a notice on the ferry that said the tower is about eighty metres high and the swing looks like it's another good ten metres on top of that.'

'All the same I'd like to go to the top and take some photographs.'

Forty minutes later they emerged from the lift on the top of the tower.

'Still fancy a swing?' asked Buchanan.

Karen turned back from taking photos of the city and shook her head. 'I'm sure it's perfectly safe, but I think I'll give it a miss this time.'

'You might, but I see a familiar face that's not scared to give it a try.'

'You mean the certain someone wearing a pink ski jacket?'

'The very same.'

They stood and watched as pink ski jacket was strapped into her seat, the chair hoisted up and out over the edge of the parapet and began to swing to and fro.'

'Makes me queasy just to watch,' said Buchanan.

'That's odd. Never knew you to be squeamish about anything,' said Karen, as they watched the swing go higher with each oscillation.

'I don't like being out of control.'

'Jack, come over here for a minute.'

'What is it?'

'Look, you can stand on this glass plate and see all the way to the ground.'

'Reminds me of the floor window in the dome of St Paul's cathedral,' said Buchanan, as Karen took photos of their feet over the edge of the glass plate.

'I think we should be getting back to the hotel,' he continued, looking over at the swing and seeing pink ski jacket climb down from the seat.

'Jack, remember, we're on holiday.'

'Yes dear, you do keep reminding me of that fact.'

Buchanan managed to get himself and Karen into the lift with pink ski jacket just as the doors were closing. On the way down he asked, 'Did you enjoy the swing?'

She looked away from her mobile phone and up at him as though deciding whether to ignore his question or not, then said, 'Yes, thanks, it was very exhilarating.'

'Get some good photos?'

'Yes, thanks.'

'Would you do it again?'

She shook her head. 'No. I think once in a lifetime is enough.' Then she returned to looking at the photos on her phone.

Karen gave Buchanan a *she doesn't want to talk to you* look.

Buchanan looked up at the ceiling and watched as the screen showed the descent of the lift. At the bottom they exited and headed for the ferry and the hotel.

The hotel lobby was buzzing with new arrivals vying for space amongst those waiting for the coach for the river boat.

'Jack, we need to get a move on with the suitcases,' said Karen, as they entered the hotel lobby. 'I think the coach for the river boat is here.'

♦

Buchanan looked at the faces of the seated passengers as he followed Karen to the rear of the coach and to his amusement the only seat left was beside the lady in pink.

'Is this seat taken?'

She looked up from her phone, glanced around to see if there were any vacant seats then shrugged. 'Be my guest,' she said, before returning to her phone.

Buchanan looked across the aisle at Karen and winked.

Since they had walked the journey to the quayside earlier they were surprised to see how long it took for the coach to get there. At least they didn't have to struggle with their suitcases as they were to be delivered direct to their cabin.

'You go on to the cabin,' said Buchanan, 'I'll join you in a minute, there's something I want to have a look at.'

'Jack, this cabin is lovely, and the bed is nice and firm,' said Karen as Buchanan entered the cabin. She sat down on the bed and bounced on the mattress. 'We should sleep well on this trip.'

Buchanan walked over to the window and pulled back the drapes. 'The veranda is not the biggest in the world, but will do nicely. I'm looking forward to sitting out in the evening as we cruise along through the countryside.'

'Thought you were going to spend your time in the bar getting your money's worth?'

'There's that of course. Then I could just spend the time reading.'

'When was the last time you read a book?'

'There's quite a good selection of books in the boat's library, we passed it on the way to the cabin, I've borrowed one of them.'

'What's it about?'

'It's one of John Mortimer's stories about his time at the bar. ITV made a series about them, starred Leo McKern as Rumple of the Bailey.'

'Any good?'

'It's well written and the characters are believable, especially Horace Rumple. I'm just getting into the first story.'

'Sounds interesting, hope the ending is satisfactory.'

'I'll keep you posted.'

'In the meantime, we have a walking trip round the city and a city canal boat-ride booked for tomorrow. We're to meet in the reception in five minutes for today's walking tour.'

'You go ahead, I'll join you in a minute.'

Buchanan descended the companionway steps to the reception to find a large group of fellow travellers standing in a tight circle round the tour guide.

'Ready Jack?' said Karen.

'Yep, what are we going to see?'

'Bridges, buildings and markets. Oh, they did mention we will pass Anne Frank's house, but we won't be able to go in. Apparently, you need to book days in advance for that.'

'OK, the walk it will be.'

♦

They arrived back on board and found another river boat tied up alongside, blocking their view across the river.

'What's first on the entertainment menu, Karen?'

'Cheese and wine tasting.'

'Sounds interesting, wonder what wines they have?'

'House wine, red and white, but you don't have to drink it. Remember we have the silver drinks package. Cheese and wine tasting finishes at five o'clock. Then we move on to the cocktail hour with live music.'

'I like this thing called, *being on holiday*.'

'We'll have many of them when you retire. What do you think of that?'

'When asked by his superior what he wanted to do with his retirement, the aged policeman said, *to lay down without a thought about tomorrow, to rest one's head on a pillow and sleep the sleep of a thousand years.* I'll sleep on that idea, my dear, what time is dinner?'

Karen picked up the *Viking News* from the bedside table. 'There is a welcoming brief at six-fifteen then dinner at seven. Oh, you'll find this interesting.'

'And pray tell me, oh excellent tour director, what am I going to find interesting?'

'There will be a clog-making demonstration after dinner.'

'Here on the boat? I'll look forward to that.'

Karen yawned and looked at her watch, 'I'm going to have a rest before dinner, been a busy day.'

'Fine, I'll go check out the boat.'

'OK. I suppose I'll find you in the bar?'

'Where else?'

'Keep out of trouble, I'll see you later,' Karen said, lying down on the bed.

◆

Buchanan collected his book from his bedside table and headed for the bar. To his delight he saw they had several of his favourite whiskies. Glass in hand he headed for a window seat and the first bit of real relaxation he'd had in years. From where he sat he had a good view of the entrance to the bar and the surrounding seating area. Why had he sat where he had, he asked himself? Then he realised it was just the habit of many years being a policeman. Always choosing to be in the right place at the right time. He scolded himself for not relaxing, took a big sip of his whisky, and started reading. He'd got as far as Rumple standing to address the jury at young Timson's trial, when he was disturbed by tense voices coming from two seats over. It was the pink lady and her partner.

'Where have you been? You said you'd be back by ten o'clock. I've had to do all the packing and unpacking.'

'Shush, I told you it could be a long meeting.'

'Next time, leave me at home.'

'Relax. It won't happen again. I told them time is running out for them. They either come in with us or be left on the outside.'

'When will you tell me what it is all about? I don't like all this secrecy.'

'You don't need to know, it's better that way,' the partner said, standing up. 'I'm going back to the cabin, I could do with a shower and a change of clothes.'

Buchanan threw back the dregs of his whisky, closed his book and stood. He waited for pink lady's partner to head for the door then followed. He walked a few paces behind, through the on-board library and along the third-deck cabins. Pink lady's partner stopped and entered cabin 312. Buchanan kept walking. When he heard the door close and lock behind him he returned to the library and walked down the stairs to the guest services desk.

'Excuse me,' he said to the receptionist. 'Mr Buchanan in 309, I wonder if you could help with a delicate matter?'

'If I can.'

'I've just seen someone I think I know, but it's been quite a few years and I wouldn't want to embarrass myself by asking them who they are.'

'And how could I help?'

'My friend of years ago was called Jim Robertson and the person I just saw went into cabin 312, just across the corridor from us in 309.'

'Let me see,' said the receptionist, while typing in the room number. 'I'm sorry, unless he's changed his name, it's not your friend Jim Robertson.'

'Are you sure? Could you check again?'

She keyed in the room number again and slowly shook her head. 'No, it's definitely not your friend. The couple in suite 312 are a Mr and Mrs Karl Mueller.'

'Ah well. At least I won't make a fool of myself by saying hello.'

'That's good, sir. Is there anything else I can do for you?'

'Is the WIFI running?'

'Yes, all the time, just use the password Viking2018.'

'Thanks.'

Buchanan climbed the companionway stairs and returned to the bar. Pink lady, or should he call her Mrs Mueller, was still sitting where he'd last seen her, staring at her phone. He ordered another whisky and returned to his chair. Instead of his book, he took out his phone and logged on to the internet. He ignored his emails and went straight to Google. He typed in the name Karl Mueller and sipped on his whisky while he waited for Google to search.

There wasn't much to learn, other than Karl Mueller was listed on LinkedIn as a financial consultant. Should he or shouldn't he? he pondered. If Karen found out, she wouldn't be pleased. He thought it would be best to get it out of his system and find out what he could while Karen was busy napping.

He scrolled through his contacts list and found the name he was looking for: Achmed Bashir. He pressed the dial button and waited. 'Yes, it's Jack Buchanan – DCI Buchanan, could I have a quick word with Mr Bashir if he's available? When do you expect him to return? OK. Could I leave a message for him? Yes, I was wondering if he knows anything about a financial consultant called Karl Mueller, lives in the Eastbourne area. Yes, he can either call me or message me back on this number, thanks.' Buchanan put his phone back in his pocket, his heart racing. He recognised the sensation: it was the thrill of the chase, something was up, and it wasn't any feathered pheasant.

He opened his book and had resumed Rumple's address to the jury when he was again interrupted, this time by his phone ringing. 'Jack Buchanan. Ah yes, Achmed, thanks for calling back. Yes, I'm on holiday – we're on a river cruise in Holland – be back in ten days. What did you find out? He is, that's what LinkedIn says – ah, I wondered if there was more to him than just that. No, I have my own resources for checking that, thanks, bye.'

Next call was to DI Hanbury. 'Hanbury, how are things back in genteel Eastbourne? Someone was what? Pistol whipped on Grove Road? And a stabbing? The poor sod. I expect I'll get the blame for stirring up a one-man crime wave. No, could you run a name through the Police National Computer? Yes, it's –' he looked up to see if pink lady could overhear his conversation, then quietly he spelled out the name for Hanbury. 'Yes, call me back if you find anything.'

Buchanan threw back the last of his drink and went over to the bar and ordered a coffee. He returned to his chair. Pink lady looked at him and then abruptly away – had she heard his conversation with Hanbury? He sat down and saw out of the window the Viking long-ship was still tied up alongside, blocking his view of the river.

He was almost done with his coffee when Hanbury called back. 'What did you find out?' asked Buchanan. 'That much? Look, Hanbury, maybe you should text me the information – thanks.'

Buchanan hung up from the call and waited for the text message. Two minutes later his phone beeped to say the message had arrived. He opened the message and read: *Karl Mueller, born England 1956, parents emigrated from Germany in 1949, no siblings. Read finance at Oxford, graduated with first class honours. Worked for various investment houses, ten years at Lehman Brothers, last recorded employer three years at Goldman Sachs. Now works as a private financial consultant. Current address listed: Meads, Eastbourne.*

Now more than ever, Buchanan was sure Mueller was the other driver, the face in his nightmares.

'Hello, enjoying yourself?' asked Karen, who'd just walked into the bar. 'I tried the upper deck, but you weren't there.'

'Was it a good nap, feel relaxed?'

'Yes, thanks.'

'Good, you're just in time for cocktails. I'm afraid there's not much left of the cheese and wine. I think I'll try a couple of cocktails then take a leaf out of your book and take a nap before we eat.

♦

'Jack, wake up, it's dinner time.'

'Didn't realise I was so tired,' said Buchanan, yawning and sitting up.

'Cheese and wine tasting coupled with cocktail hour more likely the cause.'

'C'mon, I'm on holiday, you said to relax.'

'Time for that later, we're going to be late for dinner if you don't get a move on.'

They were among the last to arrive and ended up seated at the back of the restaurant where Buchanan had an excellent view of all the tables. He noticed the Muellers were sitting alone and not talking to each other.

3

Buchanan left Karen getting dressed, but instead of going straight through to the restaurant for breakfast, he climbed to the upper deck and walked towards the bow. He stopped on the top rung of the stairs leading down to the lower deck and the Aquavit Terrace. The sky was overcast and the air brisk. The river was busy with ocean-going ships, barges laden with containers pulled by tugs and ferries plying their way across and back over the river. As he started down the steps he saw, through the glass-covered roof, Karen seated with another couple drinking coffee.

He opened the door and walked over to Karen's table.

'Jack, this is Marjorie and Charles, they're from Minnesota in the United States.'

'Good morning. Enjoying your trip so far?'

'Oh yes,' said Marjorie. 'Charles is reliving the time he worked over here with his bank. Are you going on the city canal trip this morning?'

'Yes,' said Buchanan. 'Are you?'

Marjorie shook her head. 'We're going on the guided city walk, we did the city canal trip once before.'

'This is my first time visiting Amsterdam,' said Buchanan.

'Oh, I'm sure you will enjoy it,' said Marjorie.

Pleasantries exchanged, breakfast eaten, Buchanan and Karen went ashore to get the coach that was to take them to where they were to board the canal boat.

This time Buchanan chose to sit next to Karen on the coach. He noticed that pink lady was once again engrossed in her phone, and still very much alone. This puzzled him. Why would anyone come on a canal cruise holiday, even a simple one like pottering around the city canals, and spend the time staring at a phone? What could be more interesting about what was displayed on the phone, and just where was her partner? Yesterday he'd tried to be friendly as one does when on holiday, but he got the distinct impression she just did not want to talk to anyone, especially him.

'I enjoyed that,' he said, as they boarded the coach back to the boat and lunch. He was beginning to relax and when he saw Marjorie and Charles walking towards the restaurant. He made a point of catching up with them and inviting himself and Karen to join them for lunch.

'Did you enjoy your walking tour of the city?' asked Karen.

'Yes, lots of old buildings that are now houses which were once warehouses. Some of them still have the lifting beam sticking out the wall. Guess what it's used for these days?'

'Delivering groceries?' said Buchanan, between mouthfuls of salad.

'Very funny. No, they are used to move furniture up and down when people move.'

Buchanan smiled.

'Are you doing anything this afternoon?' asked Marjorie.

'I was planning to go on the optional trip to the Delft factory,' said Karen.

'Would you mind if I joined you? Charles is still trying to get over his jet-lag and is planning to rest.'

'That would be lovely. Jack's busy in a book and I wasn't looking forward to going on my own,' replied Karen.

Buchanan watched from the bar as Karen and Marjorie boarded the coach for the trip to the Delft factory.

◆

After dinner Buchanan and Karen moved into the lounge and sat by the edge of the dance floor beside Charles and Marjorie. Next to them were another American couple Karen and Marjorie had met on the Delft tour.

'We should get a good view of the clog-making from here,' said Karen.

'Sounds fine to me. Would you like a drink, Karen?'

'Pinot Grigio, please.'

Buchanan ordered a whisky for himself and re-joined Karen. She was busy chatting to the other couple she'd met on the tour. 'Jack, this is Delia and George Kowalski, they're from California.'

'Very nice. Are you here on holiday?'

'Sort of. George's uncle fought with the 21st Division at Arnhem,' said Delia. 'Unfortunately, he was one of the many casualties. We're hoping to see the bridge where he fought and died.'

'I'm not sure if you'll get to see the original bridge. Although it survived the war, it was replaced later,' said Charles.

The sound of high heels distracted Buchanan. He looked away from the Kowalskis and saw the Muellers approaching across the dance floor. Once again Buchanan looked at Mueller's face: it was the face of his nightmares.

'Are these seats taken?' asked Mrs Mueller.

'No,' said Karen.

'I've never seen someone make clogs,' said Mrs Mueller, sitting down beside Karen.

'Neither have I,' said Karen. 'I'm Karen, this is my husband, Jack.'

'I'm Irene, and this is Karl, my partner.'

Buchanan leaned forward. 'Karl, you look familiar, have we met somewhere?'

'I doubt it, Jack.'

'We moved to Eastbourne from Glasgow last year. Eastbourne's in Sussex.'

'I know where Eastbourne is, Jack. We live in Meads.'

'Shopping? The Arndale Centre, perhaps?'

'Golf, do you play, Jack?' asked George.

'What, me chase a wee ball round a field? Not a chance.'

'How about you, Karl, you play golf?' persisted George.

'A bit.'

'What's your handicap?'

'Twenty-six.'

'Gee, I struggle to average a thirty-two.'

'Are you still working, Karl?' Buchanan asked.

Karl nodded.

'What do you do, Jack?' asked Delia.

'I'm a policeman.'

'Do you carry a gun?' she continued.

'No. I don't need to. Though some British police do carry weapons. These days with the terrorist threat we have to be prepared.'

'What do you do as a cop?' asked George.

'I catch criminals and take them out of circulation. My rank is Detective Chief Inspector.' As he informed the assembled audience at the table of this, he glanced at Irene. Her countenance had changed, now she was smiling at him; Karl was scowling.

'I've never met an inspector before,' she said.

Buchanan smiled at her. 'I'm sorry, I didn't catch your name?'

'It's Irene, Irene Adler.'

'Irene. What do you do?'

'I work with Karl, I'm his girl Friday.'

'Like a PA?'

'Sort of.'

'And what do you do, Karl?' asked Buchanan, picking up his glass while studying Karl's face.

'I'm a financial advisor.'

'Helping people with mortgages and pensions?' Buchanan was enjoying this; Karl certainly wasn't. 'Wish we'd met a few weeks ago, we've just bought a house and had the devil of a time getting a mortgage.'

'Why? I thought with you being a policeman you'd have no problems getting a mortgage,' said Delia.

'We still have a house in Glasgow, and with my possible retirement looming, some banks we approached were being awkward.'

'You should have met with Karl, Jack. He would have sorted you out,' said Irene.

Buchanan found the situation very interesting. Having gone from being ignored by Irene, he was now being used as a foil to irritate Karl, and he didn't mind one bit.

'Do you drive fast cars, Jack? You know, blue lights and sirens?' asked Delia.

'I'm provided with a car, a Ford Mondeo, nothing special. What do you drive, Karl?'

'Me, I drive a Mercedes AMG. Lovely car, just right for our country roads, holds the corners like glue.'

'You wouldn't get much use of its power on the A27,' said Buchanan.

'Oh, I don't know about that. I just put it in sport mode and nothing gets in its way.'

Not even my humble Mondeo, thought Buchanan.

'Jack, is thinking about retiring,' said Karen, realising where Buchanan was going with the conversation. 'Are you still working, George?'

'Me? No, I retired six years ago. Spent 37 years with Black and Decker. Started in the drawing office and worked my way up the ladder. I was a product manager when I left.'

'What's it like being a policeman, Jack?' asked Irene.

'It's a job.'

'You must have a quiet time – Eastbourne's a bit out of the way.'

'Not that quiet. Just last week someone was pistol-whipped in broad daylight, a few days earlier a young man was stabbed.'

'What about some of the exciting cases you've investigated?' asked Delia.

'The reason for me being in Eastbourne was I was seconded to Sussex CID to investigate the deaths of two people in the marina.'

'What happened to them?' asked Delia.

'The first was a young lady who had been drugged and thrown into the marina.'

'And the second?'

'A detective sergeant, he drowned while still seat-belted in his car.'

'Cor, sounds like an episode of *CSI*,' said George. 'Ever watch it, Jack?'

'No, sorry. I have enough crime in real life to want to sit down and watch it on television.'

'Did you catch the person who killed the girl and the policeman?' said Irene.

'Yes.'

'What happened to the killer?'

'He died while trying to escape.'

'Do you feel lucky, punk?' said George. 'A quote from the *Dirty Harry* film, Jack.'

Buchanan nodded. 'No, I didn't shoot anyone.'

'Didn't think that sort of thing went on in Eastbourne,' said Irene.

'There's been worse.'

'Do you always catch the killer, Jack?' asked Irene.

'Always.'

'And are they convicted?'

'Those who go to trial are.'

'You mean some get off?'

'No, sometimes they don't live to go to trial.'

'Jack, could I have another glass of wine, please?' asked Karen.

'Sorry, I'm doing it again, talking shop.'

'You must really love your job,' said Irene.

'Couldn't imagine doing anything else with my time.'

Buchanan went off to order a glass of wine for Karen and another whisky for himself. When he returned to his seat the evening's entertainment was about to begin: wooden shoe making.

♦

Buchanan turned off the cabin light, partially pulled back the curtain and climbed into bed.

'That was a strange evening,' said Karen.

'Wonder if those clogs are comfortable,' said Buchanan.

'That wasn't what I was talking about.'

'What were you talking about?'

'Irene. Up till the moment you said you were a policeman, she would hardly even look at you. Now she's all friendly.'

'You think she fancies me, like some women have a fixation for men in uniform?'

'No, Jack. That's not at all what I am getting at. I just think it's odd.'

'They're not married, and yet they're living together.'

Karen turned to face Buchanan. 'Lots of people live together and are not married.'

'I know, but there's something not right with their relationship. Did you notice he's wearing a wedding ring and she isn't?'

'Yes, what of it?'

'I suppose it could be a sort of self-defence mechanism. Some single men wear a wedding ring as a warning to women that they are not available for a permanent relationship.'

'Or, he really is married but either is unable or unwilling to get a divorce,' said Karen.

'I wonder if they began as a boss and secretary?'

'Happens all the time. Remember Sheila Davis? She had an affair with one of the directors where she worked. He strung her along for years till she finally got wise and called it off.'

'Yeah, I remember Sheila. What happened to her?'

'She's now married to a vicar of one of the new churches in East Kilbride. The last time I chatted to her she was expecting her third child, a boy.'

'Glad to hear it.'

'So, what about Irene? You're the policeman – what do your little grey cells tell you about her?'

'For one thing, I think she's a very complex person. When she speaks she is very careful about what she says and how she says it. I got the feeling that when I said I was a policeman, a light went on in her mind. I'm sure she's plotting something.'

'Something legal?'

'That's what I don't know. Maybe she's planning on doing the same thing as your friend Sheila.'

'Leaving Karl? And you're sure he was the one who ran you off the road?'

'Absolutely. When I saw the look in his eyes this evening, it was like I was reliving my accident. You heard what kind of car he drives: a Mercedes AMG, top speed over 190 miles per hour.'

'Lots of people drive fast cars. You would if I'd let you spend the money.'

'That's my point. You'd be lucky to get one like his for less than a hundred thousand pounds, and there's no way he could earn that sort of money selling mortgages. So, where does he get his money from?'

'Doesn't take you long, does it?'

'What do you mean?'

'You're back at work.'

♦

Later that night while lying in bed, Buchanan began to wonder about the last day's events. Irene Adler went from being standoffish to being friendly. Then there was Karl Mueller – just what did he do for a living and where did his money come from? He'd heard about London bankers making so much money that when in the local wine bars, they literally used to light their Cuban cigars with fifty-pound notes. Or could he really be so successful at gambling that he could afford to be as generous with his money as his wife said he was?

4

Buchanan woke with a start. Something was different. It took him a few minutes to figure out what had woken him. It was the sound of the main engines: the crew were getting the boat ready to sail. He looked at the time on his phone: three-fifty. He turned over and looked at Karen. She was fast asleep, blankets pulled up round her face. He leaned over and kissed her, she partially opened one eye.

'What's the matter?'

'Nothing, we're getting ready to sail. I'm going up on deck to watch. Sleep on, I'll see you at breakfast.'

As quietly as he could, Buchanan dressed in the dark then climbed part way up the steps to the upper deck to watch. He soon realised that the other long-ships that had been tied up alongside were now floating a way out in the river waiting for the berth to become available. He continued to watch as the boat was untied and made its way out into the main shipping channel and on to the port of Hoorn.

As the ship pulled away from the dock the engine note dropped as the exhaust sound no longer reverberated off the quayside. As he became used to the ambient sounds of the ship moving through the channel, he heard the sound of raised voices. They were coming from the cabin directly in front of him, cabin 312. He leaned over the rail to hear better.

'Why won't you tell her? Why should I have to spend my life as a – a – kept woman, your little bit on the side, your girl Friday?'

'Irene, how many times do I have to tell you? The time's not right. If I was to say I want a divorce, she and that lawyer friend of hers would take me to the cleaners, I'd be penniless.'

'Is that all you think about – money? Money is more important to you than me. Do you realise I'm not getting any younger?'

'Of course, I do. It's just – it's just – it's not just about the money. It's the adverse publicity that would be generated from a public divorce. It would have a detrimental effect on the project I'm working on.'

'The syndicate, that's all I hear about. Except you won't tell me about your syndicate. I'm not to be trusted, is that it?'

'Keep your voice down, the whole world can hear you.'

'I don't care who hears, if you don't do something about getting a divorce I'll –'

'You'll do nothing, do you hear me? Nothing.'

The window was slammed shut and Buchanan could feel his holiday turning into an adventure. Something was going on, and it wasn't just a bit of domestic disharmony. Time to have a meeting with his new partner in crime, Karen. He looked at the time on his phone, five-twenty, too early for breakfast, but not too early for a coffee and a pastry.

He collected his coffee and pastry from the all-night coffee station and walked through to the lounge to his chair by the window to think. Money was definitely at the root of the situation with Mueller, but how much and where was it coming from or going to? He thought back to his last major case; money was the moving force in that crime, though in that case it was all controlled by the Mafia. Could this be another? He didn't think so. Mueller was German, so in Buchanan's mind that precluded the Mafia, so what could it be? A scene from *Fawlty Towers* came to his mind, where Basil says *Whatever you do, don't mention the war*. Buchanan let his mind wander down the avenue of scenarios, such as Brexit. What effect would that have on German industries? He picked up his phone and googled for information on German exports to the UK. He saw its major exports were cars, car parts, packaged medicines and aircraft, with the UK being third in the list for export countries. The one fact that stood out to Buchanan was the total value of Germany's exports: 1.32 trillion US dollars. Now that was a lot of money at stake. Was that what Mueller was involved in, managing the movement of Germany's export revenues?

He went off down another avenue. This time he thought about the European Union and the effect Brexit was having on members of the European states. Greece was first on the list; basically it was beyond bankrupt. The German president was having problems forming a coalition government and Germany was also one of the major contributors to Greece through the IMF.

Spain was having its issues with finances. Northern Italy was contemplating becoming an independent state with local elections looming. Spain, at the eastern border with France, had the Catalan region on the edge of civil unrest following the arrest of the legally appointed government. On the southern border, Spain was still at loggerheads with the UK over Gibraltar.

Britain was struggling with a solution to the border between Northern Ireland and Eire. His home country of Scotland was in turmoil about a second referendum on independence. Buchanan thought the only logical solution was a strategy for unification. A single state, with unified governance, taxes and benefits. That way countries wouldn't have to be in debt to each other to just exist.

A distant memory from school floated into his consciousness: Germany in the nineteen-thirties. But look where that misguided philosophy ended up, between thirty and fifty million dead and countless families destroyed. Buchanan couldn't see Mueller being involved in anything like that, so what could it be?

The Romans two thousand years ago had tried to unify Europe, which ultimately failed. All that was left in his arsenal of memories was the Holy Roman Empire, with Germany being the largest territory, though that was dissolved sometime in the early eighteen hundreds. Of course, this was all speculation fuelled by an empty stomach.

The time displayed on his phone said it was now six-thirty, five-thirty back at home in Eastbourne, too early yet for breakfast, so he set off for another pastry and fresh cup of coffee, then returned to his seat by the window.

He finished his coffee and returned to his cabin with a fresh coffee for Karen. She was sitting up in bed reading the on-board news-sheet for the day's excursions.

'I brought you a coffee and a pastry.'

'Thanks,' she said, reaching out for the cup. 'What time was it when you got up?'

'Just before four o'clock.'

'Aren't you a bit tired?'

'Not really, I can take a nap later on in the day if I need it.'

'What did you do with the rest of your time?'

'I overheard a very interesting conversation between the Muellers.'

'Jack, that's not nice, eavesdropping on a private conversation.'

'I wasn't actually eavesdropping. I was standing halfway up the stairs to the upper deck –'

'Why were you standing on the stairs? Why not go up on the deck?'

'There's a notice that says not to go up on deck while the boat's going through locks and low bridges. Also, they ask passengers not to walk on the path to the upper deck during the night. The upper cabins are directly below.'

'That makes sense. So, what did you hear?'

'Basically, she is very unhappy. In her eyes, he is treating her like a servant, and when it comes to his business interests he keeps everything to himself.'

'So is she ignored or not trusted?'

'That's a good question. I think his business affairs are more than just finding mortgages and pension plans.'

'How do you know that? Have you been snooping?'

'All right, I put my hands up. I called Ahmed Bashir, you remember him, Aisha's father. He contacted a few friends and they

43

told him that Mueller is not just a simple financial advisor, he is more of what you might call a consultant financial advisor. According to what he told me, Mueller has connections in high places. He's even been seen having lunch with people such as Tony Blair, and he is a member of the Bilderberg group.'

'What, or who, is the Bilderberg group?'

'They're an international group of European and North American political and business elite. They meet once a year in various locations. There are some people who see the Bilderberg members as the forerunners of a New World Order.'

'The One World Government group?'

Buchanan shook his head. 'I don't think they're that group. But they certainly have influence, The Bush boys were members as were several other American Presidents.'

'Bashir told you all this?'

'No, I asked Google.'

'If Mueller is so well connected, why doesn't he just use private jets like they all probably do?'

'Maybe he's on a private mission, something not connected to the Bilderberg group, and that's why he's chosen this way to travel and meet his contacts.'

'You really think that's what he's up to?'

'Who knows,' he shrugged. 'I do know something, though.'

'What's that?'

'It's time for you to get ready, breakfast starts in twenty minutes.'

♦

Karen led them into the restaurant and walked over to a partially-occupied table where their new acquaintances Marjorie and Charles were seated.

'Good morning, Marjorie, Charles, may we join you?'

'Ah, Jack and Karen, certainly,' said Marjorie.

'Did you sleep well, Marjorie?' asked Karen, as she picked up the breakfast menu.

'Perfectly – till my niece called. The dear girl doesn't realise we are in a different time zone. We're at least five – or is it six – hours apart.'

'Just like my mother, except she lives in France and they are only one hour ahead of us.'

'Good morning. May I join you?' asked Irene.

'Certainly,' said Marjorie. 'Where's your husband? Will he be joining us?'

Irene scowled. 'No, he's waiting for a phone call, and for your information, we're not married.'

She sat beside Buchanan and, as she reached for a menu, her unbuttoned cardigan opened and he saw what looked like fresh bruises on her upper arm. He'd seen those type of bruises before. They were usually created by someone grabbing the arm and violently shaking the victim. Unfortunately for the victim those bruises weren't the only injuries they sustained, they were only the beginning of the abuse.

'Jack, will you order me an omelette, please?' said Karen, watching her husband.

'OK. Would you like anything with it?'

'Ham, cheese, peppers, onions, and tomatoes. Also, while you are up, would you toast me a slice of brown bread, with butter and marmalade, please?'

'Would you excuse us?' said Marjorie, standing up. 'We've got to get ready for the shore excursion and there's that safety drill before we can go ashore. Nice meeting you again, Irene.'

'Would you like something from the breakfast bar, Irene?' asked Buchanan.

'Oh, thanks, yes. What are you having, Karen?'

'I'm having an omelette. They make pretty much anything you want.'

'OK, I'll have the same, whatever it is.'

'Your wish is my command,' said Buchanan nodding.

Since their table was in the corner of the restaurant, away from the breakfast bar, Buchanan was unable to hear the conversation between Karen and Irene as he stood and watched the chef prepare the omelettes.

Buchanan returned to the table with the toast and was about to speak when he saw the *Don't ask, I'll tell you later,* look on Karen's face. He smiled back at her. 'Toast, butter and marmalade,' he said, putting the plates with toast in front of the ladies. 'Our waiter will be round with your omelette, tea and coffee in a minute. There's orange and apple juice at the counter if either of you would like some?'

Irene looked up at Buchanan. He saw the tear-stained redness of her eyes and wondered, not for the first time in his career, why did women stay with abusive men? 'Could I have an apple juice, please?' she requested.

'Karen, would you like juice?'

'I'll have orange, please.'

He returned with the juices and said, 'If you two will excuse me for a minute, I need to pay a visit to the boys' room.'

As he walked away from the table he thought Irene was more likely to talk freely to Karen if he wasn't there. He took his time and returned fifteen minutes later to find Karen sipping on her coffee, alone.

'I was wondering if you were coming back,' she said.

'Where's Irene?'

'She's gone back to her cabin. She went to say goodbye to Karl, he's been summoned to another meeting. I hope you don't mind, but I said I'd accompany her on the morning excursion. I think she wants the ear of a sympathetic woman.'

'The walking tour of the windmills? No problem, another of the Timson clan has just been arrested and Rumple has been assigned to represent him. Go and enjoy yourself, I'll be fine.'

♦

'How was the walk? See many windmills?' said Buchanan, putting his book down beside his empty whisky glass.

'It was fine, and yes, lots of tulips and windmills.'

'Anything else?'

'We had quite an interesting conversation as we walked through the local shops, then stopped for a coffee and chatted some more.'

'Should I enquire what about?'

Karen glanced around to see if anyone was in earshot. 'I'll talk to you in the cabin. Have you had lunch yet?'

'No, I was waiting for you to return.'

'Good, all that fresh air has given me an appetite. Can we sit over in the corner by the window?

'So, what did you two talk about while in town?' asked Buchanan as he closed their cabin door.

'Nothing really specific, just a lot about how she was getting tired with the way he treated her.'

'Did she say anything about him hitting her?'

'No, and that was odd. I expected her to say something about it. She just repeated the line about walking in to doors.'

'Of course, she could be on drugs. I've seen some people so out of their heads that they were convinced they could walk through brick walls.'

'I don't think she's on drugs. She was too lucid.'

'Well, either way we'll just have to keep an eye out for her. At the first sign of violence to her from Karl I'll have him arrested.'

'What are you going to do this afternoon?' asked Karen.

'Back to my book, the Timsons and the Malloys are at each other's throats, and you?'

'Marjory has asked me to go ashore with her. She's also asked to sit with us at dinner tonight.'

'In that case, I'll disappear back to the bar and my book. Shall we meet back later for dinner. The ship leaves for Arnhem at 18:30.'

'Fine, I'll see you later.'

♦

As the ship motored through the night on its way to Arnhem, Buchanan wondered where the events surrounding Irene were taking them. Too often in his career he'd seen what can happen to women who stay to long with abusive men.

He rose early for breakfast and once again decided to spend the morning on board while Karen went on ashore.

You get a good view of the bridge from there,' said Karen as she sat down to dinner beside Buchanan, 'Did you know there are still bullet holes from the Second World War in the bridge piers? The bridge isn't the original one though, that was so severely damaged during the fight it had to be replaced after the war.'

'You certainly have been doing your homework.'

'You'd find out these things as well if you went for a walk, instead of sitting here reading and drinking.'

'This is my holiday as well. You and the doctor said I was to relax, and that's what I'm doing.'

Further conversation was curtailed as the waiter appeared and passed out the menus to those seated at the table then asked about drink requests. Buchanan, ever wanting value for money, refused the table wine and asked for a glass of Prosecco.

'Prosecco, Jack?' said Karen.

'Uh-huh. It helps to cleanse the pallet, and I'm looking forward to lunch. Have you seen what's on the menu?'

'Yes, and I know what I'm going to have?'

Buchanan looked at what was on the menu and was about to speak when Irene arrived.

'May I sit with you?'

'Certainly,' said Karen, putting down the menu. 'Karl still in town?'

'No, he came back half an hour ago. He told me to go and have lunch, he needed to concentrate on some paperwork.'

Irene sat to the right of Karen and Buchanan could see what makeup couldn't conceal: a bruise on Irene's left cheek, just below her eye.

'Excuse me for asking, Irene, but are you all right?' he asked.

'What? Oh, the bruise. I walked into a door, silly me.'

'He did that to you, didn't he?' said Buchanan.

Tears formed in her eyes, her head lowered as she reached into her handbag for a tissue. 'Yes, but it wasn't his fault. I shouldn't interfere with his work.'

'But I thought you were his secretary? Surely you have to know about his work, how else can you do your job?'

'Oh, I stopped being his secretary years ago, back when I had my first miscarriage.'

Karen looked at Buchanan and slowly shook her head.

'I'm sorry, I shouldn't interfere in your private affairs,' said Buchanan.

She sniffed and blew her nose. 'I don't mind you two knowing. I can trust you not to tell anyone else my secrets. And I'm sorry to spoil your day with my sordid tale of a woeful relationship that I call a partnership.'

'It sometimes helps to talk about the things that bother you,' said Karen.

Irene looked over at the door and the adjacent empty tables before looking back at Karen. 'We used to be happy, made all sorts of plans about the future. When we met, he and his wife were living separate lives though in the same house. She was a financial consultant for HSBC. He worked for Lehman Brothers and travelled to their overseas offices quite regularly. Between them they made a considerable income but were never really happy.

'One day she announced she wanted to give it all up and settle down. You know what I mean, house in the country, children, a dog even. He on the other hand had grander ideas that did not include children and dogs. By then we had been seeing a lot of each other outside of our daily work environment. At first the travel to foreign countries, staying in top hotels, being wined and dined, meeting fascinating people was what I suppose was every girl's dream. I suppose I should have been wiser, but I fell hook, line and sinker for him. Foolishly, I thought I could change him, be the centre of his universe.'

'Is he still married?' asked Buchanan.

'Yes. He says she wants half of everything, but he doesn't want to give her anything.'

'Does she know about you?'

'What do you think? Of course she does, even sends me a birthday card every year, with a big smiley face on the front of the envelope.'

Buchanan shook his head.

'What are you doing after lunch?' asked Karen.

Irene shrugged. 'Don't know, haven't planned anything. Karl's off on another one of his meetings this afternoon, he won't be back till late.'

'What does he do in these meetings?' asked Buchanan.

She shook her head. 'I don't know, he doesn't tell me anything. I think I'm along as a diversion. We don't even sleep in the same bed anymore.'

'I was going on the afternoon walking tour,' said Karen. 'Would you like to join me, Irene?'

'I'd love to. Cosy as the cabin may be, I need to get out into the fresh air and think. I believe it's time to make a decision. I can't spend the rest of my life this way.'

Karen looked at Buchanan.

'Me? I was planning on relaxing and reading my book. The story is really getting interesting, Rumple is doing battle with judge Bullingham.'

The conversation was interrupted by the arrival of Marjorie and Charles.

'Good afternoon, have you had your lunch yet?'

''Hello, Marjorie,' said Karen. 'No, we've been too busy talking.'

♦

'How was the trial – did Rumple get Timson off?' said Karen, interrupting Buchanan's reading.

'Yes, and Timson survives for another day. How was town, more windmills?'

'No, we went window shopping and had a cup of tea in a lovely Dutch teashop.'

'How is Irene?'

'She's a very scared lady, but tough,' said Karen, as she sat beside Buchanan. 'She's going to tell him she's leaving him as soon as we get back to Amsterdam on Friday. She even threatened him with selling her story to the Sunday papers.'

'Did she say how she thought he'll take that piece of news?'

'You saw the bruises on her arms and the black eye. Jack. I'm extremely worried about her, isn't there anything we can do to protect her?'

'I don't know anything about Dutch law on domestic violence, I assume it's somewhat similar to our UK law. Unless she's willing to make an official complaint, there's not much the law can do.'

'All the same, I fear for her.'

'You think she's in that much danger?'

'She didn't exactly say so, but it was her eyes. Jack, do you remember you once took me to a fox hunt? You were there with a police team to prevent violence between the hunt and the hunt-protesters?'

51

'Goodness, that goes back a few years.'

'One of the protesters was holding a huge poster of a scared fox.'

'They were trying to unseat one of the hunters I seem to remember.'

'Do you remember the poster, the eyes of the fox, the total abject fear in its eyes? That was what I saw in Irene's eyes this afternoon.'

'I tell you what we'll do,' said Buchanan. 'This evening, we'll invite her to our table. If she tells me what she is scared of happening to her, I'll go to the captain and make arrangements for her to get a separate cabin till the morning, and a flight home tomorrow.'

'You think the captain will go along with that?'

'If Irene will go with me to the captain and tell him what she told you, I'm sure that will be the case.'

♦

'Over here, Irene, come sit with us,' said Karen, waving from the dinner table.

Irene looked behind her and shook her head.

'Jack,' said Karen, 'you're on. Time to *cherchez la femme.*'

He looked at her for a moment, then realised what Karen was getting at.

'OK.'

Buchanan stood up from the table and walked over to where Irene was standing.

'Waiting for Karl?'

'Hello, Jack, yes. How's the book, still at the Old Bailey?'

He smiled. 'Yes. All's well in the world of Rumple. Pommeroy's are still serving large glasses of Chateaux Thames Embankment, and the Timson and Malloy family are keeping Rumple gainfully employed. I've come over to see if you'd like you to join us for dinner.'

'I'm sorry, I can't. Karl will be here shortly, and he wants us to sit alone.'

Buchanan looked over her shoulder, through the restaurant doors, and down the corridor. Then he said in a lowered voice, 'Karen has told me you are going to leave Karl when we get to Amsterdam on Friday.'

She nodded and winced. Buchanan could clearly see the imminent signs of a fresh bruise forming below the existing one on her face.

She sniffed. 'I'm sorry, Jack, I just can't. Thank Karen for me for all she's done, please. You'll never know just how helpful you've both been.' Then she turned and ran out of the restaurant.

Buchanan returned to the table.

'What happened, Jack?'

'She must have already told him, there's a fresh bruise on her face where he hit her again.'

Karen stood up. 'I'm going to see her, she can't be left alone with him on the prowl.'

'Suggest to her that she stay in our cabin tonight,' said Buchanan.

'Where will you sleep?'

'The lounge. Don't worry about me. It will be just like the old days when we used to do stake-outs in hotel lobbies.'

Karen smiled. 'You certainly do love your job, don't you?'

♦

Karen left the restaurant and hurriedly walked down the corridor to cabin 312. She stopped outside the door and listened. She heard voices, thankfully not raised ones. She lifted her hand to knock on the door when it opened.

'Ah, Karl, I'm looking for Irene. I was going to invite you both to our table.'

'I'm sorry, Karen. Irene is not feeling well. She's in the shower and is going to have an early night. One of her migraines has just come on. She needs to lay down in the dark and rest.'

'Can I do anything to help?'

'No, she'll be fine. She's taken her medication and will be dead to the world in minutes. When she has these attacks it usually wipes her out. I doubt if we'll see much of her over the next couple of days. But, if there's still space at your table, I'd love to join you and John.'

'It's Jack.'

'Sorry, it's been a very busy month, and now with Irene not being well… I'll just go and see that she's all right. I'll join you in the restaurant in a few minutes.'

'OK. I'll keep a seat for you.'

♦

'No Irene?' said Buchanan, as Karen returned to the table.

She shook her head as she sat. 'Karl said she had a migraine and was going to skip dinner and have an early night.'

'Did you believe him?'

'What could I do? I heard the shower running. I couldn't just barge in and drag her out by the hair, now could I?'

'No, I suppose you couldn't.'

'Shush,' said Buchanan quietly, 'he's coming over to our table.'

'That's all right, I invited him.'

Karen stood. 'Karl, how is Irene?'

He shook his head. 'I don't know what the doctor gives her, but she was already fast asleep and dead to the world when I left her just now.'

'I hope she will be well tomorrow, we have arranged to go see the windmills and hear how the water is managed by the flood-management equipment.'

'Oh, I'm not sure if she'll be well enough for that. These attacks she has sometimes hospitalise her. With the one she has just had, I don't expect you'll see much of her tomorrow. Usually when she wakes she is so exhausted she ends up spending the day in bed dozing. They tend to knock the stuffing out of her.'

'Will you be joining us ashore for the tour to see the windmills tomorrow then?' asked Buchanan.

'No. I will be up very early in the morning before the ship leaves for Kinderdijk. I have a car coming to collect me in the early hours.'

'More meetings?'

'The needs of business I'm afraid. I won't see you again till the ship gets to Antwerp on Tuesday. I have meetings most of the day but should be back in time for dinner.'

'Not much of a holiday for you both,' said Buchanan.

'It's not meant to be a holiday, Jack. It just saves me the hassle of staying in numerous hotels and the tedium of having to deal with train schedules and airports.'

'Are these seats taken?' asked Marjorie, who'd just walked in, preventing Buchanan from continuing with his prying into the busy and private life of Karl Mueller.

'No, they're not taken. Marjorie and Charles, have you met Karl?' said Karen.

'Hello, Karl,' said Marjorie.

'Karl,' said Charles, shaking Karl's offered hand. 'Have we met somewhere? You look familiar.'

'I don't think so.'

'Paris in '03 at the Eurofidai conference. I seem to remember you were presenting a paper on…'

'Yes, you are quite correct, I was there. But I'm sorry, I do not remember you.'

'That's all right. I do remember your proposal, thought it was quite controversial. I seem to remember it created a bit of a stir. Something about individual states within states. Each with their own financial, economic, and political autonomy, free to trade with whomever they chose. But still being an integral functionary with the greater body of the parent state.'

'Yes, I'm surprised you remember the proposal. Unfortunately, it didn't get enough votes to go forward.'

'Are you still working on it? It was a brilliant idea. Something that's needed back home.'

Buchanan watched Karl closely, especially his eyes. They were darting from side to side as his mind was chasing concepts – or was it something more sinister? Was he concerned he'd said too much, given away some vital secret?

'Er, I'm sorry that Irene can't be with us this evening,' said Karl to Marjorie and Charles, as he took his seat at the table. 'It's her blasted migraines, they knock her for six. She becomes confused, hallucinates, loses her balance and falls into things, usually doors. I'd be very grateful if you didn't mention to her that I've told you about her little problem.'

'No, of course we won't,' said Marjorie, 'thanks for letting us know. We did wonder about the bruise on her face – thought she might have fallen.'

He frowned then nodded as though agreeing with the diagnosis and picked up the menu.

Buchanan stood and said loudly, 'Ladies and gentlemen, would you join me in a toast to my wonderful wife who has stood by me these last thirty-five years?'

A chorus of congratulations filled the restaurant as Buchanan pulled a card from his jacket and handed it to Karen. She opened the envelope and looked at the message inside, then read it out loud.

> I don't think anyone has ever been loved, like you love me.
> I don't think anyone has ever been cared for, like you care for me.
> I don't think anyone has ever seen the smile, that you show to me.
> And I love you with all my heart,
> forever, Jack.

Karen looked up at her husband with tears in her eyes and mouthed, *love you too.*

♦

'Did you see the look on Karl's face when Marjorie mentioned the bruise on Irene's face?' said Karen as she climbed into bed.

'Yes, I did. Wonder what that was all about?'

'What did you think about his story about Irene's migraines? Thankfully, I've never had migraines, but I doubt anyone walks into doors when they are having one.'

'Oh, I'm not so sure about that. A few months before we came down from Glasgow, I was going to lunch with a couple of the lads. As we drove down Argyle Street we got a call about a traffic accident on Stockwell Street. When we got there, we found the driver trying to explain why he didn't see the bus in front of him. He'd had a migraine attack while driving, and had temporarily lost part of his vision.'

'But a bus, how can you miss seeing a bus?'

'I don't know, apparently it's what happens to some people who suffer from migraines.'

'And are we supposed to think that's what happened to Irene?'

Buchanan reached over and turned off his bedside light. 'You know what I think? I think I'm tired, been a long time since I enjoyed dancing so much.'

'You sure it wasn't the whisky?'

Buchanan turned over and kissed Karen. 'Good night, lovely lady.'

In spite of being tired from the evening's entertainment, Buchanan couldn't get to sleep. He turned back on to his other side and stared through the window at the night scenery of the street-lit riverbanks.

Could it be that Irene was suffering from the side effects of migraine? He knew some people suffered from sight problems, and if someone could not see a bus, why not a door? But that wouldn't explain the marks he saw on her upper arms, unless…. Unless she was a self-harmer. He'd heard about some women becoming depressed when faced with the issue of being childless. An article in a newspaper came back to him about women who were childless, either by choice or circumstances. He looked over at Karen; she was fast asleep.

He picked up his phone and googled 'childless women'. An article in the *Guardian* came up and he saw that eighty percent of childless women are childless by circumstances. Either they were infertile, chose not to have children, or had a partner who didn't want the complication of children. Was that what was happening to Irene? Was she going through some horrible traumatic turmoil fuelled by the feeling of being left on the shelf? He decided, no matter what, he and Karen would see if there was anything they could do to help, though he didn't have any idea what they could do other than point Irene in the direction of proper medical care.

Of course, if he could find something out about Karl that would get him out of the way for a while, maybe that would give Irene the opportunity to find someone new. Someone who could love her and be the husband she needed. But other than getting Karl charged and jailed with dangerous driving, what could he do? He momentarily thought of calling Street, but then remembered she and Stephen were still on their honeymoon and weren't due back home till Friday afternoon.

There was Dexter, but would he be as efficient as Street? What Buchanan needed was someone with compassion, someone who'd dig as deep as needed into Karl's past. Hanbury was a possibility but, being an inspector, he'd be too busy with his own cases. No, it would have to be himself, but where to start?

♦

'Jack, are you coming for breakfast?'

'What time is it?'

'Ten past eight. You really were tired, you snored like a bear in hibernation.'

'Didn't realise bears snored,' he said. 'Sorry if I kept you awake. Have we arrived?' He said squinting through the gap in the curtains.'

'Not yet. The Viking newsletter says we don't arrive in Kinderdijk till one o'clock.'

'You go ahead, I'll join you when I'm dressed.'

'I went out for coffee earlier –'

'And?'

'There's a do-not-disturb sign on Irene's door.'

'Any sounds from the room?'

'I listened, but nothing,' said Karen.

'I was thinking about how to help her.'

'What did you come up with?'

'She definitely needs to get away from Karl, start life fresh with someone who will care for her.'

'Like you do with me?'

'Just realised we have something in common with Irene.'

'Not having children?'

'Yes, but that's not quite true for us, is it? Jill is now part of the family.'

'And Stephen – don't forget her new husband.'

'It's going to be strange having family to Sunday lunch.'

'Strange, but wonderful.'

'I think I'll go see Irene later today. I think it will be best if I go on my own, might be easier for her to talk and think,' said Karen.

'Sounds like a plan. I was thinking about looking into Karl's background, maybe he's got skeletons in his cupboard.'

'Be careful, Jack. Remember it's their relationship you will be stepping into. Or – is it you want to get even with him for running you off the road?'

'No, it's not that, at least I don't think it is. I just don't like to think of her being alone with him and him taking his anger out on her. I will go carefully, I promise. Now, if you'll excuse me, I need to get dressed. I have a breakfast date with someone special.'

'Oh, really? I wonder who that might be?' said Karen with a smile growing on her face.

Buchanan dressed and shut the cabin door behind him. The do-not-disturb sign was still on the door handle to Irene's cabin. He thought about knocking on the door, then thought better of it. He remembered what it was like to be hung over and just wanting to be left alone.

He entered the restaurant and saw Karen seated with Marjorie and Charles.

'Morning everyone.'

'Good morning, Jack. How did you sleep?'

'Fine, thanks.'

'We wondered after watching you dance with Karen last night.'

'Did we enjoy it?' he asked Karen.

'Of course, we did. Don't you remember?'

He smiled. 'Yes, of course I remember. Haven't had that much fun since, since—'

'Since Hogmanay, the last year we were in Scotland,' said Karen.

'Ah, now that was an evening to remember,' said Buchanan, leaning back in his chair and taking a deep breath.

'Jack,' said Charles, interrupting what could have been an interesting story if told. 'I've been thinking about Karl and what he does for a living.'

Buchanan sat bolt upright. 'What have you been thinking?'

'Before going to bed last night, I called my friend Mike back in the States. I asked him about Karl. Just on the off chance he might have crossed paths with him at some time.'

'And did he know anything?'

'Mike works for the US Treasury Department. His group deals with corporate money laundering. I said I was considering investing some of our savings through a financial advisor we'd met while on vacation in Holland. He asked for the name of the advisor, so I told him about Karl.'

'Did he have any information on him?'

'Nothing criminal, but he was on their watch list. Apparently, he's been working behind the scenes for and on behalf of several companies on the SDN list.'

'What's the SDN list?'

'I asked him the same question. The SDN list is a list of companies, world-wide, that the US government keeps an eye on. It also lists individuals, groups, and entities, such as terrorists and narcotics traffickers but not necessarily country-specific.'

'So, Karl is on that list?'

'Mike said no. But he has been associated with some of the companies listed. Mike said to stay well clear of him.'

'Charles, enough about work,' interrupted Marjorie 'We're on vacation and I think Karen would rather we talk about what we're doing today. Isn't that right, Karen?'

'Yes. I was looking at the *Viking News* and I see there is a shore excursion to see the windmills and how they make Dutch cheese.'

'Sounds interesting. You want to come with us, Charles?'

'Are you going, Jack?'

'Apparently so. I hear we go ashore here in Kinderdijk and are bussed to meet up with the ship in Antwerp in time for cocktail hour.'

'Then I'm in as well,' said Charles.

◆

'The do-not-disturb sign is still on the door,' said Karen, as they approached their cabin. 'Surely Irene must be feeling better by now? It's been almost twenty hours since she first said she was not feeling well,' she said pulling back her sleeve to look at her watch.

'What time is it?'

'Ten thirty-five. She should be up by now if she wants something for breakfast.'

'Try knocking. Maybe she's up and doesn't realise the sign is still on the door, and besides, she did say if she wasn't around to come and get her.'

Karen walked up to the door, knocked gently and waited. There was no answer. She knocked again, still no answer. Buchanan knocked next, using his *this is the police* knock.

'I'm going down to guest services, Karen. Something's wrong, I just know it.'

'Hurry, Jack. I'll keep trying.'

Buchanan was back in five minutes with Thomas, the hotel manager.

'Madam,' Thomas said, knocking on the door, 'it is Thomas, the hotel manager. Can you come to the door, please?'

'Something's not right, Thomas,' said Buchanan. 'You said she is shown as being on board. We've checked the bar and restaurant, she must still be in her room. Can you open the door?'

Thomas knocked again. 'Madam, it is Thomas, the hotel manager. I am going to open the door and come into your room.'

'What are we waiting for?' said Buchanan.

Thomas inserted his master key and opened the door. It was as Buchanan feared. Unfortunately, during his long career as an investigating detective, he'd seen many rooms like this. Lights off, curtains drawn. This room was no different: it was a shamble. Bed clothes were pulled to one side and lay on the floor; bloodied clothes were strewn across a chair and dresser.

'Irene?' called Buchanan, in the hope that she may be lying somewhere in the mess, 'are you in here?' It was to no avail. There was no reply to his question.

'Thomas, please don't enter. I'm a British policeman, this room is now a crime scene. Will you inform the captain, please?'

'Yes, certainly.'

'Karen, would you stand in the corridor and keep curiosity seekers away from the door, please? I'll go in and make a cursory search.'

'How bad is it, Jack?' asked Karen, as Buchanan returned to the corridor. 'Is she in there?'

'No. There's no sign of Irene being in the room. I also checked the veranda, just in case. Unfortunately, I found blood on the handrail.'

'Do you think he killed her, then threw her body over the side?'

'How about it being the other way around? They had an argument, she killed him and pushed his body over the side?'

'But in that case, where is Irene?'

'She got off the ship before it left yesterday?'

'You've spent time with her. Do you think that really likely?'

'No. I think she'd be knocking on our door asking for help if that happened.'

'That's my thought as well. The evidence in this case points to her being the unfortunate victim. But I've learned initial impressions can be quite misleading. I've seen a lot worse. This looks like a frenzied attack, not something that was premeditated.'

'Why do you think that?'

'Mr Buchanan,' said Thomas, 'this is Captain Walewska. Unfortunately, his English is not so good. I will translate for him.'

'Thank you. Will you tell your captain I am Detective Chief Inspector Buchanan, Sussex CID in the United Kingdom?'

Walewska nodded then replied, 'Inspector, Thomas says I have little English. That is so. But I understand what I hear you say, Inspector. I believe you and trust you to do what is necessary. I will inform Belgian police, they will attend in morning at Antwerp.'

'Thank you, Captain. May I have your permission to perform a preliminary investigation? It might be helpful to the Belgian police and prevent your departure from Antwerp being delayed.'

'Yes, Inspector, that makes good sense. Will you need assistance?'

Buchanan immediately thought about Street and wished she was there to work with him. 'If Thomas could find me some plastic gloves, so we don't go leaving our own fingerprints in the room.'

'Thomas, you arrange?' said the captain.

'One more thing, Captain. I think it would help the Belgian police in their investigation if no one is permitted to go ashore when we arrive in Antwerp.'

The captain nodded in agreement. 'It will be done, Inspector.'

'Who are the *we* you told the captain about?' asked Karen.

'Fancy being a CSI for the day?'

'Me? I wouldn't know where to start.'

'Don't worry, I'll show you what I want to do, it's as simple as ABC.'

'ABC?'

'Accept nothing, believe nothing, challenge every visual observation and thought.'

'Is that what they teach you at police training?'

'That and other things, like –'

'What other things?'

'Five times WH plus H.'

'Now you're making fun of me.'

'No, I'm not. It's just a way of remembering a sequence of procedures. It's the who, what, where, when, why and the how best to go about the initial investigation.'

'And what will I be doing?'

'Mostly taking photographs. I'll do all the cataloguing of the evidence using those. Oh, how I wish the team were here for this.' said Buchanan.

'Don't worry, Jack. I'll do my best. We owe it to Irene.'

'Yes, you're so right. But why didn't I see it coming? It was all too obvious, all the signs were there: the arguments, the shaking, the bruising on the face. His clandestine occupation he wouldn't tell her about, yet still expected her to act the part of his executive secretary.'

'Shall we get to work?'

'Yes, me getting angry won't put him behind bars where he deserves to be.'

'So, what's the first thing you want photographed?'

'Start at the door and get a full-width shot of the cabin.'

'Aren't you missing something?'

'What am I missing?'

'My camera. It's a mobile phone, will that be good enough?'

'Ah yes, you have a point there. I'll get my compact camera from the cabin, be right back.'

'I'll guard the door.'

'Right,' said Buchanan, returning with his camera. 'This will be better, not quite up to CSI standards, but will suffice in this circumstance.'

'Are you going to document the evidence to take back with us?'

'No, the evidence must remain here for the Belgian police to process, especially the blood-stained clothing. What we are going to do is to photograph everything, note its position in the cabin, and leave the physical evidence for the Belgian CSI's.'

'How will that help us find out what happened to Irene?'

'Tomorrow when the Belgian police get here, I imagine they will take statements from us and that will be the end of our immediate involvement. Eventually when the investigation moves to the UK, as I'm sure it will, I'll already have a visual aide-memoire and hopefully by then, a full forensic analysis of the blood samples.'

'Will that be enough for you to convict Karl?'

'That's not down to me. We collect the evidence then submit it to the Crown Prosecution Service. It will then be up to them to do the prosecuting.'

'Why not the Belgian police? The crime took place in their country.'

'It would be if that was where the crime took place. My thinking is that Karl killed Irene before he left for his business meetings and probably disposed of the body while we were still tied up in Arnhem. If that was so then the crime took place in Holland, not Belgium.'

'Shall we get to work? It's getting late,' said Karen.

'Right,' said Buchanan, 'first a wide shot from the door, then one step inside and do a panoramic shot. Make sure you get the ceiling and the floor, then we'll move into the cabin and get some detailed shots. Pity there's not a lot to go on, just some bloodied underwear and a towel.'

'Does that tell you much?'

'It will tell a lot more to an experienced CSI. I'd say she had her shower, wrapped herself in a bath towel and came out of the bathroom. That's when he hit her – see the Prosecco bottle with the bloodstains?'

Karen bent down and without touching the bottle took some close-up shots.

'Let's get out of here, we've seen all we need to – except –,'

'What is it?' asked Karen.

'Do you see what I see? Just there, on the floor, sticking out from under the bedclothes. It's a mobile phone, Irene must have dropped it during the conflagration, can you take a couple of photos of it?'

Karen took three photos from different angles, then Buchanan stepped carefully over the blood-soaked towel and carefully picked it up. 'We're in luck. It's a Samsung. Do you have a paperclip?'

'Now why on earth would I just happen to have a paperclip, and what do you need it for?'

'I'm going to pop out the memory card and copy whatever photos are on it to my own phone.'

66

'Why would you want to do that?'

'Not sure, the phone should go to the lab, but if she's like most people with a smart phone, it might tell us where she's been and who with recently. Also, if the location function was on at the time of the pictures I will be able to date and time the locations.'

'Suppose it's not hers, suppose it's Karl's phone?'

'Doesn't matter who's phone it is, it's still evidence.'

'I'll be right back,' said Karen, 'there's a couple of paperclips on the dresser in our cabin.'

She returned a few minutes later with three paperclips and handed them to Buchanan.

'That should do it,' said Buchanan, as he extracted the memory card and inserted it into his phone. Memory card copied, he put it back in the phone and put the mobile back on the floor as close to its discovered position as he could. 'Hello, what's this?'

'What's what?'

'The waste paper basket – see what I've found. Looks like the maid missed these, they're stuck to the bottom.' He carefully picked out several pieces of torn-up paper.

'What have you found?' asked Karen.

'I'm not sure, looks like an email that someone ripped in pieces then threw in the bin, assuming the room maid would get rid of them.'

'Can you make sense out of any of them?'

'Hang on, let me lay the pieces out on the dresser. It looks like we've only got the body text of an email and what looks like a separate note, pity, it would have been helpful to have had the email header.'

It took Buchanan a few minutes to arrange the pieces of the torn-up email into a readable document.

K. Apologies for last night, I was detained at the embassy by Grigoriev. Have you been indiscreet? Do you talk in your sleep? As you remember from our last meeting, we agreed you must make sure the arrangements for the import are fully understood by B, and the goods securely packed.

I can now confirm that B will meet with you in Amsterdam. Time permitting, I may join you. B will contact you with meeting place. Make sure you are not followed or recognised by anyone, remember eyes are everywhere.

The certain member of the syndicate, you know the one, is starting to be awkward and is asking questions. I am thinking it may be time to retire the individual, he has almost completed his tasks and will soon be surplus to requirements.

R

'I wonder what that's all about? said Karen. 'And who are K, B and R?'

'I think it's safe to say that K is probably Karl, no idea who B and R are.'

'What does the other note say?'

'Not much, it's just a list of names.'

'Recognise any of them?'

Buchanan read down the short list. 'There is one name I recognise, but it must be a coincidence, I'm sure there are many people with the surname of Duncan.'

◆

'That would have been fun if it wasn't for the fact that we were investigating a murder,' said Karen, as she closed the door of their cabin.

'It doesn't make sense to me,' said Buchanan.

'What doesn't make sense?'

'Why leave so much evidence behind? In my experience, most killers make an attempt to clean up behind themselves. Also, all that blood and not one set of fingerprints.'

'Maybe he cleaned them first and ran out of time?'

'Do you remember what time you went to their cabin and heard the sound of the shower running?'

'Must have been about nine, nine-thirty.'

'The ship left Arnhem at three in the morning. That gave him a window of six hours to kill her and clear up afterwards.'

'Not quite. As I came back through the library area I looked out onto the dock and saw there were people working on the dock loading fresh vegetables at ten o'clock.'

'That's right, then the band left and went ashore at ten-thirty, he must have pushed her body over the rail just before the taxi came to collect him.'

'You're forgetting your ABC's, Jack.'

'What do you mean?'

'Remember: accept nothing, believe nothing and check everything. You're letting your anger get the better of your judgement. Test all things and hold fast to which is good, and do no evil.'

'Where did you get that?'

'The pastor said it in one of his sermons a few weeks ago.'

'Good for him. Though it does make good sense, do you have any more of those sayings?'

'Come to church with me on Sunday and you'll learn a lot more.'

'Maybe. We can tighten the time even closer. I bet the crew were on deck long before we left.'

'Shall we ask the captain?' said Karen.

'Yes, let's go.'

♦

'Can I help?' asked the receptionist at the guest services desk. '

'Yes, please. Jack Buchanan, cabin 309. Could I have a word with your captain, please?'

'I'm sorry Mr Buchanan, the captain is very busy at the moment. He's dealing with an unfortunate accident. I'm sure when we get to Antwerp he'll be able to find time to talk to you.'

'I'm Detective Chief Inspector Buchanan, British Police. I'm working with your captain on the unfortunate accident.'

'One moment, please, while I make a phone call.'

She hung up and said, 'Thomas will be right here to take you to the captain.'

♦

Thomas knocked and opened the door to the captain's office. 'Inspector Buchanan to see you, Captain.'

'How can I help, Inspector?'

'I was wondering if any of your crew saw anything unusual this morning, when we departed from Arnhem?'

'I check for you, one moment.'

The captain left his office for ten minutes then returned with four crew.

'Inspector, these men were on duty when we leave Arnhem. What do you want to ask them?'

'Would you ask them if they saw anything while on the dock as they prepared to untie the ship?' Not for the first time in his life, Buchanan wished he could speak more than just one language.

'Inspector, none of my men saw anything unusual. Gabor said he remembered a taxi arriving at about two-fifteen and one of our guests leaving the ship and getting into the taxi.'

'Would you thank him for me.'

'Yes, I will. Is there anything else you wish to ask, Inspector?'

'No thank you, Captain.' replied Buchanan, looking at the time on his phone. 'I think it's time for a team meeting.'

♦

'Your usual, Mr Buchanan?' asked the bartender.

'Yes please, Aleksander, and a large glass of Pinot Grigio for Mrs Buchanan.'

'Where shall we sit?' asked Karen.

'Over in the corner, that small table with two seats. I don't want to be disturbed,' said Buchanan, pointing to a lonely table in the forward corner of the lounge.

'Your wine,' said Buchanan as he sat down beside Karen.

'Thanks,' she said, taking a sip. 'What's that on your shirt cuff?'

Buchanan lifted his left hand to look at what Karen was referring to.

'No, your right cuff.'

Buchanan looked at where she was pointing. 'Looks like blood. I must have brushed against something while I was looking around the cabin. I'll go change, and I think I'll bag this shirt as evidence. See what Dr Mansell can tell from it.'

'What next?' asked Karen, when Buchanan returned wearing a clean shirt.

'What's next is we review what we have. Of course a lot depends on what happens during the next twenty-four hours.'

'Why twenty-four hours?'

'By then the Belgian police will have arrived and commenced their investigation and maybe Karl will have returned. If he has killed Irene he'll probably say she was asleep in bed when he left. I've also asked at guest services if they would print copies of the photos we took of the inside of the cabin. They'll bring them to me as soon as they have printed them.'

'So, what are we going to do in the meantime?'

'I thought we could have a look at the photos on the memory card in the phone we found lying on the cabin floor.'

'Probably just holiday snaps. When Irene was with me she took photos of just about everything.'

'Well, let's have a look anyway,' said Buchanan as he opened the photo app on his phone. 'Ah, what do we have here? Now this is really interesting.'

'What *do* we have?'

'The phone on the cabin floor wasn't Irene's. It looks like it was Karl's phone. He must have dropped it while disposing of Irene's body.'

'What's on the memory card that's got you so excited?'

'For one thing, he *was* in Lewes the day of my car accident, and by looking at the details of the photo, it was taken not thirty minutes prior to my accident.'

'Can I see?' said Karen, reaching for the phone. 'Selfies, everyone is doing it. Who's he with? She looks familiar.'

'I think she was in the government up to a few months ago. She got unceremoniously discharged from her post for talking to the right people at the wrong time, if I remember correctly. It was rumoured that she was unofficially representing several international companies in working out post-Brexit trade deals with other non-EU countries, but it was never proved.'

'Wonder what he's drinking? They don't serve lemonade in those types of glasses.'

'That looks like The Shelleys in Lewes. I've been there a couple of times for meetings, lovely place, must take you there for dinner one evening.'

'Since we know the day and time he was there,' said Karen, 'if he was buying drinks, and putting the cost on his card, you could maybe get him charged with driving over the limit?'

'Good idea, but unless he'd been stopped and breathalysed, the charge would never stand up in court.'

'What other photos did you copy?'

Buchanan put the phone down on the table and flicked, one at a time, through the album.

'He certainly likes to drink,' said Karen, 'he's got a glass in his hand in every photo. Or maybe he just buys one and makes it last.'

'You might say that, but I wouldn't like to comment.'

'That's from the *House of Cards* television show. Do you see a connection?'

'Not really, just like the saying,' he said, continuing to thumb through the photos. 'Oh, look at this selfie, and that's definitely not Irene. Look, do you think they could be discussing the weather?'

'I doubt it. I suppose it's all the more reason to dump Irene. But that doesn't make much sense – he and Irene aren't married.'

'But maybe the one in the photo is.'

'He's such a jerk.'

'I wonder where the photo was taken?' said Buchanan as he once again looked at the details of the photo. 'This is interesting – the photo was taken three weeks ago in Mayfair in London, even has the address. The hotel is called The Mayfair, a Raddisonblu Hotel. Now let me see, if I google the hotel and date we might get lucky and find out what was happening at the hotel on that date. Can you get me another whisky while I search, please?'

'Anything?' asked Karen, as she returned from the bar.

'This is beyond bizarre,' said Buchanan, 'on that date there was a conference about international trade, post-Brexit. *And,* one of the attendees was Karl's friend from the other photo. I've also managed to find out who she is – want to know?'

'Of course I do, this is better than any television show. I can see now why you enjoy your job so much.'

'Oh, it's not always this much fun. Anyway, she's the wife of one of the members of the Russian delegation. According to a September article in the *Mail on Sunday*, she's called Tatyana Reznikov. She was attending the London fashion week. Her husband runs several export companies, one of them managing exports of his wife's line in fashion clothing.'

'Ugly-looking brute. I wonder if he knows about his wife being so friendly with Karl?'

'Who knows? Maybe she's allowed to mix with the crowd, helping to consummate deals. It does happen.'

'What a rotten way to live, being pimped by your own husband.'

'It could be her job. The marriage just in name to help with getting visas and invitations to special functions.'

'And into the competition's bed for secrets no doubt. All the same, it's nothing more than simply being a prostitute. Such a shame, she's so beautiful.'

'Probably the reason she was chosen for the job.'

'What other photos are there?'

'Not much, but there is this. The same list of names that we found on the list in Irene's cabin. I'll google a couple of them – could you go to our cabin and get my notebook and pen for me, please? They should be on the bedside table.'

'Do you want another drink while I'm up?'

Buchanan looked at his empty glass for a moment. 'Best make it a double.'

'Be right back with your drink and your notebook.'

♦

'Thanks,' said Buchanan as Karen handed him his notebook.

'What have you found?'

Buchanan opened his notebook and commenced to write down the names found in Karl's photo. 'The names of these men and women are all business leaders of British companies wanting to leave the EU. Just look at the names of the companies they represent. I'd say they are all Small to Medium Enterprises that feel they have been held back in one way or another because of EU regulations.'

'Do you think the government is getting Karl to work behind the scenes in case the Brexit negotiations collapse, and we end up leaving the EU with a no-deal?'

'More likely he's working for individual companies. See the check marks against their names on the list?'

'So, what's he really up to? He isn't in the government or running any of those businesses.'

'My bet is he's working as a go-between. Not actually working for the government, more likely has the ear of someone in Whitehall and has been tasked to set up private deals for these companies. In return the party, whichever one is involved, hopes for future support when election time comes around.'

'For a fee, no doubt.'

'Absolutely.'

Karen looked at her watch, 'I think we should be heading for bed. The ship docks at six am and I'm sure the captain has told the Belgian police he wants to be gone by eight pm.'

'I wonder if any of the Belgian police will be called Poirot and have a big moustache?' said Buchanan as he turned out the bedside light.'

5

'You realise what time it is?' said Karen, as Buchanan climbed out of bed.

'Certainly. Here on board it's five-thirty. Home in England it's four-thirty. Stay in bed, I'll go talk to the Belgian police.'

'Let me know if he has a moustache and speaks with a French accent.'

'You've been watching too much television.'

'What will you do about breakfast? It doesn't start till six,' asked Karen.

'I'll be fine. There's the coffee station, it usually has plenty of fresh coffee and pastries.'

'That's not good for your health. The doctor said you were to eat healthily.'

'I'll be fine.'

'You'll get indigestion.'

'Look, the crew will be having their breakfast, remember they have to be up for docking at six. I'll scrounge a meal with them. Please don't worry, I'll be fine.'

'OK. I'll join you when I'm ready.'

'Take your time. Remember we're on holiday.'

♦

Buchanan made his way along the corridor and down the stairs to guest services.

'Good morning. How may I help?' asked the receptionist.

'Yes, good morning. Jack Buchanan, suite 309. I was wondering if you've seen the captain this morning?'

'Are you Inspector Buchanan?'

'Yes.'

'The captain said if you are early for you to go through to the crew dining room. It's on the main deck forward. You get to it through the restaurant. I'll call Thomas to meet you in the restaurant.'

'Thanks.'

Buchanan made his way through the restaurant to the door leading to the galley, Thomas came out to meet him.

'Good morning, Inspector.'

Good morning, Thomas.'

'Ready for breakfast?'

'You bet.'

'Good, please follow me to the crew dining room. You'll find it a bit different from what you've been used to, very informal.'

'As long as there's food, I'll be happy.'

'Ah, good morning, Inspector,' said the captain.

'Yes, it is. You know something, Captain? I've never had such an exhilarating holiday as this one.'

'Not much of a holiday if you have to work, Inspector,' said Thomas.

'Work is what I do, some say it is who I am, Thomas.'

'The captain says we will be arriving early in Antwerp to meet the Belgian police. He told me he doesn't want to lose time and leave too late this evening. We have buses waiting for us for shore trips in the morning and for trips to Bruges.'

Breakfast eaten, Buchanan walked up the stairs to the upper deck to watch the ship arrive at the dock in Antwerp. He was pleased to see several police cars waiting, though how much interest he would be to the Belgian police he wasn't sure. His part in this drama was quite small, mostly just his and Karen's conversations with Irene and Karl. His thoughts about what Karl had been up to were mostly subjective.

As soon as the ship was tied up and the gangway secured, several suited individuals, followed by uniformed police, came on board.

Buchanan descended the stairs from the upper deck down two decks to the reception deck. The captain and Thomas were deep in conversation with the suited individuals.

He approached the group to introduce himself.

Thomas saw him coming over and interrupted the conversation. 'Inspector Claeys, let me introduce you to Inspector Buchanan of the British police. He has the best understanding of what has happened.'

Claeys and Buchanan shook hands.

'What can you tell me about what has happened, Inspector Buchanan?' asked Claeys.

Buchanan spent the next fifteen minutes going over the previous day's events which led up to the discovery of the dishevelled state of the cabin.

'And you haven't removed or disturbed anything?' asked Claeys.

Buchanan shook his head. 'All I did was take photos of the room, in case we have to work on the investigation back in the UK. I also copied some photos from a memory card found in a mobile phone lying on the cabin floor. The two people involved are both British citizens, Inspector Claeys.'

'I understand that, and I myself am in a difficult situation. You see, if what you have told me is correct, then jurisdiction on this crime will lie with the Dutch authorities.'

'You won't investigate?'

'Yes, we will, then turn over our initial findings to the Dutch police.'

'The partner of the missing woman said he would be joining the ship later on today, after he has completed his meetings.'

'Did he say where these meetings would be held?'

Buchanan shook his head. 'No, in fact we have no way of knowing if he is actually having meetings. For all we know he has gone on the run.'

'That is bad. Thomas, will you show us to the cabin?' asked Claeys.

'Please, follow me,' said Thomas, as he ascended the stairs to the upper deck.

Karen was just closing their cabin door as the procession approached cabin 312. She stepped back inside and watched as Thomas opened the door. Claeys was first in, followed by two of the other suited policemen. Two uniformed policemen took up station just outside the door. Buchanan grinned at Karen and waited to be invited in to 312.

Five minutes later the door to 312 opened and Claeys looked out. 'Inspector Buchanan, would you join us, please?'

'You're on,' said Karen, smiling at her husband.

Buchanan crossed the corridor and entered the cabin.

'Hello again. How may I assist, Inspector Claeys?'

'I would like your thoughts on what has happened in here?'

Buchanan slowly, with deliberation, took in a deep breath. 'On first sight, it looks like there's been a struggle and someone died as a result. The murderer disposed of the body over the side of the ship, did a cursory clean-up, then departed. I didn't examine the items of clothing and towels, as I felt that should be left to your team. If I was making an initial report, that's how I'd describe it.'

'And if you were to be at liberty to examine the articles of evidence?'

'If this was a crime of passion, I'd expect to see signs of a fight, broken items, ripped or torn clothing, but –' he said, gesturing with his hands, 'where is the evidence for that? No, I think we have three possible scenarios. First, a crime of passion, the man in this cabin has an argument, kills the woman and throws her body overboard. Second scenario, she is having an affair with someone other than her partner, someone on board, possibly a married man. She threatens the man with disclosure, he gets angry and over the side she goes. Thirdly, someone sees the man in cabin 312 leave in a

79

taxi and decides the cabin is empty. He takes the opportunity to climb on board thinking there may be valuables for the taking. What the burglar doesn't realise is that the woman is in bed with a migraine. She wakes to find an intruder in the cabin, tries to scream, but her head hurts too badly. The burglar panics and – over the side she goes.'

'Very interesting, Inspector Buchannan. It is your third scenario that I tend to agree with you on. I have contacted the police in Arnhem, they are instigating a search of the surrounding river area. Unfortunately, if the body went in the river at Arnhem, it will be miles away by now.'

'How are your investigations proceeding here on the ship?'

'Our forensics people will be complete by the middle of the day. That way Captain Walewska will be able to leave on time this evening.'

'What about the partner, Karl Mueller?'

'I will have two of my men wait on board for him. Don't be concerned, we will take care of everything, you may go on with your holiday.'

'Thank you, Inspector Claeys,' said Buchanan, pausing at the door.

'Do you have anything to add before you go, Inspector Buchanan?'

'I'd appreciate being kept informed as to the outcome of the investigation. Here are my contact details,' said Buchanan, handing Claeys his business card.

'It shall be done, Inspector Buchanan. Good day.'

Buchanan shut the door behind him and crossed the corridor to his own cabin

'Well, what happened?' asked Karen.

'I've been dismissed, like a schoolboy from the headmaster's office.'

'Bet that's not happened to you in a long time. What did Claeys actually say?'

'It's not what he said, more like what he didn't say. I get the impression he's decided that after Karl left for his meetings, an opportune thief slipped on board thinking the cabin was empty. In the process of rifling through the cabin he was disturbed by Irene. A fight ensued, she died, and the body was disposed of.'

'That doesn't make much sense,' said Karen. 'For a start, how would the thief know which cabin to enter?'

'Let's have a look at our photo evidence library. Did we get the print-outs from guest services?' said Buchanan.

'In the envelope on the dressing table.'

Buchanan picked up the envelope, opened the flap and extracted the sheets of A4 paper.

'Excellent, your photos are really good. Maybe you should come work for us?'

'No way, remember we're trying to get you to retire, not find a job for me.'

'Funny. But really, these are just what we need. Now we can conduct our own investigation. First, let's see if the evidence supports Inspector Claeys' supposition. He thinks that a thief came in through the open veranda door, but your excellent photo shows the door slid shut. And your further photo of the lock – it does look locked. Now unless he locked it after disposing of Irene's body, then casually left the cabin and walked down the corridor, past the receptionist at guest services and up the gangway... no,' he said, shaking his head, 'there's no way that could be the case.'

'That's scenario three, how about two?'

'Two. Irene was having an affair with someone on board, someone other than Karl. What do you think about that one?'

Karen shook her head. 'I spent a lot of time with her these last couple of days. I can't see anyway she could be having an affair with anyone other than Karl.'

'That then takes us back to scenario one and Karl being the perpetrator of Irene's demise.'

'If that's the case, what evidence do we have for that?'

'You went to the cabin at about nine-thirty, Karl opened the door. He said Irene was in the shower, you heard the sound of the shower running. The next time we were in the cabin was at ten thirty-five the next morning. The sign on the door said Do Not Disturb. That puts us as the first people into the cabin since you stood at the door the previous evening. Karl was seen leaving the ship at about two-twenty in the morning. Those are the facts we can verify so far.'

'Just wondering if the on-board CCTV shows anything happening in the corridor outside the cabin? That would give us a definite time for Karl's departure, and prove or disprove Inspector Claeys' theory.'

'You are catching on. I'll go check with guest services and see if there is a CCTV recording for that evening.'

Buchanan was back in twenty minutes. 'We're very fortunate. There *is* a recording. The night manager is going to run through it for us and if there is anything of interest will let me know.'

'OK, so what next?'

'Let's look at the photos. If Irene was in the shower when you arrived, I'd expect to see the evidence for that, remember Karl left a few hours after and the room hadn't been serviced.'

Buchanan shuffled through the stack of photographs and laid them out on the bed in order, as though he was following Irene out of the shower and into bed.

'What do you think from looking at these?' he asked.

'Hmm, from looking at the set from the bathroom, I'd say that it was Karl who had the last shower.'

'Why do you say that?'

'Look at the picture of the shower pan, see the bar of soap lying on the floor? That's the sign that a man was last in there.'

'Go on.'

'And look at the shampoo bottles beside the sink. Her shampoo is the one on the left, lid snapped on, as is the conditioner, and neatly side by side. Now look at his, top off and not even beside hers. Also, another bar of soap in the sink, the wrapper lying where he discarded it.'

'So, he showered after her and before he went ashore. Anything else you see?'

'You tell me. We've been married for thirty-four years – what is one of my gripes about your untidiness?'

'Towels after I've had a shower?'

'Yep. I've had a few headaches before going to bed in my time, but I'd never just dump my towels on the floor like that,' she said, pointing to the photo. 'I always hang them up to air. Those look to me like they were – just, no wait a minute. I want to try an experiment, be right back.'

Karen went into their bathroom and returned with two bath towels. 'If what I'm thinking is correct,' she said, passing the towels to Buchanan, 'pretend you've just come out of the shower and dried yourself with them. Then see if you can drop them and make them look like the ones in the photo.'

For the next fifteen minutes, Buchanan dropped and picked up the towels, but no matter how he tried, the only way he could replicate the pattern of the towels on the floor was to bend down and arrange them by hand.

'Satisfied?' Karen asked.

'So, it's your assertion that they were put there to show the blood?'

'Talking of blood, where's your shirt with the bloodstain? I'll put it in the sink in cold water to stop it staining.'

'No, don't do that. I want to take it back with us and have forensics examine it.'

'Shouldn't it be passed over to Inspector Claeys for his forensic department to examine?'

Buchanan shrugged. 'It wasn't actually evidence. I got the blood on my shirt cuff when I was looking at the blood-soaked towels.'

'So why would you want to have it examined?'

Buchanan smiled. 'There's something niggling in the back of my mind.'

'What is it?'

'Just wondering if we're missing something. Look at the photo of the bed, especially the pillow. What do you see?'

'Ah, it's been plumped, no-one has been sleeping on that. I'd say she had just come out of the shower, was getting ready to get into bed, they had an argument and he stabbed her.'

'But not through the towel, at least I don't think so. Pity I wasn't able to pick it up and examine it.'

'Maybe she'd just unwrapped it and that's when he attacked her. Look at the bloodstains on the towel, do those look like they just fell there?'

'I don't know, I'm not an expert on blood spatters, but I would have expected to see spatters everywhere,' said Buchanan shaking his head. 'I wish I had my copy of Professor Ackermann on blood spatters with me, he was the real expert on that matter.'

'Remember the time I slipped when getting out of the shower, and I banged my face on the wall and had the horrible nose bleed? Remember the mess it made?'

'Do I! You left a trail of blood across the bathroom floor. Now look at the photo of the cabin floor, and the towel.'

'I see what you are getting at.'

'So how did the blood get onto the towel, if we assume the towel was placed on the floor?'

'Are we going back to scenario three, then?'

'There is a fourth scenario we haven't thought about.'

'Is there no end to your imagination?'

'It's what I'm paid to do. My thought is – and it is just a thought – it's possible that Irene told Karl's friends that she was going to expose him. Do you remember what she said when you two were together?'

'She said she was going to sell her story to the newspaper and destroy Karl's reputation.'

'Suppose one of Karl's friends, or one of his clients, didn't want that sort of publicity to come out. Especially if it exposed Karl and those he was involved with. They tell Karl to make a fuss about leaving the ship in Arnhem, make sure he's seen leaving. Shortly after he leaves, an assassin climbs on board and kills Irene. Maybe she was only supposed to be taught a lesson about keeping her mouth shut. But, unfortunately for Irene, something went wrong, and she died. The killer made up the room to make it look like an opportunist thief was responsible then left.' He shook his head. 'The sliding door to the veranda still puzzles me though. How was it locked from the outside?'

'You know we haven't tried something?'

'What is that?'

'Hang on a minute, let me try out an idea I have. Can I have another look at the photo of the veranda door?'

'Here, not sure which one you want.'

'Ah, look see, it wasn't locked, just made to look like it was locked. So, the killer could have come in this way then exited just like they'd come in.'

'In that case, Karl could still be involved.'

'All this thinking is making me thirsty,' said Karen looking at her watch, 'fancy a cup of coffee?'.

'OK, shall we go up to the lounge and see if Marjorie and Charles want to go ashore? I've been looking at our daily newsletter and would like to see the Ruebens' paintings in the cathedral.'

'Sounds good to me, might help to take my mind off what's been going on with Karl and Irene now *that* Belgian detective has got involved.'

They were about to walk through to the lounge when Marjorie called out from the library.

'Oh, there you two are. Charles and I were wondering if you would like to join us in the shore excursion into Antwerp.'

'How funny,' said Karen, 'we were just coming to ask you if you wanted to join us.'

'Belgian chocolate is what I'm after,' said Marjorie.

'What about you, Charles?' asked Karen.

'I'm going with Marjorie. She says my taste in chocolate is in for a rude awakening. I'm looking forward to that. How about you, Jack?'

'I guess I'm going to see the Ruebens paintings – and while I'm in Belgium I hear they brew some very fine beer.'

'How about we meet in town for a late lunch?' said Karen.

'Great idea,' said Marjorie. 'Where shall we meet?'

'How about we ask at guest services before we leave?' said Charles.

♦

'What did you think of the paintings in the cathedral?' asked Karen, as they sat and watched the groups of tourists walk past their table.

'The paintings were quite impressive, but not really to my taste. Now the church building, that's something else. Just imagine what they could do with that.'

'Like what?'

'They could sell off the paintings then convert the church into apartments.'

'Jack, how could you say such a thing? That's so disrespectful of the church.'

'And having thousands of homeless, while the church leaders eat fine food and sleep in a comfy bed every night – you don't think that's disrespectful to those who pay the leaders' salaries and the upkeep of all those museums to their faith? Is that what they teach you at your church?'

'Jack, how you can be so insightful about your job, and be so ignorant about the church? This cathedral in Antwerp is Roman Catholic – they spend a great deal of money taking care of it so people like us can enjoy its magnificence, including the paintings.'

'And the poor and the homeless?'

'I'm sure they look after the poor. Remember Mother Theresa? She dedicated her life to the poor.'

'And your church, what do they do with all their money?'

'My church in Eastbourne is an Evangelical church. I grant you we don't have a huge magnificent edifice such as this cathedral. We put our money into people, not buildings. In the last few years we have helped set up two churches in eastern Europe, supported the local food bank, and run many activities in the community.'

'Such as?'

'All right, here's a couple. We run a sanctuary café for immigrants and an English language school for non-English-speaking people and children's day-care classes, which are so popular you need to book your place even before your baby is born. If you'd visit it occasionally you'd see what we're about. It's not all about wanting your money.'

'Shall we change the subject?'

'I thought you'd never ask. What shall we talk about?'

'Did you know the saxophone was invented in Belgium?'

'No. Did you know the Smurfs were created here?'

'We've been reading the *Viking News*, haven't we?'

'I'm worried about Irene. Do you think Karl killed her, threw her body over the side and then left for his meetings?'

'At this point it's strictly conjecture what happened.'

'I wonder if Karl has returned yet?'

'He'd be foolish if he didn't. It would be tantamount to him being involved with her disappearance.' Buchanan took out his phone and looked at the display. 'Twenty past two. Charles and Marjorie should be here soon.'

'I hope so, all this walking has given me an appetite.'

♦

As they walked along the quay they could see three police cars parked by the gangway.

'Looks like Karl has returned,' said Buchanan.

'I suppose you'll want to be there when they question him?' said Marjorie.

'If I'm allowed. I got the distinct impression earlier that Inspector Claeys didn't appreciate my presence.'

'But he'll invite himself anyway, Marjorie. I know him too well,' said Karen

'Come on, let's see what the inspector is up to,' said Buchanan.

They hurried on along the quay and down the gangway.

Inspector Claeys was standing with a group of policemen, Thomas and the captain. In the middle was Karl.

'Marjorie and Charles,' said Karen, 'shall we let Jack get on with business? I understand cocktail hour has started.'

'Inspector Buchanan,' said Karl, as he saw him approach. 'Will you tell these officiating bastards that I'm a British citizen and they have no right to arrest me?'

'You have not been arrested, sir,' said Claeys. 'We only wish to ask you about the whereabouts of your travelling partner, who seems to be missing.'

'Captain Walewska, do you have a more private area where the inspector can conduct his interview?' asked Buchanan.

'Can I suggest the restaurant?' said Thomas. 'It is empty at the moment and I can get a couple of my people to stand at the doors and keep passengers away.'

Captain Walewska nodded his approval and the whole entourage walked after Thomas towards the restaurant.

Buchanan turned to Karen and smiled.

'Can I sit for the interrogation,' said Karl, when they'd settled in the restaurant, 'or do I have to stand to attention?'

'Mr Mueller,' began Claeys, 'can you confirm your full name and country of residence for me, please?'

'*Jawohl, mein Herr.* It is Karl Mueller, Meads, Sussex, England.'

'There's no need to be sarcastic, Mr Mueller. It is a simple question requiring only a simple answer. Will you tell us what time you left the ship yesterday morning while in Arnhem?'

'I'd ordered a taxi for two-thirty, it was early, and I left at two-twenty.'

'How was your travelling companion, Miss Irene Adler?'

'She had gone to bed with a migraine.'

'Did you say anything to her before you left?'

'She was asleep.'

'Was the veranda door shut when you left?'

'It was shut.'

'Did you check to see if it was locked?'

'No, why should I? We're on a ship, not some downtown hotel.'

'Mr Mueller, I want you to accompany me to the police headquarters where you will make a statement.'

'Am I under arrest?'

'No, Mr Mueller, just helping us with our enquiries. When I am satisfied about your involvement in this mystery you will be returned to the ship to continue with your holiday.'

'This is outrageous! Just wait till I get my lawyer, he'll sort you out.'

'I'm sure he will, Mr Mueller. Now can we go? Sergeant Janvier will show you the way to the car.'

'Inspector Claeys, a moment before you go,' said Buchanan, as he watched Sergeant Janvier escort Karl out of the restaurant and up the gangway to the waiting police car.

'Yes, what is it?'

'There was a safe in the cabin. Did you open it?'

'Yes, we had the hotel manager open it for us, why?'

'Could I see what was in the safe, please?'

'I don't see what that has to do with the case, but I suppose it won't do any harm to let you see. The contents are in an evidence bag in the cabin. Sergeant Lapointe will show you. I have a prisoner to interrogate. Goodbye, Inspector Buchanan, I don't expect we'll meet again.'

'This way, sir,' said Lapointe smiling, as Claeys got to the top of the gangway.

'Is he always so happy?' asked Buchanan, following Lapointe along the corridor.

Lapointe nodded as he unlocked cabin 312.

The evidence of the previous day's incident was contained in clear evidence bags, laid out on the beds awaiting their removal for a forensic examination. The contents of the safe were on the foot of Irene's bed.

Buchanan saw the look of concern on Lapointe's face as he picked up the bag containing Irene's purse and smiled at him. 'It's all right, Lapointe, I'm only going to look at the items from the safe and photograph them.'

Lapointe relaxed.

Buchanan left cabin 312 and hurried down the corridor to guest services. 'Hello, I wonder if I could ask another big favour, Zofia?'

'Yes, Inspector, what is it?'

'Could you print some pictures from my memory card, please?'

'Certainly. Is it to do with the missing lady in cabin 312?'

He nodded.

'Is there any word on her yet?'

'I'm afraid not.'

'Did her husband have anything to do with her disappearance?'

'I'm sorry, I can't comment on that. You will need to talk to Inspector Claeys if you want to find out what is happening. I'm a British policeman and this is Belgium. It's out of my hands.'

'Pity. I'm sure if you were looking for her you'd find her a lot sooner than Inspector Claeys. I'm sure he thinks she's dead and Mr Mueller murdered her.'

'Do you think that?'

'No. Please don't say anything to Thomas, but one of the maids said she thought she'd seen someone waiting in a car on the dock just before we sailed.'

'That, I'm afraid to say, was the taxi waiting for Mr Mueller. He already said that he was going to be picked up about two-thirty.'

'Oh, Nadia was sure it was waiting for Mrs Adler.'

'Why did Nadia think that?'

'Because of the arguments, and the fact that Mr Mueller had already left in a taxi.'

'Did Nadia see who got in the car?'

'No, she went up on deck to see what was going on, but by the time she got out there the car was gone. Oh, here are your photos.'

'Thanks, Zofia, and don't worry about Mrs Adler. I'm sure she'll turn up soon and all will be made clear.'

'I hope so, she was always so friendly to us.'

Buchanan knocked on his cabin door and entered.

Karen was looking at her phone. 'How did you do?'

'I have photos of the contents of the safe.'

'How did you manage that?'

'I asked Claeys. I think it amused him to have me ask his permission to look at the evidence.'

'A bit conceited, isn't he?'

'Not really. He's just trying to do his job and is a bit out of his comfort zone.'

'If you say so. What was in the safe?'

'Zofia at guest services printed copies of the photos I took of the items. Here,' he said, passing Karen the stack of photos, 'have a look and tell me what you think.'

'This I assume, must be her handbag – not quite what I'd expect for someone so elegant as Irene. And this I suppose are her purse and keys. Credit and debit cards plus what looks like a few hundred Euros in cash,' said Karen, as she leafed through the photos. 'Her passport. Oh, I thought she was much younger than that. A driving licence, her phone, an open packet of tissues, a folding hairbrush, lipstick, some makeup.'

'Does that look typical contents of a handbag for someone on holiday?' asked Buchanan.

'Similar to what I have with me, why?'

'Just an idea I have.'

'What's that?'

'Do you have the photos of the lists of names we found – the ones in the phone and the other in the rubbish bin?'

'Just a minute,' said Karen as she leafed through the folder she'd set up. 'Here you are.'

'Are you sure you don't want to come work for me? Your organisational skills are excellent.'

'You're supposed to be retiring, remember?' she said, smiling at him.

'I'll place that remark where it belongs. Now, let's have a look at the names,' he said, holding the lists side by side. 'I didn't expect this.'

'What didn't you expect?'

'One of the names on the syndicate list we found on Mueller's phone, I missed it before.'

'Who is it that's got you so curious?'

'Garry Duncan,' he said, shaking his head. 'I wonder if it's the same person?'

'Who is Garry Duncan?'

'The former crime commissioner's name is Garry Duncan.'

'What's he like?'

'How can I answer that politely?' said Buchanan grinning. 'The Garry Duncan I knew is a little man with a huge ego. I once saw a copy of his file –'

'You just happened to see his file?'

'Well, he was a right pain in the arse, I just wanted to find out what made him tick.'

'And what did you find out?'

'The usual stuff, what you'd expect from someone in his position,' replied Buchanan, thumbing through pages on his phone.

'What are you looking for?'

'I kept a copy of his records on my phone.'

'You just happened to keep a copy on your phone?' she smiled. 'He must have really bothered you.'

'Ah, here it is,' he said, ignoring her jibe. 'Father was a London banker, mother gave up a career in medicine to be a stay at home mother. He was an only child, educated at private school, went on to Oxford university, obtained a first in politics. At university he captained the first eleven, quite a batsman. If it wasn't for his poor eyesight, he might have been selected to play for the county. His first employment was as a trainee manager in the Sussex Police control room.'

'So that's how he started. Bit of a high flier,' said Karen, 'like Icarus – do you think he's getting too close to the sun?'

'Good analogy. Since he started as trainee manager in the police control room he's risen to being crime commissioner and now to work in the Home Office. Where next, one wonders?'

'Prime minister?'

'Unlikely. I get the impression he likes to pull the strings as puppet master but not be in the public eye.'

'If it is the same person, why shouldn't his name be in Mueller's phone directory? If Mueller is working on post-Brexit deals and you say Duncan works in the Home Office, to my mind it's perfectly feasible they should know each other.'

'Plausible yes, legal – I'm not so sure. The only way I see it being plausible is if – is if Duncan and Mueller are working off-grid and are making private deals for each other based on the information they are exposed to in their respective capacities.'

'Why do you think that might not be legal?'

'I'm not sure. I seem to remember signing something many years ago about confidentiality. I'm sure as a government employee Duncan will have signed something about not benefitting financially from privileged information.'

'What about Mueller?'

'If he's working with Duncan he'll be just as culpable.'

'Where do we go from here?'

'I believe the curtain for act one in this drama has just come down.'

'Do I have to wait for act two to find out what's going on?'

'Come on. It's intermission time, and I need a drink before dinner. Oh, Karen, this is such a fantastic holiday, I can finally relax and enjoy it.'

Karen looked at him and shook her head. 'You go on, I'll join when I'm ready.'

♦

'Your usual, Mr Jack, Talisker?' asked the bartender, as Buchanan sat on the barstool.

'Make it a large one, Aleksander, please.'

'Have you had a good day?'

'Best holiday ever.'

'You went ashore?' Aleksander asked as he poured a large shot of whisky into Buchanan's glass.

'Thanks,' said Buchanan, taking the glass and admiring the colour. 'I stayed on board and read. Mrs Buchanan went on the tour to the palace.'

'Is it a good book?'

'Very good.'

'Did you hear about the lady in cabin 312?'

'I hear she's missing, is that right?'

Aleksander shook his head. 'The crew think she had an argument with her partner and he has killed her and thrown her body over the side.'

'Is that what you think?'

He shrugged. 'I don't listen to gossip. I'm sure she's fine, probably gone home to her mother. That's what my wife's cousin did when her husband hit her – excuse me, Mr Jack – yes, can I help?'

Buchanan turned to see who'd just joined him at the bar.

'Mr Mueller, how are you?'

'Double scotch with ice, Aleksander.' Mueller looked at Buchanan, thought for a minute, then said, 'I've been better. Do you know what that Belgian toss-pot inspector accused me of?'

'No, Mr Mueller, I don't.'

'Call me Karl – Mr Mueller is what that Belgian inspector kept calling me. He had the balls to accuse me of killing Irene. Oh, maybe I shouldn't be discussing this with you, you're a policeman, aren't you?'

'I'm on sick leave, I'm supposed to be resting, not working.'

'You look perfectly healthy to me, what's wrong with you?'

'I was in a car crash. I was run off the road by a car coming from the other direction. It was on the wrong side of the road.'

'What happened to the other driver? Did you arrest them?'

'Not yet, but I think I will soon.'

'Stupid bugger, people like that should be hung.'

Buchanan smiled. 'We no longer hang criminals, Karl. Tell me, what will you do now that Irene has disappeared?'

'I'll be fine, I was going to let her go when we got back to the UK anyway. She was no longer up to the job. I'm already interviewing a candidate to replace her. I suppose now since Irene is no longer available I'll give the new girl the job.'

Their conversation was interrupted by the arrival of Karen.

'Oh, hello Karl, have you heard anything about Irene?'

Mueller shook his head. 'Stupid girl. First the police accuse me of killing her. Then when that didn't get them anywhere they tell me they think it was a burglar who broke into the cabin. He must have woken her up, a fight ensued, he killed her and disposed of her body in the canal.'

'Since you are alone, would you like to join us for dinner this evening?' said Karen.

'No thanks, I'm going to get an early night. Don't even know where I'm sleeping. The police have taken all my stuff away and my cabin has been designated a crime scene. I need to go talk to guest services and find out which cabin I'm being given.'

'What will you do about clothing, toiletries?'

'I've got a meeting in Ghent tomorrow. I'll go shopping when I'm in town.'

'I'm sure Jack could lend you a razor and shampoo.'

'No thank you, Mrs Buchanan, the cruise line has provided me with what I need till tomorrow. Good night to you both.'

6

'How long have you been up?' asked Karen, sitting up in bed.

Buchanan was seated on the veranda with the door open, drinking a coffee while watching life on the river. 'I was woken by the noises when the ship went through the last lock-gate. We'll soon be in Ghent. Do you know what that prat said to me last night?'

'I presume we're referring to Karl Mueller? No, what did he say?'

'I was telling him why I'm on sick leave. He said drivers who run other drivers off the road should by hung.'

'You still sure he was the other driver?'

'Absolutely, and I'm sure he had a hand in the disappearance of Irene Adler.'

Karen looked at her watch. 'Eight-fifteen, time for breakfast.'

'What's on the sight-seeing list for today?'

'Hang on a minute, let me shower and I'll get the schedule. Tell you what, since you're dressed, why don't you find us a table and I'll join you when I'm ready?'

Buchanan quietly closed the cabin door behind him and saw the police tape was now gone from the door of cabin 312. He continued along the corridor towards the stairs and down one deck to the restaurant. As he entered, Marjorie beckoned him to join them at their table.

'Good morning, Jack. Is Karen joining us for breakfast?'

'Yes, she'll be along soon,' he said, sitting at the table. 'She takes a little bit longer getting ready than I do. I'm what you see, no amount of preening will help my looks.'

'Me neither,' said Charles, sweeping the few strands of hair he still had back across his scalp.'

'If Karen won't be long we'll wait to order,' said Marjorie.

'Would you like coffee?' asked the waiter.

'Yes please, just black no sugar,' said Buchanan. 'Oh, could I have two cups please? My wife will be joining us in a minute.'

'Will you be joining us ashore today, Jack?'

'No, not today. Karen said she will be going ashore, I'm going to put my feet up and read.'

♦

'How was Ghent?' Buchanan asked, as Karen returned from her shore trip.

'We actually went to Bruges. We went by coach.'

'What did you see?'

'We had lunch, walked around the gardens, and saw the church with the tall spire. Altogether, a very enjoyable day out.'

'I'm glad.'

'Oh, Marjorie and Charles are going to the evening's entertainment. It's called the Liars Club – shall we go?'

'Why not? Sounds like it will be fun.'

'Tomorrow there's a trip to see the flood museum that commemorates the great flood of 1953. Do you want to come along? It's the last tour before we return to Amsterdam on Friday.'

'Now that I definitely would like to see. Did you know they used the old Mulberry docks from the war to build a new sea defence?'

'That's my Jack.'

♦

'Seems such a long time since we were in Amsterdam,' said Karen, as they stood on the veranda and looked across the river.

'It's only been a week.'

'Would you like to do another river cruise?'

Buchanan thought for a moment. 'Yes, I do believe I would. Yes, I definitely would.'

Karen turned to face her husband. 'Where would you like to go then? What do you fancy?'

'Someone mentioned the Douro river in Portugal.'

'That was me. Shall we check with guest services about booking?'

'After breakfast. Do you still want to see the flower market?'

'Yes. I want to get some tulip bulbs for the new house.

♦

'We should come back again,' said Karen, as she glanced at the café menu. 'We could fly over on Thursday and come home on the Monday. Even better, why don't you go down to a four-day week, have every Friday off? What do you think?'

'The ACC would never approve that.'

'Oh, don't be such a wet rag. I bet your boss would jump at the chance of the reduced expense.'

'Have you decided what you want? I see the waitress heading our way.'

Karen shook her head and returned to looking over the menu as the waitress walked past their table to seat three newcomers. A few minutes later she was standing at the Buchanans' table.

'I'll have a cappuccino and a slice of coffee cake,' said Karen.

'And for you?' she asked Buchanan.

'Coffee Americano and a slice of apple pie.'

A reflection in the café window behind Karen caught Buchanan's attention. One of the newcomers to the table directly behind him was Karl Mueller. Buchanan took his phone out of his pocket and sent Karen a WhatsApp message: *'Karl Mueller is seated behind us with two other men, don't stare.'*

Karen turned her phone over and looked at the message. *'Where?'*

'Directly behind us with two other men.'

'Ah, now I see who you're getting at. It does look like him. But I thought he said he was going on the coach tour, wonder what made him change his mind?"

'He is allowed to change his mind. I still wonder who he's talking with, not anyone I've seen on the boat. Tell you what, pretend to take my photo, make

sure you zoom in on them and get a photo of the three of them and anything that looks interesting.'

Karen took several photos then showed the results to Buchanan.

'Those will do fine; the kids will love to see their parents enjoying themselves,' said Buchanan, in case the trio wondered about Karen taking the photos.

'Shall we leave? said Karen, as she put her empty cup down. 'We are still on holiday and I want to get my tulip bulbs.'

◆

'You go ahead,' said Karen as they walked down the gangway, 'I'll join you in the bar when I've freshened up.'

'Would you like me to order you a drink?'

'A large white wine, please.'

'Your wish is my command. See you when you're ready,' he said, turning to walk off towards the bar.

◆

Today on board the atmosphere was different. Gone was the frenetic activity of day one. Today, the penultimate day of the cruise, the ship was at rest. Tomorrow everyone would disembark and return to their respective homes. The ship would be prepared, and another company of guests would arrive. Most of today's guests were still ashore, taking advantage of the beautiful weather and the excitement of being in one of Europe's premier cities.

Buchanan stopped at the entrance to the bar and surveyed the room. Last evening the bar had been full of guests singing along to the sea shanties performed by two excellent folk singers. Now the bar was empty, except for one lone guest: Karl Mueller.

'How is the trip going, Karl?' asked Buchanan, sitting on a bar stool two seats over.

'Just fine. Why would you ask? Are you being a policeman?'

'Now why would you think that?'

'I saw you watching me in the square this afternoon.'

'Didn't look much fun. Was that Ivan Reznikov you were talking with?'

'Mr Buchanan, Inspector Buchanan, I understand you are here recovering from a very bad car accident. Can I offer you some advice?'

'Go on.'

'You look to me like someone who's been around the block a few times, you've got street cred. The advice I am offering you, and it is yours to do what you want with, is to retire. Do you realise you probably qualify for a full and immediate pension? Why not retire and leave it to the younger ones?'

'Thanks for the advice, Karl. I'll sleep on it,' said Buchanan, as picked up his drinks and slid off the bar stool. As he walked over to his regular table by the window, he thought about Karl's suggestion, and the fact that someone else had once used those exact words. That someone had been the ACC and she used to report directly to the crime commissioner, Garry Duncan. Were they both involved in this affair?

He watched as Karl threw back his drink, looked at Buchanan, and gave a knowing tap on his temple with his finger.

'Goodbye for now, Karl. I'm sure we'll meet again,' said Buchanan quietly, at the disappearing back of Karl Mueller.

♦

'Do you have those photos you took this afternoon?' said Buchanan, sitting up in bed.

'Yes, here,' she said, passing Buchanan her phone.

'The one in the middle looks a bit like the photo of Reznikov we saw in the newspaper article.'

'He's not quite so handsome without his Tuxedo.'

'Karl's friends don't look so happy, wonder what's got them so hot under the collar, especially the one that looks like Reznikov?'

7

'It was such a wonderful holiday, Jack. Thank you for arranging it,' said Karen, as the plane taxied to the terminal at Gatwick airport.

'Thank you for putting up with me and my being a policeman at the beginning. Old habits die hard. We should take more of these holidays, the concept of having your hotel travel with you is truly unique.'

'I still fancy Portugal and the river Douro next year. You should be retired by then.'

'Very funny. But I do like the idea of going to Portugal.'

They cleared immigration, collected their suitcases and exited through the security doors.

'Could you wait a minute?' said Buchanan. 'I just want to pop into W H Smith for a paper.'

'Holiday over?' said Karen.

He looked at her then said, 'I simply want to see how Brighton is doing.'

'Oh, yes, and I have a bridge for sale?'

He returned ten minutes later, busy reading an article on page four.

'What's got your attention?'

'An article on page four of the *Mail*. It says here that a Karl Mueller was questioned by the Belgian police about the disappearance of his private secretary. His holiday was thoroughly spoiled as he spent a day of it in a Belgian custody suite.'

'Has he been charged with Irene's murder?'

'No. They let him go, as I expected they would. There just wasn't enough evidence to get a conviction.'

'Come on, let's get a move on, the train leaves in fifteen minutes, and I've got grocery shopping to do when we get home.'

◆

As the train flashed past Balcombe station on its way to Polegate, Buchanan reflected on the strangeness of his recent holiday. As far as he was concerned, Karl had been the driver of the car that had run him off the road at the Charleston exit. But what about the disappearance of Irene? Could it be possible that Karl had been directly involved? Had they been arguing after she'd said she was leaving him and was going to sell her story to the papers? Had the argument got out of hand, Irene dying as a result, and Karl disposing of her body over the veranda railings? Buchanan wondered if Claeys would be forthcoming with information he'd learned during Karl's interrogation. He realised without anyone reporting Irene missing it would be difficult to start a missing person search, and he doubted that Karl would be willing to get involved.

The train slowed as it approached Haywards Heath. Buchanan looked up at the carriage display to verify that they were in the correct part. One to eight for Ore; they were in carriage five.

As the train pulled out of the station, minus the rear four carriages headed for Littlehampton, Buchanan resolved that first thing on Monday morning he'd open a file on Irene's disappearance. Then contact Claeys and make arrangements for the evidence to be made available for a forensics examination. And finally, he'd invite Karl to voluntarily come in and make a statement. That should get the ball rolling.

It was going to be good to get back to work. There had been the initial sick leave, post-accident, then the ten days cruising the canals of Holland. There was of course, the matter of his retirement. He knew full well Karen would like him to retire, but what would he do with his time?

He shook his head; he'd been down this road too many times. He was a cop, through and through, plenty of time to think about retirement later. Right now, there was the mystery of Irene's disappearance to resolve. He ran what he knew about the events of that Monday evening and Tuesday morning through his mind, but still couldn't put his finger on what was niggling him. Then the light came on. It was the comment by Mueller the last time they'd met in the bar. He'd used the very words used by the ACC about his retirement. Had she mentioned it to the then crime commissioner, Garry Duncan, during one of their budget meetings? Had she said, *DCI Buchanan is an expense I can't afford, tried to make him understand he qualified for an immediate pension?* But how had that message been passed to Mueller? By the time the train passed through Wivlesfield, Buchanan was sound asleep again.

He woke with a start as the train pulled out of Lewes. What if, when he went to the office on Monday morning he found he had no office, or worse still, no team? Jill hadn't said anything when Karen called to ask for a lift from Polegate station, so that was good thing, he supposed.

♦

'Thanks for the lift, Jill,' said Buchanan, as he put their suitcases in the back of her car.

'We did this once before, remember?'

'How could I forget? You picked me up from Lewes and took me to see the ACC. How is she – missing me?'

'Sort of. We got home Thursday morning so I popped into the office on Friday morning to see what had been going on while we were away and she was in the office asking about you. Wanted to know when you'd be home.'

'That was nice of her, I think.'

'She said it had been quiet since you'd been gone, no dead bodies to take care of.'

'Is that a fact? Well, we'll soon change that.'

'What he's getting at,' said Karen, from the back seat, 'is while on the cruise an English woman disappeared under suspicious circumstances and, according to Jack's reasoning, it was her partner who did the deed.'

'What is he supposed to have done with this woman?' asked Street.

'When we entered the cabin –'

'We? Who were the *we*?' asked Street.

'I was Jack's assistant CSI for a day,' said Karen. 'I did enjoy myself taking all those photos of the scene of crime.'

'What did it look like?'

'Like there had been a fight: the woman was injured and as a result, died. Then the partner threw her body over the railing into the canal.'

'Did you arrest the partner?'

'The disappearance was investigated by Inspector Claeys of the Belgian police. He interrogated the partner then let him go. Insufficient evidence to charge him,' said Buchanan.

'That's a pity. Do you think he did it?'

'That, and something else.'

'Something else? What's that?'

'He was the driver of the car that ran me off the road.'

'How can you be sure?'

'He lives in Meads and, on the day in question, thirty minutes before I was run off the road, he was in Lewes at a party. Also he drives the same car that ran me off the road.'

'Bit circumstantial.'

'All the same I'm going to invite him into the station to make a statement about his missing partner, and at the same time quiz him about the accident.'

'Now I know what we'll be doing on Monday morning.'

'So, I still have an office, and a team?'

'Yes, to both. Oh, Stephen and I have been talking and have come to a decision. I will be keeping my maiden name for work. It will just make things simpler. Could you imagine how much chaos there could be with two Hunters in the team?'

'It would make a good name for a TV programme. Just imagine it: *Hunter and Hunter*,' said Karen.

'Maybe.'

'Much been going on while I was away?' asked Buchanan.

'There was the pistol whipping on Grove Road, that's still ongoing. Hanbury is dealing with it, assisted by Morris. There were also a couple of stabbings: no fatalities, and no arrests yet.'

'How was your holiday, Karen?' asked Street.

'Absolutely lovely, we did really enjoy ourselves. In fact, we are going to book another river cruise next year.'

'Where will you be going?'

'The Douro river in Portugal.'

'When do you move in to your new house?'

'As soon as the builders have finished with the new kitchen, though there may be some repainting to do in one of the rooms. The windows should have already been replaced. How is your flat?'

'Took us a bit of getting used to. You know what it's like, everything's in a different place than you're used to. Oh, I took the liberty of getting you some fresh milk, bread and eggs, hope you don't mind.'

'Not at all, it was very sweet of you to think of us.'

8

Seven o'clock Monday morning Buchanan was in his office. Feet up on the desk, coffee in one hand and a blueberry muffin in the other. He was contented, he was back where he belonged. As was his first task on Monday mornings, he glanced at the incident board. It had been quiet, he thought. Just the usual suspects, two vans broken into with tools stolen, a missing man from Birmingham last seen on Terminus Road late Saturday night, a pensioner in Hampden Park told he needed his gutters cleaned, luckily, he called the police and reported the incident, and also a car crash on Lottbridge Drove.

Why should he retire? He was still needed and there were still bad guys to lock up. And, he reminded himself, there still was the matter of Karl Mueller and the disappearance of Irene Adler to resolve. Buchanan was now more than ever convinced it was Mueller who had run him off the A27 and was also responsible for the disappearance of Irene. He laughed when he realised it was because of Mueller running him off the road that he was at work this morning.

Had he not had the accident, his resignation letter would have been delivered. Oh, it would have been received with mock surprise. There would have been much false protestation about him being too young to retire and he should think about just staying on till a suitable replacement could be found.

Buchanan chuckled as he thought about that scenario. How could they find a replacement for him? He was unique amongst today's police officers: an anachronism, a fossil suitable only for the Natural History Museum. His previous ACC had admonished him about not delegating tasks and setting an example by being a proper line manager. He remembered the old adage: *never give an order that you are not prepared to carry out yourself.* Bollocks to all of them – he was a team player and what a team he had.

By eight o'clock he'd emailed Claeys requesting the evidence recovered in the cabin be made available for a full forensic examination in the UK. He'd also opened an incident report on Irene Adler's disappearance. Then he did a search for her and found an address in Hampden Park. He already knew the Muellers' address in Meads and had sent a text message to Mueller asking him to make contact at his office.

The peace of the morning was broken by the arrival of the newlyweds.

'Morning, Chief,' said Hunter.

'And a good morning it is, Stephen and Jill! Ready to go to work?'

'You bet. It's been a dull office without you being around here to stir things up.'

'Really? Well, let's see what mischief we can get up to now I'm back at work.'

'What's first?'

'Before we get started, did you two have a good time in Mauritius?'

Street blushed and Hunter answered, 'It was fantastic, we have photos galore to show you and Mrs – I mean Karen – when we come to dinner on Saturday. How was your holiday?'

'If you were to ask Karen, she'd probably tell you it was a busman's holiday.'

'You worked? What on?'

Buchanan spent the next hour going over the sequence of events from the moment they saw Mueller and Irene at the airport, to the moment he saw Mueller being escorted off the ship in Antwerp.

'Here are the photographs Karen took of the crime scene in the cabin, and these are the photos of the contents of Irene's handbag that had been left locked in the cabin safe.'

'And Irene Adler is still missing?' asked Street.

'There's been nothing mentioned on the Interpol website. She's just listed as missing, presumed drowned.'

'Does she have any relatives?' asked Hunter.

'I don't know. I've just started a missing person file. While you two are out, I'll do some digging.'

'What do you want us to do?'

'Firstly, I want you two to find out all you can about Irene Adler. Here's her address in Hampden Park. Then when you've done that, go see Mrs Mueller in Meads.'

'Where does she fit in to the story?' asked Street.

'She's the wife of Karl Mueller. According to what Irene Adler told Karen, they may live in the same house as each other but that is as far as the relationship goes.'

'Is her husband likely to be there?' asked Hunter.

Buchanan wondered about that. The last time he'd seen Mueller was when the boat docked in Amsterdam. Then two hours later when Mueller and two suitcases had disembarked for a taxi to the airport. 'If he is, bring him in. I want to have a word with him.'

'Suppose he doesn't want to? What shall we do?'

'Tell him – tell him he's being invited here to assist me in eliminating someone from my enquiries.'

'Suppose he asks who you are eliminating?'

'Tell him it's a delicate matter and requires the utmost discretion. That should appeal to his vanity.'

'Should we mention Irene Adler?'

'No, leave him to think what he may. When Claeys took him away, his cabin had been locked by the hotel manager after the police had removed the contents for analysis. I asked for the newspapers in the Arnhem area to be scanned to see if there were

109

any stories about wet and dishevelled women being recovered from the river, but nothing had been reported. After what happened in Antwerp he's more likely hiding out somewhere with one of his ladies. If Mrs Mueller is alone, try and get her to talk, be a sympathetic ear.'

'Do we have any information on Karl Mueller's women?' asked Street.

'There's a photo of him and a Tatyana Reznikov at a function in Mayfair last summer. She's the wife of a Russian businessman.'

'What sort of business?'

'His company exports fashion clothing amongst other things. I'm going to see if I can find out whether he's on the level or not. My thinking is it's a front for something nefarious.'

'So, other than having an affair with Reznikov's wife, why would Mueller be involved?

'I've been thinking about that quite a bit. You remember there was a government official reprimanded for having illicit talks with non-European business delegations?'

'He got the sack if I remember.'

'It is my thinking that this certain government official was working as a go-between for UK and non-European businesses. I think it possible he was setting up trade deals for post-Brexit.'

'Why would that be a problem?'

'If he was in the government, he would be working contrary to the stated aims of the Brexit talks and would cause a furore amongst the European countries that the UK is negotiating with.'

'So, do you think Mueller is working on a private level, direct with companies that stand to benefit from the possible chaos that will follow a botched Brexit deal?'

'That's highly possible. I'm going to call Aaron Silverstein when I'm done trying to find out about the background on Irene Adler. He and Bashir were very helpful with our early case.'

'The one Anton Miasma of the *Herald* called, *the case of bodies in the marina*?' said Street.

'That's the one. Bloody nuisance he is too, did you know he had the gall to publish my photograph?'

'No, when did he do that?'

'A few weeks ago, just after we arrested Giovanni Rosso. Miasma said in editorial about policing in Sussex *there should be more co-operation between the police and the press.*'

'More co-operation?' said Street. 'We give them everything they need when it's appropriate. What does he expect? A press room here at Hammonds drive?'

'Hmm. He went on to say that when I had my eye on the villain I came at the problem with both barrels blazing. Had the cheek to call me *Buckshot* – don't laugh, either of you.'

'We're not laughing,' said Street. 'Is there anything else you want us to do while we're out?'

'Nothing comes to mind. Oh, where's Morris? Haven't seen him yet this morning?'

'He called me earlier,' said Hunter. 'He's looking after the kids till his wife's sister gets there. His missis is expecting again and is suffering from morning sickness. Apparently, she had been coping, but was up most of the night throwing up. He's going to take her to the clinic to see her doctor.'

'That doesn't sound good, I'll give him a call later. How many children does he have?'

'Not sure. I think they have four,' said Hunter.

◆

Buchanan hung up from talking with Dexter and turned on his computer. He googled the name Irene Adler, and as expected found many references to the Conan Doyle story about Sherlock Holmes, but only one mention in the *Herald* where she was mentioned as being part of a group having raised a considerable amount of money for a local charity. There was a second and smaller news story about a local amdram troupe performing at the Devonshire Theatre. Irene played the part of the daughter in an abusive family. The play was called *Behind Closed Doors*. Curiosity got the better of him so he googled the play and thought that, once again, fact was stranger than fiction. The play got rave reviews and Irene was singled out for her portrayal of Sandra, the abused daughter. Pity Irene ended up being abused in real life.

Next, he looked for the name on Facebook. There were five listed. First was another reference to the Sherlock Holmes story, two were professional ladies purporting to work in Moscow, a fourth lived in Wisconsin, USA. The fifth was the Irene Adler they had met on the cruise.

Her profile was listed as an executive PA. Enjoyed all things sportive, especially marathon running, swimming and skiing. She also loved all types of cats. Her avatar showed her cuddling a huge marmalade-coloured cat up to her face and wearing not much else. He checked her posts and found her last went up the day prior to them leaving for Amsterdam. In that she mentioned she was looking forward to seeing, amongst many things, the Reich Museum in Amsterdam, and the Cathedral of Our Lady in Antwerp. Buchanan thought it a pity she never made it to Antwerp – the cathedral truly was a magnificent edifice.

Buchanan next looked through the Police National Computer. The only item that came up was an incident of twelve years ago where an Irene Adler was recorded as having been part of a hen party which had been arrested for the public order offence of being drunk and disorderly. This type of high jinks wouldn't normally be recorded as an offence but, since one of the group had thrown a glass of wine in the face of a policeman, the officer on duty had no choice but to apprehend the revellers.

Next was an email enquiry to the NHS for Irene's medical records. While he waited for a reply he contacted the Inland Revenue. He drew a blank there, all her tax returns were in order and all taxes paid. Next was the Home Office and her passport. The records revealed that two months prior to her trip to the Netherlands she had applied for a replacement passport. The reason given was that her previous one had been stolen when her flat had been burgled. He next checked the DVLA and her driving licence. As he expected that too had been replaced, the reason given was her purse had been stolen when her flat was burgled. He was about to contact her credit card company when the computer dinged, announcing the arrival of the results of his enquiry to the NHS.

The record revealed two miscarriages, the most recent a few months ago. One thing didn't make sense as Buchanan skimmed through the report: there were no records of anything about bruises or broken bones. He knew from experience that many times women would show up at their doctors' with bruises and broken bones attributed to trips and falls. Irene's records had none; in fact, her doctor had mentioned how fit and healthy she'd been, with a body of someone ten years younger than her age, the only exception being her menorrhagia. Buchanan had to google the ailment to discover what it was.

But things still didn't add up: the previous niggle, niggled again. He went back to the PNC and did a search for burglaries in East Sussex during the previous three months. He was shocked to find there had been one thousand nine hundred and ninety-eight. That equated to about sixty to seventy in the Eastbourne area during the month that Irene reported her flat being burgled. He looked up the burglary reports for the month she reported and found nothing for her address. Now why would someone not report their flat being burgled and items such as passport and driving licence being stolen? He looked at the photos of the credit cards found in her purse. There were several: a Lloyds credit card, an HSBC credit card, several store loyalty cards and a NatWest debit card. He looked at the details on the backs of the cards and called the first,

Lloyds. He read out the card number and was told that account had not been reported as lost or stolen. He got the same response from the other card issuers. Now why would that be? If his wallet had been stolen, he'd report it. Why hadn't she, especially since she'd reported the theft of her passport and driving licence from her purse?

He was pondering the evidence of his research when a loud, protesting, voice could be heard along the corridor. Minutes later the owner of the voice entered his office. Mueller obviously wasn't amused by being brought into the police station.

'Mr Buchanan, I must protest at being brought here like this. Why didn't you call me? I would have been glad to provide time for you to visit me at my office.'

'I did send you a text. But since you are here, would you like something to drink?'

'Yah, what do you have?'

'Tea, coffee?'

'I'll have coffee.'

'Stephen, would you get Mr Mueller a cup of coffee?'

'Am I under arrest?'

'Now why would you ask that, Mr Mueller?' said Buchanan.

'I don't know, I've never been to a police station before.'

'What about your recent visit in Antwerp?'

'That was rubbish. Claeys couldn't find his way out of a paper bag.'

'So, you've never done anything that might necessitate your arrest?'

'Don't be so stupid, of course not. I'm a law-abiding citizen.'

'Mr Mueller. Karl – it is all right if I call you Karl? A few weeks ago, on Friday the 27th, there was an accident on the A27, just past Middle Farm. A car travelling to Lewes was run off the road and hit a tree, almost killing the driver.'

'Why are you telling me this?'

'You were driving on the A27 towards Eastbourne on the 27th. I just wondered if you happened to witness the accident?'

'And you sent two policemen and a car to bring me here to ask that?'

'What were you doing in Lewes on the 27th?'

Mueller thought for a minute. 'Business, I was there for a business meeting.'

'What was the meeting about?'

'I don't remember.'

'Yet you remember you were driving along the A27?'

'Let me look at my diary.'

Mueller reached into his jacket and removed his phone. He keyed in his password and consulted his diary. 'The 27th, you say – yes I was in Lewes on the 27th.'

'What was the subject of your meeting?'

'None of your business.'

'What time did you leave Shellys in Lewes?'

'How did you know I was there?'

'I know lots of things, Karl.'

'Such as?'

'What is your relationship with Tatyana Reznikov?'

Buchanan watched the reaction on Mueller's face. It changed from one of arrogance to one of a man concerned he'd said too much.

'Er, she's the wife of a businessman I met.'

'Does her husband know how friendly you are with her?'

'Inspector, you've brought me here under false pretences. I was under the impression you were investigating a road accident on the A27. Now you're asking about a Russian businessman I met at a meeting in London.'

'How is the food at the Mayfair?'

'How – how did you know about that? Have you been spying on me?'

'Where is your friend Irene, Mr Mueller?'

'I don't know, she's gone.'

'Gone where?'

'How should I know? When I came back to the ship in Antwerp, that idiot Claeys arrested me.'

'Were you charged with her disappearance?'

'No, of course not.'

'Have you tried to contact her since you came back to England?'

'Her phone goes to voicemail.'

'Have you been to her flat?'

'It was locked, no one home.'

'Does she have any family?'

'You tell me – you seem to know everything.'

'The accident on the A27, Mr Mueller. On that day were you driving your Mercedes AMG? And did you overtake a vehicle on the brow of a hill, a quarter mile past Middle Farm?'

'Why would I remember that?'

'There was a witness, Mr Mueller. A reliable witness, one who saw you come over the brow of the hill, force an oncoming car off the road and headlong into a tree.'

'Where is this witness? There is no witness, you're just trying to get me to confess to something I didn't do.'

'*I'm* the witness, Karl. I was the driver of the car you forced off the road. Karl Mueller, I am arresting you for failing to stop at the scene of an accident. You do not have to say anything, but if you do it may be used in court.'

'I want to speak to my lawyer.'

'Stephen,' said Buchanan. 'Would you escort Mr Mueller down to the booking-in desk? Make sure you read him his rights and show him where the phone is – Mr Mueller needs to call his lawyer, We must make sure we do everything by the book.'

♦

Have you seen the *Herald*, Chief?' Street asked, looking up from her computer.

'No, why?'

'Miasma's at it again.'

'What's he up to now?'

'I'll read it to you, the headline says:

Man arrested in connection with the RTA on the A27 last month. Karl Mueller, a resident of Meads in Eastbourne, has been arrested and charged with dangerous driving, that of causing an accident, and fleeing the scene. The accident caused the closing of the A27 in both directions for three hours.

'He's a bit late with that. Mueller's lawyer got him out late yesterday.'

'Will it go to trial?'

'Who knows? Most of the evidence is circumstantial and, with all the cuts in forensics' budget, I doubt if he will ever see the inside of a court. No, Jill, despite our best efforts in nailing him for the road accident, he's got away with it.'

'What about Irene? Has he got away with her murder as well?'

'It's early days on that one. Unfortunately, we don't have a body or even evidence to examine. And Inspector Claeys still hasn't acquiesced to my request for the evidence to be forwarded for a forensic examination.'

'But we can't just let him get away with it, can we?'

The discussion was interrupted by Buchanan's phone ringing. 'Buchanan. She is? Thanks, Dave.'

'What was that about?' asked Street.

'My friend the ACC is on her way up. Apparently, she wants to have a word with me.'

'Maybe she wants to welcome you back to work.'

'More likely she's wondering where my resignation letter has got to.'

A few minutes later, the previously announced ACC duly arrived at Buchanan's office.

'I'll be right back,' said Street, as the ACC entered the office. 'Morning, Ma'am.'

'Good morning, Street. And good morning, Buchanan. How are you?'

'I'm fine, now I'm back at work.'

'How was the holiday? Get the chance to rest and reflect?'

'Yes, thank you. I got rest and had time to reflect on my future.'

'That's good to hear. I looked for your resignation letter, but it hasn't arrived yet. Where did you send it to?'

Buchanan leaned back in his chair and smiled at her. 'I never sent it, it was lost when I had my accident.'

'No after-effects from your accident? Company doctor happy with you returning to work?'

Buchanan thought back to his last visit to the company doctor and the subsequent discussion about retirement. *Why is it* she'd said *that when someone approaches the age of sixty, they are considered over the hill and past it? Why can't society accept that to some people, working and retirement are not necessarily ideas in conflict?* That had settled well with him. He had just passed the midpoint of his fifties himself and the idea or retirement was anathema to him. *You do agree with me, don't you Inspector Buchanan?* How could he not? After all his father at seventy-two was still fit and active, working part-time as one of the maintenance men at the Port Glasgow shipbuilding museum.

'Are you here with me, Buchanan?' interrupted the ACC.

'Sorry, Ma'am, just thinking about something, and to answer your question the company doctor said I'm fit and able to return to work.'

'Hmm, that's not quite how I read the doctor's report. This business with Mueller doesn't make good reading. Looks more like a vendetta. What makes you so sure he was the driver of the car that ran you off the road?'

'He was on the A27 at the time, and he was driving the same make and model of car.'

'Come on, you know as well as I do that the CPS would never consider a prosecution based on just those two facts alone. Could you say, with one hundred percent accuracy, that you could identify him as the driver?'

'I was going to send his phone off to forensics for analysis. Unfortunately, he took it with him when he was released. I am positive if we'd had it analysed it would show him on that stretch of the A27 at the same moment of the crash.'

She shook her head. 'Buchanan, you realise what a barrister would do with your accusation? They'd say that it was a case of guilt transference. They'd point out that you'd suffered a traumatic brain injury caused by the sudden deceleration of your car as it impacted the tree. They'd also point out you had spent several days on the ship with Mueller, who you'd taken a dislike to. And, subsequently, your brain had drawn the conclusion that Mueller had been driving the car that ran you off the road.'

That stumped Buchanan for a moment. Had the ACC got a point? Could he have actually been wrong about Mueller?

'Buchanan, I want you to write to Mr Mueller and apologise to him. I want you to explain about your car accident and subsequent confusion you have been suffering. I am going to recommend that you go on light duties till you have recovered completely. Street can take over as senior officer in the meantime.'

'You mean – I'll be working for her?'

'No, not at all. You'll still be the senior officer in the department. You'll just not be required to shoulder all the responsibilities. Just till you're back on form. Do you want me to tell her for you?'

'No, Ma'am, I can do that.'

'Good. Now if you don't have any further questions, I've got to go to phone the Home Secretary.'

◆

'How was the meeting?' asked Street, as she stood at the office door, coffee in hand.

'You've been promoted.'

'What? I'm now an inspector? That doesn't make sense, I've not sat the exam.'

'According to Madam Assistant Chief Constable, I'm past it, over the hill. You are now in charge.'

'I'm your boss?'

'That's not quite what she said, but more or less what she meant. Till I recover from my traumatic brain injury, you are the senior officer.'

'But – that's nonsense. There's nothing wrong with you, is there?'

He shook his head. 'Who knows? The company doctor said I was fine. My brain scans at the hospital were fine.'

'How do you feel?'

'She's been got at. I'll bet someone has told her to get me off the case.'

'That's the Jack Buchanan I know,' said Street, a smile growing on her face.

'I've been ordered to write to Mueller and apologise to him. According to the ACC, my brain is confused, it has assumed that Mueller was the driver of the car that ran me off the road.'

'You accept that?'

'What do you think? I'm no longer permitted to express an opinion.'

'Have you heard from Claeys yet?'

'No.'

'So, all we have at the moment are the photos Karen took of the inside of the cabin?'

'Yes. Wait a minute, there's my shirt.'

'What has your shirt got to do with anything we're discussing?'

'My shirt cuff has, or had if Karen has washed it, blood from the clothing in the cabin.'

'Why would that be helpful?'

'It's an idea I have been chasing round in my brain. Hang on, I'll call Karen.'

He hung up from the call, a smile on his face. 'She decided not to wash it, the blood was soaked right in. It was destined for the bin.'

'OK, I'm not quite following you on this, but what do you want to do with the shirt?'

'We're going to go collect it and have forensics examine the blood stain.'

'OK, that sort of makes sense.'

'Do I have your permission to proceed, Ma'am?'

'Stop that, as far as I'm concerned you're still the chief around here. Want me to drive?'

♦

'Very neat,' said Street, looking at the Ziploc bag containing Buchanan's shirt with the blood-stained cuff. 'Not often do we get the evidence already bagged and tagged.'

'I think Karen enjoyed playing CSI as much as I did.'

'I'll get this sent off for examination right away.'

'I never asked, but what did you and Stephen find out about Mrs Mueller?'

'Nothing, she wasn't in. I asked Mr Mueller before we brought him in and got the impression he really didn't know, or care, where she was. He looked like he was just there to change his clothes. I got the impression he doesn't live there much, just uses it as a convenient place to have his laundry done.'

'And where is Stephen?'

'He's gone for an early lunch, taking the car in to the garage. It wouldn't start this morning.'

'It's time he replaced it.'

'I'll let you suggest that, I've given up.'

♦

Buchanan turned on his bedside light, picked up his phone and looked at the time: five-fifteen. He pressed the answer button. 'Buchanan. Who's this? Have you called Street? She's senior officer. She said what? To call me. OK, what have you got? I'll be right there. She will? I better get dressed then.'

'What is it, Jack?' asked Karen.

'Sounds like a suicide, body reported hanging from the pier, and Jill's on her way to pick me up.'

'You'd better get your skates on then.'

♦

'Good morning, Jill. Why are we attending a suicide? That's the coroner's job.'

'Control said Dr Mansell thinks it's more than suicide.'

'In that case, what are we waiting for?'

♦

Street parked outside the pier entrance and opened the car door. 'Glad I'm wearing a coat, that wind is biting this morning.'

Buchanan pulled his jacket closed and followed Street down the steps and onto the shingle beach.

'Hence comes the grim reaper,' said Dr Mansell, as he rose from examining the body stretched out in a body bag.

'Good morning, Doctor. What have you discovered that you find it necessary to disturb my sleep?'

'You're going to like this one, Buchanan.'

'I've seen many suicides, Doctor, what makes this one so special?'

'How many suicides have you seen that were public like this one, Buchanan? If you were to ask my opinion, I'd say he had help.'

'Who discovered the body?' asked Buchanan.

'The body was seen hanging by a passing fishing boat, they tried to get close, but the sea was too rough. The skipper called 999, and control dispatched a patrol car to investigate.'

'We cut the body down, sir,' said the constable standing beside Dr Mansell.

'We?'

'Constable Atkins and I, sir.'

'Where was the body?'

'It was tied to the railing, sir. Out at the end, just beside where the old fishing pier was. It must have been in the sea; the clothes were soaking wet.'

'How long has it been there, Doctor?'

'The body was wet up to the neck. If we take that as the high tide mark, then the body's been hanging for at least ten hours. Combining that information with body temperature, I'd say he was put there after nine last night. He didn't die from hanging, his neck isn't broken. My diagnosis of death is heart failure.'

Buchanan turned to the constable. 'Know if anything was happening on the pier last night?'

'Atlantis night club was open. It was an Excellence in Industry awards night.'

'Do you know if it was busy?'

'No. sir.'

'Thank you, constable,' said Buchanan. He turned to Dr Mansell. 'Was there a suicide note?'

'Handwritten, very neat.'

'Can I see it, please?'

Mansell reached into his briefcase and handed the moist note, now safely ensconced in an evidence envelope, to Buchanan.

Buchanan read it then handed to Street

> To whoever it concerns. I can't go on. The disgrace is too much. I killed her and can't face the public humiliation.

'Can I see the body?' said Buchanan.

'Sure,' said Mansell, bending down to unzip the body bag. 'Know him?'

Buchanan nodded. 'I arrested him Monday for running me off the road. I was hoping to also get him convicted for the murder of his long-time partner.'

'Looks like he beat you to the drop. Oops, maybe an inappropriate comment, considering.'

'Anything in the pockets, Doctor?'

'Car keys, wallet, handkerchief, some loose change and a mobile phone.'

'How soon can you get your report to me, Doctor?'

Mansell shrugged. 'My initial report will be with you late this afternoon. The rest by the end of the week.'

'Right lass, back to the office.'

♦

'Good to have you back again,' said Street, as they drove slowly along Royal Parade.

'What's that remark supposed to mean?'

'I saw the look in your eyes when Dr Mansell unzipped the body bag. I saw the lights come on. Your facial expression changed, it smiled.'

'Thanks, I needed to hear that.'

'So, what's changed? You must have seen many dead people in your career.'

'The suicide note was a fake – he didn't commit suicide. No one who is contemplating suicide writes that kind of suicide note, someone tried to make it look like he'd hung himself. You know something, Jill? There is nothing better in the world than the first step in the hunt, nothing better than the thrill of the chase.'

'And you deduced all that from the suicide note?'

'That and thirty-five years of being a policeman. Time to celebrate. I think I could do with a large caramel-coffee Frappuccino, how about you?'

♦

Street was checking her emails and occasionally looking up at Buchanan. He was still smiling, except for the moments when he sucked too hard on his drink and gave himself a brain-freeze headache. He put down his drink when his computer dinged to announce the arrival of an email.

'Dr Mansell's report?' asked Street.

'No, it's from forensics. It looks like it's the report on the bloodstain in my shirt.' Buchanan started to read then said, 'Now I didn't really expect this.'

'What didn't you expect?'

'Remember I said Karen and I did a cursory inspection of the cabin?'

'Yes, but Inspector Claeys has all the evidence.'

'While I was in the bathroom, I removed a few hairs from Irene's hairbrush, not all, just a couple. When you sent my shirt off, I included the hair samples.'

'I see, you wanted to make sure the DNA of the blood samples were the same as the DNA found on the hairbrush?'

'*Précisément ma chère.* But, I didn't expect to see this in the report.'

'So, what is in the report??'

'The blood sample was menstrual blood, not arterial.'

'I don't follow you on that.'

'Don't you see? Irene wasn't murdered, she's probably as alive as you and me. Someone, probably herself, made the cabin look like there had been a fatal struggle and her body disposed of over the side. Of course, it all now makes sense.'

'What does?'

'Not only was the cabin made to look the way it did, she planned it all. Probably been working on it for months.'

'What about the contents of Karl Mueller's pockets? We haven't had a look at those yet.'

Buchanan reached over to the edge of his desk and lifted the evidence bag containing the contents of Karl Mueller's pockets. He took out the phone and, as expected, found the salt water had got into its interior and shorted out the battery.

'I'll send off the phone for analysis, I've already seen the contents of the memory card. Looks to be about eighty-five pence in cash, and,' he took the banknotes out of the wallet, 'at least three hundred in twenties and fifties. He certainly wasn't short of a bit of cash. Wonder what else is in the wallet?'

Buchanan carefully removed the contents of the wallet and spread them on the desk. 'Various bank cards, membership card for the Rhino Club in London, a Waitrose receipt for groceries, a business card for a London building firm and a library card.'

'Other than the cash, quite unremarkable,' said Street. 'What about the car keys?'

'Key fob says they belong to a Mercedes.'

'Now that's not a surprise,' said Street, shaking her head. 'I could do with a coffee

'Not the muck from the canteen,' said Buchanan, looking at the office wall clock.

'It's too early for beer,' said Street.

'Starbucks it will be then, we can have lunch at the same time.'

◆

Street waited for Buchanan to finish eating his sausage sandwich, wipe his mouth and take a sip of his tea. 'I'm ready,' she said, relaxing back into her chair.

'I believe that, maybe two or three months ago, not long after Irene Adler suffered her second miscarriage, she decided she'd had enough. Not only was she through with Mueller, she wanted revenge. She wanted him to pay for the hurt he'd caused her. I

126

suppose when he mentioned the canal trip in the Netherlands she first got her idea of how she was going to get her revenge.'

'How do you work that out?'

'I've read her NHS medical report. She's had two miscarriages in the last three years. Two months ago, she applied for a replacement passport and driving licence. On the application she said her flat had been burgled and both items stolen. I've been through the crime reports for the last three months and – guess what?'

'There were no break-ins reported at her address?'

'Got it in one.'

'But I don't see the purpose in applying for a new driving licence and passport.'

'You can't travel without one or both. Listen, let me tell you a story. There used to be a ploy used by salesmen who couldn't do their job without being able to drive to see customers. A usual requirement was they must be able to show a clean driving licence to their prospective employers. So, what they'd do, as long as they initially had a clean licence, is simply apply for a replacement. They'd make up some sort of story saying their old one had been in their wallet and it had been stolen. So, when they applied for a job, they were always able to show a clean licence. Most employers wouldn't take the trouble to check with the DVLA. Then in the future, if they were ever prosecuted for a motoring offence and received points on their licence, they'd send in one copy to the DVLA and have a clean one to show any employer who asked to see their licence.'

'But that doesn't apply to Irene Adler, does it?'

'Not quite. What I believe she has done is to get genuine replacements and leave the old ones behind for someone like Claeys to find. Then she would be free to travel on her new ones. Oh, she was so clever, and I didn't see it coming.'

'Which part didn't you see coming?'

'Right at the beginning she was standoffish, ignored both Karen and me. But, as soon as she found out I was a British policeman, well, we were bosom buddies. At least, she was with Karen. Any time Irene saw us in the bar or restaurant she'd make a beeline for us. She was setting me up to be her fall guy.'

'So, she's alive and Karl is dead. Do you think she killed him and is using the alibi of being dead to protect herself?'

'Takes a lot of imagining to see her succeed in getting Karl out to the end of the pier, then hanging him and making it look like a suicide. Nope, there's only one way to answer that question. Let's get to work.'

'Where shall we start?'

'First, when will Morris be back?'

'I talked to him earlier, he says his wife is still struggling. His wife's sister is coming down this weekend and will stay with them till the baby is born.'

'Hmm. We'll just have to get on as best as we can without him. Stephen, where's he?'

'Hanbury grabbed him. They're on a follow-up to the stabbing of a couple of weeks ago.'

'Then it's you and me, again.'

'What do you want me to do?'

'Did you get anywhere about finding Mueller's wife?'

'She wasn't in when we got there yesterday. I did ask Mr Mueller yesterday when we were there, but he said he hadn't seen her for weeks. Apparently, he only uses the address for mail and occasionally getting his laundry done. Or at least he used to.'

'Grab your coat. We'll pay a visit to Irene Adler's address first. Then we'll go see if Mrs Mueller has returned.'

'How will we get in Irene Adler's house? We don't have keys?'

'Since she's either a murder victim or a murderer, we'll get a locksmith to break in for us.'

'I've got their number, when shall I ask them to be there?'

'Twenty minutes.'

◆

It took the locksmith twenty minutes to get to Irene Adler's address and a further fifteen to open the outer front door.

'Here we go,' said Buchanan, pushing the inner front door open.

Street followed. 'I'll check downstairs, will you have a look upstairs?'

They met back in the front room.

'Find anything?' asked Street.

'Nothing out of place, how about you?'

'I'm not sure. It all looks too tidy. When I go away for any length of time I usually change the sheets, do the laundry and have a general tidy up. Upstairs, especially the bathroom. It looks like someone arranged things in a random order.'

'What's your conclusion?'

'If we work on the idea that Irene is on the run, she might have contacted a friend to get bits and pieces for her.'

'Did you check the bedroom?'

'Both. One's a single room, looks like it's used for storage, the other is the master bedroom. I went through the drawers and came to the same conclusion as I did for the bathroom. The underwear drawer looked half empty, as if someone had grabbed a handful of underwear, bra's etc. The closet contains dresses, skirts and blouses, and several empty hangers.'

'So, either Irene has been here, or a friend on her behalf.'

'That still doesn't help us locate her.'

'Did you get the key from the locksmith?'

'Yes, it's in my pocket.'

'Good, let's lock up and go see if Mrs Mueller is in.'

◆

'Her house is the second on the end,' said Street, pointing to the large mock-Tudor house with the wood-effect garage door.

'Looks like someone's home,' said Buchanan, nodding at a silver-grey Porsche sitting in front of the right-hand garage door. 'Pull up beside it.'

'That's a 911. Wonder where the money came from for that?' said Street. 'Stephen was joking about buying me one when he won the lottery.'

'How much?'

'The one he was looking at was on sale for thirty-two thousand.'

'Very interesting.'

Buchanan rang the doorbell and hammered hard on the door with his clenched fist. He peered through the frosted glass panel in the door and saw what looked like movement in the corridor. Moments later they heard the sound of a security chain being slid into place, then a bolt being withdrawn. The door opened, and the inquisitive face of a woman peered round the edge.

'Mrs Mueller? I'm Detective Chief Inspector Buchanan, and this is Detective Sergeant Street. Could we have a word with you, please?'

'Badges, you have badges?'

Buchanan and Street pulled out their ID cards and showed them to Mrs Mueller. She nodded, pushed the door closed, removed the safety chain then reopened the door.

'Come in, can't be too careful.'

They followed her down the corridor and into the front room. Mrs Mueller sat in an armchair beside the fire facing the front window. Buchanan and Street sat side by side on the settee. Mrs Mueller was nervous, she was absent-mindedly interlacing her fingers.

'Mrs Mueller,' began Buchanan, 'I'm sorry to be the bringer of bad news. Early this morning, your husband was found dead under the pier on Eastbourne beach.'

She looked up at Buchanan. He realised he wasn't the first to bring this bit of news, her face was expressionless, her eyes hard and full of anger.

'Had he been drinking?'

'We're not sure, still waiting for the coroner's report. He was found hanging from the pier.'

'Did he leave a note?' she asked, turning to stare out of the window.

Buchanan nodded. 'Your husband mentioned something in his note about disgrace and humiliation. Does that mean anything to you?'

She smiled and looked back at Buchanan. 'He led a disgraceful life and humiliated me with his every breath. I'm glad he's gone, just wish I'd pushed the bastard off the pier myself.'

'Mrs Mueller, who told you about the death of your husband?'

'A disgusting wretch from the *Herald*.'

'Did he give you his name?'

She laughed. 'Anton Miasma, Inspector. Makes me wonder if he knows the etymology of his name?'

Buchanan shook his head.

The clock on the mantelpiece struck three. Mrs Mueller sat up straight. 'Inspector, Sergeant, I forget myself. Can I get you something to drink?'

Buchanan had been wondering how he could get Mrs Mueller and Street together. He realised his presence was a hindrance to Street engaging Mrs Mueller in conversation.

'Can I make the tea?' he said, standing. 'I'm quite at home in the kitchen.'

Street almost interrupted, but when she saw the look on Buchanan's face she realised he wanted her to talk with Mrs Mueller, undisturbed by his presence.

'Yes, Mrs Mueller,' said Street, 'the Inspector does make a lovely cup.'

131

Mrs Mueller looked away from Street to Buchanan and said, 'You'll find the tea in the caddy with the butterfly design on the counter. The cups are in the cupboard above and to the left of the hob. There are biscuits in the biscuit barrel at the other end of the counter.

Buchanan smiled and left the room for the kitchen. He closed the door behind him and walked the rest of the way down the corridor and into the kitchen. Kettle filled and heating, Buchanan opened the cupboard and took out three cups and saucers. There was a tea-tray leaning against the wall at the end of the counter. He placed the cups and saucers on it and added the sugar bowl. He'd noticed a small milk jug in the cupboard beside the cups. He opened the refrigerator door and lifted the large bottle of milk. He looked at it, saw it was just over half full, thought for a minute, smiled, then filled the milk jug. He looked at the date stamp on the bottle – still three days to go – then returned it to the refrigerator. The kettle boiled, he filled the teapot and returned the kettle to the hob. He peeked in the biscuit barrel and saw crumbs at the bottom. A search of the other cupboards revealed two opened boxes of cereal and several packets of biscuits. He picked up one of the packs and looked at the price label, then grinned. He placed the pack of biscuits on the tray and returned to the front room.

Street poured three cups of tea and reached for the milk jug. 'Milk, Mrs Mueller?'

She shook her head. 'My tummy, I can't digest milk. I'll have mine black, please.'

Street handed a milk-less cup of tea to Mrs Mueller, then poured milk into the other two cups. She passed one to Buchanan and took the third for herself. Buchanan picked up the pack of biscuits to open them. He looked at the wrapper, then passed them over to Street. She saw the supermarket label, smiled, and proceeded to open them.

'Mrs Mueller,' said Buchanan, putting down his tea after a sip, 'you live here on your own?'

'Yes.'

'Your husband didn't spend much time here?'

'He'd show up when he wanted a bed for a few nights. I'd do his laundry and he'd be gone again.'

'When was the last time you saw him?'

'Four weeks ago. He showed up late at night. He'd been in a fight – least he had scratches on his face. I thought one of his girlfriends had done it.'

'Did you ask him who scratched his face?'

'No, I was just wishing they'd done a better job.'

'This is a bit of a delicate question,' said Buchanan, trying to choose his words carefully. 'Do you happen to know the names of any of his girlfriends?'

'There was one. She phoned a few days after he showed up with the scratches on his face. I assumed it was she who was responsible for them.'

'Did she give her name?'

'Arrogant bitch. I picked up the ringing phone and there she was. *This is Tatyana, put Karl on the phone.* I should have hung up, but curiosity got the better of me. I wanted to see this exotic piece of femininity that could hold my husband's attention.'

'What did you do?'

'I said if she wanted to know where my husband was she should keep a better eye on him, and if she wanted to hear all the dirt about him, she should come for a visit.'

'And did she?' asked Buchanan.

'No, but we did arrange to meet in London the next time I went up.'

'And did you go up to London and meet with Tatyana?'

'Yes, two weeks ago. She's quite pretty for her age. Too good for my husband, and I told her so.'

'Have you kept in touch?' asked Street.

She shook her head, 'Tatyana has a husband, he's a Russian businessman. She told me our husbands were working together on some business venture. She was bored and for her amusement decided to snare Karl.'

'You knew about your husband's affair with his PA?'

'Irene? Of course I did.'

'You sent her a birthday card each year?'

'Who told you that?'

'She did.'

'I liked her, pity she met my husband – she'd have made someone a lovely wife.'

'Do you know where she is?'

'She's dead, isn't she? At least that's what Karl told me. He told me he'd been arrested for killing her and throwing her body in the canal.'

'Do you think he was capable of doing that?'

'Him?' she shook her head. 'Very unlikely.'

'Was he ever violent with you?'

She shook her head again.

'We saw Irene with bruises on her face – just before she disappeared. Could Karl have hit her, if he was drunk for instance?'

'Not very likely. After a few drinks he'd be as soppy as a puppy. Got his face gently slapped a few times when he got over-friendly with the women around him.'

'The bruising? I saw it for myself.'

'Hmm, she was great with makeup, especially when she was on stage. She was probably just looking for sympathy. Or trying to deceive you.'

Buchanan nodded. 'Mrs Mueller, can you tell us who Karl was working for?'

She shrugged. 'I don't know, he never said and when I enquired how we managed to live off his income he'd tell me if I needed more housekeeping to just ask.'

'And did you?'

She smiled. 'To test him I told him the boiler needed replacing, said the gas company wanted seven thousand to do the job.'

'What happened?'

'Three days later a small package was delivered. It contained eight thousand pounds in twenties and fifties.'

'Did he ask for proof that the boiler had been changed?'

'No. There was a note in with the money, said *call if it costs more.*'

'Do you know much about your husband's early life?' asked Street.

'When we were first dating, he introduced me to his parents. They had left Germany just after the war and settled in south London. They were getting on in years, his mother died a few years ago, his father the year before. Karl was an only child.'

'Do you know much of his early years?'

She shrugged. 'All he ever mentioned about his childhood was he was bullied at school for being the son of German immigrants. They didn't know how to deal with the bullying and sent him to a private school. He did well enough to gain admission to Oxford.'

'What did he read there?'

'Economics.'

'Did your husband ever mention a Garry Duncan?' asked Buchanan.

She thought for a moment. 'I think they were at Oxford at the same time. When we were first married, we used to go to the reunion dinners. I believe that's where I met Garry Duncan.'

'Did he ever come here to the house?'

She shook her head. 'He sometimes called to talk with Karl. If they met away from here I couldn't tell you.'

'How will you manage now your husband has died?' asked Street.

'I'll be all right. I've managed to put some money aside for rainy days.'

'Will the car have to go back?' asked Street.

'Back where? Karl gave me the car when the old Volvo blew up on the M23.'

'He gave you the car! Is it on contract?'

'No. The house is mine as well.'

'Karl gave you the house as well?'

'At least I'll inherit it, he told me he paid off the mortgage five years ago.'

'Owning your home is wonderful, but there are still the maintenance costs and the council tax needs to be paid.'

'Inspector, Sergeant. I already told you about the boiler replacement money. Well, during the last four years he paid for three boiler replacements, a new roof twice, double-glazing four times, and two new conservatories. He also paid for the driveway to be re-laid four times, the garden was completely landscaped each of the last five years, all with cash and no receipts asked for. I also took out a large life insurance policy on him. I don't think I'll go short of a few pennies.'

'Did you actually have three boilers installed?'

'No, of course not, I was just seeing how far I could go.'

'And he never asked for receipts?

'No, not once.'

'If you don't mind me pointing out, Mrs Mueller, the Inland Revenue might want to know where all that cash came from?'

'Gambling, Inspector. Karl was in inveterate, and lucky, gambler.'

'Well, thank you very much for your help, Mrs Mueller, you've made things adequately clear,' said Buchanan standing. 'If there's anything else you remember, here's my card.'

♦

'Conclusions about our visit with Mrs Mueller, Jill?' asked Buchanan, as she drove them back to the office.

'I now see why she never divorced her husband for his philandering. Even though he certainly gave her all the evidence she needed.'

'I think we've found one of the strings to Karl Mueller's bow. It's money laundering. I did a quick adding up of what she mentioned – we're looking at a quarter of a million at least – and all in cash.'

'Quarter of a million! Now that's some housekeeping budget. I could do with some of that. Stephen and I have yet to work out a housekeeping budget. Wonder how much Mueller salted away for himself?'

'I found it interesting he and Duncan were at university at the same time and kept in touch afterwards.'

'If that were so,' said Street, 'what would they have in common? Mueller studied economics and Duncan diplomatic service.'

'Hang on a minute – those two subjects do complement each other,' said Buchanan. 'I imagine when we look at his bank accounts we'll find not much out of the ordinary. My bet is Mueller worked in cash economy. Anything else?'

'She was quite ambivalent to the relationship Irene had with her husband.'

'I noticed that too.'

Street concentrated, thought back over the last couple of hours spent at Mrs Mueller's. She shook her head. 'Nothing else comes to mind – except, could it be that Mueller and Duncan had more than a business venture in common? It's not unknown for that to happen at university.'

'One of the reasons I wanted you to talk to her was I wanted to have a nose around the house.'

'Ah, now I understand. You know you should take lessons on making tea, I noticed you didn't touch yours. So, what did you discover?'

'Milk in the refrigerator, and she said she didn't drink the stuff.'

'She may have had it there for her husband.'

'It was a four-pint container, half-full, and in date. Remember she said her husband hadn't been home for several weeks? There were also two opened boxes of cereal in one of the cupboards. Did you see what I saw about the biscuits?'

'Yes.'

'The store price sticker on them was a Carrefour, Calais, sticker.'

'Are you saying she drove to Amsterdam and collected Irene then drove her somewhere?'

'If I was a guessing man, which I'm not, I'd say that Irene Adler is ensconced somewhere close, or even in the house with Mrs Mueller.'

'We should be able to verify that by contacting immigration.'

Buchanan shook his head. 'I doubt if there's any record of them coming into the UK and the French, well,' he gestured with open hands.

'Oh, I just thought of something,' said Street. 'Could the two of them have killed Karl and tried to make it look like a suicide?'

'That adds another option to the *who killed Karl* list.'

'How many are on this list of yours?'

'Person or persons unknown, Tatyana Reznikov, her husband, Mrs Mueller, and now the pairing of Mrs Mueller and Irene Adler.'

'That's quite a list. Where shall we start?'

'I'm going to check on the husband, Reznikov. Would you see what you can find out about Karl Mueller's bank details? And at some point, we should chase up Karl's autopsy details with Dr Mansell.'

9

'Ah, there you two are,' said Dr Mansell.

'What brings you to the station, Doctor?'

'You seemed rather eager to hear about the method of demise of the body under the pier this morning, and since I was passing on my way home I thought I'd bring it in person.'

'Thank you, Doctor. Would you follow us up to the office?'

Mansell sat in the chair in front of the window, in between Street and Buchanan. 'What's for dinner?'

'Dinner?' said Street.

'Tradition, Jill. In the last two cases I watched you two eat dinner while I espoused the details of the death of Buchanan's first body in the investigation.'

Street looked up at the office wall clock. 'It's only five-thirty, Doctor.'

'That's fine, don't mind having an early night.'

'How about an Indian takeaway, Doctor?' asked Buchanan. 'We've found a really good Indian restaurant in the Marina.'

'What's it called?'

'The Ganges.'

'Suits me. I was there a couple of weeks ago with my wife – didn't know they did takeaway.'

Buchanan nodded at Street who produced a takeaway menu from her desk drawer and passed it to the doctor.

♦

Crumpling his napkin and throwing it in the wastepaper bin Buchanan said, 'Right, Doctor, you've been fed and watered, what's your verdict on the death of Karl Mueller?'

'As you both know, we recovered the body of Karl Mueller from under Eastbourne pier this morning,' began Mansell. 'You both saw the body, it had been hung from the railings at the end of the pier. I said then I thought the time of death to be sometime between nine and eleven o'clock the previous evening.'

'And the cause of death?' asked Street.

'Ah, now that could be a bit of a controversy. He died when his heart stopped beating, but whether it was the rope around the neck combined with the chill of the English Channel as the tide rose, or simply a dose of parnate, mixed with ecstasy, will take some further investigating.'

'I know about ecstasy,' said Street, 'but what is parnate?'

'Parnate is one of a group of drugs called MAOI's. They are prescribed for people suffering from acute anxiety disorders. They are seldom prescribed these days due to their side effects when taken with certain foods.

I looked in his wallet and found his NHS card. It was then a simple job of getting a copy of his medical records. I found out he was bipolar and had been prescribed parnate for depression. Parnate should never be co-ingested with ecstasy.'

'What's the issue then?' asked Buchanan.

'As I said MAOI's are mainly prescribed for anxiety disorders and sometimes for sufferers of Parkinson's, though there are more modern versions available for the GP to prescribe. They are reserved for people for whom the more recent drugs aren't suitable.'

'Why would that be significant in Mueller's case?' asked Street.

'When mixed with alcohol and certain foods, it can cause death.'

'Had he been eating? And if so, what?' asked Buchanan.

'Seems like he'd been at a party. When I had a look at the contents of his stomach I found, amongst other items, partially-digested cheddar cheese, liver paté and caviar, and he'd been drinking heavily.'

'Sounds like a fun party. Why would these items be important?' asked Street.

'I won't bore you with the chemical reactions in the body, but certain dairy foods, like mature cheese, meat products such as liver, and fish products such as caviar – any one of these mixed with fermented alcohol, such as beer or wine, can cause fatal high blood pressure spikes.'

'I wonder if he was a guest at the party on the pier?' said Street.

'That's one for you tomorrow,' said Buchanan. 'How was his liver, Doctor?'

'As one would expect with a lifestyle of heavy drinking.'

'Anything else?'

'I don't suppose you saw his hands when he was cut down?'

'No, they were still in the body bag, you only unzipped so we could see his face.'

'His hands were free, not tied.'

'So why didn't he just pull himself out?' asked Street.

'Not that easy when you're inebriated and struggling with a racing heart. Remember, he had a rope round his neck. He was fully dressed and barely able to keep his head and shoulders out of the sea. Think about his situation: one minute he's splashing around trying to get the noose off, the next moment as a wave passes the noose tightens and he's choking. If he stopped swimming he would start to sink, and the noose would tighten round his neck aggravating his racing heart. So, I imagine he would have reached up, grabbed the rope to take the weight off the noose, then his grip would fail and back into the water he'd go. And all the time he'd be thinking and wondering if the tide was coming in or going out, the cycle repeating itself till his heart couldn't take it anymore and he died.'

'So, your conclusion on his demise?'

'I signed his death certificate as the cause of death being heart failure due to shock of immersion in the sea. Aggravated by ingestion of an overdose of a monoamine oxidase inhibitor, cocaine, and 3,4-methylenedioxymethamphetamine. Ecstasy to you and the lad on the dance floor.'

'Glad I don't have to say that, it's a bit of a mouthful,' said Street.

'Would he be able to walk unaided, Doctor?'

'Unlikely with that concoction running round his body.'

'So,' said Street, 'I can imagine he either was invited or gate-crashed the party. He met up with at least one person who he knew, probably had a couple of drinks and someone slipped ecstasy into his drink.'

'But who led him down the pier for a swim?' said Buchanan. 'Was there anything special about the rope, Doctor?'

'No. It was just an ordinary piece of blue polypropylene three-strand. The sort of rope that contractors use to pull cables through underground ducts.'

'Was it new?'

Mansell smiled. 'Strong enough to suspend a body but probably would break under use.'

'So, probably discarded by a contractor and left lying where an enterprising assassin could pick it up without leaving a trail,' said Buchanan.

'I'll add that to my list for tomorrow,' said Street, anticipating Buchanan's request.

'If that's all, Buchanan, I'll say goodbye. I could do with an early night.'

'Goodnight, Doctor.'

'Goodnight. Till we meet again at the next body.'

'We have a lot to do tomorrow, Jill. I think an early night will do us both good, see you back here tomorrow at eight.'

♦

'Y'all right? Your usual, Jack?' said Jade, as Buchanan walked into Starbucks.

'Yes, please, but can I have a large Americano? I have a great deal of thinking to do today.'

'Are you investigating the poor bloke who hung himself from the pier?' she said, handing him his cup.

'That and other things, Jade. See you later.'

Buchanan stopped in the garage to fill up and, on the way in to pay for his petrol, he caught sight of an article in the *Mail* about the party on the pier. He picked up a copy as he went in.

To his surprise when he arrived at the office, Street was already on her computer.

'Morning, Chief.'

'What's got you here so early?'

'Couldn't sleep. Stephen was going off early with Hanbury to Winchester, so I made us breakfast and here I am.'

'Find anything about the party on the pier? There's an article in the *Mail* about it, haven't read it yet,' he said, putting the paper on Street's desk.

'I called the club on the off-chance that someone might be there, just got their answering machine. I'll call again later.'

'Anything on-line about the party?'

'Only information I could get was off their website. It says they were pleased to announce the Excellence in Industry awards were going to be held there. How about you?'

'Been thinking,' he said, sitting down at his desk and taking a sip of his coffee. 'Karl's latest fling, Tatyana, the wife of that Russian businessman. My niggler is niggling again. I can't see someone like Reznikov just letting his wife have it off with anyone she chooses – it just doesn't make sense.'

'Karl's wife didn't seem to be bothered when he did it.'

'There's more to this case than we're party to. For instance, we still don't know who Karl was working for or what he did to be able to just give his wife eight thousand pounds in cash, no questions asked. I'm going to see what I can find out about Messrs Reznikov and Mueller,' said Buchannan, turning on his computer.

Street got up from her desk and walked over to Buchanan's, looking over his shoulder at the computer screen. The name Mueller came up first, and referenced a story to be found in the *Eastbourne Herald* and a vague reference to his missing PA while on holiday in the Netherlands.

Reznikov was another matter. There were several mentions of his name, mostly articles printed in the business sections of the broadsheet newspapers, and two about charity events where he was thanked for his generosity in supporting several charities. But it was another photo they hadn't previously seen of Tatyana and Karl that drew their interest. This photo in *Hello* magazine, unlike the previous version, had a caption underneath mentioning a rumour of an affair between Tatyana and Karl. There was a second photo of an obviously angry Reznikov leaving the charity event alone.

'How about you try the PNC for the two of them?' suggested Street.

There they had better luck. Karl was listed twice, once for a DUI offence in an RTA where the driver of the other vehicle was hospitalised. Karl was found 'Not guilty' at Lewes Crown Court.

'Must have had a good counsel to be found not guilty,' said Street.

'Anyone local?'

Street scanned through the report and discovered the name of Karl's counsel. 'Got it – he was a Guthrie Burtenshaw, QC.'

'Is there an address?'

'Yes. He has his chambers in London and a local chamber here in Eastbourne on The Avenue. He has a room in the offices of Brackenstall and Stanley.'

'Good, I think I'll pay him a visit. Can you give his office a call and find out if he's available?'

'Will do.'

'What else is there about Mueller?'

'The second item was about a case where Mueller's name was linked with money laundering, though nothing was ever proved and once again Guthrie Burtenshaw, QC, attended.'

'Hmm. You know what, Jill? This case is starting to take on a form.'

'Go on.'

'Let's go back to the beginning. Nine weeks ago, I was driving to Lewes to discuss the possibility of my early retirement –'

'Discuss your retirement?' echoed Street.

'As I said, to discuss the possibility of my early retirement. As I passed the turnoff for Charleston House, I had to make a sharp turn to the left to avoid running headlong into Mueller's car. My next meeting with the late Karl Mueller was at Gatwick airport waiting to board a flight for Amsterdam. I was surprised to find he was also going to be a passenger on the same canal cruise as we were. The next surprise was his partner, Irene Adler: his PA, and on and off lover. During the first few days of my holiday, Karen and I came to know a little about Irene Adler. This information led us to suspect that Karl Mueller was a classic misogynist. After only a couple of days, this Karl Mueller leaves the cruise in Arnhem to go for a business meeting. During his absence, Irene Adler goes missing, presumed dead.'

'Have you heard from Claeys yet?' asked Street.

Buchanan shook his head. 'No, nothing yet. I suspect our Belgian inspector has more things to worry him than chasing after a missing English passenger on a Dutch cruise ship on a Dutch canal. No, Jill, we're on this chase by ourselves.'

'Like when we first met?'

'I suppose you're right. Anyway, the trail goes quiet till yesterday when the body of Karl Mueller turns up dead, hanging from the underside of Eastbourne pier. Did he kill himself, like the suicide note says, or was he given help? I think the latter, especially after talking with Dr Mansell. Mrs Mueller is obviously involved, but with which part of this mystery? Did she assist Irene Adler with her disappearance and bring her back to the UK, and is she currently harbouring her? Did they kill Karl? Or could there be a trio of assassins: Mrs Mueller, Irene Adler and Ivan Reznikov?'

'You said there was an article in the *Mail* about the party on the pier?'

'Paper's on your desk.'

Street returned to her desk and opened the *Mail* to page five and read the article. 'Nothing in here about Mueller, but there is a photo of Reznikov receiving his award.'

'What does it say?'

Street read out:

Last night at the Trans-Asian Excellence in Business awards, Russian businessman, Ivan Reznikov, was awarded the Prix d'Excellence award for his outstanding contributions to harmonising trade relationships between Russia and her near neighbours.

'Any photos?'

'There's one of him accepting the award, and another showing him with a bunch of dignitaries.'

'Could you get on to the *Mail* and see if you can get a copy of the photos taken at the awards meeting? Might be helpful if we could identify some faces.'

'What shall I tell them if they ask why I want them?' she said, looking for the newspaper's website.

'Tell them you're working on a murder investigation – no, wait a minute, don't say that, you'll have them breathing down our necks looking for a story – bad enough having Miasma to deal with. I tell you what, say you were at the awards dinner and as a surprise for your auntie in Scarborough you'd like a copy of the photos to send to her,' said Buchanan, standing and reaching for his jacket

'OK. Are you going out?'

'Thought I'd save you the phone call and go see Guthrie Burtenshaw, QC. You said his chambers are on The Avenue?'

Street nodded as she waited for her phone call to be answered

♦

The law offices of Brackenstall and Stanley were situated on a corner on the right-hand side of The Avenue, a hundred yards or so from the traffic lights where The Avenue joined Upperton Road. The building was typical of those built in the late nineteenth century: brick, rendered with lime mortar, the corners made out of render to look like blockwork. There was a basement, three floors above and a room in the attic. The bay windows of the main offices looked out on to Hartfield Square. The building, like so many others of its type, was painted in seaside cream finished with white trim round the windows with the gutters and down-pipes painted black.

Buchanan parked on the double yellow lines, locked his car and walked over to the steps leading up to the entrance. A highly-polished brass plaque beside the door proudly announced the name of the law offices of Brackenstall and Stanley. Directly below the polished brass plaque was an unpretentious laminated plastic plaque simply stating this was the Eastbourne chambers of Guthrie Burtenshaw, QC, MSc.

'Good morning. How can I help?' asked the receptionist, as Buchanan sauntered across the wide expanse of the reception lobby.

Buchanan put on his best smile and said, 'Detective Chief Inspector Buchanan. I would like to have a quick word with Mr Burtenshaw, if he's in that is.'

The receptionist frowned and looked up at the clock. 'He should be in by now. I'll see if he's answering his phone.'

Buchanan followed the receptionist's gaze. The clock said ten twenty-five. 'Is he usually this late?'

'Mr Burtenshaw doesn't drive, he had a heart attack a few years ago. He now comes in by bus – The Loop – it's not known for its punctuality.'

The receptionist pressed a few keys on his computer keyboard, looked at the screen then back to Buchanan. 'I'm sorry, did you have an appointment?'

'No, but I'd still like to see him, I won't keep him very long.'

'Can I say what about?' asked the receptionist, keying in a number.

'Yes, it's about the late Karl Mueller.'

The receptionist dialled Burtenshaw's extension and waited for an answer. 'Good morning sir, it's Matt in reception. There's a policeman here who says he would like to talk to you – said it's about the late Karl Mueller. I will. Inspector, Mr Burtenshaw is on a conference call, he said to go on up. You'll find his office on the fourth floor.'

Buchanan stood to take a breath on the third-floor landing and wondered how anyone with arthritic knees could climb the lofty heights, since he hadn't seen any sign of a lift. As he climbed the final flight, his hand slid up the bannister worn bare by many before him. What had these people been thinking, what nefarious activities were they going to see the great Burtenshaw about?

The upper landing was illuminated by a skylight that looked like it hadn't been cleaned in years. The shrill cry of seagulls wheeling above the roof penetrated the stillness of the landing. Two doors led off it. The one on the immediate left resembled that of a broom cupboard, the one on the right was half-glazed with frosted glass. There was a name in gold leaf in the middle of the glass panel: Guthrie Burtenshaw, QC. Below in less ostentatious lettering it said: *Please Enter.*

Buchanan knocked and entered. He was in a small ante-room with a desk and chair in the right-hand corner. On the desk was a blotting pad, secretary's notepad and pen, no phone. Buchanan walked over to the desk and ran his finger over the polished surface. It hadn't been dusted in a long time. In the middle of the far wall was a second, half-glazed door. This time the message on the door in gold leaf was blunt: *Private.*

Buchanan knocked on the door. When he got no reply, he went in. At the sound of the door opening, Burtenshaw looked up, obviously perturbed by being disturbed in the middle of his phone call. Momentarily distracted, he smirked and beckoned Buchanan into the office while pointing to an empty chair.

Buchanan closed the door behind him, ignored the offered chair and walked over to the window and looked down on The Avenue. Across the road in Hartfield Square a woman was throwing sticks for her over-excited dog, while her children played on the swings.

'Yes? What do you want?' said Burtenshaw, putting down his phone.

Buchanan turned to look at Burtenshaw, then at the chair, and said while sitting down. 'Good morning. I'm Detective Chief Inspector Buchanan. The lad on reception said you were in.'

'Oh, yes, so he did. How can I help?'

'I understand you have represented the late Karl Mueller in a couple of incidents?'

'The late Karl Mueller, Inspector?'

'Ah, you haven't heard. Yes, the late Karl Mueller. He was found hanging from the railings at the end of Eastbourne pier yesterday.'

Burtenshaw sank back into his chair. He was silent for a moment, then his face relaxed. 'Inspector, I am a very busy man. In fact, I'm currently engaged in a case that is demanding all my acumen. I do recall the name of Karl Mueller, but not much else. I'm afraid you'll have to remind me of the details.'

'Mr Mueller, as I said, was found hanging from the underside of Eastbourne pier. It was made to look like he had taken his own life.'

'Made to look like? Are you saying he didn't?'

'There are certain indications that lead to that conclusion. Can you think of anyone who may have wished him harm?'

Buchanan watched Burtenshaw. Without replying, he picked up his fountain pen, carefully screwed on the cap then slid the pen into the inside pocket of his jacket. 'Mr – er – Inspector Buchanan, what makes you think I would have that sort of knowledge?'

'I was wondering, since you represented the late Karl Mueller in two cases, if you may have information – not deemed important at the time – that could shed light on the present circumstances?'

Burtenshaw fiddled with the knot in his tie, rolled his shoulders and coughed. 'Inspector, if I knew that I would feel duty bound to tell you.'

Buchanan was about to mention the issue of money laundering, but instead brought up the issue of drink driving.

'Ah, that I do remember. We got him acquitted if I remember correctly. Why are you interested in that?'

'I'm investigating a recent case where he was involved in causing an accident and failing to stop.'

Burtenshaw shrugged. 'A bit of a moot point if he's, as you say, dead.'

'There's considerable property damage, and of course there's the personal injury. And let us not forget the loss of wages of the other driver needs to be considered.'

'Inspector, I fail to see the relevance of your questions, or this discussion. In fact, you're beginning to sound like one of those TV ambulance-chasing commercials that bring my profession into disrepute. I did represent the now late Karl Mueller in a completely separate case, and that was several years ago now.'

'How about money laundering? I believe there once was some talk about him being involved in that?'

'Where did you hear about that?'

'It's all on record.'

'Then you'll know that Mr Mueller wasn't involved, and I didn't need to represent him. It was the heavy-handed police investigation that dragged him into that case.'

'Then you represented the others in the case?'

'Inspector, I do believe you are fishing. I'm sure you are aware of the phrase client confidentiality,' said Burtenshaw, smiling.

'What about a Russian businessman, an Ivan Reznikov?'

'Inspector, my advice to you is to forget you ever heard the name.'

'How about Mrs Reznikov – Tatyana?'

'I know nothing about Mrs Reznikov'

'She and Mr Mueller were having an affair.'

'Inspector, I am a very busy man, I do not have time to listen to tittle-tattle.'

'The investigation of crime isn't tittle-tattle, Mr Burtenshaw. Our search for the truth takes us through the very fabric of society. We never rest, our search goes on, day and night.'

'Ah, Inspector, in that you speak the truth. Like the poor, we'll always have the criminal amongst us. Though I suppose we should be grateful to the wretches. Because of them neither you nor I will ever be out of gainful employment.'

'Is that how you see them? Just a means to an end?'

'Certainly not. We need them as much as they need us.'

'Am I hearing you correctly? Are you saying that crime is necessary for you and me to have a purpose in life? That society needs criminals and crime?'

'Inspector, you of all people should know there is no such thing as the perfect society. All the way back through recorded history, right back to the original sin of Adam and Eve, man has been at odds with what's right and what's wrong.'

'I'll agree with that.'

'Don't you see? Without bad there can't be good, and vice versa. There would be no balance.'

'What shall we say, then? Are we to continue in sin that grace may abound?'

'What's that you said? Sounds familiar.'

'Romans chapter six, verse one. One of the few verses I remember from Sunday school. Mr Burtenshaw, I'm afraid we see life from different perspectives. You of all people must know that no two witnesses will ever see the same event equally, even if they are standing side by side when the event happens.'

'That is so and can be used to great advantage when disproving eyewitness statements in court.'

'So, what can you tell me about Ivan Reznikov that I won't find in our records?'

'Interesting segue, Inspector. All I can say is, if he offers you a cup of tea, ask for water instead.'

'Tea? Are you saying what I think you are saying?'

'I'm saying nothing because, as I have already told you, I know nothing.'

'You do realise that obstruction of the police in their investigations is a crime, Mr Burtenshaw?'

'Of course, I do, Inspector. It's just – it's just I fail to see what any information I have on Mr Reznikov has to do with the death of your Mr Mueller.'

'Mr Burtenshaw, so far in my investigation I have one missing, presumed dead, woman and the body of a man who is supposed to have committed suicide but it is now looking more like murder. I am deeply concerned that there could be more deaths before this case is resolved. Now, would you please tell me what you know of Ivan Reznikov?'

'All right,' said Burtenshaw, looking around the room as if he expected to see Reznikov hiding in a corner. 'My introduction to him was through Karl Mueller. Karl asked me to arrange some import documents for Ivan Reznikov. From what I remember of the documents, Reznikov runs an export business for his wife's fashion business. He also provides security services for businessmen and dignitaries. Up till then I knew absolutely nothing about the man, let alone having actually met him. As part of the preparations for his import licence Reznikov had to provide this information on his background.'

'Did Karl Mueller have much to say about him?'

'That would be gossip, Inspector.'

Buchanan smiled. 'Mr Burtenshaw, I suspect in your world you deal in absolutes. Nothing is grey, all is either black or white, is that not so?'

Burtenshaw nodded.

'Mr Burtenshaw, when I'm investigating, I'm colour blind. Then my world consists wholly of shades of grey. That is until the sun comes out and I finally get to see the rainbow in all its glory.'

'You were correct about Karl and Tatyana Reznikov having an affair.'

'When did you realise that?'

'He showed up here once with her. She is a stunner, would look good on any glossy magazine cover.'

'Was it serious?'

Burtenshaw smiled. 'Inspector, during my many years before the bench, I met many working women, from all classes. Mrs Tatyana Reznikov would make any man shine. I did get the impression there might have been more to their relationship then just infatuation.'

'And that's all you know?'

'That's all I'm prepared to admit to knowing. If you want more information, I suggest you contact the Russian Embassy, and please don't mention my name.'

'Thank you for your forthrightness, Mr Burtenshaw. I'll keep in mind what you have said. Oh, before I go, when was the last time you actually saw Ivan Reznikov?'

'At the awards dinner.'

'You were a guest?'

'No, I wasn't a guest. Reznikov called and said he needed his documents right away.'

'What time did he call?'

'About eight-thirty, said to get there by eight forty-five.'

'Why eight forty-five?'

'I think he was getting his award at nine o'clock.'

'What was his hurry for the documents?'

'He said he had to send them to his contacts in Moscow in the morning.'

'Was he there when you arrived?'

'No. I'd ordered the taxi for eight-thirty, but it was late. I didn't get to the pier till just before nine. I had to wait till after the presentation. I had to stand there in the cold breathing in all that foul cigarette smoke.'

'There was quite a crowd at the event. Where did he say to meet?'

'He said to come to the door at the side, where the smokers stand. He said he'd be waiting for me.'

'Why all the secrecy?'

'It was the way with him.'

'Was Reznikov alone when he eventually came out?'

'No. Karl Mueller was out there on the bench.'

'Did Reznikov say anything to Mueller?'

'No.'

'Was it just the three of you?'

'There was quite a crowd out there smoking. I was only looking for Reznikov. I was in a rush to get home.'

'Did Karl Mueller say anything while you were there?'

'No.'

'How did he look?'

Burtenshaw thought for a moment. 'He looked like he'd had one too many, he kept hanging over the railing and being sick.'

'Where was he when you left?'

'Still sitting on the seat by the railing. He had his head in his hands and was swaying side to side. I thought he was going to fall off the seat.'

'What was Reznikov doing?'

'He laughed at Mueller, said he was a fool to drink so much.'

'Did Mueller say anything in reply?'

'He looked up, his face was pale, and he was drooling.'

'And were they still there when you left?'

'Reznikov said he'd take care of Mueller, not to worry and not to let my taxi wait too long.'

'And you are sure that is the last time you saw them together?'

'Yes, Inspector.'

'Thank you for being so forthright, Mr Burtenshaw. Since you are one of the last people to see Karl Mueller alive, we'll need a signed statement from you. Will you be in your chambers on Monday?'

'Yes.'

'What would be an appropriate time for us to send someone to take your statement?'

'Anytime after ten-thirty. My bus, if it's on time, gets me here just after ten.'

'One final question, Mr Burtenshaw. Where did you receive your degree?'

'That's an odd question to ask, considering our conversation.'

'Was it at Oxford?'

'Yes.'

'Do you know a Garry Duncan?'

'Inspector, if you were in court asking these types of questions, the judge would disallow them for being speculative.'

'Should I infer that you knew both Garry Duncan and Karl Mueller at Oxford?'

Burtenshaw reached into his jacket, took out his pen and unscrewed the cap. 'Inspector, I do believe you are fishing again.'

'The bait not to your liking, Mr Burtenshaw?'

'Inspector, do you have any idea as to how many students attend Oxford in any given year?'

Buchanan shook his head. 'All I'm interested in, Mr Burtenshaw, is, were you, Duncan and Mueller friends at Oxford?'

'They used to crew for me on my sailboat.'

'Thank you, Mr Burtenshaw. Goodbye.'

The sun was rising, a picture was emerging from the mist. Burtenshaw, Mueller and Duncan had all been at university together. They had all sailed on Burtenshaw's sailboat. Conclusion, they all had similar views on matters. But what were these matters? Did their association extend beyond sailing?

They were obviously pooling their resources: Burtenshaw on legal matters, Mueller on business matters and Duncan on domestic and possible international affairs. To Buchanan's mind it all pointed back towards an involvement with Brexit. The idea was that Duncan was feeding privileged insider information to Mueller, who was able to mix in the business world and free to negotiate, and Burtenshaw was keeping things just this side of legal. Buchanan didn't think there were any particular industries involved, more likely they were cherry-picking the sweetest in the bunch – those with potential to make huge profits after the UK left the European Union.

But where did Ivan Reznikov fit in the jigsaw? His wife was having an affair with the late Karl Mueller, who was also having an affair with his PA, Irene, and, as far as the Belgian police were concerned, she was now posted as missing presumed drowned. Buchanan had other ideas on this and needed to find out more about Reznikov's background. He was sure there was a more complex connection between the main participants in this play. For instance, where did Mueller lay his head at night? He must have had an apartment somewhere as it would be unlikely he was living with Reznikov's wife. Mueller had mentioned he lived in Meads, but was that just a tale to divert Buchanan from the real fact that he shared his bedtimes between his wife, Irene Adler and Tatyana Reznikov?

♦

'Jill, said Buchanan, as he entered the office, 'find out anything about the awards ceremony on the pier?'

'Just had a chat with the event co-ordinator,' she said, looking down at her notebook, 'a Ruth Samson. She's emailed me the guest list. It was an invitation-only event. I've been through the list: both Reznikovs were there, as was Karl Mueller, and so was a certain Garry Duncan.'

'No mention of Mrs Mueller or Irene Adler?'

Street shook her head.

'Was Ruth Samson at the event?'

'I asked her that. She said she was there at the beginning to make sure all was as it should be, but left before the ceremony began.'

'How about security at the event?'

'A private firm from London.'

'CCTV?'

'I said we'd be by to have a look at whatever they have.'

'I'll try the Russian Embassy,' said Buchanan, picking up his phone.

Ten minutes later he slammed down the receiver.

'No luck?' asked Street.

'They denied any knowledge of Reznikov's existence.'

'What ever happened to glasnost and perestroika?'

'That's a bit before your time, isn't it?'

'I had to take a module on politics for my degree. I chose European politics post 1940.'

'That's more than I did. I only got as far as 1066.'

'Did you talk with Burtenshaw?'

'Yes. I said someone would be at his chambers Monday morning to get a signed statement from him.'

'Was he of any help?'

'Yes, though it took quite a bit of dancing round the questions to extract the answers. I asked him about Mueller, he said Mueller was hanging over the rail being sick when he got there and Reznikov said he'd take care of him.'

'It's still circumstantial that Reznikov killed Mueller.'

'You said the club is holding the CCTV footage of the awards event?' said Buchanan.

'Yes.'

'Good, let's go see. We can have a look at where Burtenshaw passed the papers to Reznikov, and where Mueller was supposed to have hung himself.'

Buchanan parked in front of the pier in a vacant taxi parking slot. He ignored the indignant stare of one of the taxi drivers, shut his door and stopped to take in a breath. He locked the car doors and, with Street trying to keep up, they made their way out towards the end of the pier.

'What do you think about the gold paint?' Buchanan asked Street as they walked past the gold-painted lion heads on the railings.

She stopped and looked at one, then patted it with her hand. 'I think it brings a nice balance of colour. Much better than it used to look. I especially like what's been done with the domes.'

'I agree with you, and I think it's high time the residents stopped sniping at the pier owner and got behind him. After all it's his investment that's making the improvements.'

'I wonder what he's going to do with all this open space now the arcade has gone?'

'I heard there was a London restaurant interested in setting up on the pier. I wonder if that will happen now with the Arndale expansion?' said Buchanan, as they walked past the picnic tables.

'Listen to that sound,' said Street as she leaned over the railing to watch the passing waves, 'don't you just love living by the sea?'

There was a uniformed policeman standing at the entrance to the club, a line of blue and white police tape cordoning off the side of it. Buchanan walked over and showed his warrant card, the policeman undid the end of the barrier tape and let him and Street through.

'Well, well, what do we have here?' said Buchanan, stopping to look into a large yellow rubbish skip. He pushed a few black bags to the side and there, underneath, was a pile of short lengths of three-strand, blue polypropylene rope.

'Do you think that's where the rope that was used on Mueller came from?'

'Probably. Take a photo of the rope in the skip, would you? Not sure if it would be useful as evidence in a trial. Then would you call control and ask them to organise security for this skip till the SCI's have been through it.'

'Will do. What do you think they'll find?'

'Who knows? We've just found the rope.'

They stopped by the smoking zone at the side of the night club. 'This is where Burtenshaw said he handed over the papers to Reznikov,' said Buchanan, looking around. 'Damn, don't see any CCTV cameras.'

'There's one,' said Street, pointing, 'up high on the corner, see?'

'Good, that should show what went on out here.'

'Maybe that's why Reznikov chose this area,' said Street. 'Late at night, people boozed up smoking and talking – no one would notice two people talking quietly, nothing to attract attention on a CCTV screen. The perfect place to conduct a clandestine meeting. Wish I'd been a fly on the wall for that.'

'You wouldn't have lasted long with the wind out here. Let's see where Mueller died,' said Buchanan, pulling his jacket closed and walking off to the end of the pier. There was a piece of white marking-tape with the words *Police do not remove* wrapped round the railing adjacent to where the rope had been tied.

Buchanan stopped in front of the locked gates that led down to the former fishing pier. 'I presume this end of the pier is off limits at night, though there doesn't appear to be anything to stop anyone from walking back here. Hmm,' he mumbled, 'the doctor said Mueller had been drugged and probably didn't know what was going on.' He looked back at the smoking area. 'I imagine Reznikov suggested they walk away from the smokers, just to get a bit of privacy. He probably already had the rope in his pocket.'

'That means premeditation. I can't imagine Reznikov saying to Mueller, *wait here a minute, just going to rummage in the skip for a bit of rope to hang you with*. He must have planned to get rid of Mueller,' said Street, 'but why, who or what would have made Reznikov take such drastic actions? I wonder if he took the time to look for cameras back here?' She scanned the side of the building for cameras. 'It just doesn't add up. The only scenario that makes sense to me is, they came out to have a talk, their talk is interrupted when Burtenshaw shows up with Reznikov's documents. Maybe Mueller got bored waiting and went inside for a moment and when he came back out, something Burtenshaw had said to Reznikov made him act the way he did. While Mueller was inside Reznikov saw the rope in the skip and that gave him the idea of how to get rid of Mueller.'

Buchanan shrugged. 'The two of them would have sat down and while Mueller was in cloud cuckoo land, Burtenshaw tied the rope round the handrail when he wasn't watching, then Reznikov dropped the noose round Mueller's neck and pushed the dozy Mueller over the rail – it's not really very high. Reznikov probably intended that the fall with the rope round the neck would have done for Mueller. Unfortunately, the tide was in and the rope too long. Poor sod, floundering in the cold sea trying to get the rope off his neck and all the time trying to keep his head above water and not suffocate.'

160

'We are assuming it was Reznikov, aren't we?' said Street. 'It could have been anybody, an old enemy for instance. Someone who Mueller had caused to have a grievance against, saw him leaning on the railing, just happened to know where the rope was and took advantage of the situation. But anyway, we have no witnesses or evidence, just Burtenshaw's statement that he saw the two of them by the side door. And without CCTV we're out on a limb with only circumstantial evidence.'

'What time did you say we'd meet with the event organiser?'

'Ruth Samson? I said we'd be with her in the afternoon.'

Buchanan looked at his phone. 'It's three-thirty. Ready?'

They walked the long way round the building back to the entrance to the club. There was a maintenance man replacing a pane of glass in the side window.

'Excuse me,' said Street, 'we're looking for Ruth Samson.'

'She'll be in the back office. Go across the dance floor and through the second door on the left, then down the corridor and up the stairs. Her office is on the right.'

'Thanks.'

'Did you ever come here?' asked Buchanan, as they walked across the highly-polished dance floor.

'A few times to parties. I enjoyed my visits even though I felt I was a bit old for the club.'

'Second on the left he said?' said Buchanan, pulling the door open and letting Street walk past. The door opened on to a corridor with a set of stairs at the far end. They climbed the stairs and saw another corridor with two doors on each side. One of the doors on the right was open and they could hear the sound of voices. Buchanan entered and Street followed.

They walked into a room containing a single desk on the right facing into the middle of the room. A row of filing cabinets lined the corridor wall, with a steaming coffee pot sitting on top. On the left was a glass partition behind which was yet another smaller office. Directly in front was a huge window that provided a view of the coastline all the way to Hastings. Heart radio was playing. There was a young lady seated at the desk staring at her computer screen. She looked up at the sound of footsteps on the polished vinyl floor.

'Can I help?'

'Good afternoon, Tracy,' said Buchanan, looking at the name tag on the desk. 'Detective Chief Inspector Buchanan and Detective Sergeant Street. We're looking for Ruth Samson.'

'She's in her office,' said Tracy, pointing, 'but she's on the phone.'

'I see that, we'll wait.' Buchanan looked at the room and thought that as an office it might be small, but the view was postcard perfect.

'How can I help?' said Ruth Samson, opening the door to her office.

'Detective Inspector Buchanan. My colleague talked to you on the phone about the CCTV recordings of the event on Tuesday evening.'

'Ah, yes, she did. I suppose you are here to ask for a copy?'

'Please.'

'It'll take me a few minutes, so take a seat. Would you like a coffee while you wait?'

Buchanan looked at the tide rings on the coffee jug. 'No thanks.'

While they waited, Street looked at her phone and Buchanan stared out of the window at the waves pounding the shingle on the beach. He was flummoxed. Where was the investigation going? The issue of Irene Adler was, as far as he was concerned, resolved. But there was no way in his mind that Karl Mueller would have taken his own life, drunk or sober. Someone must have helped him, but was it Reznikov acting on his own? Or was there an accomplice? Could it have been Burtenshaw even – a QC? He ran down the names on the list they'd found in the other rubbish basket on the ship; there was Duncan's name, along with Mueller and Burtenshaw. Could it have been Duncan and not Burtenshaw who had been involved in the death of Mueller?'

'Here you are, Inspector, I anticipated your request. The whole evening, pretty boring watching if you ask me.'

'What about outside – the smoking area and the end of the pier? Do you have recordings for those areas?'

'Yes, but they may not be much use to you.'

'Why?'

'If I remember it was raining on the evening. Sometimes when we have those weather fronts the wind blows the rain onto the camera lens.'

'Could I have copies anyway, please?'

'I've put them on a disc, starting with the video of the event.'

'Thanks.'

◆

'You like Eastbourne?' Buchanan asked Street as they walked back along the pier.

'It's home, and you?'

He shrugged. 'It's becoming home.

'Things you like about Eastbourne?'

'Let me see, the pier of course, though I think it could do with a restaurant where the old amusement arcade stood. The Downs, that's another, not quite the Campsie Fells, but nice all the same.'

'Anything else?'

'The Devonshire reminds me of some of the old theatres in Glasgow.'

'What about the beer?'

'Nothing wrong with a pint of Harveys.'

'What about Karen?'

'Oh, I still like her too.'

'That's not what I meant.'

'I realise that, just joking. For one thing, Karen likes the afternoon tea at the Hydro.'

'Oh look,' said Street, as they approached the car, 'we have a parking ticket. You should have smiled at the taxi driver, bet he reported you. I'll take care of it when we get back to the office.'

♦

'Sorted,' said Street.

'What's sorted?' said Buchanan.

'Your parking ticket.'

'Thanks,' said Buchanan, looking at the time on his phone.

'Are we working late?' asked Street.

'If you don't mind. I thought I'd have a quick look at the video of the party.'

'Do we need a takeaway?'

He thought for a moment. 'If we were in Glasgow I'd order haggis and chips.'

'With a deep-fried Mars bar to follow?'

He shook his head. 'You know, since we've been down here in Eastbourne I've lost seven pounds.'

'That's the fresh air.'

'I'll pay for dinner, you choose.'

'Pizza. Dominoes deliver.'

'Fine by me, we can do a combo.'

'I like the garden veg. While you order I'll set up the video.'

♦

Street opened the pizza box and helped herself to a slice of the vegetable pizza. Buchanan took two slices of the Hawaiian and folded them over into a sandwich.

'Shall we get started?' said Street

Buchanan nodded, his mouth full.

The video simultaneously showed the scene from inside the club from four separate cameras, the time the display said eight-fifteen. It took a few moments of watching to identify Reznikov. He was seated at a table just to the left of the centre of the room.

'I wonder where Mueller is?' said Buchanan.

'There, over by the bar. Is that him with his back to the camera chatting to a tall woman in a green dress?'

'He is pushy. Wonder how often he gets his face slapped?'

They watched, as if on cue, the woman in the green dress throw her drink in Mueller's face then walk away. Mueller picked up a paper napkin from the bar and made an attempt at wiping the drink from his face and suit.

'Now what's he doing?' said Buchanan.

Mueller had walked off to the side of the club and turned his face to the wall.

'He's got balls,' said Buchanan. 'Look at what he's just done.'

'Not sure what you're referring to.'

'Wind the video back a few seconds.'

'Ok, what did I miss?'

'What's he got in his hand?'

'Looks like a straw.'

'More likely a rolled-up bank note. He's snorting coke in public.'

'He is a mess.'

'Keep your eyes peeled, let's see who else was there.'

They sat and watched the events of the evening unfold. The guests for the evening were seated ten to a table.'

At eight-forty, they watched as Reznikov got up from his table, bent down and said something to his wife. She nodded, then went back to her conversation with the lady seated next to her as Reznikov walked briskly across the dance floor to the smokers' exit. At eight-fifty he returned looking very agitated.

'Something doesn't look right,' said Street.

'What have you seen?'

'Can we wind back the video to where Reznikov walks across the dance floor? Good, now forward to where he walks back to his table. Do you see it?'

'Sorry, lass, no. What is it you see?'

'Can we enlarge the screen shot of his jacket pocket as he goes out, then as he returns?'

Buchanan clicked on the screen and enlarged the image of Reznikov's jacket.

'Now,' said Street, 'look at his left jacket pocket as he leaves.'

'Wish I could afford such a smart jacket,' said Buchanan.

'Now,' said Street, 'look at the same left-hand pocket as he goes to sit down. Do you see what I see?'

'He's put something in his pocket.'

'A piece of blue rope perhaps?' said Street. 'Wish we had that jacket for a forensics exam.'

'Something for us to work on,' said Buchanan. 'Be nice to hear what the band is playing.'

Eventually the reason for the evening arrived. The person in charge of the event walked over to the microphone and made a short speech, nodding towards the table where Reznikov was seated and then beckoned him to come up to the stage.

Reznikov stood to what looked like a spirited applause, pushed his chair back and walked towards the stage. He shook hands with the announcer, made a rousing speech, accepted his award, then returned to his table, where much backslapping commenced.

'See Mueller anywhere?' asked Buchanan.

'He's back at the bar bothering someone else,' said Street.

'Where's Reznikov?'

'He's not at his table – there he is – over by the door to the smokers' area. He's looking at his watch,' said Street. 'Looks like he might be going out to see if Burtenshaw has arrived yet.'

'Let's keep an eye on Mueller and see what he gets up to.'

Mueller continued in his futile attempt to pick up a companion for the evening. More than once he was confronted by security staff.

At ten past nine, Mueller stopped leaning on the bar and headed for the toilet. He was gone for five minutes then reappeared shaking his head. He stood at the door to the toilet and stared into the room like he was wondering how he got there.

'Wonder what happened in the toilet?' said Buchanan. 'He looks quite different.'

'Is that who I think it is?' said Street, pointing to a figure who'd come out of the toilet just behind Mueller.'

'It is, I'd recognise that nose anywhere,' said Buchanan.

'But why would Duncan be at the awards evening? Why would someone from the Home Office be interested?'

'I don't know, sort of makes sense if you consider Reznikov is a big player in international affairs. It is quite reasonable for Duncan to attend.'

They watched as Mueller staggered forward into the room. He got about twenty feet when someone neither of them recognised took Mueller by the arm and said something to him. Mueller looked startled then over to where they'd last seen Reznikov. Mueller shook his head and said something back. The stranger repeated what he'd said and nodded to the door to the smokers' area. Mueller's shoulders dropped, he thought for a moment then shrugged and started to walk towards the door. The time was now ten past nine. Whatever he'd been ingesting was having its effect on Mueller's steadiness on his feet. He staggered across the floor bumping into anyone in his way as he made his way towards the smokers' door.

'Did you see Duncan earlier?' asked Buchanan.

'Not sure. I did see someone resembling him occasionally going in and out of the toilets'

They continued to watch the video till Reznikov was seen standing at the bar.

'When did he reappear?' said Street.

They ran the video back to five-past nine and watched as Reznikov walked over to the smokers' door, looked at his watch, then went outside. After a further twenty minutes of scouring the various cameras they saw him return to the dance floor from the door at the end of the hall, not the door he left the building by.

'Wonder where he's been?' said Buchanan. 'If I'm correct that's the door through to the offices where we got the video from.'

'The back of the building,' said Street. 'I wonder if there is a way through to the end of the pier from there?'

Buchanan looked at the office wall-clock. 'OK, I think we'll wrap it up for today. We do need to go back to the pier and check that door. But since it's Friday evening and I have some special guests coming to dinner tomorrow, I need a good night's sleep. I'll see you and Stephen tomorrow evening.'

10

'What time did we say to Jill and Stephen?' asked Buchanan.

'Seven-thirty. Time you went and got changed.'

For Jack and Karen Buchanan, dinner this evening was going to be extra special. Though they had no children of their own, during the last eighteen months of working together, Jill and Buchanan had become closer than work partners. Jill had become one of the family. Now with her marriage to Hunter they had become the family that Buchanan and Karen never thought they'd have.

'You're looking smart,' said Karen, as Buchanan entered the kitchen while turning the cuffs up on his new cardigan.

'Got to look my best for our special guests.'

Karen looked at him and smiled, a tear appearing in her eyes. 'I'm nervous, Jack. I realise it's silly, but I can't shake the feeling. Jill bringing her new husband to dinner for the first time. I never in my wildest dreams thought I'd see this day.'

'You're nervous – what about me? I'm their boss, and I cut myself twice while shaving, haven't done that in years. Is there anything I can do to help?'

'No, the roast is in the oven keeping warm, along with the potatoes and veg. I'll do the Yorkshires just before we sit down. Oh – yes, there is something you can do,' she said, looking at him, 'you can give me a hug, then open the red wine to breathe.'

♦

Buchanan had just placed the opened bottle of wine on the sideboard when the doorbell rang. 'I'll get it,' he called, walking out of the dining room and almost bumping into Karen.

'Sorry we're a few minutes late,' said Street, handing Karen a bouquet of flowers. 'The car wouldn't start, again.'

'It just needs a tune-up,' said Stephen. 'I'll take it to Jim first thing Monday.'

Buchanan looked out the door, saw the tail lights of a departing taxi and smiled.

'Can I have your coats?' he said, closing the front door. 'I'll hang them up for you. You two go through to the lounge with Karen.'

Buchanan stood for a moment in the hall with Jill and Stephen's coats and savoured the moment. Not that he'd never hung guests' coats up before, it was simply he'd been caught up in the excitement of the moment, family to dinner.

'Would either of you two like a drink before dinner?' he asked, entering the lounge.

Stephen and Jill looked at Buchanan.

'We have wine – or something a bit stronger. I saw the taxi leave.'

'There's a bottle of Pinot Grigio open in the kitchen,' said Karen.

'Yes, please,' said Street. 'Can I help with anything?'

'I'd love that, follow me.'

'OK.'

'Stephen, what can I get you to drink?' asked Buchanan, as Karen and Jill left the room. 'Something a bit stronger than white wine? I've just opened a nice bottle of Raasay While We Wait, single malt.'

Stephen smiled. 'I've never heard of it. Is it new?'

'Hang on, let me pour you a wee dram.'

Buchanan opened the lower door on the grandfather clock and took out a bottle of whisky. 'This is a treat. The distillery just opened in 2017. I'm hoping to talk Karen into us going up there for a holiday.'

'In a distillery?'

Buchanan smiled. 'No, not in the distillery. They have accommodation on site, and next door there is the ancient and excellent Raasay House hotel.'

♦

'Here you are,' said Karen, handing Jill her wine.

'Thanks.'

'Cheers,' said Karen, holding up her glass.

'Cheers,' replied Jill.

'Well, how is married life?'

'Fine, except for that stupid car. It's as reliable as the weather. Just when you need to be somewhere it either won't start, or it overheats on the way. When I say we should replace it with something more modern and reliable, he just shakes his head and says, *women*.'

'Do you get much time together? Or does the job get in the way?'

'Not so far. We've managed to be home together each evening. Stephen's been busy with the car and studying for his sergeant's exam.'

'How about you? Do you still want to be an inspector?'

Jill shrugged and took a deep sip of her wine. 'I don't know. Once it was on the top of my list of things to achieve, now I'm not so sure.'

'Do I detect a regret in there somewhere?'

Jill lowered her head and sniffed. 'I told Stephen.'

'What did you tell Stephen?'

'I thought it would be fine – you know what I mean?'

'No, Jill. I don't know what you mean.'

'The getting married was fine, it's the sleeping together bit. I've always slept on my own, especially since – since what happened to me at boarding school.'

Karen put her glass down, walked over to Jill and put her arms round her. 'You poor dear, you told him everything?'

'I had to. I should have told him before we got married, but – but I didn't want to lose him, you see that, don't you?'

'Of course I do, but it would have been better if you had told him. How did he take the news?'

'That was the crazy bit, he said he already knew.'

'How did he know? I've never said anything, and I'm sure neither would Jack.'

'He read my diary. I'd forgotten all about it. He said he found it lying on the floor of the back of his car the day after he helped move me out of the flat. He meant to get it to me but with all the kerfuffle about the last case, then Jack's car crash and your holiday and our wedding, he simply forgot about it till weeks later when he was waiting for Jim to fix the car. I think he didn't quite know what to say, so he smuggled it into my room and hid it in one of my boxes. I didn't discover it till after we were married, and we had moved into our flat and I started emptying out the boxes of my things.'

'This was on the honeymoon when you told him?'

'Yes, of all the times for it to be brought up. He was really sweet though, even volunteered to sleep on the sofa.'

'What did you say to that kind offer?'

'What do you think? I wasn't going to spend my honeymoon with my husband sleeping on the sofa.'

Karen gave Jill a squeeze and said, 'You know, I never stop praying for you.'

'Really?' Jill said, pushing away from Karen. 'What good does that do?'

'You'd be surprised.'

'Do you pray for Jack?'

'Every morning when he goes out the door.'

'Does Jack know you pray for him?'

'Yes.'

'What does he think about it?'

'He made a fuss about it in the beginning, but when he realised how serious I was, he just shrugged and said, *whatever makes you feel good*. I've been praying for him for the last thirty-five years to come home safely and –'

'The car accident, and the incident in Glasgow, he didn't come home safely from those accidents.'

Karen shook her head. 'It did shake my faith, but I just had to keep trusting in the Lord and His promises. I have a favourite Bible verse that helps. *Trust in the Lord with all your heart, and do not lean on your own understanding. In all your ways acknowledge him, and he will make straight your paths.*'

'And you find that helps?'

'Prayer is what keeps me sane.'

'You're lucky to have a faith. With my past, no one would listen.'

'Your past is no bar to your future, not when God is involved.'

'Maybe so. Look, can we get on with the dinner?' said Street, wiping her eyes with some kitchen roll.

'Fine,' said Karen, 'I still need to bake the Yorkshire puddings.'

♦

'That was a fantastic dinner, Karen, thank you,' said Stephen.

'You're welcome.'

'Can I help with the dishes?' asked Jill.

'That's Jack's job,' said Karen.

'Yes, Jill,' said Buchanan, 'when we have guests to dinner Karen does all the preparations, I do the dishes.'

'I'll help,' said Stephen.

'Thanks, Stephen. We have a dishwasher, all we need to do is clear the table, won't take long.'

'In that case I think we ladies will retire to the lounge,' said Karen. 'Come on, Jill, let's leave the men to their task.'

'Wish I could cook like you,' said Jill.

'That's the product of thirty-five years of feeding a hungry, hard-working policeman. Don't worry, you'll pick it up as you go. And don't forget I'm always here if you need help.'

'Thanks.'

A few minutes later Buchanan and Stephen joined them in the lounge.

'Lovely dinner, dear. The kettle's on for coffee, or tea if anyone wants a cup,' said Buchanan, then, noticing a look of disappointment on Stephen's face, he added, 'I suppose you'd like another shot of whisky?'

'Please.'

'Anyone else?'

Karen and Jill shook their heads.'

'Fine, coffee for the ladies and two whiskies for the men,' said Buchanan with a smile.

Drinks in hand the four of them relaxed: Jill curled up beside Stephen, Karen put her feet up on the footrest, while Buchanan leaned back in his recliner.

'Sounds like your honeymoon went well, Stephen and Jill?

'Yes, it did,' said Jill with a huge smile. 'Didn't miss work one moment.'

'Can't say that for Jack and me,' said Karen.

'Why do you say that?' asked Stephen. 'Was it to do with the missing woman, Irene?'

'Yes,' replied Karen. 'It's a pity about her situation.'

'There's a lot of women who get in that type of situation,' said Jill.

'But they don't get murdered,' said Stephen.

Buchanan shook his head. 'What makes you think she's been murdered, Stephen?'

'I thought that's what you've been investigating?'

'No, not quite. We've been looking in to her disappearance. It's my belief she's still alive. To my mind Irene Adler found out about her employer's nefarious activities, possibly that he was in danger and so was she. The way I see the whole scenario is, she realised she was in danger and decided to get revenge on him and protect herself at the same time. She made it look like he'd killed her and pushed her body over the side of the boat. As part of her preparations she reported that both her driving licence and passport had been stolen and ordered replacements. The next item was to arrange with her employer's wife to drive to Arnhem and pick her up. They would then have driven to Calais and boarded a ferry back to the UK and Mrs Mueller's house, where I believe Irene Adler is now staying.'

'So why haven't you interviewed her?' asked Stephen.

'If she's in danger and a material witness she's better off where she is for now. We'll go see her Monday morning.'

'I envy you two,' said Stephen.

'Why do you envy Jill and me?,' said Buchanan.

'You should try working with Hanbury. Did you know he brings his own coffee to work in a thermos? He even makes his own sandwiches. There's no dropping in to Starbucks for us.'

'Do you know why he brings his coffee and makes his own sandwiches?' asked Buchanan.

'No, I just assume he's cheap.'

'Yvonne, his wife, is recovering from cancer. She's been in remission for seven months. All of his focus is either on the job or taking care of her.'

'Oh, sorry, I didn't know.'

'He likes to keep it quiet.'

As if to change the subject, Karen asked, 'Stephen, what are you and Jill doing tomorrow?'

'We're watching rugby on TV,' replied Jill, 'aren't we, Stephen?'

'I take it you're not a fan, Jill?' said Karen. 'How would you like to help me instead?'

'Doing what?'

'Come with me to church in the morning, you could help me in crèche. After church we could go have lunch, then I have a lot of packing to do getting ready for us to move into our new house.'

'I haven't been to church in years, what should I wear?'

'Whatever you're comfortable wearing while crawling on the floor. We're not a formal church, we meet in an old warehouse –'

'Oh, I know it, stopped in for a coffee while we were investigating the body in the factory. Didn't realise that was your church.'

'So, is that a yes?'

'What time should I be there?'

'First service is at nine, if you're there by eight-thirty, it will give you time for a coffee before the children arrive.'

'Well, I suppose I could clean out the car,' said Stephen. 'What about you, Jack? Will you be you going to church?'

Buchanan shook his head. 'Me? No. I'll go into the office and look over the case notes. I can't help feeling we're going in the correct direction, but on the wrong tracks.'

11

Buchanan lay on his back staring at the ceiling. In a few weeks he'd be staring at a different one in their new house. Swain's had finished replacing all the windows and upgrading the conservatory. Bowley's had finished replacing the out-of-date en suite bathroom, kitchen, and this coming week the carpets were being replaced. And very soon, Karen could finally get to cook in her new kitchen.

With the memory of dinner on Saturday evening with Stephen and Jill making him smile, he quietly got out of bed and dressed for work.

He stopped at Starbucks for his morning coffee then drove to the office.

'Your coffee,' he said, placing a cup on Street's desk.

'Thanks. Did I order one?'

'Just thought you might like one to start the day

'What a lovely thought. I –' Street's answer was disturbed by the ringing of Buchanan's phone.

'Buchanan, who's this? He is, Constable? OK, show him up.'

'You look puzzled,' said Street.

'We've been paddling in deep water. We have a visitor from the Home Office.'

'Do we know who?'

Buchanan smiled. 'It's our old friend.'

'Garry Duncan?'

'The very same.'

'I wonder what he wants? I thought we were all through with him when he quit as crime commissioner and went to work in the Home Office.'

'Apparently my enquiries about Mueller and Reznikov must have rung an alarm bell somewhere in the corridors of power.'

Moments later the desk constable escorted the former crime commissioner into Buchanan's office. 'Your visitor, Inspector.'

'Thank you,' said Buchanan, nodding at the constable.

'Mr Duncan, what brings you here this early? It's only eight thirty-five. I thought you'd be well on your way to London by now?' said Buchanan, leaning back in his chair.

'Before I do that, I have to inform you both that what I say and show you today in this office is covered by the Intelligence Services Act 1994. You may not divulge any of the information to the press or others not directly involved in your investigations. Do you both understand?'

'Sure, we do,' said Buchanan. 'What have you got for us?'

Duncan pushed some of the papers on Buchanan's desk to the side and placed his briefcase down in the cleared space. He opened the case, took three sheets of A4 paper and laid them on the table in front of Buchanan.

'I'm going out for coffee,' he said, taking off his glasses and wiping them fastidiously with his handkerchief. 'I've tried the muck you serve here before. I've also got someone to meet while I'm down here. I'll be back here about eleven to collect the document. Do not make a copy of it.' Duncan sniffed the air, turned, and walked out of the office.

Buchanan got up from his desk and went over to the window. 'Wonder where he's going for coffee?'

Street got up from her desk and joined Buchanan at the window. 'I wonder what he's looking for in the back of the car?' she said.

'Looks like he's found it,' said Buchanan, as they watched Duncan push something into his jacket pocket, lock the car and walk off in the direction of the exit gate.

'Now that is very interesting,' said Buchanan. 'Why would he not take his car?'

'Probably going to Brewers decorators on Birch Road,' replied Street. 'They have a café in the shop. The do some really yummy coffee, and chocolate cakes.'

Buchanan returned to his desk and picked up the sheets of paper. 'These could have been taken from a Wikipedia entry. Wonder why he's so concerned? I suppose it's ok to read it out loud,' he said, looking at Street and raising his eyebrows.

Street smiled, picked up her pen and opened her notebook. 'Ready to take dictation.'

'Reznikov was born in 1963 in Bogoslovskoye, a town in the district of Kalinski in St Petersburg,' began Buchanan. 'His school record was of no great significance, though he did well enough to go on to military school where he graduated with honours. He was inducted into the KGB, now called the FSB.

'In 1991 a story emerged about a confrontation he had with Vladimir Putin. Both were in the KGB as it then was called and had been serving in St Petersburg. They were working in the International Affairs section of Saint Petersburg State University, reporting to Vice-Rector Yuri Molchanov. There, he and Putin looked for new KGB recruits, watched the student body, and like all red-blooded men, vied for the friendship of any young female student they could ensnare. One night in the nightclub, Reznikov boasted he could bed any girl he fancied, even the student Putin had his eye on. Unfortunately for him, Putin took offence at Reznikov's boast. Early in the morning when he left the nightclub, Putin set on him and if it hadn't been for the other students, Putin might have ended Reznikov's career right then. From that day on, he became Putin's enemy number one.

'Reznikov served in the FSB till 1993 when he left to start his own private hire company, a cover for one of the highest-rated protection agencies in St Petersburg. With his customer base he was able to work back through their contacts till he was a key figure in all that went on in St Petersburg.'

'A male Shelob,' said Street.

'Shelob?'

'It's the name of the giant spider in the *Lord of the Rings* story. Did you see the film?'

'More than once. Anyway, back to the story of Reznikov. Apparently with all his contacts he began to be asked to mediate between warring factions in government departments. This led to him being involved with companies seeking government contracts. He became a tsar, no one could conduct business without his involvement and paying the fees he demanded for his assistance. His tentacles extended all the way into pharmaceuticals, insurance, tourism, and even the mass media. The CIA suspected him as being involved in several large shipments of cocaine across Europe from Afghanistan.'

'He was quite a busy boy,' said Street.

'Reznikov had become extremely influential within local and state-wide politics. One rumour was he intended to run for the office against his arch enemy, Vladimir Putin. The rest of the information are references to his schools and previous employers.'

Buchanan turned and looked at Street. 'You know we were told not to make a copy of the report? Pity he didn't also say not to take notes.'

Street smiled. 'I just wrote down the relevant dates and phone numbers.' She closed her notebook and looked up at the office clock as the sound of Duncan's footsteps were heard coming down the corridor. 'He's right on time, eleven o'clock.'

'Read it, Buchanan?' asked Duncan.

'Yes, thanks. Quite interesting document. Any reason he's of interest to the Home Office?'

'This comes from Thames House. Your investigations have rung an alarm bell somewhere.'

'How would they know what we're investigating?'

'I can't answer that,' he said, squinting and taking off his glasses.

Buchanan watched as Duncan pulled a tissue from a box on Street's desk and began to aggressively rub the lenses.

'Can't or won't?'

'Buchanan, I have been reliably informed you've left your size twelves all over the internet. You must realise that when it comes to the country's security, Bletchley Park and Thames House have eyes and ears everywhere.'

'They've been tapping my phone?'

'Apparently they don't have to these days. They just plug into the internet and listen. Any other questions, Buchanan?'

'Why did you bring me these documents? Surely there must be other ways of disseminating confidential information?'

'Buchanan, not everyone currently and formerly in government is excited about Brexit.'

'Does that include a certain former prime minister?'

'I'll forget you made that remark, Buchanan. All I'm suggesting is you need to get a view of the bigger picture.'

'Do I understand you correctly? You and your cronies in and out of Whitehall want me to drop my investigation into the death of Karl Mueller and concentrate on the activities of Reznikov instead?'

'Buchanan, I am reliably informed that Karl Mueller's death, though it may look suspicious, is to be treated as suicide. Caused while he was grieving the loss of his long-time friend and associate, Irene Adler.'

Street was about to speak till she saw Buchanan gently shake his head.

'Mr Duncan, I'm still at a loss as to why you have brought me this document. There's nothing in it that we couldn't find out by googling the name Reznikov.'

'Buchanan, I thought you were smarter than this. Can't you see when you've stepped over the line? Take the hint, man, and accept that Mueller took his own life while his mind was disturbed and concentrate on Reznikov instead, and make sure you keep me informed about your investigation.'

'I still don't see why you were told to bring me the information on Reznikov?'

'When it was decided to provide you with this information, and when it was discovered I knew you personally, I was ordered to bring them to you. I can assure you, Buchanan, it wasn't my idea. Now, if you found out what you want to know, I have to get to London.'

'Before you head back to London, Mr Duncan – did you know the late Karl Mueller?'

'What do you mean, did I know the late Karl Mueller?'

'It's a simple enough question.'

'He took his own life while in a disturbed state, end of story – and your involvement with his death. Do I make myself clear?'

'Oh yes, only too clearly.'

They watched out the window as Duncan left the car park before speaking.

'That was odd,' said Street. 'Why did he come here? It certainly wasn't for old times' sake. And why did he walk over to the coffee shop and not take his car?'

'It's a message, Jill. Someone has tripped over our investigations and has decided to see what we turn up. We're being used, Jill, that's what's going on. Someone in government circles wants us to pursue the matter of Reznikov to see what we find. If we get nowhere, then all well and good, everyone can sleep safely in their beds and we get pilloried for wasting police resources.'

'And if we do find something?'

'I suspect it will be taken over by the security services and we, once again, pay the price.'

'Just what are we likely to discover?' asked Street.

'Up till now I had the impression that the case had something to do with Brexit, but now I'm thinking it might not be that simple.'

'Not sure if I follow you on that?'

'We started this case by assuming that Karl Mueller had had an argument and murdered his long-time girlfriend, Irene Adler. As far as the evidence we have gathered indicates, Irene Adler is alive and well. Her whereabouts is probably known only to Karl Mueller's wife. It is my assumption that Irene Adler set about to cause the greatest discomfort for Karl Mueller by making it look like he'd been responsible for her death. She apparently, ignorant of his true business dealings, brought his name and occupation into the public eye, and this adverse publicity led to his death – which someone has tried to make look like a suicide.'

'So, who killed him and why have we been pointed in the direction of Reznikov? Just a minute, I've had a thought,' said Street. 'There is a link between them. We know Mueller was having a very public affair with Reznikov's wife. Suppose Mueller was working for MI5 and was trying to get close to Reznikov? Possibly he got a bit too close and was disposed of by him?'

'Or something else,' said Buchanan, staring out of the window. 'Reznikov could still be in the FSB and trying to worm his way into British security by the back door. But why kill Mueller? That doesn't make sense.'

'Irene Adler is the key,' said Street. 'Do you have the copy of the torn-up email you found in Mueller's cabin?'

'Yes, here,' he said, taking it out of the Irene Adler folder and handing it to Street.

'I thought so. We have already decided that the K in the email is Karl. It's my bet that the R in the email is Reznikov. No idea who the F is though.'

'I've just had a brainwave,' said Buchanan. 'Maybe Irene didn't set out to frame Mueller as such. It is just possible that she really did set out to disappear. She had found out what Mueller was up to, and realised not only was he in danger, but so was she. So, she tried to make it look like Karl had killed her, the perfect way to be absent.'

'If that's the case, she needs protection.'

'I'll call Miasma and give him a statement.'

'What will you say?'

'I'll tell him that the investigation into the missing secretary, Irene Adler, is being closed and the police are no longer investigating her disappearance. I'll say with all the evidence available and without a body to prove otherwise, the police are not taking the investigation any further and will be forwarding their conclusions to the coroner. Also, the untimely death of her co-worker, Karl Mueller, was being treated as an unfortunate incident with him being temporarily in an unbalanced state of mind.'

'Will you also copy Duncan on the statement?'

'Yep. That should give us some breathing room to find out what's really going on.'

'How will we investigate without leaving a trail and possible exposing Irene?'

Buchanan smiled. 'We'll just have to be very careful.'

'Where will we start?' asked Street, looking back at the clock, 'It's almost lunchtime.'

'Lunch is going to have to wait. I think we need to get back to Burtenshaw and get his statement signed,' said Buchanan. 'If he saw Mueller and Reznikov together moments before Mueller died, he could be in the firing line.'

◆

Street followed Buchanan into the offices of Brackenstall and Stanley and over to the reception desk.

'Good morning, DCI Buchanan. Is Mr Burtenshaw in?'

The receptionist, as before, looked up at the office wall clock then frowned. 'He should be, let me give him a call.' He dialled Burtenshaw's extension and waited, then shook his head. 'He's usually in on Mondays. I don't understand, let me check his diary.'

Opening a side drawer in the desk he took out a small diary. He turned to today's date and hummed tunelessly. 'This is not like him at all. It says here he was expecting a visit from someone in your office, then at four-thirty he was supposed to call his London junior about a case.'

'Could he still be at home?' asked Street.

'Hold on, I'll call his house.'

'I don't like this, Jill,' said Buchanan, as they waited for the receptionist to make the call.

The receptionist hung up. 'Inspector, that was his wife who answered. She said Mr Burtenshaw left for the office at the usual time this morning.'

'What was his usual time?'

'I'm not quite sure, he would usually get here just after ten.'

Buchanan looked at the office clock. 'It's now quarter to five. Didn't anyone notice he wasn't here?'

'He normally just goes straight up to his office on the fourth floor. We don't really have much to do with him.'

'How about his secretary? He has one, doesn't he?'

'Not any more. The last one quit a few months ago, apparently Mr Burtenshaw is sometimes difficult to work for.'

'In what way?'

'He had arthritis in his knees and by the time he'd managed to get to the fourth floor he would be quite grumpy.'

'Why didn't he take an office on the ground floor?' asked Street.

The receptionist made a gesture of rubbing his thumb and forefinger together, 'Money, Sergeant. Mr Burtenshaw had the reputation of being tight with money. If you go into his office, you'll see a framed ten-shilling note on the wall. Supposedly that was the first fee he earned as a barrister.'

'Where did he meet his clients if his office was a struggle to get to?'

'He'd usually arrange to meet in a coffee shop in town. He would customarily be late and have them order the coffees. That way he didn't have to pay.'

'Can you check his schedule again and see if he had any of those meetings today?'

The receptionist consulted the diary again let his breath out slowly. 'The only thing in the diary for today is the visit from your office and the four-thirty conference call.'

'You told me when I was here earlier,' said Buchanan, 'that he didn't drive. How did he get to work?'

'The Loop. It's a local bus service. He has a bus stop outside his house and there's another just down the road from the office.

'Thanks, Matt,' said Buchanan. 'We'll check with the bus company. If he's a regular someone will have seen him.'

◆

'What do you think, Jill?' asked Buchanan as they drove back to the office.

'I'm hoping we don't get a report of a body washed up on the beach.'

'Are you thinking Reznikov did Burtenshaw in as well as Mueller?'

'He was on the pier at the same time. But, that couldn't be. Burtenshaw's wife said he left for the office at the regular time this morning.'

'Would you call the bus company and ask them if the driver of The Loop remembers Burtenshaw getting on the bus this morning?'

'Will do.'

While he waited for Street to call the bus company, Buchanan turned on his computer to review the Thursday evening happenings at the awards event on the pier.

Street hung up from her call and shook her head. 'The driver has finished his shift and gone home. I've asked the company to call him there and come back to me as soon as they have talked with the driver.'

'Good. They do realise it is important?'

'Yep. Told them we were concerned for Burtenshaw's health.'

Street's phone rang. 'Sergeant Street. You have? He was? Where did he get off? He wasn't sure – the bus was busy? OK thanks, we'll check further.'

'He got on, but no one saw him get off. Must be a very busy service,' said Buchanan.

Street's phone rang again. 'Sergeant Street – it is, yes. You have? How could that happen? Where has he been taken? The DGH, thanks. Oh, before you hang up, do you keep copies of the CCTV video of passengers on the bus? Great. Make sure it's kept for me, it's possible evidence.'

'What's happened?' asked Buchanan.

'Someone resembling Burtenshaw has just been taken off The Loop by paramedics and sent to the DGH.'

'Just now? Did they say how he was?'

'They didn't know, that's all I could get from the bus company.'

'Right let's go pay him a visit.'

♦

'Remember the last time we came here?' asked Street, as they pulled in behind a parked ambulance.

'Oh yes, poor DS Nichols. I seem to remember that's where we also first met up with Dr Mansell,' said Buchanan, stopping front of the window at the emergency desk.

'Be with you in a minute,' said the nurse.

'Thanks.'

'Yes? Can I help?'

'DCI Buchanan, Sussex Police. I understand a Guthrie Burtenshaw has just been brought in?'

'I'm sorry, Inspector, we are a very busy hospital. Are you a relative?'

187

'No. This is a police matter.'

'Was he the chap on the bus?'

'We believe that is the case.'

'Wait here please, I'll go and find out for you.'

The nurse returned a few minutes later with a doctor.'

'Inspector Buchanan?'

'That's me.'

'Are you family?'

'No. We are here in an official capacity. Mr Burtenshaw has been helping us with our enquiries.'

'I see. Would you come with me, please?'

They followed the doctor through into the emergency room.

'Mr Burtenshaw is in here.' The doctor pulled back the curtain to reveal the prostrate form of Guthrie Burtenshaw, QC.

'How is he, Doctor?' asked Buchanan.

'I'm afraid we were too late. His wife is on her way.'

'What happened to him?'

'Looks like he had a heart attack.'

'Can you tell when?'

'Sometime this morning, that's my best estimate.'

'Poor bugger, riding round town all day and no one noticed. How the hell could that happen?'

'I'm sorry, Inspector, you'd need to ask the people at the bus company.'

'Wonder why he didn't call for help?' said Street. 'Did he have a phone with him when he was brought in?'

'All his personal effects are in the plastic bag at the foot of the bed,' said the doctor.

Buchanan nodded at Street, who picked up the clear plastic bag sitting on top of Burtenshaw's neatly-folded clothes.

'Not much in here, there's his wallet, set of keys, pocket diary, handkerchief, a very nice-looking fountain pen, but no phone.'

'Do you know who brought him in, Doctor?'

'That would have been one of the ambulance crews. If you ask at the desk they can probably tell you which crew responded.'

'Thank you, Doctor. We'll go and ask.'

As Buchanan and Street exited the cubicle an alarm went off somewhere in the emergency room.

'Excuse me, Inspector,' said the doctor, pushing past.

'Come on, lass. We're in the way here.'

'Do you want a coffee?' asked Street. 'The café is still open.'

'Yes, please.'

Buchanan stood in line waiting at the emergency admission desk for the new arrivals to be checked-in for triaging.

'Yes, Inspector?'

'Can you tell me which ambulance crew brought in Mr Burtenshaw?'

'That one I do remember; my brother was on that crew.'

'Is he still around?'

'He may be, try outside. Sometimes, if they are not immediately dispatched, they will take their break and hang around outside putting the ambulance back in order before their next call.'

Buchanan nodded to Street to follow him outside.

'Your coffee,' she said, handing him a paper cup. 'Why are we out here?'

'I wanted to interview the ambulance crew that brought Burtenshaw in.'

'Are they still here?'

'Hopefully. The nurse said it was her brother's ambulance that brought Burtenshaw in.'

'Shall we ask? said Street, as she walked round the only ambulance parked outside the entrance.

'Excuse me. DS Street. Are you the crew that brought in the patient from the bus?'

'Yes,' replied the female crew member.'

189

'Can you tell me what you found when you attended the patient?'

'He was slumped on the front seat of the upper deck. At first, we thought he might have been asleep. But when we checked for vital signs, none were apparent. We administered – we tried to get his heart started, but to no avail, so we transported him directly to the DGH.'

'Anything else?'

'Yes, he was holding an epipen, which doesn't make any sense.'

'Why is that?'

'These pens are used when someone has a severe anaphylactic shock.'

'Like when someone is allergic to bee stings, or nuts?'

'Exactly. The part that doesn't make sense is, if you are on heart medication you definitely should not take epinephrine.'

'How do you know he was he on heart medication?'

'He was wearing a heart attack medical alert bracelet.'

'What medication was he on?'

'You need to ask the doctor.'

'And you are sure he was holding the epipen?'

'We had to prise it out of his hand.'

'Thanks. Can we have the epipen?'

'Sure, it was going in the bin anyway.'

'Does it have a prescription label on it?' asked Buchanan.

'None that I can see. Here – what do you think?' said Street, passing the epipen to Buchanan.

'I expect that if it ever had a label it would have been on the box. Do you have the number for the bus company?'

'Hang on, it should be in my phone,' said Street, scrolling through her contacts. 'Shall I call?'

Buchanan nodded, 'Tell them I want the bus secured, nothing to be taken out, and the CCTV to be kept till we get there.'

'Yes, this is Detective Sergeant Street – yes, it was me who called earlier. There was a passenger taken ill this afternoon on The Loop – yes – we're at the hospital. I'm sorry, but he didn't recover. The reason I'm calling is we need to search the bus – no, it's a police matter. Can you lock the bus and keep it locked till we get there? Shouldn't be more than twenty minutes, also – yes, I was going to ask – a disc will be fine, goodbye.'

'I take it the bus is back at the depot,' said Buchanan.

'We have been fortunate. It was the end of the day's run and the bus was due to return for cleaning and fuelling. They will make sure nothing is removed till we get there.'

'Good. I've just called control, they're going to organise a CSI team to go to the bus garage. In the meantime, let's go see if Mrs Burtenshaw is here yet.'

Buchanan stopped at the desk. 'I wonder if we can have a word with the doctor who was attending the patient who had the heart attack on the bus?'

'Do you remember the doctor's name?'

'Sorry, no,' said Buchanan.

'I'll have to find out who the doctor was. Please wait in the waiting area.'

'Not sure I like this,' said Buchanan, staring out the waiting room window, 'she's been gone fifteen minutes and we need to get down to the bus garage.'

'I'll go see if I can find out anything' said Street, 'I'll be right back.'

Street returned ten minutes later with the doctor.

'Inspector, I'm sorry to have kept you waiting, it's been manic around here today.'

'Do you know what killed Mr Burtenshaw?'

'His medical history says he shouldn't have survived for as long as he did. I saw from his records that he'd had a triple bypass four years ago.'

'Has his wife been informed?' asked Buchanan.

'She's with him just now, saying her goodbyes.'

'Doctor, please don't take this wrongly, but I want our police surgeon to perform a post-mortem on the body of Mr Burtenshaw.'

'You think someone has been negligent? If so, I can assure you everything was done by the book.'

Buchanan shook his head. 'Relax, Doctor, I believe there may have been causes other than just blocked arteries that led to Mr Burtenshaw's demise.'

'Such as?'

'This, Doctor. The ambulance paramedic said that someone in Mr Burtenshaw's condition should never be given a shot of epinephrine. It is possible someone injected Mr Burtenshaw with one of these,' he said, holding out the epipen for the doctor to see.

'Especially with that dose,' said the doctor. 'It's amazing his heart held out as long as it did. Don't worry, Inspector, I'll make sure his body lies untouched in the mortuary.'

'Thank you, Doctor. Would you mind waiting a minute? What is it, Jill?'

'Just got word that the SCI team are on their way to the garage.'

'Good, and could you also contact Dr Mansell and ask him to have a look at Mr Burtenshaw's body?'

'Doctor,' said Buchanan, 'at some point we need to interview Mrs Burtenshaw. Would it be advisable for my sergeant to have a word with her now?'

The doctor thought for a minute. 'I saw her a few minutes ago. She's a strong woman, I don't think she'll mind. Sometimes in situations like this it helps the grieving person to have someone to talk with. If you follow me, Sergeant, I'll take you to her. It will be good for her to have someone to chat with while she waits for her sister-in-law.'

'I'll wait here for the sister-in-law,' said Buchanan.

Street followed the doctor through the emergency area and over to a curtained cubicle and waited while the doctor entered.

'Mrs Burtenshaw, there's someone from the police outside wanting to know if you are up to being asked a few questions?'

'I'm not sure what I can tell them. I wasn't with Guthrie when he had his heart attack.'

The doctor stood back and beckoned Street to enter.

'Oh,' said Mrs Burtenshaw, ' I don't know why, but I expected a uniformed policeman.'

'This is my ID,' said Street.

'Thanks. Please come in, or would you like to ask your questions somewhere a little more pleasant?'

'I'm fine here if you are.'

'I've said all I need to say,' she said, leaning forward to kiss her dead husband's forehead. She gently pulled the sheet up over his face. 'Goodbye, my dear, see you in the next life.' She leaned back in her chair, breathed out slowly then stood. 'Shall we go? There's nothing here for me now.'

'The coffee shop is still open,' said Street.'

'That would be fine, I can't leave for a while anyway. I'm waiting for Guthrie's sister to come over from Brighton. She doesn't drive and is waiting for her nephew to collect her.'

Mrs Burtenshaw stood for a moment at the curtain to the cubicle, sniffed and smiled. 'Ready?'

'What would you like to drink?' asked Street. 'They don't have a great selection – there's tea, coffee or a soft drink?' she said, looking at the food counter.

'Could I have a cappuccino, please?'

'OK.'

'Thanks, sorry – I don't know your name?'

'Jill Street.'

'I'm Lydia.'

'I'm sorry to hear of your loss, Lydia.'

'Thanks, Jill,' she said, taking a tentative sip of her coffee. 'I'm at a loss – why are the police involved in Guthrie's death? I know he had a bad heart, the doctor said Guthrie could go at any moment. But why the police?'

'Mr Burtenshaw was helping us with another case we are working on. We had arranged for him to meet with someone from our office today. When we heard he had been brought into the DGH we came in to see if he was all right.'

'Was he important to your investigations?'

'We're still working out where your husband fits in to the overall picture. Were you married long?'

'Thirty-two years.'

'Children?'

She shook her head.

'Where did you and your husband meet?'

'Oxford, I was reading classics. We met, like so many students, in one of the city pubs. I seem to remember it was called something like The Angel and the Greyhound. Though for the life of me, I can't understand what an angel and a greyhound would have in common.'

'We have some interesting-named pubs here in Eastbourne.'

'Do you think he suffered?'

'I don't know, Lydia. You would have to ask the doctor that question. You said you met Guthrie at Oxford, was he reading law?'

'Yes. He was in his second year studying for his BA. We waited for him to graduate before we got married.'

'Did he have any friends at university?'

'Not many, he preferred to study over partying. I don't think he liked university life very much. He found it difficult to settle, he used to complain about there being too many hooray Henrys and boorish toffs, and not enough serious students. Though there were two that he did sort of get along with.'

'Was that before you came into his life?'

She thought for a moment. 'I suppose it was. There were six of us: Guthrie and myself, Garry Duncan and Karl Mueller with their respective girlfriends. I don't remember the names of their girlfriends, they changed them like horses on a merry-go-round.'

'You and Guthrie stayed together?'

'Oh yes,' she said, laughing, 'for better or worse.'

'Did either of you stay in touch with Guthrie's friends?'

She shook her head. 'There were a couple of incidents that happened in his senior year that ended the friendship. Though ironically it was his profession that brought them back into his life later on.'

'What caused the rift in the friendship?'

'As I said, Karl and Garry changed girlfriends quite regularly. Unfortunately, Garry thought I was one of the girls on the merry-go-round. He tried to rape me one evening.'

'What happened?'

'We were at an end of term party at someone's house, I don't remember whose. You can imagine the atmosphere: all that pent-up frustration being outworked in one frenzied alcohol and drugs-fuelled evening. I told Guthrie I wanted to leave as the party was getting out of hand. He just smiled and said, *Let's go then.* I excused myself to go to the toilet and when I came out Garry was standing outside the door, two empty champagne glasses in one hand and an open bottle in the other. I was petrified when I saw the look in his eyes. I stepped back and tried to close the door, but he pushed himself forward and me back into the toilet. Luckily for me, Guthrie saw Garry follow me up the stairs and managed to break the lock on the door and rescue me.'

'That was a close shave, What did Guthrie do?' asked Street.

'If you'd met Guthrie recently, you would have seen a tall, stooped man. Well, when he was at university, he was a very fit man. He played cricket, was a regular on the rugby first eleven, and loved sailing. That evening when he got me out of the toilet, he waited for me to get my blouse buttoned up and tidy my hair, then he sent me downstairs. The next time I saw him he was in shock, his face was white, his knuckles were scraped bare and bleeding profusely.'

'What about Garry Duncan?' asked Street.

'He was in hospital for a week with a broken jaw, four broken ribs and a punctured lung.'

'Did the police get involved?' asked Street.

'No, Guthrie said if Garry made a complaint, he would report Garry for attempted rape. Garry told the ambulance crew he'd been drinking heavily and had fallen down the stairs. There was bad blood between Guthrie and Garry from then on. It took all of Guthrie's tact to continue socialising with Garry.'

'You said Guthrie sailed while at university. Did he have a boat?'

'Yes, in the early years at university he used to sail on the Farmoor Reservoir, or at least he did when he could find people to crew the boat.'

'I'd have thought there would be no shortage of volunteers.'

'There were plenty of eager sailors, but most of them were already involved in sailing.'

'What did Guthrie do?'

'He tried advertising in one of the local free-press papers, but nobody would commit to regular crewing. So, in a mood of desperation, he swallowed his pride and asked Karl and Garry to crew. At first, they said they weren't interested, but soon changed their minds when Guthrie said they could bring their girlfriends along.'

'Did that work?' asked Street.

Mrs Burtenshaw's reply was interrupted by the appearance of Buchanan.

'Excuse me, Mrs Burtenshaw, I'm Inspector Buchanan. Your sister-in-law has arrived and is in the waiting room. She has asked to say goodbye to your husband. The nurse will take her through then bring her here.'

'Thank you, Inspector.'

Buchanan bought a coffee and joined Street at the table.

'You were telling us about Guthrie's sailing adventures?' said Street.

'Unfortunately, it backfired on Guthrie. As soon as the boat had the sails up, Karl, Garry and the girlfriends scuttled down into the small cabin to drink and smoke marijuana and whatever else their minds took to.'

'So, Karl and Garry weren't much help?' said Buchanan.

'Garry wasn't much help, he was more adapted to sitting at his desk with his feet up rather than doing anything physical. Karl wasn't a fit man either, too much partying had taken its toll on him. If it hadn't been for some of Guthrie's friends steering him away from Karl and Garry, Guthrie might have ended up on the other side of his profession.'

'In jail.'

'Yes, let me give you an example. Guthrie had arranged to go out with Karl and Garry one evening. They went into a pub and Karl tried to pick up a girl. Unfortunately for Karl the girl already had a boyfriend, who was a local bricklayer. Karl must have been on something, because he insulted the boyfriend who challenged him to step outside. Karl spent a month in hospital with three broken ribs and three missing teeth. Guthrie made a strategic decision, he slipped out the back door and back to his rooms.'

'Justice was administered,' said Buchanan.

'That's an odd remark for a policeman to make.'

'Some might say I'm an odd policeman, Lydia. You said that Karl and Garry came back into your husband's life, in a professional way?'

197

'About five years ago, Guthrie had a call from another lawyer friend of his. He said a Karl Mueller had been involved in a car crash, and asked for Guthrie to represent him.'

'Karl Mueller? The same Karl Mueller from university days?'

'Yes.'

'So, what did Karl Mueller do, and why ask for Guthrie?' asked Buchanan.

'Guthrie was always getting Karl out of scrapes while they were at university. I guess the memory of those days lingered on. Guthrie said it sounded like Karl was desperate, the other driver had died. Karl had been charged with driving under the influence and would probably go to jail if found guilty. Guthrie represented him and got him off. He told me later he had thought about deliberately losing the case. He really disliked the two of them.'

'What else did Karl do at university that had caused the trouble with their friendship?'

'Karl had got a girl pregnant. Guthrie mediated between Karl's parents and the girl's parents. In the end the girl lost the baby in a miscarriage. Karl laughed at the news, Guthrie was disgusted and said never to ask for his help again.'

'Was that the last time their paths crossed?'

'No. Karl never seemed to understand just how much he annoyed people, I think he just lived in his own world. A couple of years later, a friend of Karl's called to say that Karl was being investigated for money laundering.'

'Do you recall the friend's name?'

'Duncan, Garry Duncan, and yes, it was the same Garry Duncan.'

'Did Guthrie help?'

She took a sip of her coffee and put the cup back on the saucer. 'That case never went to trial.'

'And these were his friends from his university days?'

'That was what Guthrie told me.'

198

'Do you know if Guthrie saw either of them recently?'

'I believe he was working on something for a friend of Garry's, something very important about import-export licences.'

'That's not the sort of thing that comes to mind when you think of a QC.'

'Guthrie had become a bit of an expert in European Union Law, I imagine it was something related to that.'

'When was the last time you met his friends?'

'The last time I saw them was at the Lawyer Awards Evening in 2007. Guthrie had been seconded to a team working for some offshore clients. The team was up for the Offshore Award, I never found out what Garry and Karl were doing there. We made a point of staying out of their way all evening.'

'You mentioned something about another incident that happened during their senior year – what was that?'

'Ah yes, I did. Thankfully, Guthrie had nothing to do with that affair.'

'With what affair, Lydia?'

'There was a terrible scandal in Oxford university, a young woman died from a drugs overdose.'

'Were Karl and Garry involved in her death?'

'I'm not sure, nothing was ever proved.'

'What happened?'

'It was in the newspapers at the time. The university said someone was selling heroin and other drugs to the students. They put out a newsletter warning about the drug culture, also they said the university would not protect anyone caught dealing or consuming illegal substances. I can only guess at the connection between the death of the student and Garry and Karl. Guthrie told me Karl and Garry financed their way through university by dealing in drugs. Garry was the business brain of the duo; I believe Karl saw it as a way of supporting his habit.'

'What about Guthrie? How did he finance his studies?'

'He hated the whole drug scene, he had a friend from grammar school who overdosed on LSD and jumped off the roof of the school. Guthrie's parents weren't wealthy; his dad was the manager of a branch of Boots the chemists during the day, and tutored maths students in the evenings. Guthrie's mother was the deputy head at the same local grammar school he went to.'

'Who paid his university fees?' asked Street.

'The local education authority paid most of Guthrie's fees, plus each year he received a substantial grant. His parents made sure he never went into the red. I suppose Guthrie was a bit of a bore to those around him at university.'

'What about sports?'

'As I said, he was good at cricket, rugby and sailing.'

'And you think it might have been his friends who supplied the heroin that killed the unfortunate student?'

'Guthrie was only a few months away from graduating, he told them he needed to get on with his studies and wouldn't have time to socialise.

'Did they say anything?'

'I don't know. Guthrie got stuck in to his studies, and I in mine. We married the month after graduation and moved away from Oxford.'

'Lydia, I don't know if you have heard, but Karl Mueller has died. His body was found hanging from the pier earlier this week. Guthrie was one of the last people to see him alive.'

'The last person to see him alive?'

Buchanan shook his head. 'No, I said *one* of the last.'

'Was that Tuesday evening?'

'Yes.'

'Guthrie went out Tuesday evening. I remember we were just sitting down to watch some old *Rumpole of the Bailey* videos when the phone rang.'

'Do you know who called?'

'Guthrie said it was a Russian client; he sometimes brought work home with him.'

'What else did Guthrie say?'

'He said the Russian needed some of the documents that evening as they were to be sent to Moscow the next morning.'

'I understand Guthrie didn't drive. Did you drive him?'

'No, he got a taxi.'

'Do you remember which taxi firm he used?'

'Yes, Call-A-Cab, Guthrie always uses them, they're very reliable.'

'Do you remember what time this was?'

'I think the phone rang about eight o'clock, Guthrie went out about a quarter to nine.'

'Do you remember when he returned?'

'It was late, the news was about to start.'

Their conversation was interrupted by the arrival of Burtenshaw's sister-in-law.

'Thank you, Lydia,' said Buchanan, standing, 'I'll leave you to chat.'

'Thank you, Inspector.'

'Are we done here?' asked Street, as they watched Mrs Burtenshaw and her sister-in-law settle down to another round of coffees.

'Yes, time to move on.'

'The SCI's should already be there at the garage, and Dr Mansell said he'd attend to Mr Burtenshaw.'

♦

Street turned off Lottbridge Drove on to Birch Road and followed a number 55 bus to the garage. She backed into a spare parking slot beside a white Ford SUV.

'That's what I like to see,' said Buchanan, as he got out of the car. 'Our team is already at work.'

They walked into the car park and over to where the bus had been parked. The white-suited CSI team were talking to an individual in a grey suit.

'I assume that must be the depot manager,' said Buchanan, as they got closer to the group. 'Good afternoon.'

The grey suited individual turned to see who'd just arrived. 'Who are you? This is private property.'

'Detective Chief Inspector Buchanan, and Detective Sergeant Street.'

'Oh, sorry. Graham Marsh, depot manager. I was just asking your people how long they're going to be, this bus needs to be serviced and sent out again.'

'How are we progressing?' Buchanan asked one of the white-suited CSI's.

'Ten minutes at the most, sir.'

'Good. Find anything of interest?'

'A mobile phone, a wallet and this,' he said, holding out an empty epipen box.

'Good, can you catalogue them? I'll take them with me and send them off for analysis when we get back to the office. Mr Marsh, have you been able to contact the driver?'

'Yes, he's just returned, he's in the office waiting for you. Please don't keep him long, it's a very busy night for us.'

'Lead on, Mr Marsh – mustn't deprive the bus company of its hard-earned profits.'

Buchanan said goodbye to the CSI's and he and Street followed Marsh into the office.

'Andy,' said Marsh, 'these policemen want to ask you some questions. I'll be in my office if you need me, Inspector.'

'Hello, Andy, I'm Inspector Buchanan and this is Detective Street. Been a long day?'

'No more than usual. What do you want to know?'

'Can we start with your full name and address, please?'

'Andrew Benson, Flat 5, Honeysuckle Close, Shinewater.'

'Are you a regular driver for the bus company?'

'Yes.'

'Always, The Loop?'

'Have driven it for the last year and a half.'

'Do you get to recognise regular passengers?'

'Some.'

'How about this person?' said Street, showing Andy a photo of Burtenshaw.'

'Of course I recognise him. He's the guy who passed away on the bus today.'

'Do you know his name?'

'Sorry, no.'

'Which stop does he get on and off at?'

'He gets on at Linfield Road and off at The Avenue.'

'Always the same stops?'

'Yes.'

'Does he sit in the same part of the bus each time?'

'He goes up on the upper deck, sits at the front.'

'Do you know why?'

'People who sit at the front like the view, I suppose.'

'When he got on this morning at Linfield Road, how many passengers were already on board the bus?'

'Not many, that's a quiet part of the morning round. The bus pass doesn't start till nine-thirty. I'd say there wouldn't have been more than half a dozen.'

'Any of those passengers on the upper deck?'

'Nah. They were most elderly, they usually choose to sit downstairs.'

'So, there wasn't anyone on the upper deck?'

'There was one gentleman, never seen him before.'

'Where did he get on?'

'Langney shops.'

'Do you know where he got off?'

'He stayed on all the way round town to the Tesco roundabout.'

'Any particular reason you remembered him?'

'I don't think he was used to taking the bus.'

'What made you think that?'

'For a start he didn't have change, he only had a twenty-pound note. Most bus users either have a bus pass, day rider ticket, or the correct change.'

'Can't you give change?'

'Can you imagine how much change I would need to carry?'

'Twenty, thirty pounds?'

'In the summer, Eastbourne is awash with foreign students, sometimes there may be twenty of them waiting to get on the bus.'

'Ah, I see. So, what did you do with this passenger?'

'I managed to make change this time, told him the next time to bring the correct amount.'

'Anything else cause you to remember him?'

'Asked if the bus went past Lindfield Road.'

'Why would you remember that?'

'He came down the stairs twice to ask.'

'Could you identify him if you saw him again?'

'Yeah, I think so.'

'Could you give us a description of him, please?'

'Not quite as tall as you, black hair swept back at the sides, I think he used hair oil. Clean shaven and wearing a dark grey suit. He also wore wire-rimmed glasses, narrow skinny ones like you'd find in the Pound Shop and a hat that didn't quite fit him.'

'Jill, would you show Andy the photo of Mr Duncan?'

'Do you recognise this man?'

'Not sure. The guy on the bus looked scruffier, and he was wearing a hat.'

'Can you tell us about your round?' asked Buchanan.

'I drove round Winkney Farm, took on a couple of passengers at the stop just before the railway crossing.'

'Where did those passengers sit?'

'Top deck. They were a couple of young girls, nurses I think, they got off at the DGH.'

'Did you pick up any other passengers who went up on the deck?'

'There was an older fellow, had a cane. He struggled up the stairs, and Mrs Markham. They got on at the first stop on Broderick Road.'

'Mrs Markham?'

'She's my wife's cousin.'

'Where did she get off?'

'Terminus Road.'

'Do have contact details for her? We'd like to have her tell us what she saw.'

'It'll be in my bag in my locker, shall I get it?'

'In a minute. What do you remember about this morning's incident?'

He shrugged and let out his breath. 'All I heard was the sound of a scuffle and raised voices, then it went quiet. That's all.'

'Where did the man with the cane get off?'

'He got off at the DGH.'

'Did you pick up passengers at the DGH?'

'Half a bus load; dropped most of them off in town at Terminus Road.'

The interview was interrupted by the entrance of the depot manager.

'Your people are very thorough, Inspector. They cleaned the bus out better than any of our cleaners do.'

'I'll send you the bill,' said Buchanan. 'Mr Marsh, do you keep the CCTV videos of the cameras on the buses?'

'Yes, would you like a copy from The Loop?'

'Yes, please.'

'Do you need Andy for anything else, Inspector?' said the depot manager.

'Thanks, Andy. We'll be in touch to take a statement from you.'

'I'll get my wife's cousin's address for you.'

'Thanks, Andy. Mr Marsh, can we have a copy of the bus schedule, please?'

'Just The Loop? Each route has its own schedule.'

'We'll have whatever you can give us.'

'Anything else, Inspector?' said the depot manager, handing Buchanan a handful of bus timetables.

'No, we're done for now.'

'Did Andy give you his wife's cousin's address,' asked Buchanan, as they drove back to Hammond's Drive.

'Yes, including her phone number.'

♦

'Do you know if Stephen and Morris are available yet?' asked Buchanan, as he turned on his computer.

'Stephen should be done with Hanbury tomorrow, not sure about Morris.'

'Could you give him a call and find out how his wife is doing? We could do with having them on this case. Also, could you get on to the *Herald* and have them put a message in the paper about the fracas on The Loop this morning?'

'Will do. I'll call Morris before I go home.'

'Thanks. I'll see you in the morning, I need to leave a bit early. Karen says the kitchen fitter has had an idea about something in the kitchen and needs our approval before he goes ahead.'

'No problem, see you in the morning.'

12

'Good morning,' said Street, yawning.

'Late night?'

'Stephen took me out for dinner and a movie. We didn't get home till gone midnight, then we sat up and talked till gone two in the morning.'

'Did you get the message off to the *Herald*?'

'Yes, shall I read it to you?'

'Please.'

> Following the unfortunate death of a passenger on The Loop bus service, police are interested in talking with anyone who got on the bus on Monday morning at about nine o'clock, between Gardners Books and Lindfield Road.
>
> Anyone with information can call Sussex CID on 01273 470101 or call 101. Information can also be reported anonymously to Crimestoppers on 0800 555 111 or online at crimestoppers-uk.org.

'That'll do. How about Stephen and Morris?'

'They're both downstairs with Hanbury.'

'You did explain to them we need them?'

'Yes. Stephen said he's looking forward to getting back to some real crime.'

'That's what I like, a man with a sense of humour,' said Buchanan, as Hunter and Dexter entered his office.

'Morning, Chief,' said Hunter. 'Did I miss something?'

'No, you didn't. How's the missus, Morris?'

'She's fine now her sister is there to look after her and the little ones.'

'Good. You awake, Stephen?' Buchanan asked Stephen as he yawned.

'Definitely. What do you have for us?'

'First I want you to follow behind The Loop bus and see who gets on and off. I specifically want you to follow the one that leaves the Langney shopping centre at nine forty-six. I'm particularly interested in two young ladies, possibly nurses, who joined at the stop just before the railway crossing, and an older man with a cane who got on at the first stop on Broderick Road. There's another woman who got on the bus at the Broderick Road stop, this is her name and address.'

'Jane Markham, Freeman Avenue, Hampden Park. Do you want us to talk to these people?' asked Stephen.

'Yes, one of you get on the bus if you have to. If you manage to find them, I want you to ask about what they saw on the bus yesterday morning.'

'What are they supposed to have seen?' asked Morris.

'Someone being murdered in the front seat on the top deck.'

'Surely they would have reported it?'

'They may not have realised what was going on, Morris. I want you to get them to just say what they remembered. I definitely don't want you to tell them what to remember.'

'The same with Jane Markham and the man with the walking cane?'

'Yes, and after lunch I want you to – just joking. If you manage to get statements from the four witnesses, I would like you to go to a dispensing chemist and see if you can find out who this prescription for epinephrine was subscribed for,' he said, passing Dexter the epipen box. 'And lastly, go to Call-a-Cab and find out the details of a fare for a G Burtenshaw booked for last Monday evening at about eight-thirty. The times on that booking are critical to the investigation.'

'Shouldn't we do that first?' asked Hunter.

'I need the witness statements from the bus passengers before they forget what they saw.'

♦

'You got the keys, Morris?' asked Hunter.

'In my jacket. I suppose you want me to drive?'

'Please, these police cars bore me.'

'How's the Talbot? Did you get the roof fixed?' asked Dexter as they walked through the car park.

'Had to have a whole new canvas fitted. Jill's not too pleased about it, she had the money earmarked for a new sofa. I think I'm doomed to sell it and buy something boring and less likely to break down.'

'You did have fun while it lasted. What will you get to replace it?'

'There's a Golf GTi in the police compound with a for sale sign in the window, thought I'd see how much they want for it.'

'You sure that's what Jill means by *less likely to break down*?'

'Oh, she'll not notice, she's a woman.'

Dexter grinned. 'You have a lot to learn about women, Stephen. I'd buy a four-door Ford Focus, plenty of room in the back for child seats.'

'Give us a chance, we're just married.'

'Do you want to wait here at the Gardners' bus stop for the bus?'

'No, keep going and see who we see at the stop just before the railway crossing. That's where the driver said the two young women got on.'

'Could those be our two young ladies?' asked Dexter, watching two young women standing at the bus stop.

'Let's find out. Pull in at the garage, don't want to block the bus stop.'

'Excuse me ladies,' said Stephen. 'Are you waiting for The Loop?'

'Yes. Why?' replied the shorter of the two.

'Could we have your names, please?' asked Dexter.

'Cheeky, trying to pick us up are you?' said the taller of the two women.

'This is police business,' said Hunter. 'Could we have your names, please, and a contact phone number?'

'I'm Judy, Judy Wadsworth. We're nurses. You can get us at the DGH if you need to ask any more questions,' said the taller one.

'Thank you, Judy. And your name, please?' he said, turning to the other lady.

'Emma Thomson.'

'Thank you, Emma.'

'Do you always catch The Loop at this time of the day?'

'Yes.'

'Yesterday?'

'Judy just told you we do. Why are you asking?'

'Where did you sit yesterday – on the bus that is?'

'Up top, where we always sit,' replied Emma.

'Did either of you notice anything out of the ordinary?'

They looked at each other as if there was a joke in the question somewhere.

'There was something that happened just after the bus turned onto Lindfield Road,' said Emma.

'What was that?'

'There's a nice old man who quite often gets on the bus at that stop. He always sits at the front on the right. Well, yesterday someone came from the back of the bus and sat beside him. They must have known each other because they started chatting.'

'Did either of you hear what they were chatting about?'

'No,' said Judy.

'How about you, Emma?'

'No, I was too busy talking to Judy. Besides, the bus can be noisy.'

'So, was that was what caught your attention?'

'Not quite. After a while they started arguing about something, the old man got quite agitated and tried to push the other man off the seat.'

'Did he succeed?'

'No. As quickly as it started, they stopped their fight and sat quietly together.'

'Did either of you think what had happened, odd?'

'Constable, these days two men arguing on a bus, then sitting quietly together? A lover's tiff?'

'Did either of you remember seeing them get off?'

'We got off at the DGH, they were still sitting together.'

'Were they talking?'

'Don't think so, the older man had his head on the other man's shoulder.'

'Would you recognise the man who came from the back of the bus and sat with the passenger in the front seat?'

'Don't think so. I only saw the back of him.'

'How about you, Judy?'

'No, same thing, I only saw his back.'

'Did any of the other passengers talk to them when they were arguing?'

'There was only George upstairs with us. He just sat and read the Metro.'

'You know George?'

'He works in the kitchen at the hospital, not quite sure what he does,' said Judy.

'Where does George join the bus?'

'The stop after us, the first on Broderick Road. Here's our bus, 'bye.'

'Thank you, Judy, Emma. We'll get in touch for a statement,' said Stephen.

They returned to their car and watched Judy and Emma get on The Loop. 'Where to now?' asked Dexter.

'Let's go and see if Jane Markham is at home.'

♦

'This looks like where she lives, nice house,' said Dexter.

'Not bad if you like living in a housing estate. Where would you park your car?'

'In the street like everyone else, you snob. Not everyone can afford their own driveway.'

'I'm not a snob. I just don't like parking my car in the street. I've lost too many wing mirrors because of that.'

'Enough about cars, we've got a job to do. I for one don't want the chief breathing down my neck.'

'He won't do that to you.'

'You might say that, you're his son-in-law. I plan to keep my nose to the wheel and stay out of trouble.'

'Either way, we've got work to do, c'mon.'

Dexter pressed the door bell and waited for a response. Somewhere in the back of the house a dog barked excitedly. A voice shouted at the dog to be quiet, two minutes later the door was opened.

'Yes?'

'Mrs Markham?'

'Yes, is something wrong?'

'PC's Hunter and Dexter. We're following up an incident on The Loop bus service yesterday morning. Were you on the bus yesterday morning?'

'Yes, why?'

'Can you tell what time you caught the bus?' asked Stephen.

'The usual time.'

'Can you be specific?

'Look, I just ride the bus, I don't time them. The Loop is quite erratic about when it arrives. I think there's one every twenty minutes. I usually get the one that comes about a quarter to ten.'

'Did anyone else get on the bus with you?'

'Yes, there was a chap with a cane, I think his name is George.'

'Is he a regular?'

'I suppose he is. He's there most mornings when I'm there. I've seen him say hello to another couple of regulars. I think they all work at the DGH.'

'Where does he sit, if he's a regular?'

'Upstairs just behind the stairs. I think he has a problem getting up the stairs with his bad leg.'

'Where do you sit?'

'Towards the back upstairs, I prefer to be on my own.'

'Did you notice anything unusual?'

'"The bus was on time?'

'Is that all?'

'Yes.'

'Was there anyone else upstairs?'

'I seem to remember someone sitting at the back reading a newspaper.'

'Could you describe them?'

'Sorry, no.'

'Thank you, Mrs Markham, that's all for now. We'll be in touch if there's anything else.'

'A bit of a wasted morning,' said Dexter, as they did up their seat belts.

'With the chief there's no such thing as a wasted morning. I suppose, Morris, we're like kitchen staff in a big fancy restaurant. We gather all the ingredients for the meal and present them to the master chef. He consults his recipe book, then trims and cuts and mixes everything together into a gourmet meal.'

'A good analogy, Stephen. I think someday I'd like to be a chef.'

'How are you doing on preparing for your sergeant's exam?'

'You kidding? With four kids to chase round the house, another due any minute and my sister-in-law trying to keep my wife from going crazy? I'd be better off studying in the middle of the M25 at rush hour.'

'That bad, huh?'

'Not really. Now Jean's sister is staying with us it's got a lot better. Enough about me, where to next?'

'The DGH and George.'

Dexter parked behind a taxi at the main entrance. 'Try asking for him at the information desk,' he said.

'Can I help, Constable?'

'Yes. We would like to talk with a man who works here at the hospital. He walks with a cane and we believe he works somewhere in the kitchen, first name George.'

'You don't have to look far, he's in the coffee shop. Over there with his back to us, sitting with the two orderlies,' said the receptionist, pointing at a broad-shouldered man wearing a white work coat.

'Thanks,' said Dexter.

'Excuse me, George?' said Hunter.

'Yes? What do you want?'

'Could we have a word with you, please?'

'Yeah.'

'Do you come to work on the bus?'

'Yeah.'

'Which one?'

'The Loop, when it's on time.'

'Same time each day?'

'Yeah. I catch the one that comes just after nine.'

'Did you do that yesterday morning?'

'Yes, I just told you I do.'

'Did anyone else get on with you?'

214

'Yeah. A lady, she quite often gets the same bus.'

'Where did you sit?'

'Up top.'

'Any particular seat?'

'I like to sit on the right behind the stairs.'

'Do you remember how many people were up there with you when you got on?'

'Judy and Emma, they're nurses. They work here at the hospital, and the old fellow who sits up front.'

'The old fellow?'

'I think he's a banker or something. He sits there on his own reading the *Financial Times*.'

'No one else?'

'Ah, yes, there was. There was someone sitting at the back, never seen him before.'

'Did he get off anywhere?'

'Not while I was on the bus. Odd thing was, I think he was waiting for someone.'

'Why do you say that?'

'When the old fellow got on, this chap at the back came forward and started talking with him.'

'Did you happen to hear any of their conversation?'

'Nothing that made much sense.'

'Such as?'

'I think the new chap was angry, said something about the old fellow being *stupid to have done it,* and *expected more from someone like you,* and then he asked a question.'

'What did he ask?'

'It sounded like, *are you sure you didn't say anything to anyone else?*'

'What did the old man say to that?'

'I didn't hear, but it must have been something that annoyed him because he tried to push the new chap off the seat. They struggled for a moment. I was going to see if I could do something but before I could grab my cane, they stopped arguing and just sat there quietly like they were tourists out for a day trip.'

'Did the new chap get off the bus?'

'No, he was still sitting with the old fellow's head on his shoulder when I went down the stairs. I figured they were a couple of gays who'd had an argument and made up.'

'Would you recognise the new chap?'

'Not sure. I was more interested in hearing what they were saying.'

'How about you try and give us a description of him?'

'Tall, about your height, Constable, and quite thin. Dark oily hair combed back at the sides. He was wearing a dark grey suit. That's about all I remember. Oh, he was wearing glasses, thin wire frame type and a hat that looked two sizes too small for him, made his ears stick out.'

'Thank you, George, we'll be in touch. We will need a statement from you.'

'Do we have time for a coffee?' Dexter asked Hunter.

'Starbucks on Terminus Road?'

'Sounds fine to me. The prescription the chief wants us to trace was issued at the Boots pharmacy on Terminus Road. Maybe they can tell us who prescribed it and who it was prescribed for. Then we can go check with the taxi company about Burtenshaw's taxi ride.'

They parked outside Brufords on Cornfield Road and walked back to Starbucks.

'Stephen, how come the chief always goes to Starbucks for his coffee?' asked Dexter, as they stood in line waiting for their drinks.

'I think it's something to do with the atmosphere, though this place doesn't have anything to shout about.'

'That must be why we have meetings at the Pevensey Starbucks,' said Dexter.

'What did you think about the statements from the bus passengers?' asked Hunter as he drank down the last of his coffee.

'It all points to the mystery passenger who sat with Burtenshaw. Do you think he was a client or someone who was more than just a friend?'

'We won't know the answer to that till we find him and ask. He doesn't sound much like a client, more like a friend of many years, or could even be a family member. Shall we get on with the day?'

They left Starbucks and walked along Terminus Road to Boots. They had to wait for the pharmacist to be free.

'Yes, officer, how can I help?' asked the pharmacist.

Hunter passed the pharmacist the epipen box, still in its evidence bag. 'Any chance you can tell us anything about who this was prescribed for and by whom?'

'Can I take it out of the bag?'

'Sorry, no.'

The pharmacist put on his glasses and studied the epipen box through the clear plastic evidence bag. He looked closely at it for a few minutes then looked at Hunter and Dexter then passed the bag back. 'I'm sorry, I can't tell you much. Standard issue of epinephrine, date of prescription as stated on the box and it looks like it was issued to a Miss Bridget Standish. Other than that it's what it says on the box.'

'And these pens can only be dispensed by prescription?' said Dexter.

'They are, but if you are enterprising enough they can be bought online.'

'Is that what has happened in this case?'

'No. This prescription is genuine.'

'And you can't tell me who it was prescribed for?'

'Just the name on the box, Bridget Standish, I'm sorry. If you had the prescription receipt I could dig through our past prescriptions and maybe find what you are looking for.'

'Do you keep a record of who prescriptions are prescribed for?'

'Yes, but this one is almost six weeks old.'

'It is important.'

'I'll have a look, but it will take time. Do you have a phone number that I can call if I find out anything?'

'Just call 101 and ask to be put through to the incident room in Hammonds Drive.'

'I will.'

'Shall we walk to the taxi rank or collect the car first?' asked Dexter, as they exited Boots on to the Terminus Road precinct.

'I seem to remember the taxi rank is just up Terminus Road on Lismore Road, the short walk will do you good. These last couple of weeks sitting at home have taken their toll on your waistline.'

'Cheeky.'

'Can I help, Constable?' asked the taxi-rank receptionist, from behind her glass screen.'

'Yes, we're checking on a booking for a week ago Tuesday evening.'

'Who was it for?'

'A Guthrie Burtenshaw.'

'He's a regular, says it's cheaper to go by taxi than to waste money buying a car,' she said, looking back through the bookings on her computer. 'Ah, here it is, called at seven fifty-eight and asked to be collected at eight-thirty and taken to the pier, driver to wait for return trip.'

'Does it say what actual time the pickup was?'

'Unfortunately, the Hampden Park crossing gates were stuck and the driver had to go around, I think he was a bit late for the pick-up. The only way to get the actual time would be to ask the driver.'

'Is he working just now?'

The dispatcher looked up at a board beside the desk. 'Yes, he's just taking a fare to the station, should be available in ten minutes. Want me to text him?'

'Yes, please.'

'He'll be here in two minutes,' the dispatcher said, putting down her phone.

'Thanks.'

As if on cue, Burtenshaw's driver arrived.

'Charlie, these are the two policemen wanting to talk to you.'

'Good afternoon, Charlie. Can you remember a fare you drove last week to the pier?'

'You are kidding? Which day, what time?'

'Tuesday evening, Charlie. You picked up a fare on Lindfield Road.'

'Ah yeah, I remember, cheap git, no tip. I got there at eight forty-five and he was waiting. Dropped him at the pier at eight fifty-five. Told to wait as he'd only be a few minutes.'

'Do you remember how long you waited?'

'He didn't show up again till nine-thirty and I dropped him back at his house at nine-fifty, still no tip.'

'What state was he when he returned?'

'Out of breath, had a strange look on his face.'

'Drunk, or did he look unwell?'

'He wasn't drunk, I don't let those sorts in the cab. No, I'd say he looked, not unwell, more like he'd just had a shock. I remember, his hands were shaking, almost couldn't get the door open.'

'Thanks, Charlie. We'll get your statement typed up and come back with it for you to sign.'

'Sure, no problem, always willing to assist the police in their investigations. Shame he died, though better it was on the bus than in my taxi.'

♦

'Strange people, taxi drivers,' said Hunter, as they climbed the stairs to Buchanan's office. 'The invisible beltway in society. We all use them but never really see them.'

'Being a bit philosophical for this time of day,' said Dexter, looking at the time on his radio. 'You need to go lie down.'

'Who needs to go lie down?' asked Buchanan.

'No one, Chief,' said Hunter, 'just a bit of banter.'

'How about you banter about what you've been doing?'

'Hello, Stephen,' said Street, looking up from her computer screen.

'Hello. You been busy?' he asked, sitting down on one of the empty chairs in the office.

'Yes, how about you two? How did the interviews go, did you manage to track everyone down?'

'Yes, and there are some surprises.'

'OK, let's get going,' said Buchanan, unscrewing the cap from his pen. 'I don't want to be here all day.'

Hunter and Dexter read from their notebooks detailing the day's witness interviews.

'Very interesting,' said Buchanan, looking at the notes he'd written down when Hunter and Dexter had completed their retelling of the interviews. 'I would like all those statements typed up and signed by the end of the day. Leave me copies on my desk before you go out. Jill, do we have the preliminary report from Dr Mansell yet?'

'No, do you want me to call him back? He's still at the DGH.'

'Yes please, tell him I just need his impression for now.'

'Will do.'

'Stephen and Morris,' said Buchanan, 'what was your impression about the chap who sat behind Burtenshaw and the stranger?'

'A possible,' said Morris. 'As soon as we have typed up the witness statements we could take a photo from the bus CCTV and Stephen and I could go round and see if he recognises the chap.'

'Great idea. How soon will you be done?'

'Ten minutes for me. Stephen?'

'I'm done. Shall I do the photo?'

'Doesn't matter who does it,' said Buchanan, 'just get it done.'

'Do you mind if I ask you a question – sort of a personal one?' asked Street, after Dexter and Hunter had gone to get the witness statements signed.

'Sure, go ahead.'

'I notice I seem to do a lot of the driving lately. Are you OK with driving?'

'Yes, I'm fine, just prefer to think, and I do that better when you're doing the driving.'

'Oh, OK. What are you thinking about just now? You do look a bit bothered.'

'The amount of time Burtenshaw was on the pier the night Mueller died. When I talked to him in his office last week, he gave me the impression that all he did was deliver the papers to Reznikov then return home. The taxi driver's statement clearly shows Burtenshaw was on the pier for at least thirty-five minutes. Now why would a lawyer, a QC mind you, make such a mistake?'

'Maybe he was enjoying the view. Stephen and I have wandered out to the end of the pier at night when the stars are out.'

'Do you remember what the weather was like that night?'

'Yes, wet and windy.'

'So, what was he doing?'

'Shall I have a detailed look at the CCTV video?'

'We both will. We've missed something, and I want to find it.'

♦

'Right, this is eight pm, said Buchanan, glancing up from the computer screen and writing the time on the whiteboard. 'What time did Burtenshaw book the taxi for?'

Street looked through the notes. 'Eight-thirty.'

'That matches. Next?'

Street skipped between the four cameras and watched till the time got to just after nine. 'There's Reznikov and his wife, Tatyana, and there by the bar is Mueller,' she said.

'Wait, camera three,' said Buchanan. 'Is that Duncan?'

'Where?'

'Seated at the table by the side of the stage. Look, he keeps looking at Reznikov's table. It looks like he's trying to get his attention.

They continued to watch and were rewarded by Reznikov nodding acknowledgement at Duncan, rising from his seat and heading for the toilet. Duncan followed.

'I wonder what's so important that they need to talk in the toilet?' said Street.

'We know Reznikov was inside for the presentation, wonder what Burtenshaw was doing?'

'If Mueller was still alive, Burtenshaw could have been talking with him.'

'I don't think that's likely given what we've heard about their relationship. Just had a thought though. Suppose Burtenshaw delivered the documents to Reznikov, headed back to the taxi and got caught short, needed to pee. So, when no one was watching he went for a wander out to the end of the pier. He unzipped and stood close to the railings pissing into the sea. Just imagine what went through his mind as he stood there relieving himself, and what went through his mind when he saw Mueller leaning over the railings being sick.'

'That's a bit gross,' said Street. 'It's one thing to not like someone, but to have the presence of mind to go look for a piece of rope, return and put it round Mueller's neck then shove him over the railing. . .'

'Suppose Burtenshaw saw it in the skip when he arrived? said Buchanan. 'Being a sailor, he just picked it up and put it in his pocket.'

'It fits the timeline. Shall we see if Duncan shows any sign of being involved?'

They spent the next two hours going through the CCTV video, but to no avail. Duncan kept appearing then disappearing yet he never talked with Reznikov or left the building till the end.

'You know what his behaviour says to me?' Buchanan asked Street.

'He's dealing?' said Street. 'I wonder if he was supplied by Reznikov when they met earlier?'

'Fits the pattern of a high-class dealer,' said Buchanan. 'A 2014 survey revealed that a high percentage of adults in the UK have done drugs. I suspect that a good percentage of them still do – as would many of the hundreds at the event last Tuesday evening.'

'Who was doing drugs?' asked Hunter, as he and Dexter charged into the office.

'Just going over the events of the evening when Mueller was murdered,' said Street.

'Oh,' said Dexter.

'And we now have a fairly good idea of what happened.'

'I thought we were sure it was Reznikov who killed Mueller?' said Hunter.

'We still are. We've been reviewing timelines and it is quite possible that what took place was Burtenshaw lied about going straight home. He may or may not have seen Reznikov actually kill Mueller, but we believe he may have seen Mueller at the end of the rope and did nothing to help,' said Buchanan.

'We also have positively identified Garry Duncan as being at the event and possibly dealing,' said Street.

'Could there be a connection between the three of them?' said Hunter. 'Something went wrong and both Duncan and Reznikov killed Mueller? Burtenshaw saw what happened and he was killed to shut him up?'

'Plausible,' said Buchanan. 'But we haven't yet established that Burtenshaw was murdered. It is even possible that Mueller did take his own life. No, we're still a page short of a novel. Tomorrow morning, I think we'll go right back to the beginning and go through all the evidence we have. The coffees are on me. See you all at eight.'

13

Buchanan arrived at seven fifty-five and placed the coffees on his desk. He was the first one into the office. Three minutes later Street arrived, followed closely by Hunter and the ACC.

'Seen Morris anywhere?' asked Buchanan, momentarily taken aback by the ACC's presence.

'He went to Cavendish Bakers for the doughnuts.'

'Good morning, Ma'am. Didn't expect to see you here this morning.

'That's why I'm here. Don't worry about my coffee, I brought my own,' she said, holding up a travel mug.

'Good lad,' said Buchanan, when Dexter walked in with a large bag of doughnuts.

'Thought this would help us to think better,' he said, offering the doughnuts around and doing a double-take as the ACC smiled at him and took a bite of her doughnut.

'Did you know there's a National Doughnut Day in the US?' said Hunter.

'Who cares?' said Buchanan. 'If they're as fresh as these, I'll eat them any day.'

'Where do you want to start?' asked Street.

'Please ignore me,' said the ACC. 'I've just popped in to see how you are all getting on.'

'Let's start with what we have on Irene Adler and Karl Mueller,' said Buchanan. 'You have the floor, Jill.'

'Irene Adler was Karl Mueller's secretary and mistress. She has little prior dealings with the police, just a nebulous record of her flat being burgled and her passport and driving licence stolen, more on this in a minute. As yet, we do not know what spooked her into doing a runner. We suspect that her partner, Karl Mueller, was involved in some sort of business deal with a Russian oligarch, Ivan Reznikov. We also suspect that Karl Mueller was going behind Ivan Reznikov's back and was going to double-cross him. Irene Adler found out about the double-cross and decided to go underground. She must have realised that if her boyfriend was in Reznikov's sights, so was she. During their years of being together, she suffered two miscarriages, the most recent about two months ago.'

'Sorry for interrupting, Jill,' said the ACC. 'How do we know all of this?'

'Inspector Buchanan and his wife met Irene Adler and Karl Mueller while on holiday. It is Inspector Buchanan's belief that Irene Adler used their brief friendship to make her disappearance look like a murder, with her body being disposed of in one of the Dutch canals.'

'Buchanan,' said the ACC, 'do I understand you aided and abetted this woman to make it look like she'd been murdered by her business partner?'

'Not quite, Ma'am. Karen and I were used. Miss Irene Adler is a very smart woman.'

'Where is she now, if she isn't dead?'

'I'm looking into that, Ma'am,' said Street. 'We are working on an assumption that Karl Mueller's widow is harbouring her.'

'Why would you think that?'

'Mrs Mueller and Irene Adler are friends; Mrs Mueller sends Christmas cards to Irene each year.'

'Have you been to see Mrs Mueller, Buchanan?' asked the ACC.

'Initially to inform her about the death of her husband.'

'Ah, I understand that incident has been determined to be a suicide, due to his state of mind after losing his – friend.'

Buchanan let his breath out slowly while looking at the ACC.

'Yes, Buchanan? You have something to add?'

He shook his head. 'No, Ma'am. If you say suicide, then who am I to argue the point with you?'

'How did you find out about the miscarriages, Jill?'

'We looked at Irene Adler's medical records. We also believe she had been planning to disappear for several months.'

'Why do you say that?'

'The passport and driving licence. As soon as they had been reported stolen she applied for replacements.'

'That's perfectly logical, I'd do the same.'

'Her lost passport and driving licence were found in the cabin safe on board the cruise ship.'

'What else?'

'The cabin looked like a charnel house,' said Buchanan. 'The cabin had blood-soaked items strewn everywhere. I did a cursory search; my wife took detailed photographs of everything while the boat sailed on to Antwerp. In Antwerp Inspector Claeys, of the Belgian police, took over the investigation. As of yesterday, we have not had any information from him as to his progress in his search for Irene Adler.

'Karl Mueller was briefly detained by Claeys, but when there was no evidence to connect him with Irene Adler's demise, disappearance, Claeys let Mueller go.'

'So, Mueller returns to the UK full of regrets, goes to the business awards dinner and in a depressed state takes his own life? End of story, right Buchanan?' said the ACC.

'If you say so, Ma'am. I couldn't possibly comment.'

'Would you three leave the Inspector and I alone for a minute, please?'

They looked at each other, stood up and left the office. Dexter grabbed the doughnut bag and closed the door behind him.

◆

'So, you didn't just happen to be here this morning, Ma'am?'

'You need to drop this investigation, Buchanan. You are wasting too many resources. You know the press are hounding us about our staffing levels.'

'More bobbies on the beat. I've read the papers and according to some of them we are currently at a potentially perilous undermanned state. Did you know that many policemen are taking early retirement to become train drivers?'

'No – you're pulling my leg.'

Buchanan shook his head. 'Sadly, it's very true. Higher salaries, better working conditions, and proper breaks. That leaves many cases being shelved because there simply aren't enough investigators available.'

'Yes, I've read the same reports. With some budgets being cut twenty percent, thousands of victims are being let down as thousands of suspected felons go free to commit more crimes that we cannot investigate,' she said, shaking her head. 'Just one big vicious circle. Policemen becoming train drivers – what next?'

'I heard that Scotland Yard have asked former CID officers to return to work as the force is overloaded with incomplete investigations that need to be cleared up.'

The ACC nodded. 'I heard the same report, and I see that smirk on your face. I suppose that pleases you?'

Buchanan shrugged. 'It only pleases me from the point that I see my job being secure for a while longer, but it saddens me that we have allowed the situation to get this bad. What hope is there for the futures of Hunter and Dexter?'

'I've seen some of the reports on them, quite impressive. Their dedication to the job stands out a mile.'

'Yes, they're exceptionally good at what they do. Someday they'll be the detectives that solve crimes we can't even imagine.'

'And that's one of the reasons I'm here. Hanbury says Hunter has been a great help so I'm lending him to Hanbury to help with clearing up the recent spate of burglaries in the area.'

'And Dexter?'

'He's going on leave to be with his wife.'

'But her sister is staying with them.'

'Buchanan,' she said, shaking her head, 'let it go. You've had a good run, it's time to hang up the cuffs.'

'Is that what you think, Ma'am, or has someone been whispering in your ear?'

'Buchanan, I'll put that remark down to – to your present condition.'

'My condition – what the hell is my condition? Will you please tell me that?'

'Buchanan, please. The doctor says you are overwrought, your accident – '

'That was two months ago, and why are you talking to my doctor?'

'The company doctor, actually. Listen, this, this is not easy for me, but –'

'Let me finish your sentence for you, Ma'am. I'm being suspended. Am I correct?'

'I'm sorry, Buchanan, it's out of my hands.'

'For how long?'

'I can't answer that.'

'Can't or won't?'

'Were you aware that the Procurator Fiscal in Glasgow is reviewing the circumstances surrounding the deaths of the two men under a police car?'

'I thought that was all put to rest?'

'Apparently not; and there's more.'

'More?'

'Someone has come forward to say you pushed Rodney Richardson into the harbour and left him to drown.'

'That's bloody nonsense. There are three witnesses to the fact that he dived, voluntarily I might add, into the harbour.'

'There's also the issue of you hounding Karl Mueller into committing suicide.'

'Suicide? That's nonsense. Mueller was murdered.'

'Can you prove that?'

'Not at the moment but, given time, I'm sure I will be able to. What you haven't heard yet is Burtenshaw was also murdered.'

'Who is Burtenshaw?'

'Guthrie Burtenshaw, QC, Ma'am.'

'Explain?'

'Karl Mueller, Guthrie Burtenshaw and Garry Duncan were all at Oxford together.'

'Wait, wait – wait a minute. Are you referring to Garry Duncan, the former Sussex Crime Commissioner?'

'Yes, Ma'am, I am.'

'You're madder than a March hare,' she said, shaking her head and walking over to the window and staring out. 'Buchanan, you can't go making these type of accusations, without proof. You could end up being dismissed from the force, or worse.'

'Please hear me out, Ma'am. As I said, all three of them attended Oxford: Mueller read economics, Burtenshaw read law and Duncan read politics. According to Mrs Burtenshaw, Mueller and Duncan financed their way through Oxford by dealing in drugs. A student died of an overdose during that time. Mueller was working on a business deal with an Ivan Reznikov. He's a Russian businessman with a criminal record worse than anything I've ever come across.'

'Who told you that nonsense?'

'What – the part about the business deal, or Reznikov's past?'

'Either will do.'

'Garry Duncan, that's who.'

She turned back from the window and thought for a moment. 'Buchanan, I came here this morning to put you on sick leave. You were going to be pensioned off – '

'But –'

'Wait, don't say anything you'll regret. What I am going to tell you is, now listen carefully, I'll only say this to you. This morning I arrived at the station to reprimand you and send you home on gardening leave. Unfortunately, when I got here you were out on a call, and as I had a flight I could not afford to miss, I left you a note on your desk which the cleaners put in the wastepaper basket. Do I make myself completely clear?'

'What about Hunter and Dexter?'

'I'll leave the issue about Dexter to you, and as for Hunter, I'll stop in on Hanbury on my way out and explain he only has Hunter for today and tomorrow. I'm afraid you and Street will just have to do the best with what you've got.'

Buchanan smiled and nodded.

'I'm going to be away for a few days, it's a personal matter. I won't be back till next Friday morning. It is my wish not to come back to find you've arrested the whole government and taken over the running of the country.'

'Thanks, Ma'am. I'll do my best not to.'

'Now, where's Dexter got to with those doughnuts? I've missed breakfast because of you.'

♦

Buchanan watched out of his window as the ACC's taxi left the compound and headed for the airport.

'It's all right, you can all relax,' he said, as the team filed into the office. 'I'm not going anywhere, But I'm sorry to say Morris and Stephen will be. Stephen, you've been seconded to work with Hanbury till Thursday, and Dexter you're on compassionate leave starting as from now.'

'Chief?' said Dexter.'

'Yes?'

'With my wife's sister looking after things, I'm sort of in the way at home. Do I need to go on leave?'

'That's up to you. Not every day does someone get compassionate leave.'

'But this case we're working on,' said Street, 'we need Stephen and Morris.'

'I'm sorry, my hands are tied. The decision was made before the ACC got here this morning.'

'That stinks,' said Street.

'Then I choose to refuse my leave,' said Dexter.

'Excuse me a minute,' said Buchanan, as he picked up his ringing phone. 'Really? Fine. Thanks.' He put the receiver down and smiled. 'That was Hanbury. He said he can manage without Stephen.'

'So, we are a team again,' said Street.

'Shall we continue? We have ten days to clear this mess up.'

'We thought she was going to fire you,' said Street.

'So did I, for a minute. I tell you all, there's something going on, call it a conspiracy if you will, but I for one want to get to the bottom of it. Jill, it's back to you.'

'Not sure where I got to.'

'Irene Adler's miscarriage,' said Dexter.

'Continue, please, Jill.'

'The next event is when the Chief returns here and sets up a missing person report on Irene Adler. Her flat is searched, resulting in us concluding that someone has collected clothes for her new life, wherever that is.

'Mrs Mueller is interviewed, and we get to hear about the background of Karl Mueller and Ivan Reznikov and their friendship at Oxford. From there the trail leads us to the door of Guthrie Burtenshaw, who has now died. The three of them passed through the three years of Oxford as sort of friends, though Burtenshaw was more studious than Mueller and Duncan.

'Mueller met Reznikov somewhere and took a shine to his wife, Tatyana; the feelings were apparently reciprocated. We have a suspicion that Reznikov was totally aware of this relationship and maybe even encouraged it. They all get together on the evening of the Business in Excellence Awards dinner on the pier – all that is except Guthrie Burtenshaw. He had been preparing an import licence for Reznikov and is summoned to the awards dinner to deliver the papers. The reason given for this is Reznikov needs to scan and send the documents to his contact in Moscow in the morning.

'Burtenshaw arrives and meets Reznikov and Mueller. Mueller is either drunk, high on cocaine, or both. For whatever reason, yet unknown, Burtenshaw waits for thirty-five minutes on the pier before returning to the taxi and his home. Next morning Mueller is found hanging form the pier, then two days later Burtenshaw is found dead on the bus.'

'Well done, Jill. An excellent recounting of events as we know them.'

'What do you want us to do, Chief?' said Hunter.

'I want you and Morris to do the rounds with the witness statements and get them to read the statements then sign them. Jill and I are going to do what we should have done last week, we're going to shake the Mueller tree and see what falls out.'

'Do you still think she's harbouring Irene Adler?' asked Dexter.

'Who knows, Morris? Either way we'll get it sorted this morning. Any word from the pharmacy?'

Dexter shook his head.

'Get on to that while you two are out, will you?' said Buchanan, as he rubbed his hands together. 'We've only got ten days to wrap this case up, and there's still a lot of investigating to get on with.'

Dexter crumpled the doughnut bag and tossed it into the wastepaper basket, then stood up. 'Ready, Stephen?'

'See you two later,' said Hunter, as he and Dexter left the office.

'Right, Jill, shall we go see Mrs Mueller?' said Buchanan.

◆

'Good, she's home,' said Buchanan, as Street turned off the road and on to the driveway beside the Porsche.

'Still like this house, I wouldn't mind living here,' said Street, turning off the engine. 'Just look at the place, must be in the region of four, five hundred thousand. Just as well Mueller paid off the mortgage before he died.'

Buchanan pressed the doorbell and waited. The inevitable sound of the door chain being attached preceded the opening of the door. 'Mrs Mueller, It's Inspector Buchanan and Sergeant Street, we have some more questions. May we come in?'

'Just a minute,' she said, closing the door to remove the security chain then reopening it. 'Come in.'

'Thank you, Mrs Mueller.'

They followed her through the same room as before. Mrs Mueller sat in her chair and motioned Buchannan and Street to sit. 'Do you want a cup of coffee or tea?' she asked.

'That would be nice, shall I make it?'

'Why not? You've seen my kitchen.'

'Why don't I?' said Street. 'The Inspector has some important questions to ask.'

Mrs Mueller nodded. 'Go ahead.'

'How are you, Mrs Mueller?' asked Buchanan.

'Fine.'

'I'd like to bring you up to date on our investigations into the death of your husband if you don't mind?'

She shrugged. 'No.'

'We are now quite sure he did not take his own life. The evidence points to him being pushed over the railings and left to drown in the sea.'

She shook her head. 'Not likely, he was a good swimmer.'

'Mrs Mueller, when he was discovered, he still had a noose tied round his neck. Even if he had managed to stay afloat, when the tide went out he would have been strangled.'

'Would it have been a slow death? Would he have suffered?'

Buchanan nodded. 'Certainly.'

She looked up at Buchanan, smiled and said, 'Good,' just as Street returned carrying a tray with three cups of coffee.

'Hold on, you haven't tasted it yet,' she said, as she put the tray down on the small table.

'I was referring to my late husband's demise,' said Mrs Mueller.

'Oh. Would you like sugar in your coffee? I remember you don't take milk.'

'Two spoons, please.'

'Mrs Mueller,' began Buchanan, 'I have a dedicated team who have been working round the clock on the case of the death of your husband, and additionally the disappearance of Irene Adler. Based on our investigations we have drawn certain conclusions. And one conclusion in particular has brought us here to your door. We believe that Irene Adler is very much alive, and we also believe you know of her whereabouts.'

'I suppose it doesn't matter anymore. Yes, she's alive.'

'Is she, by chance, staying here with you?'

'Certainly not.'

'Then could you please tell us where she is?'

'I can't tell you as I don't know.'

'Mrs Mueller, you have already caused us a great inconvenience by withholding evidence. I could, if I decided, charge you with obstructing the police in the conduct of their duties.'

'What I mean is I'm telling the truth when I say I don't know where she is. I left her at the train station in Arnhem.'

'Where was she going?'

'Barcelona.'

'Does she have family there?'

'Listen. You know I knew all about her and Karl. I was just pleased he could finally make someone happy. But he was a real shit, treated her like dirt. Did you know she had two miscarriages? Well, when I found out the first time she was pregnant, at first I was angry. Why should she have his child and not me? See – we couldn't have children, my fault, not his. When she told him, he said to get rid of it. She told me she was going to keep the child regardless if he wanted it or not. Unfortunately, she lost the baby and life resumed as it was.'

'Where did Tatyana Reznikov enter the scene?'

'Karl was working on a new business venture with a pal of his from university days.'

'Do you know the name of this pal?'

'Garry Duncan.'

'Just him?'

'I believe there was a third, Tatyana's husband, Ivan Reznikov.'

'Who was the driving force in the relationship?'

'It was Tatyana's husband, Ivan.'

'Anyone else involved?'

'I believe there was a lawyer, another of their university pals.'

'Was he actually involved in the deal?'

'No, he was just taking care of the paperwork,' she shrugged, 'that's all I know about the affair.'

'Do you know when the last time was Karl met with any of the others?'

'The night he died, it was at the awards dinner on the pier.'

'You said Irene went to Barcelona. Why did she run away?'

'She was afraid.'

'Of what – or who?'

'One of Karl's friends.'

'Did she say who?'

'No. She called me from Amsterdam in tears. She said she must get away and hide for a while and could I help her.'

'How were you to help?'

'She asked me to go round to her flat, collect enough clothes and a suitcase to last a couple of weeks, then bring them to her in Antwerp. She was very insistent that I should tell no-one.'

'How were you to meet?'

'She said the boat would be tied up just past the bridge in Arnhem. I was to wait in the car with the lights off and she would come to me.'

'Did she say what time?'

'She said she wasn't sure when Karl was going ashore, apparently he was going on another business meeting. I think it was about two in the morning when she got in the car.'

'And you then drove her to the station?'

'Yes.'

'How was she?'

Mrs Mueller smiled. 'I'd never seen her look so happy.'

'Have you heard from her since?'

'No, but that's all right, I know she's safe now.'

'What do you mean by safe?'

'She's on a cruise ship, away from anyone who knows her.'

'Do you know which cruise line and the name of the ship?'

'That's part of the fun of the story. While on the canal cruise, she used Karl's credit card to book a first-class sea cruise on Viking. I believe the ship is headed for Stockholm.'

'Jill.'

'I know what to do.'

'Mrs Mueller, twice we've been here and been offered something to drink. Both times you've declined milk in your drink. Yet, when I checked your refrigerator there was a four-pint bottle of milk in the door. If you don't drink milk, and Irene Adler is not staying with you, who drinks the milk?'

'I keep it for visitors, like you and your sergeant.'

'A four-pint container? How many visitors do you get in a week? Or – do you have someone staying with you, someone you don't want us to know about? I can get a search warrant, Mrs Mueller.'

'I sometimes have visitors stay overnight.'

'Someone I may know? Shall I go down the list of suspects?'

'It's Ivan.'

'Ivan Reznikov?'

She nodded. 'It's all above board, he just stays here when he's in town.'

'Did you husband know?'

She smiled. 'No.'

'How often did Ivan stay here?'

'Mostly when he came down to talk about syndicate business.'

'Can you tell us about the syndicate – who was in it for instance?'

'I know Karl and Ivan were in it, and there was the lawyer but I don't think he was directly involved like the others.'

'Was the lawyer's name Guthrie Burtenshaw?'

'Yes, that's him.'

'How about a Garry Duncan?'

She thought for a moment, then nodded. 'Yes, he was one of them.'

'Did they meet very often?'

'I don't know anything about that.'

'And Ivan Reznikov was only an overnight guest, nothing more?'

'That is none of your business, Inspector.'

'Mrs Mueller, last week your husband was murdered and one of the last people to see him alive was Ivan Reznikov. You've just told us he stays here, but you refuse to explain what your relationship is with him. Can you understand why I'm pursuing this line of enquiry?'

'We are just friends. His wife was having an affair with Karl. At first Ivan thought it was just another of her infatuations, she'd had several. We used to sit and talk about how fickle people can be. I think Ivan preferred the peace and quiet of Eastbourne to the bustle of London.'

'Let me ask my question again. How often did Ivan stay here with you?'

'Whenever he wanted to. I'd get a phone call from the airport and he'd say he was in town for a week, could he come for a visit?'

'Was Karl ever here when Ivan came for a visit?'

'Never in the house. Karl spent most of his time on the road or staying with Irene.'

'When Ivan is in the country and not staying here, do you know where he stayed?'

'Somewhere in London. He once told me there are flats near the embassy that visiting Russians could use. He owned one and rented it out when he was away.'

'Did you ever visit him in London?'

'Once or twice, he'd take me out to dinner. Oh, it wasn't that kind of relationship. I think what we had was more platonic. When he stayed here he would bring me gifts from Russia and a bottle of vodka for himself. Do you like vodka, Inspector? I have some left from his last visit. Oh, of course, you can't drink on duty.'

Buchanan smiled. 'Thank you for offering, I prefer whisky.'

'We'd just sit and talk, mostly about him. I was married to Karl for more years than I want to remember, but in the few times Ivan stayed here I learned more about him than I ever did about Karl.'

'What sort of things did he talk about?'

'His childhood and how Russia has changed since the fall of the USSR, especially now since that man has taken over running the country.'

'Was he referring to Vladimir Putin?' asked Street.

'Yes. Did you know that his wife, Tatyana, is a cousin of President Putin? She's the daughter of one of Putin's cousins. As long as they stayed married and Tatyana was happy, Ivan was safe in the knowledge nothing untoward would happen to him. Let me tell you, Inspector, that Tatyana had him wrapped round her little finger, could get anything she wanted.'

'Now that we didn't know.'

'Do you know what his favourite song was?'

Buchanan thought for a moment. '*Kalinka*?'

'No, it was, *Yesterday*, by the Beatles.'

'Pop music?'

'Think about the words, Inspector: yesterday, all my troubles seemed so far away, now it looks like they're here to stay, oh I believe in yesterday.'

'He sounds a bit of a romantic, dreaming of things gone by.'

'You have a lovely voice, Mrs Mueller,' said Street.

'Thanks, that's what Ivan also said. On one of the few times we met in London, he took me to his favourite Russian restaurant. He said it was the best for traditional food and music. He made me sing karaoke with him after dinner, in Russian.'

'Sounds like what my family do in Scotland, except we sing in Gaelic.'

'I'd like to hear that sometime.'

'Maybe when this investigation is over, Mrs Mueller,' said Buchanan, standing. 'Thank you for being so frank with your answers. Sergeant Street will come back with your statement for you to sign. Oh, before we go,' he said, taking the photo Karen took in Amsterdam at the restaurant out of his jacket pocket, 'can you identify any of these men in the photo?'

She looked at it. 'The one on the left is Karl, seated next to him is Ivan, I don't know who the third one is.'

'Thank you, Mrs Mueller.'

♦

'I should have seen that coming,' said Buchanan, as Street drove them back to the office.

'What should you have seen?'

'Reznikov and Mrs Mueller. Karl and Tatyana were having an affair, why shouldn't Reznikov and Mrs Mueller comfort each other? I think it's high time we had a word with Ivan Reznikov.'

'How will you do that? You called the Russian Embassy, they denied any knowledge of him.'

'Tell you what, when we get back to the office, I would like you to call the Russian Embassy and say you are putting on a party for some old friends who used to live in Russia and you would like it to be authentic as possible.'

'I don't follow you.'

'Listen – tell them you would like a recommendation for a London restaurant that has authentic Russian food and entertainment.'

'Surely there must be more than one restaurant in London like that?'

'Maybe, but have a go at it. If they give you several, get their names and phone numbers.'

'OK.'

♦

'You know, said Street, as she stared at her computer screen, 'we still haven't talked to Tatyana Reznikov and heard her side of the events.'

'I'm with you on that,' said Buchanan looking away from his computer screen. 'Fortunately, she's quite prominent on the internet. So far I've found her fashions being sold in two shops on Oxford Street in London and a website for her UK company.'

'Does it give contact details?'

'For the company, yes. But it won't necessarily provide details for her.'

'I'll try Facebook,' said Street.

'Thanks. Facebook leaves me cold. All it seems to do is show what people ate and what their dogs are doing. You fancy a coffee?'

Street nodded. 'Frappuccino, please.'

♦

'Your coffee,' said Buchanan, placing the cup on Street's desk. 'Any luck?'

'Not sure yet. I've found her Facebook page and sent her a friend request, now it's a wait and see what happens.'

'How about Stephen and Morris, heard from them?'

'Stephen called and said the pharmacist found the doctor who prescribed the epinephrine.'

'Local doctor?'

'Yes, Stone Cross. Stephen said he will let me know how they get on.'

'Good. Get anywhere with Viking?'

'Just got off the phone with them.'

'And?'

'Irene Adler is a passenger on the *Viking Star*.'

'Did you get her cabin number?'

'Uh-uh, no cabin for this lady. Miss Irene Adler has her own penthouse veranda suite, courtesy of Karl's credit card no doubt.'

'Bet that wasn't cheap.'

'Seven and a half thousand.'

'I wonder who'll get stuck paying for that? After all you said it was his card that she used and that's fraud when you use someone else's card without their permission.'

'I suppose she could say he'd already agreed? After all, he was still alive when she did the booking. Not much chance of interviewing her till she gets back, then. When is that?'

'It's a twenty-two-day cruise, but you don't need to wait that long.'

'Why?'

'Because the ship docks in Amsterdam the day after tomorrow. It will be there for two days.'

'Fancy a visit to Amsterdam?'

'Who's paying for that?'

'I'll talk to the ACC. I'll explain I need to have female company when interviewing a major suspect, simple.'

'OK, I suppose.'

Street's computer dinged. 'Success, I'm now friends with Tatyana Reznikov. I'll have a browse through her posts and see what she's been up to.'

'Keep a look out for pictures of her and Karl Mueller. I'm going to call the ACC.'

'Will do.'

Buchanan put the phone down and looked at the clock. 'She's in a meeting and can't be disturbed. *Please leave a message or call back later.* What's the point of having a phone if you don't answer the bloody thing?'

'You leave her a message?'

'Yes. I said we're flying to Amsterdam to interview the missing witness in the Karl Mueller murder case.'

'That should please her, especially since that case is supposed to be deemed a suicide.'

'Let's not worry about it, we'll have it sorted before she gets back.'

'I've got good news on the Tatyana front.'

'Tell me, I need some good news.'

'She's launching a new line in clothes in London tomorrow.'

'Wonder how we can get an invitation?'

'No need, it's an open event at the Selfridges store on Oxford Street.'

Buchanan looked at the time on the computer, 'Tell you what, if we are going to London tomorrow, why don't we have an early night?'

Street smiled. 'Brilliant, I can go home and make dinner for Stephen and me. Be a change from takeaways. What time should we meet in the morning, and where?'

'How about I pick you up at eight? We can park at Eastbourne station and catch the London train from there.'

'Sounds fine to me, see you in the morning.'

'Goodnight.'

14

Buchanan rang Street's doorbell and waited for a reply. It came three minutes later with Hunter opening the door and looking guilty about not already being out at work.

'Just debriefing Jill about what we found yesterday, Chief.'

'I'll believe that, just don't take it for a vote. Is she ready?'

'Right behind me.'

'Morning, Jill.'

'Good morning. Stephen really was telling me about what they found out yesterday.'

'I believe you. Let's go, you can fill me in on the train.'

♦

'I miss the old trains,' said Buchanan, trying to stretch his legs without disturbing the sleeping passenger across from him.'

'Really? The old slam-door trains were cold and draughty.'

'I'm referring to the days of steam. The compartments were all heated with steam from the engine, and the seats were proper seats, not these plastic bucket things.'

'I didn't realise you were that old,' said Street, enjoying the banter.

'I'll have you know the last steam train in service was in 1968. I was a young man then.'

'I thought they were supposed to be unreliable, cramped, and in winter smelled of wet dogs?'

He shook his head. 'Not the trains I rode between Glasgow and London – those were the days.'

'Stephen talked with the doctor who prescribed the epinephrine,' said Street.

'That prescription was written six weeks ago.'

'I know that. But what we didn't know was who Bridget Standish was.'

'And we do now?'

'Yes, she was Karl Mueller's niece, but there's a twist to the story.'

'Go on.'

'Bridget Standish almost died from anaphylactic shock four weeks ago.'

'Because she didn't have her epipen?'

'Not according to the doctor. He issued her with another prescription after the first one went missing.'

'Do we have dates when the replacement was issued?'

'The doctor prescribed the replacement the day after the first one went missing, which was well before her attack.'

'So, we can assume that during the week after her first prescription was issued, someone stole it,' said Buchanan. 'I wonder if her parents can think of anyone who might have done that? Jill, I think we need to ask the parents if they knew Burtenshaw.'

'Maybe she simply lost it? Kids do that.'

'That's also possible. But it still doesn't answer the question of how it ended up in the hands of Burtenshaw, and why he injected himself.'

'Maybe he wanted to die and asked a friend to bring him the epipen,' said Street.

'I suppose if Mueller was still alive we might assume it was him on the bus with Burtenshaw. But since we know it couldn't have been, we need to look for another link. The question of how Mueller's niece's prescription ended up in Burtenshaw's hand is a puzzle. I need to sleep on this one. Do you have any ideas?'

Street sat silent for a moment. 'Nothing comes to mind at the moment. I'll get the parents' details from Stephen and give them a call.'

'A kleptomaniac QC? What next?' said Buchanan, as he turned to stare out of the window.

♦

'How do we get to Selfridges?' asked Buchanan, as the train arrived at Victoria Station.

'Victoria line to Green Park, then change to the Jubilee line to Bond Street, then it's a short walk along Oxford Street.'

'Ever been to one of these?' Buchanan asked Street, as they walked through the doors to Selfridges.'

Street shook her head. 'No, have you?'

'Do you know where to go?' asked Buchanan.

'I was told the fashion show would be taking place on the third floor in the area where they sometimes have the Christmas display.'

Buchanan walked behind Street trying not to look out of place as they rode the escalators up to the third floor and over to the fashion show area. A viewing salon had been set up behind temporary screens, each hung with posters of models, presumably wearing some of the clothes to be modelled this morning. They were forty minutes early and found they had a wide choice of where to sit.

'Front row seats?' asked Street.

'I suppose the models will come out from behind that screen at the end of the catwalk,' said Buchanan. 'See that table to the side?'

'Yes, why?'

'There's a microphone sitting on it. For my money that's where Tatyana will be to describe the clothes worn by the models. Be a pity to come this far and have her disappear out the door.'

'Why don't we just arrest her as a material witness?'

'I'd rather take her to lunch and have her amenable to my questions.'

'Can't imagine what your expense claim is going to do to the ACC's blood pressure when she sees it?'

'Neither can I. C'mon, let's grab our seats before they get taken.'

As they took their seats, a young man came over and asked if they were guests of the house. It took Buchanan by surprise, but not Street.

'Yes. We're here as guests of Tatyana. Would you let her know we're here and looking forward to treating her to lunch?'

The young man looked puzzled for a moment then recovered his composure. 'Oh, I thought she was seeing the buyers right after the show.'

Buchanan smiled and said, 'She is. Lunch is a special surprise to celebrate the launch of the new line. Ivan thought it might be a nice gesture, let's not spoil her surprise.'

'Ivan, her husband?'

Buchanan smiled. 'Yes, her husband, Ivan Reznikov. You know what he's like when anyone spoils his arrangements.'

All semblance of emotion now departed from the young man's face. He nodded in assent, shivered, then left to show guests to their seats.

'That was telling,' said Street.

'Definitely. The last time I saw that kind of reaction was when a local thug, called Maxi, was told that Nicker wanted back the fifty pounds he'd borrowed. Maxi boastingly said that Nicker could shove that request up his arse.'

'What happened?'

'What Maxi didn't realise, was that Nicker, who was a good foot taller than Maxi, was standing directly behind him, his right fist poised ready to slam it into Maxi's face.'

'Did he?'

'Maxi pissed himself, then ran out of the pub.'

'Oh dear, how embarrassing for Maxi. Did he ever pay Nicker the money he owed?'

'He sent it via an intermediary the next day.'

'Not sure I'm looking forward to meeting Ivan Reznikov now.'

'Don't worry. That breed of thug has one great weakness.'

'What's that?'

'Their vanity. Don't worry. This is Britain, he's on my turf and will play by my rules.'

'I hope you're right on that.'

Their conversation was cut short by the sound of a disco track being played through the sound system. Faces of the assembled audience turned towards the opening in the screens at the end of the catwalk. They broke into applause when the focus of the morning came into view.

'Good morning, ladies and gentlemen. Thank you for being here this morning. Please, sit back and feast your eyes on my new creations.'

Buchanan and Street sat for the next hour watching models parade the latest creations from the design table of Tatyana Reznikov. There followed a short sales announcement saying that complimentary lunch would be served directly after the sales had been completed.

Before anyone left, Buchanan and Street went behind the screens in search of Tatyana Reznikov. They found her in the middle of a throng of excited models, each celebrating with a glass of champagne.

'Excuse me,' said Buchanan, trying to be heard above the babble of voices. 'Tatyana, can I have a quick word, please?'

She turned to see what this male voice was doing in amongst the bevy of female chatter. 'This is a private party, please leave.'

Buchanan pushed his way into the throng of partially-dressed models and produced his warrant card. 'Detective Chief Inspector Buchanan and Detective Sergeant Street, Sussex CID. Is there somewhere a little more private to talk, please? It's about Karl Mueller'

Before she could answer, two well-dressed, suited women pushed in between Buchanan and Tatyana.

'It's OK,' said Tatyana, to the one on the left. 'They're here to talk to me about Karl. I'll be fine. Meet me back here after lunch?'

They nodded and left.

'My minders, Ivan takes my security seriously.'

Buchanan nodded. 'If you wouldn't mind giving me a few minutes of your time, we will be gone.'

The models drifted away to find more champagne while the two minders backed away and stood poised like coiled springs ready to uncoil at any provocation.

Tatyana turned to them and said, 'It's all right, you can go and have lunch, these two people are friends of Karl.

'So, Inspector, Sergeant – I would like to think you came here to look at my collection, but that would be an idle thought. What is it you want to know?'

'It is lunch time. Could we buy you lunch?'

'I'm not sure,' she said, looking at her watch. 'I can't really leave while there are still buyers here.'

'We could have lunch here at Selfridges,' said Street. 'Their menu in the roof garden is very good.'

'That's fine for me,' said Tatyana.

Street and Tatyana, followed by Buchanan, made their way up to the fifth floor. Even though it was lunch time they were able to find a table.

Buchanan watched and listened as Street and Tatyana ate and swapped stories about clothes. As they were finishing their lunch, Buchanan began with his questions.

'Tatyana, can you tell me how you and Karl met each other?'

'It was at a trade show at Olympia in London. Ivan was there as a member of a Russian trade delegation, I went along to keep him company. It was an engineering show, the company Ivan was representing specialised in CNC machining. By lunch time of the first day I was bored and went for a wander round the exhibition. Karl's company, or at least the company Karl was representing, specialised in injection moulding. I saw him as I approached his stand and had the opportunity to watch him in action. He intrigued me with his sales patter and I saw someone who could be helpful with the distribution of my line of fashions in the UK.'

'I fail to see the connection between injection moulding and high fashion, Tatyana?' said Buchanan.

'There isn't. What I saw was someone who was very much at ease talking to people. I walked up to him and asked him about injection moulding, of which he very soon concluded I knew nothing about. That was when I saw him at his best. Within a few questions he ascertained where my knowledge base was and then proceeded to explain all about injection moulding.' She blushed at a memory. 'I'm sorry, something just came back to me. Anyway, I introduced myself and asked him if he was freelance or worked for the company.'

'I don't understand?' said Street.

'Quite often companies will hire in professional presenters for trade shows. That way they only have to send a couple of experts to answer the difficult questions.'

'Oh, I didn't know that.'

'Well, Karl said he worked for himself and would be pleased to meet me after the show closed for the day to discuss what I was looking for.'

'Did Ivan go along to the meeting?' asked Buchanan.

'Yes. Before I went to see Karl I had a talk with Ivan and explained what I'd found out about Karl's expertise in marketing and sales. I said Karl would be an ideal contact for future exhibitions. Ivan liked the idea and agreed to meet Karl. The meeting went well and Ivan took Karl's details with a promise to get back in touch within the week. Ivan then left for another meeting. That left Karl and I to spend the rest of the evening together.'

'What did you talk about?'

'The usual sort of things, his childhood, his time at Oxford university, his early life in business, going from job to job till the day he decided to go into business for himself as a consultant.'

'Did he talk much about his personal life?'

'Are you asking did he tell me he was married?'

Buchanan nodded.

'Yes. The marriage was in name only. Like so many couples they found living together a lot different from dating. It wasn't long before they drifted apart into separate lifestyles.'

'Did he ever mention his secretary?'

'Irene? Did you know Karl was arrested and questioned about her death? What a stupid idea that was. His arrest almost destroyed a huge business deal Karl was working on.'

'Do you happen to know what the business deal was, or the name of who he was working with?'

'No. It was a private matter between him and Ivan and some other private investors.'

'Did Karl talk much about his life at university?'

'Yes, but I think he held back some things from me.'

'What sort of things did he talk about?'

'Mostly about his studies. Did you know he got a first in economics? He even fancied working in government.'

'In any particular capacity?'

'Tony Blair was his idol, although he had already left before Karl arrived at university. Karl did manage to do some consulting work for the TBI a few years ago.'

'What's the TBI?' asked Street.

'Tony Blair Institute.'

'Oh. Bit pretentious, that.'

Tatyana shrugged. 'Karl seemed to enjoy it, he even got to meet his hero once.

'Tatyana, did Karl ever talk about his friends, past or present?'

'Karl didn't have many friends, the only two I recall were a Garry Duncan and a Guthrie Burtenshaw.'

'Was there anything special about those two friends?'

'Guthrie Burtenshaw was a lawyer used by the syndicate, Garry Duncan had his government connections. Karl said they were the only two friends he had at university. He said he got on well with Duncan, but Burtenshaw was a swot.'

'Did you ever meet either of them?'

'I met Garry Duncan a couple of times. I think he and Karl rekindled their friendship while Karl was doing the consultancy for the TBI.'

'You and Karl, it was more than a business relationship?'

'Yes, we were in love with one another, silly at our age, and both of us married.'

'Didn't your husband say anything about you having an affair with Karl?'

'We have an arrangement, what's called an open marriage. Ivan has his girlfriends, mostly a bunch of tarts that he gets drunk with. Inspector, why do you think Karl killed himself?'

'What do you think?'

'I was told it was because of Irene Adler's death,' she said, shaking her head. 'But that couldn't be. He told me he had broken with her several months ago. He said she had become impossible to be with after her miscarriage

'Who told you about Karl's death?'

'His friend Garry called to say he'd read it in the newspaper.'

'Why do you think he called you? According to what you've told us you hardly knew the man.'

'He said Karl used to talk to him about me, said he was going to divorce his wife and marry me.'

'What about you and Ivan? Were you getting a divorce from him?'

She smiled. 'My marriage to Ivan is one of convenience arranged by the government. It is easier for spouses of businessmen to get visas that way.'

'So, you and Ivan aren't really married?'

'On paper, yes. Though Ivan sometimes seems to think he can take liberties.'

'What do you do when he's like that?' asked Street.

'I tell him to go find one of his whores if that is what he wants.'

'Did you tell Ivan about Karl being dead?'

'Garry must have told him. I mentioned it and he said he'd already heard.'

'Could it have been Burtenshaw who mentioned it?'

Tatyana shook her head. 'I think they only communicated over Ivan's import licence paperwork.'

'Do you happen to know where Ivan is just now?' asked Buchanan.

'He's due back from Amsterdam this morning.'

'Can you tell me where he will be staying?'

'We have a flat in Notting Hill.'

'Will he go straight there?'

'Probably, but just to drop off his bags. I imagine he'll head for the Embassy after that, you could give the Embassy a call.'

'I've tried there before. As far as the Embassy is concerned, Ivan Reznikov doesn't exist.'

'He usually goes out to dinner, you could try calling around. There aren't too many real Russian restaurants in London.'

'Thanks, we'll give it a go.'

'Oh, is that the time? I have to go, Inspector,' said Tatyana, looking at her watch, 'Been nice talking with you.'

'Er, how long will you be? I have some more questions to ask.'

'Who knows? If there are lots of buyers it could be a couple of hours, at least.'

'It's two-thirty now,' said Buchanan looking at his phone. Could we meet back here at five-thirty? That should give you plenty of time.'

Tatyana looked perplexed. 'What questions do you still need to ask?'

'Five-thirty, Tatyana. I'll explain then, don't worry, it's just to clear up some questions arising from your earlier answers.'

'OK, till five-thirty.'

'What answers did she give that have caused you to want to ask more questions?' asked Street as they watched Tatyana thread her way through the afternoon visitors.

'I'm sure she knows more about what Karl was up to than she's said so far.'

'What are we going to do for the next two hours?' asked Street.

Buchanan smiled. 'We're moving in to our new house soon. I thought you could help me find a suitable moving-in gift for Karen.'

♦

'I know we said five-thirty,' said Tatyana, arriving flustered, 'but I simply couldn't turn away the buyers. Now what are these questions you've been dying to ask me?'

'You said Karl's friend Garry told you about Karl's death. How did he get your phone number?'

'When Karl was on his business trip in Holland, he lost his phone and asked me to get a replacement for him. He gave me his friend Garry's number and said to call him when I had the new phone.'

'Did you deliver it?'

'Sort of. I called him, and he told me give it to Ivan.'

'Why Ivan?'

'Ivan was going to meet up with Karl and Garry at the awards dinner.'

'Did you go to the dinner?'

'I was intending on going with Ivan, but he had me deliver a package to a friend in Milton Keynes, so I didn't get there till just before the awards were given out.'

'Didn't that sound a bit odd at the time?'

The muscles on the side of her mouth tightened. 'He was like that, besides, you never say no to Ivan.'

'You know what my next question is?'

'Did I wonder if Ivan killed Karl?'

'Was he capable of doing that?'

'That and more, Inspector. When I heard that Karl had killed himself, I was shocked. I did momentarily think Ivan might have killed him, but then I changed my mind. Karl was on the brink of the biggest deal in his life. He said as soon as it was completed, he would retire, I could get rid of Ivan and we could *buy a yacht and sail over the horizon.* Ivan just couldn't have killed Karl, he needed him for whatever the syndicate were working on. Karl was Ivan's UK partner.'

'What about Garry Duncan? Where did he fit into the picture?'

'I've no idea. All I knew was Karl didn't trust him.'

'Do you know why?'

'Karl told me a story about when they were in their final year at university and how they were going to arrange to smuggle dope into the UK from Holland. It was going to be their final deal and was to make them enough cash to set themselves up in business after university. Karl borrowed the money from friends to buy the dope and gave the money to Garry, who was to fly over and meet with the seller and make all the arrangements for it to be shipped to the UK.'

'I take it something went wrong?' said Street.

'Garry came back and said the deal went badly wrong. When he met with the buyer he was told to hand over the money and to forget he'd ever been in Holland. Garry told Karl he'd been mugged by a Bulgarian gangster and had all the money for the deal stolen.'

'What did Karl do?'

'What could he do? He certainly couldn't complain to the police. As soon as Garry went out, Karl called the contact in Amsterdam to check Garry's story. The contact said that Garry never showed up.'

'So, he just did nothing other than to make a phone call?' said Street.

'No – not quite. Karl has a bit of a temper when roused. He waited for Garry to return to the lodgings then he accused him of being everything under the sun. Garry has a thick skin and shrugged most of the insults and accusations off. That was until Karl accused him of double-crossing him and keeping the money for himself.'

'What did Garry do?' asked Street.

'He picked up a chair and hit Karl over the head. Thankfully the scout heard the noise and called the police.'

'Scout?' said Street.

'That's what they call the person who looks after the students' accommodation, sort of a housekeeper,' said Buchanan.

'Karl wasn't seriously hurt,' continued Tatyana. 'He refused to press charges, so that was the end of that and their friendship.'

'Were you aware that Ivan and Burtenshaw were the last two people to see Karl alive?'

'Are you saying one of them killed Karl? Because if you are …'

Buchanan shook his head. 'No, I'm not. When he was last seen, Karl appeared to be either drunk, drugged or both. The official report into his death will be listed as he took his own life while in a disturbed state over the loss of his long-time friend, Irene Adler.'

'That's nonsense.'

'Which bit? The bit about being drunk, the bit about the drugs, or the bit about being disturbed about the loss of his friend Irene Adler?'

'You're the one with all the answers, you tell me.'

'Do you know the names of any of the other syndicate members?'

She shook her head.

'Do you know what the syndicate was about?'

'No. All I remember Karl saying was, it would make a few people very rich.'

'And you have no idea who was in the syndicate or what it was about?'

'No.'

'How about the initial investment? How much did Karl put in?'

'Ah, that I do have an idea about. We were going to buy a house in Chelsea for an investment. We were about to complete on the deal when Karl said he'd found a much better investment.'

'Nothing else?' asked Buchanan.

'No, sorry.'

♦

'Where did Tatyana say was the best place for true Russian food?' asked Buchanan, as they headed for the underground.

'Solyanka. I've just had a look at their website. It has been around since 1965. Tatyana said it's where the embassy staff take their friends when they are visiting the UK. The website boasts that the restaurant is one of the oldest Russian restaurants in the UK,' said Street.

'Does the website have a menu?'

'Yes, it says they serve many traditional Russian dishes, including pancakes with caviar, cabbage rolls, cabbage soup, and even Russian champagne.'

'Sounds promising, continue.'

'There is also live, traditional, Russian music. The bar menu boasts an excellent selection of genuine Russian vodkas. And you'll like this – at the end of the evening you can join in singing karaoke with songs in Russian.'

'Can you imagine what it would sound like, me singing Russian in a Glaswegian accent?'

'I think you'd be great.'

'Enough of that.'

'Shall I call and see if he's there?'

'Yes, why not.'

They stood outside Oxford Street underground station, trying to stay out of the way of the late commuters heading home.

'They were a bit cagey,' said Street, hanging up. 'I said I was a friend of Tatyana and had a message for him. They said they don't know if he'll be in this evening and to try again some other time.'

'He's a wary character, but I suppose you have to be when you're in his line of business. Which station are we headed for?'

'Back to Oxford Circus, Victoria line to Green Park, then it's the Piccadilly line to Knightsbridge, followed by a brisk walk down Brompton Road. We go past Harrods then right on Beauchamp Place.'

'Ever think about being a tour guide?'

'I'll think about that, got your ticket ready?'

♦

'Ever shopped in Harrods?' asked Street. as they passed the magnificent frontage of the store.

'Once, bit expensive for my taste.'

They turned on to Beauchamp Place, crossed the road and stood outside the restaurant.

Street looked at her watch. 'Let's hope he likes to eat early, it's only seven-thirty.'

Buchanan climbed the steps to the front door, stopped and looked at the menu displayed in the glass-covered holder. He only recognised a couple of the dishes and realised this evening's dinner was going to be interesting. He held the door open for Street and followed her in. He had imagined the restaurant to be a bit bigger, but decided it looked just right.

Street asked for a table for two at the back, but the waiter apologised saying they didn't have any tables available at that moment. Street explained they'd heard Ivan Reznikov usually ate there when he was in London and, since they had travelled there especially to meet with him, they wouldn't mind waiting for a table.

'The name of Reznikov opens doors, and gets tables in full restaurants,' said Buchanan quietly, as the waiter left them to get the menu.

'I wonder what else it gets you?' said Street.

'A bath in the English Channel?' said Buchanan.

'Are you now thinking it could have been him? I thought you were leaning towards it being Burtenshaw who pushed the unfortunate Mueller over the rail?'

He shook his head. 'I'm still working on it. We need to talk with Reznikov first, he has the penultimate piece to this jigsaw.'

The waiter returned with the menu and asked if they wanted drinks.

'Large white wine for me,' said Street.

'I'll have a whisky – Talisker, if you have it,' said Buchanan, 'and a glass of water.'

'I've just realised something,' said Street.

'What's that?'

'This the first time you've taken me out to dinner. We usually end up at the end of the day getting a takeaway.'

'You're absolutely right, but don't get used to it. My expense account only stretches so far, and let's not forget our trip to Amsterdam the day after tomorrow.'

The waiter returned with their drinks and a menu for each of them.

'Quite basic, the menu,' said Street.

'All part of the ambience,' replied Buchanan. 'See anything you fancy?'

'It's not so much what do I fancy. It's more like what do I recognise. For instance, what is shashlik?'

'That I do know, it's a kebab. They have lamb, pork or chicken.'

'How about you chose for us? I'm out of my depth here.'

'Shall we start with soup?'

Street shrugged and nodded, while taking a sip of her wine.

'As far as I am able to translate, we have the choice of beetroot, a spicy sour soup and mushroom.'

'When in Rome, do as the Romans do. I'll try the beetroot soup.'

'And for your main?'

'How about the beef Rasputin?'

'I admire your spirit of adventure.'

'What about you?'

'I'll try the mushroom soup and follow with the lamb kebab.'

Buchanan looked up from the menu and in the mirror on the wall behind Street. He saw the waiter make a beeline to a group at a table at the other end of the restaurant. He leaned over one guest in particular and, to Buchanan's eye, looked like he was whispering something in his ear.

The guest had the shoulders and neck of a rugby player and a head as bald as a billiard ball. Two heads turned and looked directly at Buchanan. As they did the waiter nodded at Buchanan's table. The guest said something to the waiter, who nodded again. The guest pushed his chair back and stood up from his table and made his way over to Buchanan and Street. A professional wrestler thought Buchanan, as he watched him approach their table. He walked with the rolling gait of an aged sailor, a walking mountain.

Buchanan slowly shook his head at Street as the man mountain approached and placed his hand on Buchanan's shoulder. Instantly he knew what a sheep feels as the talons of an eagle dig into its flesh. Buchanan continued to look at the man's reflection in the mirror, smiling as he recognised the face of the third man in Karen's photograph taken when they were in Amsterdam.

'Good evening,' he said, pushing down on Buchanan's shoulder while maintaining his talon-like grip. 'I understand you are looking for someone? Maybe I can help?'

Buchanan reached up to the man's wrist and wrenched it free from his shoulder and turned it palm up. Using the forefinger of his free hand, Buchanan traced the lines on the man's palm and shook his head. 'Not good, my friend. See here, this line is your lifeline, and look at this line, the fate line. Do you know what it means?'

'No.'

'You have had had a good life, got things your own way for many years. You've been very successful at your work, but,' he said, shaking his head slowly again, 'this line here, the fate line, see where it intersects with your lifeline? You are going to meet a stranger, someone from a northern country. This person is going to cause you a great deal of grief, it's all downhill from here my friend. If I were you, I'd give it all up and retire to your dacha in the country while you still can.'

The man pulled his hand away and sneered at Buchanan. 'You joke with me. No one has ever bested me.'

'Till now, perhaps. The palm never lies.'

'What do you want?'

'Let's start with your name. You do have one, don't you?'

'Georgi.'

'Where's your boss, Georgi – Ivan Reznikov?'

'He'll be here when he's ready.'

'Did you enjoy the awards dinner?'

'Why are you asking that?'

'It's a simple question, Georgi. I imagine a man of your intelligence should be able to answer it.'

Georgi shook his head. 'You really should be careful who you talk to and how you talk to them – Mr Policeman.'

'Excuse me,' said the waiter, as he walked off to greet a new arrival.

'Ah, I see your boss has just arrived,' said Buchanan. 'How about you go and introduce us? I'm Detective Chief Inspector Buchanan, and my friend here is Detective Sergeant Street.'

'Round one to me,' said Buchanan to Street as Giorgi went over to Reznikov's table. He watched with interest as Georgi explained about the purpose of the people seated at the far table. After much gesticulation and shrugging, Georgi returned to Buchanan's table.

'Mr Reznikov asks, would you join him for dinner?'

Buchanan nodded at Reznikov. 'Come lass, round two.'

'Is this your first visit to this restaurant, Inspector?' asked Reznikov in a deep baritone voice, as the waiter pulled out two chairs for Buchanan and Street at the table.

'A friend of mine recommended this place for really good Russian food and live music.'

'They were absolutely right,' said Reznikov. 'The borscht and solyanka are to die for. I'm pleased you choose to join us.'

'Are you sure we won't be interfering in your evening?' asked Street.

'Not at all, come experience true Russian hospitality,' he said, passing Street a menu.

'We've already ordered,' said Buchanan.

'What are you having?'

'I chose the beetroot soup and the beef Rasputin,' said Street.

'Good choice. And you, my friend,' he asked Buchanan, 'what did you choose?'

'Mushroom soup and the shashlik.'

'And to drink? You are drinking, aren't you?'

'Beer and wine,' said Street.

'What? You come to a Russian restaurant and you are not drinking vodka?'

'Yuri,' he said, to the ever-present waiter, 'bring us a bottle of Snow Queen and five glasses.'

Street shook her head. 'Not for me, thanks.'

'Why not?' said Reznikov, looking disappointed.

'I'm pregnant.'

Buchanan looked at her. 'Why didn't you say? I'd never have brought you here if I'd known.'

'I'm a big girl, I can look after myself.'

'Well, we'll just have to drink to your health,' said Reznikov.

A toast to Street's health was drunk, followed by one for the baby and a third to mother Russia.

'Mr Reznikov,' began Buchanan, 'this visit isn't all pleasure. I do have some questions to ask you.'

Reznikov nodded as he sipped on his soup. 'I know that. What do you want to ask?'

'You were at the Excellence in Industry awards dinner in Eastbourne last week?'

'Yes. I was there to receive my award.'

'What time was that, do you remember?'

Reznikov shook his head. 'It was late in the evening. Check with the organisers, I'm sure they will tell you.'

'Were you with anyone?'

'I was with hundreds of people, it was a very busy evening.'

'How about members of the syndicate?'

Reznikov stared straight at Buchanan. 'That's none of your business.'

'Why did you ask Guthrie Burtenshaw to bring you the documents he was working on for you?'

'I was flying to Amsterdam the next day. The papers had to be registered with my import export lawyer in Moscow. If you've ever tried to export goods from Russia, you would understand the chaos that comes from dealing with Russian bureaucracy.'

'Karl Mueller, did you invite him?'

'Why would I?'

'That was my next question.'

'There were lots of business people there that evening.'

'Garry Duncan, was he there as your guest?'

'I don't know anyone called Garry Duncan.'

'Oh, I think you do.'

'What does this Garry Duncan look like?'

'He's about five-foot ten, thin, dresses smartly. Has dark oily hair swept back and he wears narrow steel-rimmed glasses. He works in the Home Office.'

'I may have met him. I meet lots of government officials in my line of work.'

'Just what is your line of work?'

'I run an import-export business.'

'I understand you are arranging for your wife's fashion business to get a licence to export to the UK?'

'Ah, yes, yes, now I remember where I met Mr Duncan. He is one of the officials in the Home Office. He is helping me with my application to import to the UK.'

'And Karl Mueller, where does he fit in to your life?'

'Mr Buchanan, you ask a lot of questions.'

'It's my job to ask questions. Karl Mueller, Mr Reznikov?'

'He and my wife are having an affair.'

'Really? Could it be that you actually front for her operating as an FSB agent?'

Reznikov snorted. 'You've been reading too many James Bond stories, Inspector. Tatyana is a fashion designer, nothing more.'

'Her affair with Karl Mueller, did you condone it?'

'Inspector, there is a ten-year age difference between my wife and me. She has certain urges that only a younger man can satisfy. She'll tire of him and come home begging me to forgive her.'

'She hasn't already done that?'

'What do you mean?'

'You haven't heard about Karl Mueller?'

'Heard what?'

'He's dead. Committed suicide the evening of the awards dinner.'

'Stupid man.'

'Are you trying to get me to believe you didn't know about his death? It was in most of the newspapers.'

'I don't read your newspapers, they're all rubbish.'

'Did you see Karl Mueller that evening?'

'I don't remember.'

'Try, Mr Reznikov, dig deep into your memory of the events of the awards evening last week.'

'I may have seen him at some point during the evening.'

'About nine o'clock perhaps?'

Reznikov shrugged. 'It's possible.'

'Where did you meet with Guthrie Burtenshaw?'

'What do you mean, where did I meet Burtenshaw?'

'You asked him to bring you the papers for your lawyer.'

'Outside. It was private, no one's business but mine.'

'Was it just the two of you?'

'No, your Queen and her husband were there. Of course, we were alone – I just told you it was private.'

'So, you simply called Burtenshaw and asked him to bring you the papers he was preparing for you? When did you call him?'

Reznikov thought for a moment, 'It was before the awards ceremony, probably about eight.'

'Why didn't you do it during the day?'

'I was going to Amsterdam the next day and I thought if the papers were ready I could take them with me.'

'Why not go to Moscow with the papers?'

'I'm no longer welcome in Moscow, I told my lawyer to meet me in Amsterdam.'

'Where did you ask Burtenshaw to meet with you?'

'I told you, outside.'

'Where exactly?'

'Outside where people smoke.'

'How was he to let you know when he'd arrived?'

'When I called him, he said he would be there within thirty minutes. I simply went outside and waited for him.'

'Was he there when you went out?'

'No, he was late.'

'And you went out on your own?'

'Yes, I told you that already.'

'How many people were out on the deck smoking?'

'I don't know.'

'Try, Mr Reznikov.'

'Six, seven maybe.'

'How about Karl Mueller? Was he out there?'

'No, not when I went out.'

'Did he come out after you?'

'Yes.'

'Did he say anything to you?'

Reznikov shook his head. 'The slob couldn't say much to anyone. He was drunk, drugged – or both.'

'Did you say anything to him?'

'No.'

'Did he talk to any of the smokers?'

'He was in no state to talk to anyone. He staggered over to the railing, knelt on the seat and vomited over the railing.'

'What did you do next?'

'I went back inside; the ceremony was about to start. After the presentation I went back out to meet Burtenshaw.'

'Was Mueller still there when you met up with Burtenshaw?'

'I think so – yes, he was. When Burtenshaw arrived, he said hello to Karl. Karl looked up, shook his head and leaned forward as if he was trying to focus. He mumbled something then leaned back staring at the raindrops blowing off the roof.'

'How much time did you spend with Burtenshaw?'

'Not more than ten minutes. He made a remark about Karl needing to look after himself or he might have an accident and hurt himself. He then handed me a large manila envelope with the documents. I peeked inside, I didn't want them to get wet, said thank you and went back inside.'

'And Karl Mueller and Guthrie Burtenshaw were still outside when you went back inside?'

'Yes. Inspector, I reckon you are an intelligent man and have already put two and two together and have decided that poor Karl probably leaned over the railing one time too many. Am I correct?'

'That is one possibility, except for one small detail.'

'And what is that small detail?'

'When he was found, he had a rope round his neck. Are you sure you didn't take him for a walk? Maybe to help him sober up a bit?'

'No. Have you thought about asking Burtenshaw if he took Karl for a walk to sober up?'

'That won't be possible. Guthrie Burtenshaw died yesterday afternoon from a heart attack.'

'How sad for you, Inspector. Your only possible killer dead.'

♦

'What did Stephen say when you broke the good news?' said Buchanan, as they walked down Beauchamp Place.

'I'm not pregnant. One of us had to stay sober, I just said what came into my mind at the time.'

'Oh.'

'Disappointed?'

Buchanan was quiet for a few steps. 'I suppose I am. For a moment I was going to be a grandfather. Ah well, that's life. What did you think about the meal?' he asked, as they entered the Knightsbridge underground station.

'Service was helpful and very friendly, though I wonder how much of that was because we were sitting with Reznikov. You seemed to enjoy the music, I thought it was a bit too loud.'

'Live music was just perfect for me – I didn't find it too loud. It reminded me of the ceilidhs we used to have back home in Scotland. I realise it wasn't cheap, but that's what you pay when you want authenticity. All in all, I thought it was worth it. Just hope the ACC does as well when I put in my expense claim.'

'How much of what Reznikov said can we believe?' asked Street, as the train rattled on its way to Eastbourne.

'He definitely was at the awards dinner, he definitely met Burtenshaw to collect the papers, and Karl Mueller was present at the meeting, and most likely unable to fend for himself. Karl Mueller knew both men so probably would have been amenable to the suggestion of taking a short walk. The question that remains is: which one of them helped poor Mueller over the rail?'

♦

'Good morning, Jill. You're in early,' said Buchanan. 'If I'd known you'd be here I'd have brought you a coffee.'

'I already did that,' she said, pointing to her cup on the desk. 'Wanted to get the interviews with Reznikov and Tatyana typed up before we get started with the day. Also, Claeys called.'

'What did he have to say?'

'They are dropping the investigation into Irene Adler's disappearance.'

'Did you tell him what we've found out?'

'Yes. He said he wasn't surprised. I told him we were coming over to Amsterdam tomorrow to interview Irene Adler.'

'What did he say to that?'

'He gave me a name and contact details for an Amsterdam police inspector who may help us. His name is Biermann, Inspector Klaus Biermann of the DNR,' she said, looking down at her notebook. 'The DNR is the Dutch national police force. Claeys is also going to send over all the evidence collected in the cabin.'

'A bit late for that now. Still, Karl's phone should be in there somewhere, maybe we can have a deeper look at its memory.'

'And prove you correct about it being Karl who ran you off the road?'

'There is that. Can I have Biermann's number? Better let him know we're coming.'

'You might ask him to detain Irene Adler, just to make sure she's there when we arrive.'

'A very good idea, thanks.'

15

'Got your passport?' asked Buchanan, as Street climbed into the car.

'Yes, in my pocket.'

'OK, let's go see what Irene Adler has to say for herself.'

'I would have liked to have seen her face when Biermann knocked on her cabin this morning, bet she was surprised.'

'Bet she'll be even more surprised to see me.'

♦

The taxi dropped them at the ship's gangway. Buchanan paid the driver while Street went over to the security guard and introduced herself, then waited for Buchanan to join her.

'The guard is calling guest services to have them let Biermann know we have arrived.'

'Good. Ever thought of going on a cruise?' said Buchanan, looking up at the side of the *Viking Star*.

'Stephen and I have talked about it. But with trying to save for a deposit for a house, we just can't afford one right now.'

Their conversation was interrupted by the arrival of a uniformed policeman. 'Inspector Buchanan?'

'Yes.'

'I'm Sergeant Smuts. Inspector Biermann is waiting for you in the main lounge on deck seven. If you'll follow me, I will take you to him.'

Buchanan walked behind Street as she followed the sergeant up the gangway. He stopped at the top, talked with a uniformed ship's officer, then beckoned Buchanan and Street to follow. They rode the lift to deck seven, then walked forward to the lounge.

Biermann and Adler were seated by a window on the port side, obviously deep in conversation. They stood as Buchanan and

Street, walking behind Sergeant Smuts, approached from the entrance doors.

'She looks a bit worried,' whispered Street to Buchanan.

'And so she should be,' he replied.

'Good morning, Inspector,' said Biermann, extending his hand. 'Klaus Biermann.'

'Good morning, Klaus. Jack Buchanan, and this is Detective Sergeant Jill Street.'

'Miss Adler you know,' said Biermann.

'Yes indeed. How are you, Irene?'

'I'm fine, thank you.'

'Would you like something to drink, Inspector?' asked Biermann.

'Coffee, if there is any.'

Biermann turned to Smuts. 'Coffees for the visitors, Sergeant.'

'Enjoying your holiday, Irene?' asked Buchanan.

'Yes, thanks. But before you begin, can I apologise for putting you and Karen through the ordeal of thinking I'd been murdered? It was wrong I know, but I was quite desperate at the time.'

Buchanan nodded. 'Accepted. But it would have been better if you had confided in me at the time. Are you aware of what has happened to Karl?'

'He's dead?'

'Yes.'

'When was this?'

'Last week.'

'Oh – how did he die?'

'The official line is he committed suicide while the balance of his mind was disturbed.'

'Really? I find that difficult to believe. Karl was the most single-minded, self-centred man I knew. Suicide? I don't think so, Inspector. Please – tell me what really happened.'

'We're still waiting for the autopsy results. I'm sorry, that's all I can say at this time.'

She shrugged and leaned back in her chair.

Smuts returned and stood waiting for Buchanan to finish speaking. 'The drinks will be here in a minute.'

'Thank you, Jan,' said Biermann. 'Inspector Buchanan, we will leave you while you interview Miss Adler. I have some phone calls to make, I will rejoin you in half an hour.'

'Thanks" said Buchanan, as Biermann and Smuts made their exit over to the far side of the lounge.

'Irene,' began Buchanan, 'will you start from the beginning and tell us what really happened on the night you did your disappearing act?'

'It started – well I suppose it started when Karl and I first met, but that's not really pertinent to why you're here. Anyway, when I started working for Karl it was all proper and above board. He had an office in Eastbourne and I would show up for work each morning, just like any secretary would.'

'What was he doing? What was his line of work?'

'Consulting for local government agencies. Then one day, about five years ago, he landed a consulting contract for a Russian businessman.'

'Do you remember the name of this Russian businessman?'

'How could I not? It was Ivan Reznikov.'

'Any particular reason you would remember the name?'

'It was his wife that I remember the most.'

'Why is that?'

'Karl became smitten with her. They were having an affair right under her husband's nose.'

'Did he know about the affair?'

'That was the bit that puzzled me at the time. I'm sure he did,' she said, a smile growing on her face. 'But Ivan got his own back.'

Street looked up from taking notes and leaned forward, eager to hear.

'Ivan was taking care of Karl's wife, if you understand my meaning.'

'I do understand your meaning,' said Buchanan. 'Do you know much about their relationship?'

'There wasn't much of a relationship. When Ivan needed to get out of the limelight or to meet someone private, he would go to Eastbourne and stay with Karl's wife.'

'So, he wasn't living with her?'

'No, Ivan has a luxury flat somewhere in west London. I believe it's near the Russian Embassy.'

'What did Karl have to say about his wife and Ivan Reznikov?'

'I don't know, he didn't talk to me about it. I simply would answer his phone calls. Sometimes she would call me to find out if Karl was likely to be home during the week.'

'Must have been difficult for you, being cheated on by your employer and having his wife call to see if the coast was clear for her to cheat on him?'

'I'd lost all illusions of ever having a meaningful relationship with Karl by then. When I lost my first baby, Karl was quite attentive. When it happened again a few months ago – he more or less dismissed me from his life. I simply became a safe port in a storm.'

'Can we discuss why you went to such an elaborate subterfuge in pretending to be murdered and point the blame at Karl?'

'I used to listen in on his phone calls, but that's not quite all I did. Being his PA, I used to take care of everything associated with running the office, and this included mobile phones. One morning he showed up at the office in a right state. He'd been out celebrating a customer paying him early, or something like that. He showed up at the office, much the worse for wear, and told me how he'd been mugged and had his phone taken. As his PA, it was down to me to organise a replacement for him. He said to get one for myself as well, since I'd been using my own quite a bit for business.'

'Perfectly normal solution,' said Street.

'Yes, it was. I went to the phone shop and ordered two smart phones and had them put on the same account. What I didn't realise till later was, when someone called his phone, my phone rang at the same time. At first this was a novelty, I was taking his messages and doing what a PA should. I later realised he just ignored his incoming calls and had his phone set to call-forward on no reply to my phone.'

'What about your own phone?' asked Street.

'I'd just leave it turned off at work. I'd simply turn it on if I wanted to make a personal call.'

'Did you answer all his calls?' asked Street.

'No. By then I knew the numbers of his friends and the numbers for the clients he was working for. Others? I'd just let those just ring through to his voicemail.'

'Did you listen to his messages?'

'Yes. After all it was my job to look after him.'

'So, what led you to take such drastic action?' asked Buchanan.

'It was several things. I knew Karl was working with Ivan on some sort of deal where Ivan was arranging to have Tatyana's fashions imported into the UK. Karl was making all the necessary connections'

'How was he doing that? After all he was just a consultant.'

'He has contacts, people he knew from his university days.'

'Do you remember their names?'

'Yes. The lawyer's name was Guthrie Burtenshaw, QC, he has an office in London and another somewhere in Eastbourne. There's also someone he knows who works in the Home Office, a Garry Duncan.'

'That all sounds above board,' said Street. 'What went wrong?'

'Karl went wrong,' Irene said, looking round. 'I suppose you know already, but the business of importing Tatyana's fashions was a front for smuggling drugs into the UK.'

'How did you find that out?' asked Buchanan.

'I was angry with him, you know what I mean – him and Tatyana?' She shook her head and took another sip of her drink. 'But what annoyed me was the fact he really was in love with her, and she with him.'

'Oh, that must have really hurt,' said Street.

'It certainly did at first. But the more it went on, the more intrigued I became. I had become the jilted lover, something totally new for me to experience. I suppose that was when my friendship with Mary grew.'

'Mary, Karl's wife?' said Buchanan.

'Yes, strange that – anyway, I would listen in to all of his messages – I know, I know, I was jealous.'

'Did you ever confront Tatyana?'

'No, by then there wasn't much point. When I came to my senses it dawned on me I'd lost him years ago.'

'So sad,' said Street. 'What did you do next?'

'When it finally dawned on me that Karl and I were no longer a couple, I decided I'd had enough and made up my mind to end the relationship on my terms.'

'This holiday on the cruise ship?' said Street.

'That and other things. The final straw was when I realised Karl was going to cheat Ivan. I sensed something dreadful was likely to happen, call it woman's intuition. Especially since I googled Ivan Reznikov's name and to my surprise found he had his own Wikipedia page.'

'Really?' said Street. 'What did it say about him?'

'It described his childhood, time in the military and – his association with Vladimir Putin …'

'Vladimir Putin – the Russian president?' said Street.

'The very same,' said Irene.

'You are much better out of that mess,' said Biermann, who'd just returned and was sitting beside her.

'Thanks,' said Irene, looking at him and smiling. 'Tatyana didn't realise I was listening to his messages and phone calls.'

'Do any of them stand out in your memory?' asked Buchanan.

'Yes. A few weeks ago, she called and said they needed to be careful, Ivan was suspicious.'

'But you said her husband knew about their relationship, why would they have to be careful?' asked Street.

'She and Karl were going to double-cross Ivan on the drugs deal.'

'How were they going to do that?'

'Not everyone who graduates from university goes on to be upstanding pillars of society, Inspector. I think when Karl realised just how much money could be made from dealing drugs big time, it just went to his head. A week after he and Ivan had made their arrangements Karl started to scour his list of contacts. With the promise of much to gain he set about re-establishing contact with his former university contacts.'

'The same students he used to sell to?' asked Buchanan.

'No, not the students. Karl went after the dealers he used to buy from. At first, he found it hard going as most of them were either in jail or dead from ingesting their own products. After a couple of false starts he managed to work his way back up the supply line to a couple of dealers who said they were prepared to work with him.'

'That was risky – how could he trust them?' asked Street.

'That was Karl, blinded with the thoughts of riches beyond his imagination.'

'So, how was he going to work the deal and not have Ivan breathing down his neck?'

'The deal was, as I understood it, Ivan would take care of the supply to the UK and Karl was responsible for the distribution. I think he and Ivan had agreed upon a price based on the delivery cost, plus a fifty percent split in the profit after sales. Ivan knew how much had been delivered and what the street price was, so it was a case of simple maths and percentages.'

'But I don't quite see how Karl was going to cheat Ivan?' said Street.

Irene shrugged. 'I suppose the answer to that question died with Karl.'

'Other than the two names you have already mentioned; do you remember any more names that might help us solve this case?'

'There were some strange texts. No names were ever mentioned, but I always knew who it was though. The phone would buzz, and the display would be addressed to Icarus. When Karl replied to the caller he would text back someone called Daedalus.'

'So, Karl was Icarus. Could Daedalus have been Ivan?'

'I suppose so, but why use those names?'

Buchanan smiled. 'It's an old Greek myth. King Minos invited Daedalus to build a maze for his pet, a minotaur. Some children managed to abduct the minotaur and Daedalus and his son Icarus were jailed for assumed complicity. Daedalus designed two sets of wings with feathers attached to frames. He and his son flew up into the sky. Daedalus had warned Icarus not to fly too close to the sun. But unfortunately for Icarus, he disregarded his father's advice and flew too high. The heat of the sun melted the wax that held the feathers to the frame and Icarus fell into the sea and died.'

'But,' said Irene, 'if Karl was this Icarus and Ivan was Daedalus, who is Minos?'

Buchanan shook his head. 'That's just another piece of this jigsaw for us to discover.'

'This story about Icarus, are you saying that is what has happened to Karl? He got too big for his boots?'

'Karl was found hanging from a railing at the end of Eastbourne pier. When he went over, the tide was in.'

'That was just like Karl, always reaching for the sun.'

'I've asked you this before, but now you've had time to reflect, do you think Ivan Reznikov could have killed Karl?'

'All I knew was Tatyana was very insistent that Karl be careful, and to make sure he was never anywhere alone with Ivan, only if others were with him.'

'There has been a mention of a syndicate. Do you know any of the names in the syndicate?'

She looked at the froth on her coffee, took a sip, then said, 'I once saw a list of names on an email from Reznikov and asked Karl about them. He was quite evasive at first then said something about them being prospective clients. But, you see, there was a problem with that, three of the names were already known to me: Duncan, Reznikov and of course Karl himself.'

'What about Burtenshaw?'

'No, I'd have recognised that name,' said Irene, as Smuts rejoined them and sat opposite her.

'Do you remember the other names on the list?'

'No. But I may still have the email on my phone.' She saw the questioning look on Buchanan's face. 'It wasn't only our phone calls that were connected, emails as well. Let me have a look.'

'Inspector – Jack,' said Biermann, while Irene scrolled through her emails, 'maybe we can work together on this? Amsterdam has, unfortunately, quite a reputation for drug smuggling.'

Buchanan took the photo out of his pocket that Karen had taken while they were in Amsterdam and passed it to Biermann. 'Recognise anyone?'

Biermann leaned back and nodded. 'Two of them. The one in the middle is Ivan Reznikov, the one on the left is Giorgi Borislav, a Bulgarian gangster, don't recognise the third one. Borislav is well known to us for his involvement in drug smuggling, one amongst many evils.'

At the name of Borislav, Irene looked up. 'He's mentioned in the list of names on my email.'

'What are the other names?' asked Buchanan.

'Tajali, Atkins and Ansari.'

Buchanan shook his head. 'They're not familiar to me. How about you, Jill?'

'Same here. We could run them through the PNC when we get back to the office.'

'The third one's name, Klaus, is Karl Mueller,' said Buchanan, pointing to the photograph. 'He's currently residing in the Eastbourne morgue.'

'That's not good. I take it he's your former employer, Miss Adler?'

'Yes.'

'How did he die, Jack?' asked Biermann.

'As I said, he was found hanging from Eastbourne pier. We don't have a conclusive diagnosis yet, forensics are overstretched and underfunded. All the police doctor will commit to is heart failure.'

Biermann gave an understanding nod at Buchanan's evasiveness of response. 'Police budgets are always under attack, you'd think that those who finance and make the funding decisions for our police forces were working for the other side. I read last week that the UK police budget is to be cut by seven-hundred million pounds by 2020. Just how the hell are you supposed to fight the current epidemic of the drug culture with its knifings and shootings?'

'Just keep doing our job, Klaus. Putting one foot in front of the other, day after day, week after week, month after month, plodding along shovelling up the detritus left from what some call the *it's my life, and my body. I'll do what I damn well please with it,* enlightened society,' said Buchanan.

279

'What garbage! I'd like to take some of those naïve, mentally-blind morons to see what happens to families when drugs and alcohol takes over the life of someone in the family. I'd like them to see how children suffer, sometimes growing up to replicate what they saw their elders do.'

'Inspector Buchanan,' said Irene, 'is there anything else you wish to ask me? I'm supposed to be going ashore for a tour of the city.'

'When will you be back?'

She shrugged. 'I was going to have lunch, then just wander round the city. If you remember I was preoccupied the last time I was here.'

Buchanan turned to Street and asked, 'What time is our flight back?'

'Eight-twenty this evening.'

'Klaus, could we avail ourselves of someone in your office to type up Miss Adler's statement?'

'Certainly. I was going to invite you both back for lunch and give you a bigger picture of the smuggling problem we have here in The Netherlands.'

'Irene, how about we meet you back onboard here at about five o'clock? I should have your statement typed up by then for you to sign.'

'That would be fine.'

'I can drive you back, Jack,' said Biermann, smiling at Irene. 'I may have some further questions for Miss Adler.'

She smiled back and said, 'The ship will be here for two days, I've nothing planned for tomorrow except a lie-in. How about we meet at lunch time? You could ask your questions then.'

Biermann smiled. 'I'll be here for twelve?'

'Lovely. I'll book a table for two, so we're not disturbed.'

Biermann stood, smiled and bowed. 'Ready, Inspector Buchanan, Sergeant Street? Sergeant Smuts will drive us to my temporary office.'

'Where is your main office?' asked Street.

'The DNR are based in Utrecht, but we use outlying offices when we are working on cases. Currently my office is on the fifth floor of the Burgwallen police station.'

♦

Street and Buchanan followed Biermann down the corridor and into his office. They waited patiently at the door as Biermann cleared two chairs and moved them into position in front of the desk. 'Please, take a seat while I go and find someone to type up Miss Adler's statement.'

'He's being very helpful,' said Buchanan.

'Did you notice how he was looking at Irene?'

'Puppy-dog eyes?'

'I think he likes her, I wonder if he's married?'

Buchanan looked at Biermann's desk and at a double wide photo frame adjacent to a single photo of a young woman. Buchanan picked up the double wide frame and showed it to Street just as Biermann walked in to the office.'

'Ah, my daughters, Silvia and Tasha; sadly, my wife passed away four years ago. Those two are the joy of my life.'

'You never remarried?' asked Street.

'Who'd marry a policeman my age? Especially one already with two daughters, beautiful as they may be.'

'You might be surprised one day,' said Street. 'Most women I know would love to have two beautiful daughters and a husband who has a steady job, especially someone like you who obviously loves his work – oh, sorry – not me, I'm already married to a policeman.'

'He's a very lucky man, what's his name?'

'Stephen.'

'And he's also a policeman?'

'Yes, we even get to work together – sometimes, don't we?' she said, smiling at Buchanan.

'Lucky you. If you'll give me your notes, I'll have them typed up for you.'

'Thanks,' said Street, as she handed Bierman her notebook.

When Biermann was out of earshot, Buchanan asked, 'What was all that about, children and marriage? Are you still thinking about your comments of the other night at Solyanka?'

'No, not at all. Call it a hunch, woman's intuition, but I think Biermann has fallen for Irene.'

'And you get that from – what?'

'He's the father of two young girls, he has a good steady job, he said his wife passed away four years ago, ergo he is single. Irene is single, would like children and is about the same age as he is. A match made in heaven. Didn't you notice how intense they were in conversation this morning when we arrived? And that nonsense about him interviewing Irene tomorrow, table for two, bet it's his day off.'

'You really think that? I just assumed he was questioning her about why we were there.'

Street smiled. 'I just hope we get an invitation to a wedding.'

'Who's getting married?' asked Biermann, as he entered his office.

'Just someone I met recently,' said Street.

'Oh. Well – I hope they have a long and happy life together. Now, Jill. Your interview should be typed in a few minutes. I've asked for it to be brought back here to my office when done, then I can take you to lunch.'

'Thanks, and my fingers thank you.'

'So, this wretched business of drug smuggling we Dutch are saddled with,' said Biermann, relaxing into his chair. 'I'll give you four recent examples that happened in just one year,' he began.

'The first: on the second of May, a Rotterdam port inspector was arrested on cocaine charges, in connection with an attempt to smuggle two hundred kilos of cocaine into the Netherlands. Our investigations discovered he had access to large areas of the port and had allowed criminals to enter. The cocaine was concealed in a coal shipment.

'Second: in July, a former customs officer was convicted for his part in the smuggling of three thousand-four hundred kilos of cocaine in shipping containers. His share in the deal would have amounted to three and a half million Euros.

'Third: in November, cocaine worth over twenty-five million Euros were found hidden in a sea-container refrigeration unit. The cocaine was hidden in amongst boxes of fruit. All six men involved are currently in restricted custody.

'And fourth: in December, the captain of a trawler was given seven years for cocaine trafficking. The crime he was found guilty of was about the transportation of seven hundred kilos of cocaine. The street value of just these four events comes to somewhere in the region of one hundred and thirty billion Euros.'

'Whew, that's a fortune,' said Street.

'It's much, much more than that. Just think if that amount of money was legitimately spent by the public on goods and services in the shops. Then think about these items that have been purchased, they would all have had sales tax levied on them. Millions of Euros in much needed cash would be raised. Factories could be working overtime to supply the public needs. Just think of the teachers, nurses, and doctors who could be trained and made available to society. Hospitals, schools, parks for children to play in could be built. Those are just a few items that come to mind. Of course, these are some of our successes, for every shipment that gets stopped, many more get through. It's almost a waste of my time chasing these scoundrels. What does it matter?'

'Can I tell you a story?' asked Street.

'Certainly.'

'A father and daughter were walking along a beach at high tide. They came to a place where a shoal of starfish was beached and drying out. The daughter bent down and picked one up and threw the starfish into the water. Her father said that it was a futile gesture, it just wouldn't make any difference, there were thousands of them. The daughter looked up at her dad and said, *It made a difference to that one.*'

Biermann nodded while picking up the photo of his daughters. 'You are so right. Even if we only stop one shipment, it will be one less for the demons to use to destroy the lives of those addicted to the stuff.'

'You do have lovely daughters,' said Street.

'They're my raison d'être,' he said, looking away from the photo, a tear in his eye. Do you have children, Jack?'

Buchanan smiled and looked at Street. 'Jill is the closest my wife and I will get to having children. Jill's parents died when she was young and since we have no children of our own, we've sort of become family.'

'That's lovely,' said Biermann.

There was a knock at the door and the typist brought Irene's statement and handed it to Biermann. 'Thanks, Trudy.'

Biermann glanced at the typewritten report and handed it to Buchanan. 'Those names that Irene, I mean, Miss Adler, mentioned, shall I have a look on our computer to see if they show anything?'

'Certainly,' said Buchanan, turning to Street. 'Did you write them down?'

She gave him a *do you think I was born yesterday* look. 'Yes, they are, Tajali, Atkins and Ansari.'

'I'll have a look at Reznikov while I'm at it,' said Biermann, as he studiously typed in the names.

Buchanan got up from his seat and walked over to the window. Down below in the street were police cars, motorcycles mixing with bicycles and many tourists. He reached into his jacket pocket and removed a well-mangled tube of fruit gums. He slowly and carefully unwound the twisted foil wrapper and extracted a lemon gum. A memory from childhood popped into his head – what had happened to the blackcurrant gums? He was sure he remembered as a child sucking on them when he had a sore throat.

'Got them,' said Biermann.

Buchanan returned to his chair and waited for Biermann to begin his dissertation.

'The name Atkins comes up as a drug dealer living in Birmingham, in the UK. Harold James Atkins, born 17th April, 1958. His criminal career started at the age of eight when he was arrested with two other boys while breaking in to a sweet warehouse in east Birmingham. He received a short custodial sentence. He next appears as a getaway driver in a post office robbery. He then was caught pimping underage girls. Ten years ago, he was caught in a police dragnet for drug dealing and prostitution. He's currently out of jail on licence. Tajali has a similar profile and is based in the Manchester area, he also is currently out on parole. Ansari also has form. He is currently serving a ten-year sentence for GBH, drug dealing and gambling. He has five months to run on his current sentence. His area of operation was in Liverpool.'

'That's very interesting,' said Buchanan. 'With Mueller operating from London and his cohorts in Birmingham, Manchester and Liverpool he would have a huge area for distribution.'

'I've also had a look at Reznikov. Now there is a career gangster if ever there was one. 'He retired from the military and started an escort agency …'

'Ran an escort agency?' said Street. 'How does that make him a career gangster?'

'I will explain,' said Biermann. 'When the report says *escort agency,* it doesn't mean he provided girls for visiting businessmen. What he was providing was an armed protection limousine service to top echelon businessmen and politicians, including Vladimir Putin.

The service even extended to criminal leaders, giving him a direct line to those who ran the criminal underworld. From the escort agency he branched out into arms dealing and, along with the arms, came drugs and people trafficking.'

'Is he still doing that?' asked Street.

'No. He was becoming an issue for the establishment so has gone into voluntary exile in the UK.'

'By the establishment, you mean the Kremlin and, by that association, you mean Putin?' said Street.

Biermann nodded. 'Before he became so influential, he and Putin worked in St Petersburg university looking at students for their suitability to become KGB candidates. Apparently, there was one student in particular that caught Ivan's attention, her name was Tatyana.'

'The same Tatyana?' said Street.

'The very same. She is Putin's niece. Putin was furious with Reznikov and threatened him with dire consequences if he mistreated her.'

'Another reason to go into exile,' said Street.

'Apparently, to cross swords with Putin is to be the holder of a poisoned chalice. A great many people who have passed through his web of activity have come to a sticky end.'

'Like who?' asked Street.

'Though there is no direct evidence to prove Putin's involvement, government agencies say that the Russian and Bulgarian mafia was used as an agency to enforce Kremlin doctrine by assassinating people after the *Project Moscow* property deal went sour. These included such notorieties as Boris Berezovsky, Alexander Litvinenko, a former FSB officer who defected to the UK, Roman Tsepov, who was making money from gambling licenses and acting as an intermediary between businesses and Putin, and, more recently, the attempt on exiled spy Sergei Skripal, living in England.'

'This is nuts, Klaus,' said Buchanan. 'All these facts may be true, but – I think my investigation is being led down the garden path. Down a rabbit hole and away from the truth of what we should be investigating. If you don't mind, I think it's time we returned to the UK, and to where the real crime is happening.' He looked at the clock on the wall. 'In fact I think we should be getting to the ship for Irene to sign her statement.'

'Oh, there's still plenty of time,' said Biermann. 'Let's have lunch first? Tell you what, why don't we invite Irene, I mean Miss Adler, out to lunch? There's a couple of questions I'd like to ask her as well.'

Street looked at Buchanan and smiled.

'If it's all right with you, Klaus, I'd be happy for you to take Miss Adler out to lunch. But this investigation has gone too far off the tracks to take time going out for lunch. I've got collars to feel. We can make our way to the airport and a flight back to the UK.'

'Shall I check first and see if there are any flights?' asked Street.

'Ah, hadn't thought of that,' said Buchanan, 'go ahead.'

'In the meantime,' said Biermann 'I'll arrange a car for you.'

Buchanan turned and looked at Street.'

She shook her head. 'Nothing, we're too late.'

'Great,' said Biermann, 'lunch it will be.'

♦

As before, Smuts drove up to the ship's gangway and parked.

'Wait here with Smuts,' said Biermann. 'I'll go and see if Irene is ready.'

'You've already asked her?' said Buchanan.

'Yes, shortly after we arrived back at the station.'

Biermann saw a look of confusion on Street's face. 'I have her mobile number,' he explained.

'Oh, smart policeman,' replied Street.

'Just doing my job. I'll be right back. We can have lunch then I can drop you off at the airport.'

'Just look at her,' said Street, as Biermann escorted Irene Adler down the gangway. 'She looks like she's dressed for a summer tea at Buckingham Palace.'

Buchanan squeezed up against the door of the police car to provide room for Street and Irene Adler to sit beside him on the back seat. He looked forwards and could see the smile on Biermann's face in the mirror.

16

'I think you are right about Biermann and Irene Adler,' said Buchanan, as they waited to be called to board their flight back to Gatwick.

'You noticed.'

'How could I not? They were like a couple of love-struck puppies. Did you see them holding hands under the table?'

'I saw,' said Street. 'So, what's got you thinking we're being led down the garden path on this case?'

'From experience I've discovered that when you meet no resistance in an investigation, it is usually because you are on the wrong track or, more likely, someone is trying to divert your attention away from the truth of a situation. Remember my example of the killdeer bird with the broken wing?'

'Remind me.'

'The killdeer is a bird found in parts of Canada and the USA. It makes its nest on the ground near human habitation. When a mother killdeer senses danger from some animal or person it will drag its leg and pretend to have a broken wing, then it will try to lead the predator away from the nest with the young – a trick sometimes employed by other birds.'

'So, by using your example, who or what is the killdeer?'

'Duncan, that's who.'

'That's not going to go down well back home.'

'Nonetheless, he's my choice for now. By the time we get back to Eastbourne,' Buchanan said, looking at her boarding card, 'it will be too late to follow up today. Monday morning, before you do anything else, I would like you to do a full background check on Garry Duncan.'

'Will do,' replied Street. 'How far back do you want me to go?'

'As far back as there are records.'

289

♦

'What time did you come in?' asked Buchanan, placing a large coffee on Street's desk.

'Thanks,' said Street, taking the lid off the cup and adding a sachet of sugar. 'About six-thirty. Stephen's got the day off and has gone fishing with his dad, so here I am.'

'Find anything yet on our boy?'

'Just basic school stuff.'

'Elucidate me.'

'Big word for eight-fifteen?'

'I'm in a good mood. What do you have?'

'He was born in 1965 in Southampton. Mother was a schoolteacher, dad worked for Lloyds. Parents divorced when he was eight, father died a year later in a car crash. His mother never got remarried but did have a lasting relationship with a headteacher she worked with, who wasn't married at the time. Young Garry never took to the new man in his mother's life and became withdrawn. There are some reports of him being caught shoplifting, mostly sweets from the newsagent. Sort of thing lots of kids get up to. It did earn him the nickname of magpie.'

'So sad,' said Buchanan, 'happens too often these days, fathering without responsibilities. What next?'

'Next, young Garry was shipped off to private boarding school while his mother and her partner went on archaeology field trips round the south of England. Garry would come home on holidays but the relationship with his mother's partner stayed frozen. He did make what appears to be a lasting friendship at school with – are you ready for this?'

'Go on.'

'Karl Mueller.'

'Strange kind of friendship, since we know what happened during their years at university. Anything show up on the PNC?'

'Not very much. Mueller seems to be the instigator of mischief in the friendship. The only information on file is a couple of reports about the usual teenage pub brawls, and a couple of incidents where there was a suspicion of them supplying drugs at parties.'

'Nothing about a fight at the end of university?'

Street shook her head. 'Looks like it was never reported.'

'Did Stephen and Morris find an address for Bridget Standish?'

'Should have. Let me have a look in the file. Ah, yes here it is. Hmm.'

'What does "hmm" mean?' asked Buchanan.

'It means they have a lovely house in Hankham.'

'Hankham?'

'At the top of Gallows Lane in the village of Westham.'

'That's not far from where our new house is. Shall we go visit, you drive?'

Street parked on the Standishes' wide driveway beside an empty horsebox tethered to a Land-Rover Discovery.

Buchanan looked inside the horsebox and shrugged.

'What?' asked Street.

'Not long empty, those are fresh droppings on the floor.'

'Shall we try the front door?' said Street.

'By all means,' said Buchanan.

Street pressed the doorbell and knocked, with no response.

'Let's try round the side of the house,' said Buchanan. 'It's quite likely they have taken their horse round to its stable.'

'You're assuming it has a stable,' said Street, as she followed Buchanan through the open gate and along the side of the house.

Walking past the end of the house they saw that there was indeed a stable. It was one of three situated beside a large paddock. In the paddock were two people and presumably the horse that had just exited the horsebox.

As Buchanan and Street neared the paddock. the man holding the horse's bridle looked up, passed it to the other person and walked towards them. When he got to the fence he said, 'Can I help?'

'Detective Chief Inspector Buchanan and Detective Sergeant Street. Sorry to disturb you, we won't keep you long.'

'What's wrong?'

'Nothing is wrong. Can we start with your name, please?'

'John Standish, and that's my wife holding the horse. Do you wish to speak to her as well?'

'Yes please, Mr Standish,' said Buchanan.

'Yes, well, OK, I'll be right with you.'

Mr Standish returned to his wife and the horse. He said something to her and pointed at Buchanan and Street. She turned and stared at them, said something to her husband then led the horse into the stable.

'Nice horse,' said Street as they watched Mrs Standish.

'It's an Arabian,' said Buchanan. 'You can tell by their wide forehead and large eyes, short back and arched neck.'

'Interesting,' said Street, as Mr and Mrs Standish approached across the paddock.

'Inspector,' said Mr Standish, 'how can we help?'

'It's a small thing really. We understand your daughter has been prescribed epinephrine?'

Tears formed in Mrs Standish's wife's eyes. 'Bridget is highly allergic to nuts; the epinephrine was in case of emergencies.'

'Is she well? I understand she had an anaphylactic event a few weeks ago?'

'Yes, she's going to be fine. She's currently at a special clinic being treated for her allergies, we're hoping for a complete cure.'

'Can you explain the relationship between your family and Karl Mueller?' asked Buchanan.

The Standishes looked at each other then back at Buchanan. 'Karl is, was, my wife's cousin, Inspector,' said Mr Standish.

'He was the son of my wife's mother's sister. He was a likeable character, but we only ever saw one side of him. The horse you saw us put in the stall was his gift to Bridget, she is getting it ready to compete in dressage.'

'When was the last time you saw your cousin, Mrs Standish?'

'I suppose it was a few weeks ago. He stopped by to tell us he was working on a new deal.'

'Was that usual for him?' asked Street.

'I think he saw us as the family he never had and liked to get confirmation that all was well.'

'In what way?'

'We've been happily married for nineteen years,' said Mr Standish. 'I run a very successful business and of course there is Bridget, our beautiful daughter. Everything he never had.'

'Was he ever inappropriate towards your daughter?' asked Buchanan.

'No, never,' said Mrs Standish. 'He doted on her, hence the horse.'

'Horses, especially fine ones like your daughter's, don't come cheap,' said Buchanan.

'He was wealthy, money never seemed to be an issue for him.'

'Do you know if he had any friends?' asked Buchanan.

Mrs Standish shook her head. 'If he did, they were few and far between. Though there was one who sometimes would come along with him.'

'Could you describe him for me?' asked Buchanan.

'He was a quiet man. I think he was shy. About your height, Inspector, always seemed to be wearing the same grey suit,' said Mrs Standish. 'But quite slim, with dark greasy hair brushed back at the sides.'

'Do you know his name?'

'Karl only referred to him as Garry.'

'Mrs Standish, I understand there was an issue of your daughter's epinephrine going missing. Can you remember the details?'

'We always kept the epipen in the drawer of the side table in the front hall. That way everyone knew where it was if needed.'

'Everyone, Mrs Standish?' asked Buchanan.

She smiled. 'We had a piece of paper with a big red arrow pointing down at the drawer with the words *Epipen Here*. We reasoned if something went wrong anyone could find it.'

'A few weeks ago, when the pen went missing,' said Buchanan, 'was that before or after Karl's recent visit?'

'Just what are you implying, Inspector?' said Mrs Standish.

'A simple question. Did the pen go missing before or after Karl's last visit?'

She thought for a minute, Yes, I think it did.'

'Mrs Standish,' said Street. 'The last time Karl was here, was he alone?'

'No – he wasn't. His friend Garry was with him.'

'Can you remember if Garry was alone at any time?'

'Are you saying he took the epipen?'

'We're just making enquiries?'

'It's possible. I seem to remember we were all out at the paddock watching Bridget put her horse through its paces. We weren't watching out for Karl's friend.'

'Jill, can you show Mr and Mrs Standish a photo of Garry Duncan?' asked Buchanan.

'I think I should have a recent one on my phone,' she said, scrolling through her photo album. She stopped at a recent photo of Garry Duncan and showed it to Mr and Mrs Standish.

'Yes, that's him. Have you met him before?'

Buchanan smiled and said, 'Oh yes, we've certainly met Garry.'

17

'We have the lock, we have a key, now all we have to do is to find out if the key fits the lock,' said Buchanan, as Street drove them back to the office.

'You really think Duncan could be our killer?'

'I'm not saying that – yet. Where are Stephen and Morris?'

'They were investigating a couple of break-ins in Herstmonceux,' said Street. 'I talked to Stephen a few minutes ago and he said they were just about to head back to the office.'

'Well, in that case, since it's such a nice day, let's make a detour by the Castle Tearooms. While you drive I'll call Stephen and Morris and have them join us.'

♦

'Table for two?' asked the waitress, as Buchanan and Street entered the tea room.

'No,' said Street, 'we have two others joining us. That one in the corner would be fine if it's available?'

'Certainly. I'll be back to take your order when your friends arrive.'

'Do you remember our last visit here?' said Buchanan, as he made his way round the table to the back.

'How could I forget? That poor man nailed to the tree.'

'Yes, it was a bit gruesome, can you pass the menu?'

Buchanan stared across the table and out into the car park thinking about the last time they had been here and what transpired after the discovery of the body. At least the case had been successfully resolved. His daydreaming was curtailed by the arrival of Dexter and Hunter.

They made an interesting group thought Buchanan. He and Street in plain clothes sitting at the table. Hunter and Dexter in full uniform, complete with stab vests and yellow-handled tasers sticking out of their holsters standing at the door.

'Come sit down,' beckoned Buchanan, 'you'll give the patrons the wrong idea.'

Hunter and Dexter sat down, and the waitress reappeared. 'Thought you two were about to be arrested,' she said, with a huge grin on her face.

''He's the chief,' said Dexter, nodding at Buchanan, 'we're here on a case.'

'I thought that investigation was all done?' said the waitress. 'At least that's what I read in the *Herald*.'

'Which case are you referring to?' asked Buchanan.

'The one the paper called the case of the laminated man – did someone really get nailed to the tree?' asked the waitress.

Buchanan smiled at the thought his cases were becoming notable, 'The paper was correct, that case is closed, and yes, unfortunately there was an incident about nails and a tree.'

'Oh, how interesting. Are you looking for more bodies today?'

'No. Today we're just here to have a chat and a cup of tea, when you take our order.'

'Oh, sorry. What can I get you?'

Buchanan looked round the table at the faces then said, 'Tea and scones for four, but could we have extra scones please, one of us,' he said, looking at Stephen, 'has a penchant for homemade scones.'

'Certainly. Jam and cream as well?'

'Absolutely.'

'One of us has a penchant for scone?' said Stephen. 'I was just being polite and besides, I didn't want Mrs Foscatini to be disappointed.'

'I'm sure you didn't,' said Street.

'So, what's the meeting about,' said Dexter.

'I believe we have found the key to the unlocking of the case we're working on,' said Buchanan as the waitress reappeared with a tray laden with two teapots and a plate of scones with butter, jam and cream.

'Let me know if you want more,' she said, then departed.

Dexter picked up the cups, put them on saucers then passed them round the table while Street picked up a teapot and began to pour.

'I wanted for us to meet here and have a chat. I'm sure you are all aware of the staffing levels we suffer from.' Buchanan saw a look of concern fleet across Dexter's face. 'Please, relax, nobody's going to be let go. In fact, I'm trying to establish a permanent investigation group with me as a sort of mentor.'

'Is that what you told the ACC the other day?'

'No, I've just thought about it, and that's why it's important that we don't muck up this investigation. For the next hour we can relax, but when we get to the office, it will be all hands to the pumps.'

Hunter made a face and shook his head. 'Bit of an odd metaphor, Chief?'

'I don't think so, Stephen. We either bring this case to a conclusion by Friday or – I'll be digging dandelions out of the lawn.'

'Talking about dandelions and lawns,' said Dexter, 'when will you and Mrs Buchanan be moving in to your new house?'

'A timely question, Morris. We have the keys and plan to move in a few weeks time. Thankfully the movers will be doing the lion's share of the work as our furniture has been in storage for over a year.'

'What have you been using in the mean time?'

'The house we have been renting is fully furnished. So that just leaves clothes, bedding and sundries for us to move.'

'All the more reason to wind the case up this week,' said Dexter.

'Exactly. Have you had enough scones, Stephen?'

Street smiled at Hunter at Buchanan's good-natured jibe.

'Yes, thanks. They certainly are very good, almost as good as Mrs Foscatini's.'

'In that case,' said Buchanan, taking out his wallet, 'let's get to work. I'll see you back in the office in twenty minutes.'

♦

Buchanan put the phone down as the team entered his office and sat facing him.

'I believe we discovered the key this afternoon,' began Buchanan, 'when we visited the parents of Bridget Standish. They live in the village of Hankham. Their daughter is the niece of the late Karl Mueller. The relationship is through the mother. Mrs Standish's mother and Mueller's mother were sisters.'

'How does that help us?' asked Hunter.

'You remember we found an epipen clutched in the hand of Guthrie Burtenshaw?'

'Yes, he injected himself.'

'That pen was prescribed for a Bridget Standish, the niece of Karl Mueller. He's the friend of Garry Duncan.'

'Well, yes, we know that already.'

'But what we didn't know was on the day the epipen went missing, both Karl Mueller and Garry Duncan were visiting the Standish family to see Bridget's new horse. We are going on the observations of Mr and Mrs Standish that while they and Karl Mueller were out in the paddock looking at the horse, Garry Duncan was in the house and saw the opportunity of stealing the epipen.'

'But why would he steal an epipen?' asked Dexter.

'That is what I intend to ask him. Now, as you are aware, I am, once again being investigated with regards to the two deaths in Glasgow and someone has said they saw me push Rodney Richardson into the marina.'

'But that's nonsense,' said Dexter, 'we were there, we saw what happened. Can I ask who this mysterious witness is?'

'That is sub judice according the ACC, who I must add made a point of reminding you that she will be back on Friday.'

'Are you saying we only have what's left of today and till Thursday evening to wrap up the case?' said Hunter.

'Yes. So, we are going to have to use our time and resources wisely. Stephen and Morris, once again it will be down to the two of you to do the leg-work. Jill and I will rattle cages where necessary, OK?'

'Fine by me,' said Hunter. Dexter nodded.

'Jill, did you call Duncan?'

'Yes, he's at home this afternoon.'

'What did he have to say?'

'He wanted to know what I was working on and was I still wasting my time working with you.'

'Cheeky sod, we'll soon sort him.'

'Are we going after Garry Duncan? Is he the mastermind in this case?' asked Dexter.

'I wouldn't actually use the expressions *go after,* or *mastermind,*' said Buchanan. 'It's going to be more of a stalking game at this point. Jill has done some preliminary work on the background of our protagonists: Ivan Reznikov, Tatyana Reznikov, Karl Mueller, Irene Adler, Guthrie Burtenshaw and Garry Duncan.

'So far, I think we can safely eliminate Mueller and Burtenshaw, as they are no longer with us. Irene Adler had a part to play but I'm quite sure she is no longer involved. That leaves Tatyana Reznikov, Garry Duncan and Ivan Reznikov.'

'Where do we fit in?' asked Hunter.

'I would like you two to make enquiries about Garry Duncan. Jill has the file with his details.'

'How will we do that without him knowing what we are up to?' asked Hunter.

'That's just it. I want him to know. If I were to call him and request his presence to answer questions about the deaths of Mueller and Burtenshaw, you two would be doing traffic duty, Jill would be sent on a sergeant's retraining course and I – well, your guess is as good as mine as to what I would be doing.'

'I like this,' said Dexter. 'Where does Duncan live?'

'Somewhere past Hove off the A27 on the way to Chichester. We need to put him off guard, get him off-balance, keep him guessing. Park in a prominent place in his driveway and have your lights on as you arrive.'

'Any suggestions on how to start?' asked Hunter.

'You could start with something innocuous such as – I know – the old trick of investigating a road traffic incident in the area. What kind of car does he drive, Jill?'

Street scrolled through the Duncan file. 'A black Audi Quatro.'

'Tell him you are making enquiries about a report of someone driving an Audi Quatro erratically on the A27 the previous evening. Ask to see his car, look for damage, get him to talk about cars. Stephen – that should be easy for you. Then poke around the property, open and close windows and doors, you might want to make comments about how valuable some of his household contents are. Ask him if he's sure he has enough insurance, be nosey, get him flustered.'

'This is going to be interesting,' said Hunter.

'Do either of you play golf?' asked Buchanan.'

'I do,' said Dexter.

'Good. After you have rattled his cage at home, go visit his golf club. Start by asking if he's a member, then if anyone asks you why you are there, continue with the storyline about investigating a report of someone driving a car like his erratically on the A27. Ask in the office about membership and say you only want to be a member of an honourable club. Get them chatting in the office, ask about how Duncan plays. Intimate that you heard from someone that he likes to drink a lot.'

'Bet he'll be angry when he hears that,' said Street.

'I hope so,' said Buchanan.

'You really think he's guilty?' asked Hunter.

'He's definitely guilty of some part of this sorry affair,' said Buchanan.

'What do you want me to do?' asked Street.

'I would like you to get in touch with Tatyana Reznikov again. Tell her – tell her that after reading her statement there are a couple of unanswered questions that have come up.'

'Then?'

'Then, get her to talk about her and Karl and when she's chatting steer the conversation round to Garry Duncan. I suspect if you can, she'll open up and you may find she reveals a whole different Garry Duncan to us.'

'Suppose she says she wants to talk face-to-face?'

'Fine, go with the flow, as long as you get her to talk.'

'We'd better get going,' said Dexter, 'I need to be home by a reasonable time this evening. Mother-in-law is going out.'

♦

Buchanan stood at the window looking down on the car park as Dexter and Hunter climbed into their car to go put the plan into gear. He saw Street's reflection in the window; she was busy tapping the keys on her phone. A grin grew on her face as she talked with Tatyana.

Buchanan looked back out the window, across the rooftops and over to Sovereign Harbour. That was where what he now had as a career had got started – *the case of the bodies in the marina*, the *Herald* had called it. Then there was *the case of the laminated man;* he wondered what handle Miasma, the crime reporter for the *Herald,* would hang on the present case. Poor Miasma, chasing round in the dark trying to piece together what Buchanan and his team were up to, all the time hoping to get the scoop that would transform his career.

How fortunate I am, thought Buchanan, I've probably got the best team a policeman could ever have, and all the more reason to get to the bottom of the case.

The trace on Mueller's phone had placed him at the scene of the accident. Strange, thought Buchanan. Though there was no joy in this fact, there was at least a sense of completion that he'd been right all along, but no joy in the thought of how Mueller must have suffered as he died.

The death of Mueller disturbed him. Usually by now there would be clear evidence pointing to the killer, with only the leftovers of the investigation to bring it to a successful conclusion. But not this time. He had three suspects: Reznikov, Burtenshaw and Duncan. All had a motive and were present at various times during the evening.

Of the three, Reznikov was the prime suspect, with Burtenshaw second and Duncan a close third. But what about motives? Reznikov was being cuckolded by Mueller and was about to be cheated on in a business deal. Burtenshaw seriously disliked Mueller, but was that enough to want to kill him? Duncan was a business partner and without Mueller would be out in the cold

There were of course the other members of the syndicate, but none were close enough to be involved in Mueller's death, besides they weren't at the event dinner.

The CCTV footage at the pier was inconclusive but did point to Reznikov as the perpetrator of Mueller's murder. But why would he eliminate his main partner – unless he already had someone else in mind? Burtenshaw or Duncan, those were the only two fitting the bill: Burtenshaw was dead, so that left only one name: Duncan.

'OK, 'bye,' said Street, hanging up from her call and catching Buchanan's attention.

'Sounds like you two hit it off,' he said.

'I suppose we did. She has agreed to talk to me – alone, and away from her husband.'

'Where and when?'

'Tonight. She says she will meet me in the reception of the Sofitel hotel at Gatwick airport.'

'Strange place to meet.'

'She said she has urgent business in Moscow and won't be back till next week.'

'What time are you meeting her?'

Street looked at the office clock. 'Phew, better get my skates on, she said her flight was at five twenty-five.'

'Will you take the train or drive?' asked Buchanan.

'I think I'll take the train. If she decides to have something to eat and a drink, I won't be putting myself in danger of being over the limit. Also, alcohol tends to loosen tongues.'

'Good point. Any idea when you'll be back?'

'She said her flight was at five twenty-five. So I imagine I should be back by about six thirty-seven.'

'Shall I pick you up from the station?'

'Please.'

'I better get my coat on if I'm going to give you a lift,' said Buchanan.

♦

Buchanan stood on the platform and watched the train pull out of the station. For a fleeting moment he saw his career leaving the station and him left standing on the platform. He shook his head and returned to the car park. He shut the door, put the key in the ignition and glanced across at the new Arndale shopping centre construction. He recollected the desk sergeant had described it as a WW1 German battleship.

Buchanan drove back to his office to await the results of Hunter and Dexter's interview with Duncan. To his surprise Dr Mansell was waiting for him in his office.

'Ah, there you are,' said Mansell, 'thought you'd gone off on holiday again.'

'Fat chance of that. To what do I owe this visit?'

'Just on my way home and thought I'd stop in and go over my ideas about the deaths of Mueller and Burtenshaw with you.'

'Something new post-autopsy?'

'Just some random thoughts that might help you with your investigation.'

'OK, I'm all ears.'

'My first thought was about the rope that was used to hang Mueller. I had it examined by the lab. Turns out it was just plain blue polypropylene, the stuff used extensively by the construction industry.'

'We already came to that conclusion,' said Buchanan.

'What we didn't realise at the time was the rope in question was beyond its useful life and had begun to deteriorate. If you'd looked closely at it, you would have seen the surface was rough. This was due to the surface strands breaking and anyone who handled it would probably have tiny shards of polypropylene on their hands and clothes. When I looked closely at the neck wounds on Mueller, there was a slight necklace of blue pieces of rope embedded in the skin.'

'Now that could be useful if we could get Ivan Reznikov in custody. Anything else?'

'The knot where the rope was tied to the railing was called a round turn and two half-hitches – a sailor's knot. Any of your suspects sailors?'

'Burtenshaw, Mueller and Duncan.'

'Garry Duncan, the former crime commissioner?'

'The very same.'

'I heard he's a high flyer in the Home Office. Fancies himself for the position of Home Secretary one day,' said Mansell.

'Not if I have anything to do with it. Besides, I thought you had to be a serving member of parliament to get that position.'

'That's a bit vengeful. What's he done to deserve your ire?'

'He got up my nose. Tried to steer the investigation off down a rabbit hole.'

'You think he killed Mueller?'

'He's just one of the suspects.'

'Just one? How many are there?'

'Two with a possible third. Do you have any other thoughts on the evidence?'

'You realise Mueller's suicide note was a fake?'

'Uh-huh, the majority of genuine suicide notes I've seen tend to try and make some sort of justification for their actions. Such as *I'm sorry I've made a mess of things, make sure my prize coin collection goes to, etc.* Besides, when did he write it and with what? There was no pen or paper in his pockets when we searched his clothes. Was there anything interesting about the paper?'

'Glad you asked. The top of the paper had been torn off, leaving a trace of a phone number. I had it analysed and the number on the paper is that of the night club. The ink of the note is non-conclusive, though it does match that of the complimentary pens used in the club.'

'So, the death of Mueller is looking more like it wasn't premeditated, but rather a spontaneous event. Someone saw Mueller in a distressed state and went looking for a way to make it look like suicide.'

'Just one person?' asked Mansell.

'Probably not,' Buchanan said, while writing on a notepad, 'I'll pay them a visit tomorrow morning. This has been very helpful, anything else?'

'There were DNA traces on the rope and the epinephrine box.'

'What sort of traces?'

'I'll deal with the rope first. There were several distinct DNA samples on the rope where it went round Mueller's neck. At the other end, where it was wrapped round the railing, the lab also found several distinct DNA samples. Several of the samples at the noose end matched the knot on the railing end. I also had some of the rope bits found in the skip tested and they matched all but two of the samples tested on the rope that was used to hang Mueller.'

'So, from that you deduced the multiple samples were those of the workmen who had last used the rope and the two individual ones are those of the two who were instrumental in the demise of Mueller?'

'Exactly.'

'How about the note – was there any DNA on it?'

'Inconclusive, I'm afraid. It was cheap paper and its structure had started to break down.'

'So, all we need to do now is match the DNA on the rope with that of our killers. What about the epinephrine syringe and box?'

'Once again we have several samples and a clean handprint. There were six DNA samples on the box and two on the syringe. One of the samples on the box also matched the sample on the syringe. The second sample on the syringe matched that of the DNA of Guthrie Burtenshaw, as did the handprint.'

'Good, we're getting somewhere. The paramedic said he had to prise the syringe out of Burtenshaw's hand – glad the paramedic was wearing gloves. Looks like it's another visit to the Standish family for DNA samples for elimination purposes. So whoever stole the epinephrine box, also handled the syringe?'

'Looks that way.'

'So, are you saying Burtenshaw stabbed himself with the pen?' said Buchanan, looking at the gold nib of his fountain pen.

Mansell shook his head. 'Unlikely. From what we could determine Burtenshaw was right-handed. From looking at the pattern of Burtenshaw's handprint on the pen he would have had to reach right over his body to stab himself in the left leg. The injection mark was down low on the left upper thigh. I would suggest the killer sat beside him and just stuck Burtenshaw when he wasn't watching. Burtenshaw felt the sting, looked down and saw the epipen, realised what had happened, and after a struggle grabbed the pen from the hand of his killer.'

'That works as a hypothesis,' said Buchanan. 'So, to recap, on the night of the events dinner, killers one and two meet and decide to get rid of Karl Mueller. One of them sees the rope in the skip, picks it up and puts it in his pocket. Possibly killer two is inside the venue and finds the notepaper and pen, writes the suicide note and re-joins killer number one. Either they convince Mueller to go outside, or they see him go out for a cigarette and follow him.' He looked up from taking notes. 'Did Mueller smoke?'

'From looking at the insides of his lungs, I'd say about twenty a day.'

'Interesting. Where were his cigarettes and lighter? They weren't in his pockets either.'

Mansell shook his head. 'That's your side of the equation.'

'So when he's outside, one, or both, suggest a stroll out to the end of the pier. While one of them is engaging Mueller in small talk, the other, the sailor, fashions a noose and then ties the other end to the railings. They wait while Mueller needs to lean over the rail to vomit, rope around the neck and heave-ho, over you go, exit Karl Mueller.'

'Was Burtenshaw at the event?' asked Mansell.

'He wasn't invited to the actual event but was summoned by Ivan Reznikov to deliver papers that he was working on. Oh – how perfect this is.'

'What is?' said Mansell.

'There was a delay in Burtenshaw returning to his taxi. I just wonder if he wandered back to Reznikov with a question or something and saw Muller being dispatched over the railing. As a result of him walking back he was seen and was now perceived as a threat. Especially since Burtenshaw already didn't like Mueller and Duncan and by extension that also meant Reznikov. But which one of the two of them killed Burtenshaw?'

'That's your domain,' said Mansell, standing to leave as Hunter and Dexter wandered into the office.

'Afternoon, Doctor,' said Hunter.

'You two look pleased with yourselves.'

'We've had a good afternoon, we've been sniffing around a suspect.'

'Is that standard procedure?'

'It is if you're working for the chief,' said Dexter.

'I take it your truffle hounds are referring to our earlier conversations, Buchanan?' said Mansell.

'Truffle hounds – they've never been called that before! And yes, it's about the deaths of Karl Mueller and Guthrie Burtenshaw,' said Buchanan, looking at a text message on his phone. 'Stephen, would you go meet Jill at Hampden Park station? Her train has just left Lewes.'

'OK. I suppose we are meeting back here?'

'Yes, I'd like to hear what the three of you have found out and make a decision about our next move. Fancy waiting for Jill to get here, Doctor? It will probably be pizza for dinner tonight.'

'Beats heating up leftovers in the microwave. My wife is out tonight visiting with her sister. I'll call her and let her know I won't be home for dinner,' said Mansell.

'Be right back,' said Hunter, picking up the car keys from the desk.

♦

Mansell sat at Street's desk and picked up the phone to call his wife. Buchanan leaned back in his chair, picked up his notebook and reviewed the notes he'd taken while Mansell gave his briefing on the deaths of Mueller and Burtenshaw. He was disturbed by his desk phone ringing.

'Buchanan. And to what do I owe this phone call? Yes, I did. No, they were checking on a report about an Audi Quatro being driven erratically along the A27. There was an earlier report about a hit and run on the Polegate bypass. The golf course? I don't know, maybe one of them is looking for a golf club to join. Certainly, Mr Duncan, I'll have a word with them when I next see them. Goodnight.'

'Was that who I think it was?' said Dexter, returning from a drinks run to Tesco.

'Yes,' said Buchanan, 'that was the first of many calls I expect to get from Mr Duncan over the next few hours. You two did a good job of lighting the touch paper of his anger.'

'Whose anger?' said Street, as she and Hunter returned from Hampden Park station.

Buchanan looked at her and smiled. 'That was Mr Duncan, he's not a happy chappy. Pizza will be here in a few minutes.'

'Good, I need something to soak up what I've been drinking.'

'No food?' asked Dexter.

'Nothing other than bar nibbles. She certainly could knock back the vodka.'

'She?' asked Mansell.

'Tatyana Reznikov, wife of the Russian businessman at the centre of the present case,' said Buchanan.

'Ah, thanks.'

'Pizzas are here,' said Dexter. putting the phone down.

'I'll give you a hand to carry them up,' said Hunter.

◆

'Right, Stephen, Morris,' said Buchanan, 'I've already heard from Duncan. Let's hear your version of your visit.'

Hunter looked at Dexter and grinned. Dexter had a slice of pizza halfway to his mouth.

'We got off on a bad foot,' said Hunter. 'Mr Duncan was extremely annoyed that we'd pulled into his driveway with our blues on. We strolled slowly up to his front door. By the time we got there, and he'd opened the door, his neighbour across the road came over to ask if everything was all right. That really pissed Mr Duncan off. He did quieten down a bit when Morris went and turned off the blues. By then his neighbour on the left had arrived and there were several people standing at the front gate, most with their phones out taking photos.'

'That must have taken his annoyance to a new level,' said Street.

'It did. When we mentioned why we were there he quickly ushered us into his house. I think the spectacle of him being questioned by uniformed policemen in his driveway hit a raw nerve. I got the impression it's not the first time it's happened.'

'We've never checked to see if he is, or has been, married,' said Buchanan.

'We sort of did,' said Dexter. 'On the way out there were still a couple of the neighbours standing by the gate. They wanted to know what was going on. I mentioned we were just checking on the Audi Quatro story when one of the neighbours said they wondered if Duncan and his cousin were fighting again.'

'Cousin?' said Buchanan.

'Yes, cousin,' said Stephen. 'But there was no sign of him while we were there. The neighbour said there had been frequent arguments over the last two years about him moving out. They went on to say that the cousin had fallen on hard times and Duncan had said he could stay till he got back on his feet. That was four years ago.'

'That must be causing friction,' said Buchanan, 'something else for us to investigate. Did you get a name for the cousin?'

'Harold Beaumont. I checked the PNC, there's nothing known,' said Dexter.

'We were about to leave when I looked out of the French windows and saw his Audi sitting on the driveway at the side of the house,' said Hunter. 'Without asking, I opened the door and went out to look at the car. I surreptitiously leaned on the bonnet and found the engine was still warm.'

'I casually asked him what it was like to drive the car,' said Dexter. 'how it handled at speed, all the usual questions that get asked when petrol heads get together. Duncan replied he'd not driven for several days. That statement didn't make sense. Why would he say that when it was obvious it had been on the road as the engine was still hot? I waited till we were on the way back then did an insurance check on his car, and bingo! His insurance expired two weeks ago.'

'Now why would he do that?' said Buchanan, a smile growing on his face. 'He should know better. The risk he's taking driving with no insurance could certainly mean the confiscation of his car and even loss of his job. Wonder what's going on in his mind that's distracting him from his responsibilities?'

'The deaths of Mueller and Burtenshaw?' said Street.

'Probably,' said Buchanan. 'Anything else to report about your visit to Duncan?'

'He has a huge bar-bill at the golf club. According to the club secretary, Duncan likes to be the life and soul of the party, always standing people for drinks. The secretary said it was as if Duncan was trying to buy votes at an election. Do you think what we're doing is going to have any effect?'

'Mr Duncan has already phoned to say how much he's enjoyed the game so far. No, actually I think we've really rattled his cage. Thanks, guys. Jill, how did you get on with Tatyana?'

'My first impression was she was wired, you know, on something like speed. She couldn't stop chattering. I put it down to her celebrating with too many vodkas. After a while she relaxed a bit and told me she was finished with Ivan.'

'How was that?' asked Buchanan. 'I thought they had an open relationship?'

'She had lunch with her husband yesterday. She told him it was all over, she was going to leave him and since there was nothing to keep her in England she was returning to Moscow.'

'What about her fashion line?'

'I asked her about that. She said she has done the initial work by being at the launch and could send one of her associates to run the show from here.'

'That must have annoyed Ivan.'

'It did. He started to pick on her, made fun of her relationship with the *Kraut* as he referred to Karl. That was a big mistake, she said.'

'What did she mean by that?'

'She started to cry, and of course it just made matters worse.

'How?'

'Ivan kept on attacking Karl's memory. The final straw was when she accused him of killing Karl. He denied it at first but then he made his big mistake. He even boasted how easy it had been to get Karl plastered and then push him over the railings.'

'Did he say if he did it on his own'

'No, that was all she said about Karl's death.'

'So, there isn't any evidence of him murdering Mueller other than a drunken rant?'

'She wouldn't say directly. But she did mention that Ivan had been in phone contact with Garry Duncan, who had told him about the deal Karl Mueller had done with his UK distributors.'

'So, it looks like Duncan ratted on Mueller to Reznikov,' said Hunter. 'Probably trying to cut himself in on the deal.'

'I don't understand,' said Mansell. 'If this Tatyana knows her husband had something to do with the death of Karl Mueller, why is she flying off to Moscow instead of making a complaint to the police?'

'I've been puzzling that myself all the way back from Gatwick,' said Street. 'The only thing that comes to mind is – and this is the bizarre bit – she said by the time she was back in Moscow, Ivan would be regretting what he'd done.'

'I don't like this one bit,' said Buchanan, reaching for his notepad. 'If I'd known she knew what she did, I'd have brought her in as a material witness. Poor lass, she's probably worried sick she'll be his next victim. I think I'll call Reznikov in the morning and warn him about being too hasty in dealing with his wife's outburst.'

'What do you want us to do tomorrow, Chief?' asked Hunter.

'Follow up on Duncan's cousin. It might go nowhere but should get him rattled when he realises we're still checking up on him.'

'Do you want us to pursue the lack of insurance?' asked Hunter.

Buchanan shook his head. 'No, leave that to me. I'll mention it to him the next time he calls –as I'm sure he will when you start chasing the cousin.'

'What about me?' said Street.

'I would like you to arrange for someone in the SCI team to go visit the Standish family and collect DNA samples, so we can eliminate them from the epipen box and pen. Then you and I will make a return visit to the pier and do further investigations into Mueller's suicide note. Other than that, I think we're well and truly done for the day, see you all tomorrow.'

18

'Will you be home late today?' asked Karen, as she sipped on her breakfast coffee.

'Depends on what we find out at the pier,' replied Buchanan. 'Jill and I are going back to see if we can shed any light on Karl Mueller's supposed suicide note. Then I've got to try and track down Ivan Reznikov and warn him off from doing anything he might regret with regards to his wife.'

'Why, what's going on with them?'

'They had a very public row in a restaurant. She accused him of murdering Karl Mueller. He apparently didn't take nicely to the accusation. Jill thinks she's gone back to Moscow to stay out of his way and to get protection.'

'This is just like that television series, you remember, *McMafia?*'

Buchanan shook his head, 'I remember. It was too much like real life for me. What are you doing today?'

'I'm going over to our new house to check the measurements for the living room curtains and see if Rich Bowley has started painting the spare bedroom. Can't quite get my head around the fact that we are moving in to our house in a few weeks.'

'It's been nice staying here in the Marina, but it will be even nicer to get into our own home and I'm sure your sister and husband will be pleased, they'll be back from Paris soon.'

◆

'Your morning coffee, Jill,' said Buchanan, taking the cup out of the Starbucks holder.

'I was wondering where you'd got to. Thanks. The SCI's are booked to go see the Standishes this afternoon.'

'Good. We'll head over to the pier after I make this phone call.'

'Who are you calling?'

'Mrs Mueller. I'm presuming she has a phone number for Ivan Reznikov. Damn.'

'What's the matter?'

'I've left my phone at home. Be right back.'

◆

Buchanan drove into the car park at Hammonds Drive and saw to his annoyance the ACC's car parked beside his slot. What was she doing back so soon? It was only Tuesday, he was supposed to have until Friday morning. The name Duncan came to mind – he must have got to the ACC before Buchanan could complete the investigation. Drastic action was needed, he thought, as he climbed the stairs. Walking down the corridor, he saw the door was open and female voices were emanating from the office. At least they weren't raised, he thought.

He stopped in front of a picture of Eastbourne pier. He looked past the picture at his reflection and made sure his tie was straight, hair laid back where it should be, and smiled. He liked what he saw, even the wisps of hair that curled up past his ears – they gave him a certain gravitas. He reached into his jacket and removed a fruit gum from its wrapper, popped it into his mouth, rolled his shoulders and continued down the corridor to his office. He was ready, let the battle commence.

Street was at her desk. The ACC was standing looking out the window. 'I tell you Jill, your boss has gone one step too far this time. I told him he had till Friday morning to complete his investigations and wrap up the case. But attacking Garry Duncan of all people! Did you know he may be the next Home Secretary?'

'Not while I'm still around,' said Buchanan, as he marched into his office and into his chair. 'I presume you being back early means you have been hearing from Mr Duncan, Ma'am?'

The ACC turned and stared at Buchanan, then at her wristwatch. 'Are you accustomed to arriving at work at eight forty-three?'

'No, but maybe I could give it a try.'

She was about to say something when Buchanan put up both his hands in a conciliatory gesture. 'Excuse me, Ma'am. That was uncalled for.'

'I should hope not, Buchanan – this is not something I wanted to do –'

'Wait, Ma'am. Please don't say anything till I have brought you up-to-date on our investigations – please.'

The ACC looked at Street, saw the look on her face, the tears forming in her eyes. 'OK, one last time, and it better be good. Jill, would you mind getting me a coffee? Your boss and I have things to talk about.'

'Oh – sure. White without and an Americano? be back in fifteen minutes.'

◆

Street shut the door behind her and headed off to Starbucks wondering just how bad it was for Buchanan. She would miss working with him if they forced him to retire. But they couldn't do that, he was the core of the team.

◆

The ACC picked up a chair and placed it directly in front of Buchanan's desk. 'Right, Buchanan, let's have it, warts and all. Where are you with this investigation?'

'The deaths of Karl Mueller and Guthrie Burtenshaw are related to a friendship that developed many years ago. While at university, Mueller, Duncan and Burtenshaw started and maintained a somewhat strained friendship,' said Buchanan. 'Burtenshaw drifted away from the friendship of the trio, but he did continue to get involved in their lives, mostly from a legal perspective. The death of Karl Mueller is definitely murder. The death of Guthrie Burtenshaw is also murder. The two deaths are, in my mind, inexorably linked. It is my contention that the murder of Karl

316

Mueller was carried out by at least two protagonists and one of those is also responsible for the death of Guthrie Burtenshaw.'

'And the names of these protagonists are?'

'In the case of Karl Mueller, it is my belief that Garry Duncan and Ivan Reznikov were involved. In the case of Guthrie Burtenshaw – it is my contention that he was killed by a lethal injection of epinephrine by Garry Duncan.'

'All right, let's begin with the death of Karl Mueller. What evidence do you have?'

'First, who instigated the review of the Glasgow incident?'

'I've already said that was sub judice.'

'All right, let me mention a name, you don't have to respond, I'll just look at your face. Someone who works in the Home Office? Garry Duncan – I thought so.'

'Buchanan, you have to end this vendetta.'

'I was right about Karl Mueller running me off the road, and I'm damn sure I'm correct about Garry Duncan.'

'Karl Mueller, you were telling me about your evidence?'

'All four of them, Reznikov, Burtenshaw, Mueller and Duncan, were at the awards event on the pier. We have CCTV evidence that Karl Mueller was outside in the smoking area just before he went over the railings. Shortly prior to this, Ivan Reznikov called Guthrie Burtenshaw at home and asked him to bring him the papers he'd been working on. Burtenshaw was to meet Reznikov outside the door to the smoking area. During the evening we have been able to track Mueller and Duncan inside the event. From experience, watching them going in and out of the toilets, it would appear they were both dealing in drugs.'

'Have you told anyone else about your thoughts?'

'No one except the team. How else are we to do our job?'

There was a knock at the door.

'Come in,' said Buchanan.

'Your coffees,' said Street. 'I also got some biscuits.'

'Thanks, Jill,' said the ACC. 'You may as well stay while your boss reveals all.'

'Thanks,' said Street, as she went over to her desk.

'Jill,' said Buchanan, 'while you're here, could you give Mrs Mueller a call and ask her for Ivan Reznikov's phone number?'

'Will do.'

'Do you have any sugar in the office?' asked the ACC.

'Top shelf in the cabinet,' said Street, pointing to the cabinet behind the open door.

While the ACC dug in the cupboard for a sachet of sugar, Street called Mrs Mueller. Buchanan and the ACC waited for Street to conclude her call.

'I have Reznikov's number,' she said, 'but there is a problem.'

'We don't like problems,' said Buchanan.

'She was expecting him down to stay last night, but he never showed up. He called her yesterday afternoon and said he'd had an almighty row with his wife. Apparently, he'd said things he shouldn't have, and she'd stormed out of the restaurant.'

'Did Mrs Mueller give you any indication as to what was said?' asked Buchanan.

'He told her he'd boasted that he'd taken care of his wife's lover, Karl Mueller.'

'Did she say what was meant by *taking care of?*'

'Mrs Mueller didn't say. By eleven-thirty he still hadn't shown up, so she called his mobile number, but didn't get an answer.'

'And this Ivan Reznikov is a prime suspect in the murder of Karl Mueller?' asked the ACC.

'Yes, Ma'am,' said Street.

'Can I have the number?' said Buchanan.

Street passed the note she'd written the number on over to Buchannan.

Buchanan keyed in the number and pressed the call button. The sound of ringing came out of the speaker. Buchanan was about to hang up when the call was answered.

'Ivan Reznikov?' Buchanan asked. 'Then who am I speaking to? DI Anderson? Who am I – this is Detective Chief Inspector Buchanan, Sussex CID. I'm trying to find Ivan Reznikov. You can't? Then would you call me back on a secure line at the Incident Room on Hammonds Drive, Eastbourne? Good, we'll wait for you to call, goodbye.'

'What was that all about, Buchanan?'

'I'm not sure why a DI Anderson is answering Reznikov's phone, Ma'am. DI Anderson said he could not talk to me on an unsecured line. He will call us on an internal line in a minute.'

No one spoke, all three of them sat sipping their drinks waiting for the phone to ring.

It was ten minutes before it did.

'Put it on the speaker, Buchanan,' said the ACC.

'This is DCI Buchanan. Who is this?'

'It's DI Anderson, sir.'

'Thanks,' said Buchanan. 'I have you on the speakerphone, and with me is Alison Gilbert, the Assistant Chief Constable of Sussex, and DS Street. What can you tell us about Ivan Reznikov?'

'Ivan Reznikov was found slumped against the wheel of his car on the A22 at just after four-thirty yesterday afternoon. First impression of the attending officer was that Mr Reznikov had been drinking and had passed out while waiting for the lights to change. It quickly became apparent that all was not well with Mr Reznikov, an ambulance was called, and he is now in intensive care at the Princess Royal Hospital in Haywards Heath. We have no news at present as to his condition as the hospital are running blood tests.'

'This is DS Street, Inspector. Does it look like he's had a heart attack?'

'No. The hospital is checking for poisoning. Mr Reznikov has been moved into an isolation ward.'

'Not another one,' said the ACC.

'Are you referring to the recent case in Salisbury?' said Anderson.

'The very same. Has the Home Office become involved yet?'

'I believe they have been informed. But until we know the cause, we are keeping a complete news blackout.'

'Why wasn't I informed?' asked the ACC.

'I'm sorry, I don't have that information, Ma'am. This case has only broken in the last twenty minutes.'

'What do you mean by that? I thought you said Reznikov was brought into the hospital during the early hours of the morning.'

'He was, but initial diagnosis was alcohol or drug related. It wasn't till he was seen by one of the senior doctors that something more sinister was suspected.'

'Thanks, Anderson. Do you have the name of the doctor in charge at the hospital?'

'Yes, it's a Stephen Whittington.'

'Thanks. We'll make our own enquiries from here.'

'Well, that's a strange turn of events,' said the ACC. 'I think you need to tell me the rest of what's been going on.'

'Could you wait a minute on that, Ma'am?' said Buchanan. 'There's a couple of things that need to be taken care of immediately. Jill, could you get on to the Princess Royal Hospital, find out from the doctor in charge when we might know what ails Ivan Reznikov. Make sure he understands this is an official enquiry.'

'I'm on it.'

'Now, Ma'am, as I was saying. We have CCTV footage that shows Mueller outside sitting on the bench where the smokers congregate, the only designated smoking area on the pier. Would you like to see it?'

'Certainly.'

Buchanan rotated his computer screen, so it was visible to both the ACC and Street, who'd rolled her chair over.

'Here you can see Mueller sitting, head in hands outside the exit door to the smoking area. The footage is, unfortunately, quite grainy as it was misty that evening. From what we can see on the video Reznikov exits the venue and stands looking around; he notices Mueller but doesn't say much to him.'

'Reznikov seems to be waiting for someone,' said the ACC. 'He keeps looking at his watch then towards the end of the pier. He doesn't look like someone who is about to commit murder.'

'If you'll continue to watch, Ma'am, you'll see he is waiting for Guthrie Burtenshaw. Ah, there he is. Burtenshaw hands over what looks like a large envelope, they chat for a moment, Burtenshaw leaves and Reznikov goes back inside the venue.'

'Buchanan, all that appears to be above board, I didn't see any signs of Mr Mueller being thrown over the railings with a rope round his neck.'

'The smoking area wasn't where he died, Ma'am,' said Street. 'It was towards the end of the pier where the former fishing pier is situated.'

'So, what's the point of the video?'

'It shows Mueller, Reznikov and Burtenshaw were all together just before Karl Mueller was murdered.'

'Or decided to take his own life. Buchanan – I'm sorry, but you haven't shown me anything that would convince a jury that Ivan Reznikov killed Karl Mueller. And when it comes to your vendetta against Garry Duncan, you haven't shown me anything at all.'

Buchanan raised his hands and said, 'Please, wait, I haven't finished yet. We now shift to the CCTV footage from the end of the pier. This is twelve minutes after Reznikov goes back into the event leaving Karl Mueller slumped on the smokers' bench. Unfortunately, this camera shot is not as good as the previous one as it has now begun to rain. Karl Mueller has moved from the smokers' bench to the bench beside the gate to the former fishing pier.'

'How can you make that out, Buchanan? It's raining and dark.'

'Just wait a moment, someone moves, the lights come on. See, this time it is different, if you look you can see he is looking up as though he is listening to something or someone. Watch, he shakes his head and then lowers it back down as though he is having trouble staying awake. If you look carefully you can just see the knees and right shoulder of someone who has just sat down beside him. They say something to Mueller that makes him look up, unfortunately there is a wind squall that obscures what happens next,' said Buchanan, staring at the screen. 'When the vision returns Mueller is gone and all we can see is the leg of someone disappearing out of sight.'

The ACC shook her head. 'Buchanan, I still don't think you have evidence that would stand up in a trial.'

'But, Ma'am, you saw what we saw. Karl Mueller listening to someone, a figure runs into view and Karl Mueller goes over the railing. There were three of them on the end of the pier, Reznikov, Duncan and Mueller. Then in a flash Duncan and Reznikov were gone, and Karl Mueller was hanging from a rope fighting for his life.'

'That is a bit better, but it still doesn't show either Reznikov or Duncan being involved. And, have you given thought to this, the two figures we see on the screen could have been trying to prevent Mueller from going over the railing?'

'If that were the case, Ma'am,' said Street, 'don't you think one of them would have called the emergency services?'

'A valid point, Jill,' said the ACC, taking a long sip of her coffee. 'Now, what about the death of Guthrie Burtenshaw? Where does that death fit in to the scenario you are espousing?'

'Burtenshaw told us he had been summoned by Ivan Reznikov to bring the documents he'd been preparing down to the events evening on the pier. I checked with the taxi firm and the taxi driver about the timing of his trip. We matched the times of the taxi to that of the CCTV footage and the arrival and delivery of the documents to Reznikov match. But,' she said smiling, 'there is a gap of about twelve minutes between him walking off and arriving at the taxi. I walked and timed what it takes to get from the end of the pier to the road. The difference in times would have given Burtenshaw time to walk round the end of the pier and see what happened to Mueller, and also be seen by Reznikov and Duncan.'

'Are you now saying that one of them also killed Burtenshaw?'

'No, Ma'am,' said Buchanan, 'just Duncan.'

'How on earth do you arrive at that conclusion?'

'I can answer that, Ma'am,' said Street.

'The floor is all yours.'

'On the day that Guthrie Burtenshaw died, we had an early morning visit from Garry Duncan.'

'I thought Burtenshaw died on a bus?' said the ACC.

'He did. Ma'am, if you'll let me continue.'

'Sorry, you have the floor.'

'Garry Duncan was only here for a few minutes then left to meet someone. I checked the bus timetables and it is just possible for him to have walked through the Tesco car park to Seaside Road and caught the number 1A going towards Langney shopping centre. At the shopping centre he would have only had to wait a few minutes for The Loop, the very same bus that Guthrie Burtenshaw took.'

'What about the epipen? Burtenshaw died from a severe reaction to an injection of epinephrine?'

'The epinephrine was prescribed for a Bridget Standish, she is sort of a niece of Karl Mueller. On the day the prescription went missing, both Karl Mueller and Garry Duncan were visiting with the Standishes. Mrs Standish said they were all out in the paddock looking at Bridget's new horse that her uncle Karl had bought her. During that time Garry Duncan was in the house. We did a background check on Garry Duncan as a teenager and found he was prone to shoplifting. His school nickname was Magpie.'

'Do you have any evidence Garry Duncan was actually on the bus?'

'Not the 1 or 1A, but we do have CCTV of someone sitting beside Burtenshaw on the bus and several witness statements complete with physical descriptions of the person who sat beside Burtenshaw and apparently argued with him. All the witness descriptions could be of Garry Duncan.'

'Do we have a frontal view?'

'No, just from the rear, and he was wearing a hat.'

The ACC shook her head. 'You are going to require a great deal more if you are going to try and prove Garry Duncan to be the killer of Guthrie Burtenshaw.'

'We are waiting for DNA tests on the epinephrine box and pen,' said Buchanan.

'Do you have any DNA samples to compare it with?'

'Not yet,' said Buchanan. 'I'm waiting for the time we can get him in custody.'

'How will you achieve that?'

'I sent Hunter and Dexter to question Duncan about a traffic offence and quite by accident discovered he is driving on the public roads without insurance.'

'Really. If that is true it is very silly of him,' she said, getting up and walking over to the window. 'Was he cautioned?'

'No. This fact didn't come up till after they had left him.'

'Where are Hunter and Dexter just now?'

'I sent them to find out about Duncan's cousin, Ma'am. Apparently, he's been lodging with Duncan for the last four years, caused quite a bit of friction between them.'

'It might be a good idea to get in touch with them,' said the ACC. 'Garry Duncan has just driven into the carpark.'

Buchanan got up from his chair, went over to the window and looked at the spectacle that was developing in the car park. Hunter and Dexter had just followed Duncan into the carpark and had stopped directly behind his car, blocking him in. Duncan gesticulated about having them move the squad car. Hunter shook his head said something to Dexter then the two of them walked off towards the entrance to the station. Duncan shouted something then climbed back in his car then exited with his mobile phone to his ear.

Buchanan returned to his chair to wait for the inevitable arrival of Garry Duncan.

'I think it would be better if I made a swift exit,' said the ACC. 'If I am correct, that phone call will be directed to me. I'll be downstairs with the duty crew. Call me if things get nasty – no, maybe you should call me if nothing happens.'

Hunter and Dexter were the first to arrive.

'You'll never guess who's here?' said Hunter.

'You lose,' said Buchanan, 'I was watching out the window, Duncan looks thoroughly angry. So, before he gets here, what did you find out about the cousin?'

'He came out of the Navy six years ago and wasn't able to settle. Four years ago he moved in with Garry Duncan. He's got a reputation of always caging money from friends and acquaintances,' said Dexter.

'You'll like the next bit,' said Hunter. 'It is he who has been driving the Audi, has done for the last three years.'

Buchanan leaned back in his chair, reached for a fruit gum. 'So, cousin has been driving the car for three years, maybe paying for the petrol, but who was responsible for paying the tax and insurance? You checked that the car is still uninsured?'

'Yes,' said Hunter, 'I did an ANPR check while following it down Lottbridge Drove.'

'This is just perfect. Duncan has just driven into the police station, in plain view of two policemen, in a car with no insurance.'

'Why is that an issue?' said Hunter. 'All he'll get is a fine and points on his licence.'

'Failure to prove you have insurance for a vehicle driven on the public highway can get you a fine and points. But it also can get you arrested and your vehicle impounded. I think I'll start with the no-insurance issue and go from there. But, while I wait for the man to arrive, how about you two go to the office next door? I'll shout if you're needed.'

Street settled back into her chair and smiled at Buchanan.

'Why are you smiling?' he asked.

'It's all over your face, the smile of the gladiator just as he's about to dispatch his foe on the floor of the coliseum.'

'A gladiator; never been compared to that before. Maybe I should go out and buy a sword.'

Street's answer was prevented by the arrival of an extremely agitated Garry Duncan.

'Ah, Mr Duncan, how nice of you to pay us a visit. How are you today?'

'How am I? You ask that when your goons have been harassing my family and friends with their insinuations?'

'Oh, and what might these insinuations be?'

'C'mon, you sent them out to badger me and my cousin. Now what's this all about?'

'Did you drive here today?'

'Of course I did.'

'In an Audi Quatro, vehicle ID echo, alpha, six –'

'Yes, yes, of course I did. What of it?'

'Can I see your driving licence?'

'Why?'

'Mr Duncan, you have just admitted to driving your car on public roads. Do you have your insurance certificate with you?'

'No, of course not. My cousin drives the car normally, he has the insurance documents.'

Buchanan smiled. 'Mr Duncan, can I see your driving licence, please?'

Duncan, possibly sensing Buchanan had the upper hand, acquiesced to his request and handed his driving licence over.

'Good, at least you have a current licence. It's a pity about the insurance.'

'What do you mean about the insurance?'

'You don't have any. You've just admitted to driving on the public roads without insurance. Hunter, Dexter,' shouted Buchanan, 'my office, now!'

At the sound of the summons, Hunter and Dexter appeared at the door.

'Ah, there you two are. Would you please write Mr Duncan up a ticket for operating a motor vehicle on public roads without holding a valid insurance policy? Here is his driving licence.'

Street pretended to be on a phone call while Hunter dutifully read Duncan his rights and wrote out his ticket.

'When you produce a valid insurance certificate you can get your car back,' said Hunter. 'In the meantime your car will be impounded.'

'How am I to get home?' asked Duncan.

'Who said you were going home?' said Buchanan. 'Mr Duncan, is that the suit you were wearing the day you brought us the file on Ivan Reznikov?'

Duncan looked down at his jacket, then back at Buchanan. 'Yes. What of it?'

'You are sure about that?'

'Yes, of course I am. It's the one I always wear to work. Why?'

'Could you take it off for a moment?'

Duncan stared at Buchanan for a moment. 'No, I certainly will not.'

Buchanan smiled. 'Mr Duncan, it would be most beneficial to you if you would take it off.'

'And if I refuse?'

'If you refuse, I will ask Constable Hunter and Constable Dexter to remove your jacket for you.'

'Buchanan, you've finally lost it,' said Duncan, sliding his arm out of his jacket.

'Jill, could you find a large evidence bag?' said Buchanan.

'Evidence bag? What's that for?' said Duncan.

'It's for a forensics exam. Oh, and your tie, let's not say we weren't being careful. And the contents of your pockets, including your car keys.'

'Careful? Careful about what?'

'Garry Duncan, I am arresting you on suspicion of the murder of Guthrie Burtenshaw and involvement in the murder of Karl Mueller. You do not have to say anything, but it may harm your defence if you do not mention when questioned something which you later rely on in court. Anything you do say may be given in evidence. Constable Hunter, would you escort Mr Duncan down to the cells, please?'

The colour drained from Duncan's face as he realised what was happening.

As he was being escorted out of Buchanan's office he came face to face with the ACC.

'Ah, Mr Duncan. Is there a problem?'

'You ask me is there a problem? Of course there bloody well is. Buchanan has finally blown a gasket. He seems to think I've got something to do with Guthrie Burtenshaw's death. Tell them to let me go – immediately.'

'I'm sorry, Mr Duncan, my hands are tied. Can I suggest you engage the services of a lawyer?'

As soon as Duncan had been escorted out of the office the ACC said, 'I hope you know what you are doing, Buchanan. Garry Duncan could be the ruination of your career and reputation.'

Buchanan smiled. 'He's guilty, there's no doubt about it in my mind.'

'Your mind maybe. But remember you still have to convince the CPS and then a jury.'

'Oh, we will, we will.'

'What are your next steps in the investigation?'

'Jill and I are going back to the pier. There is the matter of Mueller's suicide note and the pen he wrote it with.'

'I thought the suicide note is a fake.'

'It is, but someone wrote it on club notepaper with a club pen.'

'A bit of a nebulous search, those sorts of things are usually strewn everywhere in offices.'

'Nonetheless, Ma'am, we must exhaust all avenues.'

'And you are sure about Duncan?'

'Absolutely, I'll stake my job on it.'

'You may be doing just that. Based on the evidence you have presented to me, you have my approval to continue to hold Duncan for a further twenty-four hours,' she said, looking at her watch. 'That gives you till eleven o'clock on Thursday morning to either charge him or let him go.'

'Thanks Ma'am. I can assure you, Garry Duncan isn't going anywhere.'

'If that's the case, I'll meet you back here Friday morning at eight-thirty sharp, and mine's a medium latte with one sugar.'

Buchanan smiled. 'See you Friday morning.

As the ACC left, Hunter and Dexter wandered into the office.

'How is our boy?' asked Buchanan.

'All tucked in and comfortable in his cell. What do you want us to do next?'

'His car keys are on my desk, have a look through his car. You may find something, but probably not if his cousin has been driving it for the last couple of years, worth a go anyway.'

♦

When Street and Buchanan arrived at the pier, as before he parked in a spare taxi slot. This time Buchanan walked over to one of the waiting taxis and produced his ID. 'DCI Buchanan, keep an eye on the car for me, thanks.'

'You do know how to endear yourself to taxi drivers,' said Street, as they entered the pier.

The main entrance door to the club was closed so they walked round the building to the rear and up the stairs to Ruth Samson's office. Street knocked on the outer office door and went in, Buchanan followed.

Tracy was seated at her desk opening the post, but there was no sign of Ruth Samson. 'Good morning, can I help?' asked Tracy.

'I hope so. DCI Buchanan and DS Street. We were here a few days ago about the unfortunate incident at the end of the pier.'

Tracy nodded.

'We are wondering if you have any complimentary note pads and pens?'

'Phew, haven't had any of those for months. We're getting a new logo soon and till we do there won't be any complimentary pads or pens.'

'Mind if I look around?' asked Street.

'No, go ahead.'

While Street gave the office the once over, Buchanan asked, 'Do these CCTV cameras work?' He pointed to the camera up in the corner of the room.

'Yes, they're on a separate system to the ones outside and the dance floor.'

'Would you still have the recordings for the night of the awards event?'

'It's possible, it was only a few days ago, I'll have a look.'

'Got them,' said Street.

'Got what?' asked Buchanan.

'The notepad and pen, they had fallen down behind the filing cabinet. See the front of the pad still has the top of the sheet attached? Should be a simple job for forensics to match the paper. Whoever wrote the note must have done it in a hurry, and just tossed them down on the top of the cabinet where they just simply slid over the edge and down the back,' she said, while carefully putting the pen and the pad in an evidence bag.

'You're in luck, Inspector,' said Tracy. 'The video hasn't been recorded over.'

'Could we have a copy of it please?'

'Yes, would you like to look at it while I make a copy?'

'That's all right, we'll have a look when we get back to the office.'

♦

Hunter and Dexter were waiting in the office when Buchanan and Street returned from the pier.

'Find anything,' asked Buchanan.

'His cousin should try cleaning out the car, it's a right tip inside,' said Dexter. 'You have any luck?'

'Jill thinks she has found the notepad and pen that was used to write the suicide note.'

'Where was it?' asked Hunter.

'It had fallen down the back of a filing cabinet. I'm going to get it off to forensics, we have till Friday morning to wrap the case up.'

'Why Friday morning?'

'Because that is when the ACC will be back to either congratulate us or put us out to pasture,' said Buchanan. 'We have Garry Duncan in custody, and I don't need to remind you that we can only hold him for forty-eight hours without charging him.'

'So, what can we do?' asked Dexter.

'Not sure. It's highly unlikely that forensics will have anything for us within the next twenty-four hours, even if I tell them it's an emergency. And you're sure there's nothing in the car?'

Dexter shook his head. 'It's difficult to tell, the car really is a mess inside.'

'All right, let's have a look at the CCTV of the club office.'

Street plugged the USB drive into her computer and pressed the play button. The time displayed on the screen said five-thirty.

'Fast forward to about eight-thirty,' said Buchanan.

The screen darkened, and the office was now lit only from the lights in the corridor. The clock in the corner of the screen moved slowly on till just after nine a shadow disturbed the light coming from the corridor. As the person entered the club office a gasp went round Buchanan's office: it was Garry Duncan followed by Ivan Reznikov. They watched fascinated as Duncan and Reznikov rummaged round the office till Reznikov finally found what he was looking for. He picked up a notepad and pen and gesticulating to Duncan passed them over. Duncan hastily wrote something on it, tore the bottom of the note from the pad and threw the pad and pen onto the filing cabinet. Street smiled as she saw that her summation of the events was correct in all details. The pad and pen slid across the top of the filing cabinet and disappeared over the edge and down the back.

'Perfect,' said Buchanan. 'That is the first piece of hard evidence we've got in this case.'

'What about the CCTV from the bus?' said Street. 'We haven't shown that to Stephen and Morris yet.'

'Why not? But I don't think it will add anything to what we know. All it shows is someone sitting beside Burtenshaw.'

'It only takes a few minutes,' said Street.

This time the CCTV footage was bright and clear, although it only showed Burtenshaw from the back. As the passenger sat down beside Burtenshaw, Dexter said, 'We know that hat. That's the same hat that's in the back of Duncan's car, I'm sure of it.'

'Bingo!' shouted Buchanan. 'Morris, go retrieve the hat and put it in an evidence bag. Stephen, when Morris gets back, I want you two to get the evidence off to forensics and make sure they understand what we are looking for and that we need the results back by Thursday lunchtime.'

'They're not going to like that.'

'Like it or not, this is urgent. I've only got permission to hold Duncan for a maximum of forty-eight hours without charging him.'

♦

Dexter returned with the hat in an evidence bag then he and Hunter departed for the forensics lab.

'What do you want me to do next?' asked Street.

'Have you called the hospital to find out the condition of Ivan Reznikov?'

'No, been busy, I'll get on to it right now, and you?'

'I'm going to prepare the paperwork for holding Garry Duncan for a further twenty-four hours. Thankfully I have pre-approval from the ACC to hold Duncan if the evidence supports the charge.'

'And does it?'

'It better.'

While Buchanan worked his way through the necessary paperwork to hold Duncan, Street managed to track down the doctor in charge of Ivan Reznikov.

'Any luck?' asked Buchanan as Street put the phone down.

'No. Unfortunately he's not able to give a condition report till after the latest blood test results had been completed, and that won't be till sometime tomorrow morning.'

'Ok, that will just have to be. First thing tomorrow we'll go see Reznikov,' said Buchanan. 'I want to make sure he is actually in hospital and not trying to worm his way out of the charge of murder.'

19

'Nice place to have a hospital,' said Street, as Buchanan managed to find a parking space in the visitors' car park. They walked through to the A&E department and waited in line at the reception desk.

'Yes, can I help?' asked the receptionist.

'Good morning, Detective Chief Inspector Buchanan. Could I have a word with Doctor Whittington, please?'

'I'm sorry, he's not available this morning.'

'We're investigating the circumstances behind why one of your patients, an Ivan Reznikov, has been taken ill.'

'Oh. Please wait a minute and I will go see if the doctor is available.'

'Fancy a coffee?' asked Buchanan.

'Why not? I have a feeling we are going to be here quite some time.'

Buchanan purchased two coffees from the café and returned to the A&E, handed one to Street then wandered down the corridor to the toilets. When he returned Street was talking to a bald-headed man in a white coat. As Buchanan approached Street turned and pointed at him.

'Doctor Whittington?' asked Buchanan.

'Yes. I was just explaining to your sergeant how difficult it has been in determining the cause of Mr Reznikov's symptoms.'

'Why is that?'

'We are not equipped for this type of blood analysis. But since the Home Office became involved we now are in a position to state what is wrong with Mr Reznikov.'

'And that is?' said Buchanan.

'Mr Reznikov has been poisoned with thallium. It is an odourless, tasteless chemical that is generally used in rat poison.'

'Why did it take so long to detect?'

'Initial symptoms are like many ailments common to man. Mr Reznikov had been out to lunch, he drank quite a lot of alcohol, he was found in his car slumped over the steering wheel. So, when he was brought in to the A&E, the initial diagnosis was mild alcohol poisoning. It wasn't till he didn't respond to treatment that I was called in to give a second opinion. I've just had the results and it is definitely thallium poisoning. Unfortunately, several hours have passed between the ingestion of the poison and the initial treatment.'

'Will he die?' asked Street.

'It's too early to tell, it was quite a large dose.'

'Are the Home Office people still here?'

Whittington shook his head. 'No, as soon as I said it was plain thallium, and not radioactive, they didn't want to know and left. If I were you, Inspector, I'd be looking for a jealous lover, not a spy wearing a black coat with a hat pulled down over their eyes.'

'Thanks, Doctor. When will you know if he is going to pull through?'

'It's a case of how long is a piece of string? Since we do not actually know how much he ingested we can only go by continually monitoring his vital signs. But, from my experience, I'd say he has only a twenty percent chance of surviving.'

'That bad, eh? Thanks, Doctor. One of us will check back with you daily, if that is all right with you?'

'No problem, just don't expect me to be hanging on to my phone waiting for you to call.'

'I understand, thanks.'

As they drove through Lewes on the way back, Street said, 'Thallium, that's the main component in rat poison. Quite fitting if you give consideration to the possibility that he was given it by his wife.'

'A modern-day Lucrecia Borgia,' said Buchanan. 'If she was responsible, it's unlikely we'll see her back in the UK again.'

◆

'Mr Duncan's lawyer is waiting for you, sir,' said the desk sergeant, as Buchanan and Street entered the station.

'Where is he?'

'I've put him in interview room two.'

'Where's Duncan?'

'Still in his cell.'

'Good. Has the lawyer been waiting long?'

The sergeant looked over at the station clock, smiled and said, 'Only about fifty minutes.'

'Is that all? Thanks. We'll go see him shortly,' said Buchanan. 'Jill, could you scoot up to the office and see if we've heard back from Forensics. I'll be in with Duncan's lawyer.'

'Ok, see you in a minute.'

'Sergeant, could you rustle up some coffee and biscuits for Street and me?'

'Yes, sir. I'm sure we can manage that. Shall I bring them to the interview room?'

'Yes, please.'

Buchanan opened the door to the interview room and looked at the lawyer seated at the interview desk.

'Inspector Buchanan,' began the lawyer, but Buchanan put up his hand in a gesture that would stop a motorway full of traffic.

'Before you begin,' said Buchanan, 'I would like you to know your name?'

'August Pennington.'

'Where's your client, Mr Pennington?'

'He – *er* – decided not to be present at this interview.'

'That's his choice,' said Buchanan, sitting in the chair directly opposite Pennington. 'Mr Pennington, from our investigations, it is our professional opinion your client is guilty of at least one murder and probably the complicity of a second. Now, you wanted to say something?'

Before Pennington could speak the door opened and a constable brought in two mugs of tea and a small plate of chocolate biscuits and laid them in front of Buchanan.

'Inspector Buchanan,' began Pennington for the second time, 'I have reviewed the charges under which you are holding my client and I have to say that what you have, would, in my experience, not stand much of a chance in court. What evidence or witnesses do you actually have?'

'CCTV on the bus, and several witnesses who will all put Mr Duncan at the scene of the crime, plus other items which I am not prepared to divulge at this time.'

'So, you are not going to let him go?' said Pennington, looking at the clock.' Your forty-eight hours are up, Inspector.'

'So they are. How observant you are, Mr Pennington.'

'Then I insist you either charge my client or let him go.'

The sound of the interview room door being opened interrupted Buchanan's answer. It was Street and she was grinning.

'Is it what we thought?' Buchanan asked.

'Yes, everything as we thought.'

'Good. Jill, would you mind asking the sergeant to escort Mr Duncan here?'

'You're going to let him go?' said Pennington. 'Good. I'm glad you've come to your senses, Inspector,'

'What on earth made you think that, Mr Pennington? I'm just about to charge Mr Duncan with the murder of Guthrie Burtenshaw and with complicity in the murder of Karl Mueller.'

'But I thought –'

'Not quite enough, apparently. We now have CCTV, fingerprint and DNA evidence that any jury would find conclusive in finding your client guilty of the charges I am about to bring.'

While they waited from Duncan to be brought through from the holding cell, Pennington scanned through his file on him. Ten minutes later a very dishevelled Garry Duncan was ushered into the interview room. He was about to say something when Pennington interrupted and said, 'Please do not say anything, Mr Duncan. I'm sorry to say you are about to be charged.'

Duncan stood still, shoulders slumped and stared down at his feet.

Buchanan stood and walked over to Duncan. 'Garry Duncan, I am charging you that on the evening of the 12th of this month, with one other person did murder Karl Muller and then on the 14th of this month, by lethal injection, caused the death of Guthrie Burtenshaw. You do not have to say anything, but it may harm your defence if you do not mention when questioned something which you later rely on in court. Anything you do say may be given in evidence. Do you understand?'

Duncan nodded.

'Is that a yes, Mr Duncan?' asked Buchanan again.

Duncan looked up, his eyes red and sunk in their sockets. 'Yes, I understand.'

'Sergeant,' said Buchanan, 'would you return the prisoner to the cells, please?'

'Don't worry, Garry,' said Pennington to Duncan as he was led out of the room, 'we'll beat this one. They don't really have anything.'

'Now if you've got nothing else to discuss, Mr Pennington, I'll bid you good day,' said Buchanan, reaching for the last chocolate biscuit.

20

'Your coffee, Ma'am,' said Buchanan, placing a large latte on the desk.

'Thanks.'

'Where's your team?'

'Jill will be here shortly, Stephen is working with Hanbury this morning and Dexter is on the way to the hospital to be with his wife, hopefully before she gives birth.'

'Well, while we wait for Jill, let me get the unpleasant part of my visit over with. Since Garry Duncan has been charged with the murder of Guthrie Burtenshaw and being complicit in the murder of Karl Mueller, his credibility has gone out the window.

'With the investigation into the incident in Glasgow underway, I'm unable to interfere with it. But I have talked with the Procurator Fiscal, and he has said from looking at the file he doesn't see why the Home Office was pushing for another enquiry into the matter. He said it should be all over within two weeks and he doesn't see any reason for you to be reprimanded.'

'Well, that's good to hear.'

'Though I think it might be a good idea if you were to be scarce for the next two weeks. Do you have any annual leave left?'

'I've still got two weeks from last year I wasn't able to take.'

'Good, take them starting from tomorrow. The Glasgow thing will be over by then and you'll still have several weeks before Duncan comes before the court. Any ideas as to what you'll do?'

'We were supposed to move into our new house next weekend, but Karen's mother is sick again, so she will be visiting with her in France.'

'Will you be going with her?'

Buchanan shook his head. 'Before all this blew up, we'd arranged for the removal company to get our furniture out of storage and delivered to our new house next week. But with Karen's mother not being well again and Karen going to be with her, I'll be staying behind.'

'Will you stay in your new house?'

'No, I'll probably go up to Castlewood and see if I can get a ride on one of the horses.'

'What will Jill be doing while you are away?'

'With all the overtime she's worked, Jill has a few days in lieu and will be going with Karen to see Karen's mother.'

'Good, and good work winding up the case,' said the ACC, changing the subject as Street entered the office.

'Good morning, Ma'am,' said Street.

'Good morning, Jill.'

'Your coffee is on your desk,' said Buchanan.

'Thanks.'

'Right, Buchanan. Arresting someone is one thing. What sort of evidence do we have for a conviction?'

'Jill, how about you update the ACC?' said Buchanan.

'OK. I'll begin with Inspector Buchanan's road accident on the A27. It is …'

♦

'You're home early – quiet day?' asked Karen.

'I've been told to go home and keep out of the spotlight till the investigation in Glasgow is concluded.'

'What investigation?'

'Glasgow, you remember, the fight in Porters bar.'

'Of course, I remember. That's what got us down here to live in Eastbourne. But, Porters bar, Glasgow – that was over a year ago. You don't work there anymore.'

Buchanan shook his head and said, 'Relax, Karen. The Assistant Chief Constable said that since someone in the Home Office had instigated the reactivation of the previously suspended case, they must go through the motions. It should be all over within a couple of weeks.'

'But who'd be so spiteful as to do that?'

'She wouldn't reveal who, all she would say was the matter was sub judice.'

'So you don't know who's behind it? My bet would be Gary Duncan.'

Buchanan smiled at his wife and said, 'She said that since the complaint had been made, and the Glasgow press had got wind of it, they had to go through the motions, that's all.'

'That Gary Duncan has a lot to answer for.'

'Don't I know it? But at least he's now beyond making any more trouble. Look on the bright side, I've been sent home for the duration on full pay. I'll have plenty of time to do the jobs around the new house that you've been going on about, and I'll be there when the movers deliver our furniture on Thursday.'

'You're a bit late for doing any decorating. Rich Bowley has already started painting the spare room.'

'Oh.'

'I have an idea,' said Karen, smiling. 'Why don't you come with me and Jill to see mother?'

'I was told not to leave town.'

'Really?'

'Well, they did say I could be called to give a statement and not to go too far.'

'What will you do while we're away? The new house won't be ready to live in till I get back and we get the curtains up. Then there's the new bedding, we still haven't decided on the patterns for the duvet covers.'

'All the more reason for me to stay here, I can make sure the movers put the furniture in the correct rooms. As for somewhere to sleep and eat, I'm going to Castlewood and taking up Nathan's offer to go riding. He's always saying I should get out and about more often.'

'Good, maybe taking time off will rub off on you.'

'The discussion about my retirement is a closed subject, my dear. All I intend to do is sleep well, eat well and relax, nothing is going to interfere with that.'

The End

1

What a day it had been thought Buchanan. He'd seen Karen and Jill off on the early morning Newhaven ferry, then gone over to their new house to see if all was ready for the moving company to deliver their furniture on Thursday.

He'd gone from room to room taking in the smell of fresh paint fighting with the smell of new carpets and thought one of the first jobs would be to buy air freshener. The living room sported a huge open fire and he looked forward to the winter months sitting with his feet up on the stool and reading one of the many *will read some day* books he had on his list.

He finished his tour in the spare room and saw that the decorator had already made a start by filling the nail holes and scratches on the walls and skirting boards. He returned to the dining room and walked into the conservatory. He knew exactly where he would situate his recliner. In his imagination he saw himself relax back into it, look out across the garden, suitably laid out and planted with excellence by Karen, and watch the sun set over the roses clinging to the top of the neighbour's fence.

Now it was time to head to Castlewood for a week of horse riding, reading and relaxing, and nothing was going to get in the way of that.

To be continued...........